ASH

A DESTINED NOVEL

ASH
A DESTINED NOVEL

SHANI PETROFF & DARCI MANLEY

Copyright © 2015 by Shani Petroff and Darci Manley

Cover design by Sammy Yuen
Interior designed and formatted by E.M. Tippetts Book Designs
ISBN 978-1-940610-32-0
eISBN 978-1-940610-42-9

First hardcover edition March 2015 by Polis Books, LLC
60 West 23rd Street

POLIS BOOKS

In dedication to the billions killed during the Event.
You are destined to live on in our hearts.

AMENDMENT 41

An annual tax shall be imposed upon each family that chooses to keep a child whose status determines they will be unable to contribute to society. The tax imposed by this amendment shall be used to fund credits, grants, and other financial support to improve upon the system.

AMENDMENT 44

Those who refuse, or otherwise fail, to accept and follow those destinies ascribed to them by the Department of Specialization may be prosecuted, and if found guilty, fined or imprisoned, as the Ministry of Seven shall dictate.

AMENDMENT 44, ARTICLE A

The Department of Keepers shall be authorized to punish noncompliance of destiny fulfillment with immediate and summary execution.

ONE

—

Dax

"Don't let them ruin this for you," I told Laira, trying to keep her eyes focused on me instead of the gathering student body. I forced myself to sound confident. "Just pretend like they're not there, okay? You've waited seventeen years for today, and it's going to be ultra, no matter what."

We stood on the front lawn of our school's sprawling, perfectly manicured lawn, while the higher rings gathered about twenty feet down from us. They maintained a forced separation that I, for one, preferred.

"Why did the Ash cross the road?" a Purple shouted from across the lawn.

"To waste our time," a Crimson screamed back.

I shook my head in disgust. The only thing you could count on the upper rings to agree on was their superiority over the lower rings. I was about to point this out to Laira when I noticed the horrified look on her face. She shuffled from one foot to another, trying to avoid the glares of our classmates.

"Oh Dax," she said, her voice barely a whisper. "This was such a bad idea. They're all angry to be stuck after school because of me. I was so stupid to pick this place."

"No you weren't," I assured her. "Spectrum Academy is perfect. I mean, it must be, right? You had this location approved by the Department of Specialization."

She hung her head, and I frowned. It was bad enough Laira's family couldn't be here to witness her Destiny Day. They couldn't afford to miss work—that was the Ash ring for you. But there was barely anyone here to support her. Only a handful of lower ring students attended Spectrum, and the upper rings weren't exactly lining up to make friends. But there was no way I was letting any of that spoil my best friend's day.

"What is it the Seven always say?" I asked her, trying a different approach. "'The gift of destiny is a perilous responsibility. With it comes the power of the future.'"

The Ministry of Seven had endless slogans promoting ring unity, and this was one of Laira's favorites. It seemed to work, because she raised her head back up and tried on a tiny smile.

"It's going to be great," I continued. "I mean, just look at you. You look like a million ostows." And she did. Laira had twisted her auburn hair into an elaborate crown that looked completely upper ring. And her shift dress wasn't the usual gray that most of us Ashes wore. It appeared almost silver and sparkled in the sun.

"Really?" she asked.

"Absolutely." I glanced at my own patched shirt and pants. I wished I had a dress like that—or any dress for that matter. But today, like every day, I wore bleached hand-me-downs from my seven older brothers. "Though I might not be the best judge of fashion," I said, grinning.

The corners of Laira's mouth twitched up, and the color crept back into her face.

"Come on already," another Purple interrupted.

"We've got a race to get to," a second voice added.

I turned to the crowd and yelled back. "And Laira's got a time stamp to follow, so take it up with that guy if you think she should break it."

I motioned to the closer of two Destiny Keepers who would monitor Laira's destiny today. He was a block of a man. Solid and square with so many muscles I was surprised he was able to find a uniform that fit. A stun stick was slung through his belt, although I doubted he'd ever need to use it.

No one said another word. They all knew too well the consequences of messing with destiny.

"Thanks Dax," she said, holding onto her grin, but only just. "You know," she continued, "somehow I thought being in front of the school would make me feel special or important or something. That this might be the one day the higher rings would actually care. But I didn't think about the date. No one wants to be here when the race of the year begins in three hours. I can't believe you're even here. Aldan's destiny is what matters today."

"No way," I said, shaking my head emphatically. "Your destiny is just as important as my brother's. Believe me, Aldan would say the same thing. A destiny is a destiny. And it's double reason to celebrate."

"I'm destined to cross the road, Dax," she said wryly. "Your brother is destined to win a worldwide championship. It's not exactly the same thing."

"You might be right," I said. "But what if you're not?" I held up a finger to silence her protests. "You *never* know. That's why I got you this. To remind you." I opened up the flap of my tattered messenger bag, digging inside until my hand closed around

Laira's gift. It was a book. The real kind. With pages and a hard cover and everything.

Laira laughed. "You've got to be kidding," she said.

I shrugged. "It's vintage." I thrust the book toward her.

"It's *old*," Laira replied, giggling.

"It's about destiny," I explained. "Written about Dr. Og's first destiny extractions. It talks about everything—how he was able to scan the brain and retrieve and interpret each person's fate, how time stamps and other details could be lost if the process took too long, and even info on some of the really famous early triggers."

I took the book from her, opened it to the chapter on the trigger effect, and scanned the first page. "See, this chapter is about an Ash who was destined to read a poem out loud. It inspired Mula Olan to come up with hover technology. There wouldn't even be a loop race today if she hadn't heard that poem."

"Do you really think I could make something like that happen?"

"Absolutely," I said.

"It's ultra, Dax. Really," she said, grabbing me in a quick hug. As she released me, the bell began to toll. We looked in unison up at the clock tower. You could see it from most of the rings. All, in fact, but the one Laira came from. And the one where I would wind up eventually—the Ash ring. But that hardly mattered right now. It was two o'clock, and Laira's time stamp was scheduled for 2:03.

"Ready for this?" I asked her.

"Oh, please," a priggish voice answered instead. It belonged to a tiny slip of a Purple named Portia. What she lacked in size she more than made up for with an extra large mean streak. "This is such a waste of time. We shouldn't have to watch a bottom feeder do some mundane task. Especially some charity case the school thrust on us."

I whirled around to face her. I might have been at the bottom of the color rings, but it didn't mean I had to sit idly by while she flung insults at Laira. I clenched my fists at my side and took a step. Which is when I caught the eyes of the closest Destiny Keeper and stopped. I wasn't insane—no matter what people said. Still, just because I couldn't pound some sense into Portia, didn't mean I couldn't tell her off. I opened my mouth to speak, but Madden Sumner beat me to it.

"Portia, enough," she chided her friend.

Everyone immediately grew quiet. Madden was destined to be a future Minister of the Seven, one of the country's top commanders, but for now simply held court as our school's resident royalty. And one of my least favorite people. "Laira has a right to be excited," Madden continued. "It *is* her Destiny Day, and Ash destinies have their function, too. After all, even the smallest destinies have *some* meaning."

She gave Laira a condescending, close-mouthed smile and flipped her chestnut hair over one shoulder with a clattering of her bracelets. She wore seven bangles to represent each of the rings. They stacked in descending order—purple, crimson, green, yellow, brown, slate, ash. She was the only person I knew who was allowed to wear all of the colors at once. It would have been a nice symbol of harmony if I thought she meant it.

I rolled my eyes, turning back to Laira to resume my pep talk. I stopped when I noticed her expression. She looked determined, like she was on a mission, and she was nodding her head at Madden's words. She had actually taken them as a compliment.

For reasons I hadn't been able to grasp, Laira worshipped Madden, and was able to delude herself into thinking the future minister actually cared. But I knew the truth. I'd gotten a behind the scenes look at Madden when she'd dated my brother, Link. Still, I wasn't about to get into that with Laira. Not now. Not when she was about to fulfill her destiny.

I watched as the hands on the clock tower moved to the three-minute mark.

"It's time," Laira said, taking a deep breath and placing her foot onto the road.

"Good luck!" I called as she took another tentative step, her eyes moving from me to the crowd to the clock tower. She had to make it fully across before 2:04 hit, but she didn't want to rush the moment either. You only get one destiny. Well, most people anyway.

The street in front of Spectrum circled around the school sharply. Laira had made it about halfway across the road when I heard the unmistakable purr of an engine. At first I didn't register the sound. Cars weren't that common. Besides, the Destiny Keepers had cordoned off the streets, so the sound of an approaching vehicle was odd enough that I simply blocked it out.

But then I saw it. A white government-issued van racing around the bend.

Everyone stood frozen, almost transfixed. The upper rings were silent. The Destiny Keepers were silent. Laira was silent. She stood paralyzed in the middle of the street.

My voice shattered the quiet. "Laira, move!"

The van fishtailed over the pavement in a shriek of squealing tires. Laira was still frozen as it hurtled toward her, each second bringing it closer and closer to impact.

There was nothing I could do. I was too far away.

"Jump!" I screamed.

TWO

Madden

The van barreled straight for the Ash. I knew I should close my eyes, I didn't want to see this, but I couldn't turn away. Why wasn't she moving? Dax Harris was screaming for her to run, but Laira didn't budge. I braced myself. She was going to get hit.

With a fraction of a second to spare, Laira came to life and lunged out of the way. The van made a sharp turn in the opposite direction, the wheels squealing against the pavement. It skidded out of control, skipping over a curb and slamming into a bench on the side of the road with a loud crunch of metal. Smoke leaked from the front.

Laira reached the opposite side of the road right as the clock tower hit 2:04. I breathed a sigh of relief. I'd been annoyed when the school had required us to watch an Ash destiny take place— we had Keepers for that—but I was glad to see her succeed. It was imperative to our society that no one strayed from their calling.

We couldn't afford another Event. I shuddered to think about the problems that could develop if anyone failed to meet their destiny. *But Laira made it*, I reminded myself, and turned my focus back to my classmates.

There was a mad rush of chatter. One of my best friends, Portia, clutched at my hand. Her porcelain doll's mouth was puckered into a perfect O as she waved toward the crashed car. "Did you see that?" she asked, her eyes glued on the vehicle.

"Of course she saw it," my other friend, Lavendar, answered for me. She crossed one arm over the other. The amethysts on her fingers sparkled in the afternoon sunlight against her dark skin. "We all saw it. That PAE van practically ran down the Ash."

"Do you think the driver's okay?" someone nearby asked.

The driver. I looked over at the vehicle. A worrying billow of smoke continued to drift up from the hood. Was it possible I knew him? My father was head of national security. He worked with the Preventing Another Event division, or PAE, all the time. I'd met many of the officers when stopping by the UV building to see him over the years. "I don't know," another voice answered. "That was a pretty bad crash."

I stood straighter, making sure to appear calm and composed. My training prepared me for this. After all, I was a future Minister of the Seven. My duty was to lead. "Everyone just stay where you are," I said, trying to keep the concern from my voice. "I'll go check out the situation."

I strode over to the Destiny Keeper closest to me, careful to walk not run. He was all muscle, with a stocky frame that reminded me of a tree trunk. "How is the driver?"

"Seems okay," he said, to my relief. "One of my men is with him now. He's…"

"Excuse me," Dax Harris interrupted. She hurried toward us with her Ash friend in tow. The girl was shaking. "What happened?" Dax demanded. "Laira was almost killed. Weren't there blockades? Something?"

"Watch yourself," he replied, the warning clear in his tone.

I looked at Dax in disbelief. Was she seriously questioning if the Keepers did their jobs? There was a reason they were nicknamed Removers. And no one in their right mind mouthed off to them, especially not someone of Dax's standing. But that was the thing about my ex-boyfriend's little sister. She never had any sense of boundaries or social grace.

"We're just trying to understand how something like this could take place. No disrespect meant, sir," she said. I could tell she didn't mean it, but apparently she fooled the Keeper, because he humored her.

"The street was blocked off," the Keeper continued. "I don't know how the van made it through."

Dax glanced at the still smoking wreck, and seemed taken aback, almost as if she was noticing it for the first time. "Is the driver okay?"

"As I was telling Ms. Sumner, he appears to be uninjured. Perhaps his involvement was part of the girl's destiny."

"Do you think I could have triggered something?" Laira asked.

The Keeper shrugged and Laira's eyes widened. "I knew I had a bigger purpose than just crossing the street," she said in excitement. "If this turns out to be something, maybe I can petition to get moved up a ring. How ultra would that be?"

I stifled a groan. A man was possibly injured in a crash and this was what she cared about? She didn't belong anywhere higher than Ash. Not that she would get the chance. Having your color designation changed was extremely rare. A quorum of Destiny Specialists, on the advice of a Keeper, had to decide that the person's destiny triggered something so big that they deserved to be raised a rung. It only happened about once every five years. The only other way to switch rings was to give birth to a child with a destiny above your own ring, like my parents did. But that also rarely happened. In fact, other than my family and Dax Harris's, I couldn't name any.

"Maybe you could help me with the status change request?" Laira continued, badgering the Keeper. "You did monitor my destiny and the crash."

This was really too much. I attended Spectrum to learn ring appreciation, but after all my years here, it only reaffirmed what the government said—rings were in place for a reason. Ashes would be best served by remaining with other Ashes. Laira's exposure to Purples had given her delusions of grandeur, rather than focusing on what mattered—her successful contribution to society as a whole. It was a disappointing lesson on ring relations. Still, there were more important matters to tend to right now.

I'm going to go check on everything, okay?" I half asked, half told the Keeper.

"Of course," he said, and I left him to deal with the Ashes alone. The second Keeper stood next to the van. He was a long, lanky man, and he moved to the side as I approached. His purple uniform was perfectly creased, his black boots shined. "Don't worry, Miss Sumner. He's fine. His van may need some work, but it looks mostly cosmetic. I think it'll run."

I peered in at the driver. I didn't recognize him, but that wasn't too surprising. He was older than me by several years. Dark, curly hair framed his face, and the beginnings of a beard shadowed his jaw. It struck me as odd. The PAE had strict codes. Cropped hair, clean shaven. Maybe he had been on special assignment.

"Are you alright?" I asked.

He smiled back. "I'm just fine. A little embarrassed, I guess. The Keeper was telling me I interrupted a destiny in progress.

I somehow missed the signs. A lot on my mind. What with the loop championship today." He laughed a loud, booming laugh. "Speaking of which, I should really get moving. I'm supposed to be meeting some friends to head over to the stadium together."

There was something about his speech that sounded forced and I paused, looking at him harder. "How long have you been driving for the PAE?" I asked.

"Not too long," he said. "Just a few months."

I was probably being paranoid, but I asked another question to make sure. "Is Robin still managing the office over there?"

"You know it," the man said, shaking his head and smiling.

"How's he doing?" I asked, my body tensing.

"He's as good as ever."

A wave of nervous energy pulsed through me. "Robin's a woman," I said. "And she retired last month." I wasn't paranoid. I was right. This man wasn't who he said he was.

His loud laugh boomed from the van again. "I'm just a little mixed up from the crash."

A bead of sweat trickled down his temple, and he reached up to wipe it off, displaying the band that circled his left wrist. Only I could see that it was a retired model. The shape of this man's tracker was a perfect square, rather that the rounded corners that had been part of the last hardware update. I stepped back from the van.

"He's not wearing a proper tracker," I told the Keeper. "He's not PAE. He's probably not even a Purple."

The Keeper snapped to attention, immediately pulling his stun stick from his belt. The small wand crackled to life. "Miss Sumner, please return to the lawn. Sir, step out of the vehicle. Slowly."

I did as instructed, but the driver didn't. He shot out of the van and went straight for the Keeper's throat. But he only ended up with a blow to the side of the head for his efforts. The Keeper had been ready with his stun stick. He quickly cuffed the man, while his broader partner opened the back of the van. He glanced inside and immediately slammed the doors shut. I couldn't get a look, but it had to be something important, because he promptly tapped a message into his tracker. Moments later two additional PAE vehicles screeched into the scene. A woman stepped out of the first, got into the wrecked van, and drove off.

The suspect was then hauled into the second car. He looked right at me, and a strange smile played over his lips. I shuddered at the attention. I was glad to see him driven away.

Around me, the student body buzzed with nervous energy as they tried to understand what had happened. I was just as curious. The two Keepers who had served as Laira's monitors remained behind. They rejoined our group when the vehicles were out of sight.

"What's going on?" I asked.

"You were right, that man was an imposter," the taller one said, his face expressionless. "He's being taken to the holding cells for questioning."

I was overwhelmed but did my best to hide it. Destiny enforcement had virtually wiped out crime for decades. It was hard to imagine anyone stepping out of line in this day and age. Sure there were the occasional purple collar offenses—financial scams, gambling, that sort of thing. But there was nothing violent. Nothing that put anyone's life at risk. And nothing that a large fine and tighter monitoring wouldn't put a stop to.

"It's nothing to worry about. We've got it under control," the Keeper continued. "You have a good eye, Ms. Sumner. Thank you for your help today."

"Way to go, Madden!" Lavendar yelled, then began to clap. Portia joined her and a moment later the applause spread through the crowd.

I turned and gave a mock bow, which resulted in more whistles and shouts. I tried to remain poised, but a smile tugged at the corners of my mouth. I couldn't wait to tell my dad what had happened.

"Don't you mean way to go, Laira?" Dax Harris interrupted, trying to take away my moment. "Without her destiny, this would never have happened.

"You must be joking," Portia said, coming to my defense. "That *Ash* didn't do anything but almost get run over. If it wasn't for Madden, that criminal would have just driven off."

Dax wouldn't let up. "That *Ash* has a name. It's Laira. And she triggered the whole thing."

"Why am I even bothering talking to you?" Portia muttered in annoyance and turned her back on Dax. "Way to go, future Minister Sumner," she said, giving me a knowing smile.

We walked away from Dax and joined the rest of the Purples. Several other friends congratulated me before I noticed my boyfriend, Bastin, walking our way. Portia nudged me.

"Good looking *and* knows how to dress," she sighed. "It's not fair, Madden."

I just smiled. Bas looked good today. He always did. Sandy brown hair, perfectly-fitted shirt, tanned from his many tours around New City—a chore of being on the prestigious Rebuilding Tomorrow committee.

"Hey," he said as he approached. He stopped beside me and put his hands around my waist. He leaned down to kiss me, but I gave him my cheek.

I couldn't go around kissing in public—not even with my boyfriend. As a future minister, I had an image to protect. I couldn't very well risk being snapped in a lip-lock with my boyfriend, no matter how handsome he was. It just wasn't good PR.

He knew that too, and shook his head in defeat. "What's with the Destiny Keepers over there?"

"An Ash destiny," I said.

Lavendar butted in before I could say anything else. "Madden caught a criminal."

Bas frowned, his blue eyes clouding. "Are you okay?" he asked me.

"I'm fine," I assured him.

"Really?" Worry knitted his brows together.

"Yes, I promise." It was cute the way he was so concerned.

"What happened?"

"A guy took a PAE van, and—" I waved a hand as I saw Bas's disbelief. "It was nothing. He was immediately taken into custody."

His expression relaxed. "Big day at Spectrum, huh?" he said.

"You don't know the half of it," Portia said with an evil grin. "The guy almost ran down some Ash in the process."

Bas raised his eyebrows. "Seriously?" he said, starting to laugh. "Sounds like I missed out on some ultra fun."

Several students laughed around us, and I immediately held my hands up. I knew my friends were joking, but Lavendar, Portia, and especially Bas could get downright mean when it came to the lower rings, and we were in mixed company. "Come on now. You know it's not the lower rings fault they can't improve society in the same way we can. They may not make much of an impact, but it doesn't mean they don't have a purpose."

"Yeah, to infect our ring," Bas said. "We'd probably have been better off if that Ash did get run over. Ashes and Slates shouldn't be allowed in the Purple zone. It's that simple. Don't tell me you don't agree."

I didn't get a chance to answer. Dax Harris saw to that.

THREE

Dax

My fingernails stabbed my palms as I watched Laira's face crumple. She had just completed her destiny. She might have even triggered something huge, but no one would remember her part of the story. The focus had shifted, like it always did, to a Purple. And not just any Purple. To the queen of the pack, Madden Sumner. Laira met my eyes for a moment, shrugged, then looked away in defeat. Madden and her friends didn't care that Laira could hear their conversation. They didn't care that their words would be what she remembered from her Destiny Day. Bastin Worthington was the worst of them all.

He didn't go to school at Spectrum, but everyone knew who he was. Not only was he dating Madden Sumner, but he was the grandson of a Minister of the Seven. I was so sick of people like him. Which is when an idea popped into my head.

Bastin knew an Ash destiny was happening, but he didn't

know what it was, or if it had been accomplished yet. And the Keepers were still standing across the street talking. I unclenched my fists and smiled. This was going to be fun. Before I had time to change my mind I was running toward him, my arms wide open.

"It's you! At long last, I've finally found you," I said, flinging my arms around him and burying my head into his chest. His muscular chest, I couldn't help but notice. Too bad it was overshadowed by his ego.

"Crilas," Bastin cursed. "What the—" He looked at me in shock, and I returned it with wide-eyed adoration. "Who, who are you?" he sputtered. "Get off of me." He tried to pry me away, but I held on for all I was worth.

"He said get off," Madden said through gritted teeth. The students who had started to drift off stopped and turned back around to watch, much to her horror. And my delight.

"I can't," I told her, my hands now clinging around Bastin's neck. "Today is Thursday, September nineteenth." I looked over at the clock tower for added effect. "And it is almost 2:15, is it not?"

Bastin's eyes flicked to the clock in confusion. "What is this about?" He finally peeled himself away from me and took a step back, adjusting his tie.

"I'd like to know that myself, *Dax*," Madden said. I could tell she was trying to stay calm, but her eyes had narrowed into slits. I've had my share of run-ins with our future minister and once the eyes narrow, it means she's started to boil. Which was exactly what I wanted.

"Well, *Madden*," I said, matching her tone, "he may be *your* boyfriend, but he's *my* future."

"You have no future," she spat back.

Technically she was right, but her boyfriend didn't know that. And so I moved toward Bas, reaching out for him possessively.

He grabbed my wrist before I could wrap myself around him

again. "Will someone *please* tell me what is going on?" The vein near his temple jumped in fury. It was just the reaction I was hoping for—and the perfect place to drop the final bomb.

"But darling, can't you feel it?" I answered as dreamily as I could. "You're my destiny." I clasped my free hand over his. "Tall, light brown hair, blue eyes, purple tie? My file says we're to be married. I've been waiting for this moment all my life. We're destined to spend eternity together. Now where could the Keepers have gone off to? Technically my destiny isn't scheduled for another two minutes." I glanced up at the clock tower. "Well, one minute now. Don't you just love this system?"

The color drained from Bastin's face. He was totally falling for it.

The students around the lawn were snickering. People rarely paid attention to Ashes, but when you were an Ash with a Blank destiny like me, you developed a kind of notoriety. My classmates knew I was lying, but it didn't matter. They were still riveted.

Bastin turned to Madden, opening and closing his mouth, trying to form words. Nothing was coming out.

Madden turned her wrath toward the crowd and the laughter immediately stopped. "Enough," she growled.

I ignored her. "Bas, sweetie?" I said as innocently as possible. "Honeybun? Say something, won't you?"

But it wasn't Bas who answered.

"I'll plan the bachelor party," a voice called out. It belonged to Sol Josephson, the only other Ash besides Laira and me at Spectrum. Roars of laughter met Sol's suggestion, and I struggled to keep a straight face.

"She's messing with you, Bas," Madden told him. "She's a Blank. One who's just overstepped her bounds."

I stepped back and held my hands up. "Guilty," I said, smirking.

Bas turned to me, his paralysis quickly turning to fury as he registered Madden's words. For a moment I wondered if he'd actually hit me. But then Madden stepped in between us, glaring for all she was worth. Madden was short. Even in four-inch heels, I had a good two inches on her. I made sure to look down my nose at her. You use what you can in these situations.

"Don't make me call the Keepers back over here, Dax," she threatened.

"I can see the *New City Times* headline now," I shot back. "Future Minister of the Seven Locks Horns with Lowly Blank. What an honor. We'll be joined together for life."

She hesitated. Most Purples went to great lengths to avoid being linked with those beneath them. And you could bet your colors they didn't mix with the likes of me—despite the fact that we all attended Spectrum Academy. We all knew the ring unity mantra was for show. Just like I knew that Madden was bluffing. "What?" I pressed. "No comment?"

I was enjoying Madden's embarrassment enough that I didn't notice Laira creeping up to my side. "Dax," she said softly. "What are you doing? You have to stop. And apologize." She turned to Madden. "She's sorry. Right, Dax?"

I gave Laira an incredulous look. Had she forgotten what the Purples had said? Didn't she understand that she was the reason I'd made a scene to begin with?

"You should listen to your friend," Madden said, finding her voice again. "Seriously, Dax. What would your family think if they saw you right now? Are you trying to get them another fine? Or do you just want to bring them down to your status?"

And now I hesitated. I was the only Ash in my family, and they got enough flack for having a Blank to take care of. The last thing any of them needed was to pay another fine because of me. Besides, Link would kill me if he knew I was starting up with his ex. But I was still angry. And I'll be the first to admit that I make bad decisions when I'm angry. Instead of apologizing, I smiled and made sure my words sounded extra sweet when I reminded her of something. "It didn't seem to work when you tried to lift them up to your status," I said. "Unless, maybe I'm confused? It was Link who dumped you, not the other way around, right?"

Madden's earlier anger was now tucked behind an expressionless wall. "It's time for you to go. Laira, why don't you be a dear, and see to it that Dax gets home."

Laira nodded. Traitorously. "Of course," she said. She cleared her throat. "Before we go, do you think that maybe you could sign this?" She thrust the book—the book I'd given her—toward Madden. "So I could keep it as a memento from my Destiny Day?"

"I'm afraid I don't have a pen," Madden replied.

"Oh," Laira said. "But maybe you could take it home and sign it?" she rushed on, holding the book toward Madden hopefully. "Whenever is fine."

Madden looked at her, then looked at me and pursed her lips. She plucked the book from Laira's hand. "I'd be happy to," she said.

With that, Madden turned and walked away, Bas right behind her. Once she was gone the rest of the group dispersed.

"Dax, what were you thinking?" Laira moaned once we were alone. "Are you trying to ruin my life?"

"Are you serious?" I asked, stunned. "Did you hear the way they were talking about you? Bas laughed about you getting *run over*, Laira."

Laira shook her head. "It was just a stupid joke. I know he didn't mean it. And Madden stood up for me."

I took a deep breath. Laira's ability for self-deception was staggering. "Laira, I saw you. Madden and her boyfriend practically had you in tears. Just because they were born with ultra destinies doesn't make them any better than us."

"I don't know, Dax," Laira replied. "Remember what Doctor Og always says? 'The deeper a destiny carves the path, the more responsibility it demands.' The Purples work hard to make our lives better. All of our lives."

I didn't need Laira's particular brand of cheering up right now. "That's one way to look at it. Or you could say they need to work that much harder to be better people. Bastin Worthington deserved what he got."

Laira groaned. "Dax, you just can't go around making fun of Bastin. Or Madden. If anyone knows that *everyone* matters, it's Madden. She's going to be one of the Seven. They know that every destiny is important—even an Ash's. That's why *everyone*...'" She stopped as she realized what she was saying. "Um, never mind." She dropped her head down and kicked a pebble with her shoe.

"It's okay," I said. "You can finish. That's why everyone matters. Because everyone has a destiny. Everyone but a Blank."

"That's not what I meant," she said, still not looking up. "You know that doesn't matter to me."

"It's fine," I told her, and I actually meant it. After all, I was one of the .001 percent in our society who was born a Blank—someone who had no destiny to harvest at birth, no purpose, no future. I was used to people ripping on my status; even most Ashes didn't want to be associated with me. But Laira never cared about my standing, and she hadn't meant anything by it. "I don't want to fight," I told her. "You just completed your destiny. And my brother's about to complete his. We should be celebrating." I took a breath and put on a smile. I really did want this to be a good day. "So tell me," I said, "what does it feel like triggering something that could have major consequences?"

Just like that the mood lightened. "It's pretty ultra," she said. "To be honest, I was a little worried about what would happen once I completed my destiny. I've been waiting my whole life for it, you know? What am I supposed to do now that it's over?"

I nodded. It was a common reaction of the Post-Destiny crowd, and if I couldn't exactly understand, I could still empathize.

Laira grinned. "But if I triggered something, can you imagine? My destiny could ripple, affect other people, maybe even the world. Dax, my ring could even be reassigned. It means there's something to look forward to again."

The chances that her ring designation would be altered were slim to none. But Laira was happy, so I went along with it. "You never know."

"And don't worry," she said, linking her arm through mine. Her voice took on a teasing tone. "We can still hang out when I'm a Purple. I'd never judge someone by their ring."

I just laughed. "Come on, walk faster. Aldan's race starts in less than three hours. If I don't get home and ready soon, my mom will kill me. We can't be late."

"That's right," she said. "You wouldn't want to miss a nanosecond of Theron Oliver's announcements."

"It's not about Theron," I protested. "It's about Aldan." I could feel my face reddening.

"Uh huh," she said as we walked further down the lawn toward the light rail. "And that's why you borrowed a dress for the race—to impress your brother?"

She'd kind of hit the nail on the head with her Theron comment. I *did* want to wear something to catch his attention. My mom rarely let my family spend our limited funds on clothes for me. Especially not on something as frivolous as a dress, not when there were months we could barely pay our bills. She said it was a waste when my seven older brothers had "perfectly good" clothes they had outgrown.

Which is to say that she'd long ago perfected the art of

bleaching and dyeing my brother's hand-me-downs to appear Ash-appropriate. Even though I knew there was no real future for me and Theron, I still wished it could happen. There were times I swear I'd catch him looking at me—and not like his friend's kid sister. If wearing one of Laira's dresses would get him to really notice me, I was willing to give it a try. There was no way I was admitting it, though.

"No. I just feel like dressing up, that's all," I lied as we walked on.

"Sure," she agreed between giggles. "It has nothing to do with how funny he is or popular... or what was it you said last week? Something about how cute guys with freckles are?"

My answering glare just made her laugh all the harder as we approached Sol. He was still stretched out on the stone wall surrounding the school, busily tapping something into his wrist tracker. Ink black hair spilled down over one of his eyes, and he tucked it behind his ear as we approached.

"Nice one out there," he told me. "That was a Revenant move if ever I've seen one." He karate chopped the air with a flourish.

"Yeah, right," I said with a grin. The Revenants were a myth, though times like today I wished they were real. I gave the air a few jabs of my own in response—a left hook, then a right, pretending it was Bastin Worthington's head.

"I take it back," Sol said. "With moves like that, you couldn't pay them to take you."

"Hey!" I said, but laughed all the same. Sol could be funny when he wanted to be. Especially for a guy who wouldn't be around much longer.

"Though while I have your attention, perhaps you'd be interested in a friendly

wager on tonight's race? I already have a grid going on speed, times, rankings. I haven't been able to get anyone to bet on first place yet. Dax, how about it?"

Laira rolled her eyes at him. Partially because what he was asking was ridiculous and partially because gambling was illegal. Not that Sol really cared about the rules; he had a whole side business hacking into the school's computers to steal exams and change grades.

"No thanks," I said, fluttering my fingers in a wave as Laira and I turned to go.

We all knew who tonight's champion would be. And I knew better than to bet against destiny.

FOUR

Madden

"Be ready at four-fifteen sharp," I told Bas as I gave him a quick kiss on the cheek and ran toward Perse Manor. Times like this—the times that I'm off schedule even by a few minutes—my home can feel more than a little overbearing. It sits back several hundred yards from the road and all but the third story turrets are hidden by the surrounding hedges. I raced up to the front door, anxious to tell my father about my part in today's arrest. I knew he'd be proud. I was taken aback to see him standing in the foyer waiting for me with folded arms.

"You're late," he said.

"I know, but—"

"I don't want excuses," he said, before I could explain my tardiness.

"If you'd just let me—"

He cut me off again. "Look up there."

Above my head hung a crystal chandelier, and from that

hung an old-fashioned sundial. Time's shadow stretched over the purple veins in our marbled floor, stopping next to my feet. I was twenty minutes late.

"I keep that in our entranceway as a reminder," my father said. "A reminder of how important time is. You, of all people, should understand that." His voice echoed through the large space.

"I have a good reason," I answered softly.

He shook his head. He wasn't looking for an explanation; he was looking for an apology. "You knew you were supposed to be here twenty minutes ago. There is a schedule to keep. You have responsibilities to this country, as do I."

No kidding. He reminded me of them every single day. All that mattered to him was his precious schedule.

"It'll be fine," I replied. "I don't need a full two hours to get ready. I set my hair last night and Nora already laid out my dress." I wanted to add that this conversation was wasting more time than it took me to get home, but I stopped myself. You didn't mess with my father when he had that look in his eyes.

"That's not the point," he said. "It's my job to make sure you're safe and where you need to be when you're supposed to be there."

I studied a particularly wide vein of purple cutting through the floor. I wondered how he'd feel when he found out I'd had a run-in with a criminal. So much for keeping me safe. But I wasn't going to say anything. Not now. He could find out from someone else. "It's not like you didn't know where I was," I said instead. "My wrist tracker was turned on. You could have pinged me. You would have seen I was still at school."

"I shouldn't have to ping you. You're going to be one of the world's most important leaders next year. You shouldn't need your father tracking you down like some delinquent Ash. You are Madden Sumner, future Minister of the Seven."

His chest swelled as he said those last five words. It was like my destiny was all he cared about. Well, aside from his own.

"I know that."

"Then act like it. You owe it to your people."

I hated to admit it, but he was right. He was *always* right. I had a responsibility. I shouldn't have wasted time dealing with Dax Harris.

"I'm sorry," I told him. "I won't be late again."

"Good," he said. "Now go get ready. The car will be by to pick you up shortly."

"Aren't you coming with me?" I looked up at him in surprise.

His eyes were cold and impatient. "I've given up my seat. Tonight's race isn't the only thing happening in this city. I have important business to attend to at the UV."

"You're not coming at all?" I asked. We were finally going to do something fun together, and I'd been looking forward to it since last year's championship.

"My duty is to all the rings, not just you, Madden. Try to remember that."

"Of course," I replied, biting back the words I really wanted to say. *Don't you remember what it used to be like? When you still laughed once in a while? When you thought of me as your daughter instead of a future minister?*

But he probably didn't. The laughter had left the house right around the time my mother did. Vanders Sumner didn't mess around with fun and games anymore. His destiny was to guard and protect, and since my mother's death he took it seriously. He was the government's Chief of Security. He would protect his country. He would protect his daughter. And at the rate he was going, he would protect himself from ever feeling anything, ever again. I was used to his approach to parenting by now. After all, it had just been the two of us for fourteen years, if you didn't count Nora. But even after all this time, I still kept hoping he might warm up.

Instead he gave me a formal nod, then turned and walked away.

"Dad," I called after him. "Sorry again."

He didn't answer. He didn't even turn back around. He just continued down the hall.

I bit my lip and marched up the curving staircase. Today was not going the way it was supposed to. Instead of being proud, my father was mad at me. And to make matters worse, I'd lost control of a conversation in front of an audience. All because Dax Harris had decided to make a point that no one cared about.

I walked down the long hallway leading to my wing. I stopped to adjust one of the series of Monet paintings hanging from the wall. They were some of the only original artworks to survive the Event. I stared into the water lilies and gave myself a chance to compose myself. I wasn't successful. Hot, salty tears still pricked at my eyes as I entered my bedroom.

"There you are, Madden," Nora said. "Let's get you dressed. We don't have much time."

I tossed my schoolbag onto the floor as Nora bustled around the room. The book that Laira had asked me to sign peeked out from one corner. It was a symbol of everything that had gone wrong today and I took a deep breath, trying not to lose control.

Nora made her way to me and began tugging at the laces that tied the bodice of my day dress. "Here we go. Free at last. Now, let's—" She grabbed my face in her hands. "Honey, what happened? Why are you crying?"

"I'm not," I protested, plastering on a smile. Ministers of the Seven did not cry and definitely not in public. "Just something in my eye," I said, composing myself.

I hoped Nora would leave it at that, but she knew me too well. She sat down on the edge of my bed and patted the seat beside her. "Come tell me what's wrong."

"It's nothing. Honest." I walked over to my closet instead. A dark purple silk gown hung outside my closet door. "Wow. Willa outdid herself this time." My stylist definitely knew how to provide the perfect outfit for any occasion. My championship dress was no exception. The top was fitted and flared down into a fringed organza A-line skirt that reached the floor. Although I could have added accessories in black or white, I always felt for a future minister a full purple ensemble was the way to go. Aside from my signature zone bracelets, of course. Today's outfit would be game-stopping. There were going to be just as many eyes on me as on Aldan Harris. "Help me put it on."

Nora got up and lifted the dress over my head. "Don't try changing the subject. You can't fool me, Maddy. The others, yes. But I know better."

I smiled at that. Nora was the only one who called me anything but Madden. Well her and Link. But he hardly counted any more. Nora only used the nickname when I was upset. She always knew if something was bothering me, even if no one else could tell. After all, she'd practically raised me. My family moved from the Crimson to Purple zone, and straight into Perse Manor, when I was born. My mom and dad were both Crimson, but my birth, my destiny, made the zoning council reevaluate. My parents were quickly bumped up to Purples, both in status and living situation, and Nora kind of came with the house.

Her destiny was to serve those higher than her, and in the government's book that meant serving Purples. But while she won't say it to anyone, I know that's not how she sees it. Nora believes in a higher power that goes beyond science, but I don't say anything. I wouldn't want to get her in trouble.

"So are you going to tell me what happened?" she asked, smoothing out the bottom of my dress. "You know you can always talk to me."

"It's just my dad being my dad. It's like he doesn't see me anymore. All he sees is my destiny." I wanted to say more, but I felt myself getting choked up. "Never mind."

Nora sat me down into a rocking chair in the corner of my room and kneeled before me. "Now you listen to me. Your father loves you very much. Do you understand me?" I twisted my colored zone bracelets, and Nora put her hands over mine. "He just has a hard time showing it now." My eyes darted to the cube on my dresser and Nora followed my gaze. Pictures of my mother filled each side, changing shots every ten seconds. Nora went and picked it up. "You look just like her, you know. Same chestnut hair. Same wide smile. It makes it harder for him." A younger Mila Sumner—everyone always said that, but I didn't see it. We looked similar, I supposed, but my mother had this energy, this fire that you could see even through a photo. I had nothing like that. Maybe she could have taught me had she lived longer, but I was only three when she died. My father wouldn't talk about her or any of her family now. Sometimes it felt like Nora was all I had. I stood up and gave her an impulsive hug.

"Thanks, Nora," I said.

"Of course, sweetheart. Now it's time to cheer up. You hear me?" she said grabbing on to my chin. "You have a big function to go to, and more than one boy to impress, am I right?"

"Just Bas," I told her.

"Mmhmm," she said and gave me a wink. "But let's make Link jealous all the same." I couldn't help but smile. I hadn't told anyone that I was nervous, and admittedly a tiny bit excited, about seeing Link again tonight. But Nora sensed it.

She whisked me over to my vanity and got to work, and I watched the transformation with my usual amazement. "You get prettier every day," Nora said when she completed her handiwork.

"I can't believe you're almost seventeen. You look so grown up." Nora had done my makeup to perfection. The liner made my brown eyes look sultry and mysterious, without looking sooty. And that was just the start. My cheekbones appeared razor sharp, my lips the perfect bow shape, and my skin clear and dewy. My hair tumbled in waves, softly framing Nora's work. I thought about giving her another hug, but it was getting close to leaving time and my father would walk in any minute. He didn't approve of friendships with lower rings. While Nora wasn't an Ash or even a Slate or Brown, she was a Yellow—and the help. He'd just yell at her again for treating me like a child instead of an up-and-coming leader. Plus, it was my fault we took so long getting ready. Portia and Lavendar wouldn't stop pinging me, and I had to coach Lavendar through a wardrobe crisis. After all, it wouldn't have been very minister-like to ignore a friend in need. Portia's pings, however, I let sit unanswered. She'd laughed at Dax Harris's prank, which I wasn't going to forget any time soon. My lack of response said more than any message.

"One last finishing touch," Nora said, reaching into my closet. "You said you wanted something a little different for your hair tonight, so I had Willa make something special." She took out a hatbox and opened it up, revealing a wreath made of fresh lilies, my mother's favorite flower.

"Nora, it's ultra. Thank you!" She carefully placed the halo on my head and the sugar-sweet smell of the flowers washed over me. I truly felt special.

"Your Aunt Maeve loved flower wreaths. When she moved into the house with your parents, she had Willa design her one every day, even if she wasn't going anywhere fancy. Maeve was—"

"What is that?" my father said. He stood in the doorway, arms crossed in front of him, and glowered at Nora.

"Oh hello, Mr. Sumner," Nora said in surprise. "We're just

finishing with Madden's hair. Doesn't she look beautiful?"

He shook his head, ignoring the question. "You know better than to bring *that* woman's name up in my home. I will not have my daughter made up to look like her. You and I will speak about this later, Nora."

"Oh, sir, I'm sorry. I didn't think about it that way. We just wanted to try something new tonight for the occasion."

My dad just glared. "Take it off and have her downstairs in five minutes. The car is waiting, and she cannot be late."

Nora bobbed her head. "Yes, sir."

My father left, slamming my door shut behind him.

"I'm sorry, Maddy," Nora said, rushing to my side and removing the wreath. "I should have known better."

"It's not your fault." I watched Nora gently place the wreath back in its box with a twinge of sadness. "He was overreacting. If it wasn't about Aunt Maeve, it would have been about something else, I'm sure."

Although Maeve really was a touchy subject. The last time I'd seen my mom's sister was when I was five. My father refused to even speak her name, let alone tell me anything about her. There'd been rumors about her being crazy and fleeing New City to live in the woods. That was before it had become illegal to go off grid. No one had ever told me the real story.

"Was Maeve really that bad?" I asked Nora.

Nora glanced at the door, then lowered her voice. "At the end, I suppose. But once upon a time, she was very wise, very brave, like your mother. Like you." She patted me on the back. "You should get going. You don't want to keep your father waiting."

I certainly didn't feel very brave, but it helped that Nora believed in me. It reminded me that, if nothing else, I could fake it better than anyone.

FIVE

—

Dax

I reached the tree at the end of my street and checked my wrist tracker. Thirty-eight minutes-fifteen seconds. A personal best, and I wasn't even out of breath. By the end of the year, I was sure to shave my run home down to an even thirty. The thought gave me an extra burst of energy, and I almost sprinted to my door, but a sea of red dresses blocked my path. As luck would have it, a gaggle of Crimson girls, no more than ten years old, were gathered on the pavement near my home.

My family lived in one half of a two-story aluminum duplex, identical to all of the others on the block. This time of day, the sunlight hitting the solar panels made the area's rooftops sparkle. The girls didn't seem to know what to do with all of the uniformity. Crimson neighborhoods weren't pre-fab like mine. They were giggling to themselves as I made my way around them.

"I'm pretty sure this is where he lives," the tall one with bushy eyebrows squealed. "I was able to track him this far, but he's not in my ping circle, so I don't know which house is his."

While it wasn't typical to see this many Crimsons in my area, it wasn't exactly out of the norm. Aldan's fans—especially the girls—had a tendency to hunt him down, even if it meant coming to the Yellow ring.

"You can ask her," the tiny one said when she spotted me watching them from the doorway. She sucked the end of her cherry red braid as she waited for her friend to answer.

For a second I actually thought I'd help them. Give them the thrill of their life and call my brother down to say hello. That was until I saw their expressions.

"Are you nuts?" Bushy eyebrows asked. She lowered her voice in disgust. "She's an Ash."

"But I really want to see Aldan," the little one whined.

"Fine," Bushy eyebrows relented. "Everyone put out a fist." They did as she instructed and she began that old childhood rhyme I detested. "*Purple, Crimson, Green, Yellow, Brown, Slate, Ash, touch one from the outer rings and you'll get a rash. You are out.* Ha! Rose, you're it, go ask her."

A skinny Crimson with tight blonde curls and a red pleated dress to match her ring affiliation took a few steps toward me. "Ash," she said, giving me a condescending look, "where does Aldan Harris live?"

"A few buildings that way," I replied, pointing down the street, toward the garbage dumpster at the end of the block. It would smell particularly ripe with the warm weather we'd been having. "Can't miss it – it's the one with the metal door."

I closed our own metal door behind me just as Rose exclaimed, "But, wait, they're all metal."

Welcome to the Yellow Ring, I thought. We were probably the only mixed-ring household in the entire area. All of my family was Yellow, except for my brothers, Link and Aldan, who were both Purples. After they'd been born my family had been bumped up two rings, to Crimson. It hadn't lasted long though. Once I came along, we were rezoned back to Yellow, so that's where we lived. I threw my bag down and let out a grunt thinking about the girls. *Touch one from the outer rings and you'll get a rash.* So much for a color tolerant society.

I took a deep breath. I understood the reason for the rings. Stories from the Event had been hammered into my head for as long as I could remember. About forty years ago, one person's failed destiny wiped out most of the world. Billions died. The stories and footage were terrifying. I knew the color system helped monitor the entire destiny matrix to keep us safe, but hearing the upper rings make fun of my standing still made me want to hit something.

"Dax, that better be you," Link shouted, interrupting my thoughts. "You're late."

"Coming," I hollered back, forgetting one annoyance and remembering another.

I hoped he hadn't heard about what happened with Madden. For reasons that continue to baffle me, my brother took it upon himself to fall for her a couple of years ago when he was a junior and she and I were freshman. He has a soft spot for her even now. I mean, don't get me wrong—the girl is pretty. Even I could admit that. But her whole superiority complex kind of negated her looks if you asked me. Whatever the case, today's courtyard performance was just the sort of thing that tended to get back to my brother. I took my time wandering to the kitchen, rehearsing possible defenses.

My parents and Link were sitting around our kitchen table. The plastic extender had been placed in the center of the table to open it to full width. I had to turn sideways to squeeze past as I walked in. My dad was, as usual, distracted by a book—sonnets by the look of it—while my mom and Link were fixated on the cube in the center of the table. My mom looked up as I came in. "Where have you been?" she demanded, scrubbing one hand through pale blonde hair the exact same shade as mine.

"It was Laira's Destiny Day today, remember?"

"That still should have put you here ages ago," she said.

"I know. It's a long story." I really didn't want to get into what had happened at school. Fortunately, my mom didn't want to hear about it either.

"Never mind," she replied, waving me off. "The race is in two hours, and we need to get there early to support Aldan."

My dad looked up absently, rubbing his hand over the few wisps of hair still clinging to his balding head. "As the bard says, 'better three hours too soon than a minute too late.'"

"The Tempest?" I asked, grabbing a box of Rice Puffs from the counter. My dad loved quoting Shakespeare. It was a fascination I'd never shared, though I did try to humor him.

"The Merry Wives of Windsor," Link corrected me.

"Very good," my dad said to Link in approval. "Nice try all the same, honey."

"Thanks, Dad," I replied and nodded to the beer he was drinking. "One of Carlen's?" My oldest brother, Carlen, worked for a brewery in NoPur, the dividing line to the north of the Purple zone, right where it transitioned to Crimson. His destiny had been to make a commemorative beer for the inventor of the destiny system, and one of the founding ministers, Dr. Jebidiah Og. He completed it two years ago when he was twenty-six. If rumor could be trusted, the brew was still a ministry favorite. On special occasions my dad could usually be found with one of Carlen's brews in hand. I could even talk him into a sip when Mom wasn't around.

"You bet," he answered. I could see the pride on his face as he turned once more to his book.

"So what's the number up to?" I leaned over Link's shoulder to look at the cube's screen.

"He just broke five million," Link said, clearly oblivious to my Madden run-in.

"Not bad," I said, plopping down in the chair next to him. I shoved a handful of puffs into my mouth. "Any good mail?" I asked between chews.

"Somehow they keep managing to top the last ones," Link replied, turning back to the screen facing him. "This one comes from our very own New City. *Dear Aldan, watching your dedication to loop racing has been truly motivating. Anyone can fulfill a destiny, but the way you've prepared for yours with such grace and commitment has been an inspiration. You've taught my children how important it is to work hard, even if destiny has already paved a path for you. You're a true role model. A true hero.*"

"Aaaaldan," I yelled in the direction of his room, "You're a true hero. And role model. And inspiration."

My mom looked up and shook her head. "Dax, don't yell at the table."

Link punched the screen again and snorted.

"Let me see," I said, spinning the cube in my direction. I clapped a hand over my mouth to keep from laughing as well. "Here's one from New Vegas." I raised my voice an octave. "*Dearest Aldie, you are the most handsomest, smartest, nicest loop racer the world has ever known. Every night I go to sleep looking at a cube filled with you doing your greatest tricks. I even named my stuffed clock tower after you, so that I can say I kiss Aldan every night. One day I hope to do it for real. But we can't tell my daddy. The last boy I kissed he—*"

"Dax, I was using that screen," my mom said, exasperated. She spun the cube back around. "I've got our tickets pulled up," she continued. "We have three spots in the Box. Link will take one. Your father and I will take the other two."

She tapped the top of the cube so that all of the sides now showed the seating chart. "We've got spots for the rest of your brothers here."

"Where are they, anyway?" I asked. Link and Aldan were my only brothers living at home, but the others still lived in the Yellow zone on the opposite side of town. I'd thought everyone would be at the house in preparation for Aldan's race, but so far I'd only seen Link.

"Ald's in his room," Link replied. He rolled his eyes. "Talking to *her.*"

We exchanged a grin. Aldan had been spending more and more time chatting with a mystery girl, but neither one of us could pry any details from him.

"Strom, Pel, and Kai are already at the loop making signs or something," he continued, ticking our brothers off on his fingers. "Carlen is at the brewery getting ready for the after-party tonight. And Shay is running late at work. There's some emergency at the park he had to take care of. They'll meet us there."

I nodded my head as I looked at the chart again, steeling myself before I spoke. "Where am I sitting?" I knew what the answer would be, but I still had to ask.

"Yeah, Mom," Aldan said, appearing in the doorway. He was already wearing his purple jersey with the number "1" stitched onto both sides. While it was crisp and ironed—my mother had seen to that—his hair looked like an overturned bird's nest. "Where's Dax sitting?" He readjusted one of his signature purple arm cuffs as he waited for her response.

My mom sighed, and with that tiny exhalation of air I had my answer.

"It's alright." I shrugged. "I already made plans. I told Laira

I'd sit with her."

She gave me a bright smile. "Well, there you go," she said.

"No way," Aldan said. He walked to the table and jerked a chair out, flipping it around backward before sitting down. He propped his elbows on its back and fixed my mom with a steady look. "I thought you asked for a family pass."

Her smile fizzled. "Honey," she said. "I've got the rest of your brothers all together, which was hard enough. I'd like Dax to sit with the family as much as you, but this is a very visible event. I hardly think this is the kind of publicity you want today."

Or any day, I thought. My mom and I weren't exactly close. She tolerated me at best. If I just had a destiny—any sort of destiny—she probably wouldn't hate me so much. But I don't. And whether I'm out in New City, or in my own home, I will never forget that detail. Neither will she.

"I don't care about publicity," Aldan said. "What I care about is my family feeling like they're part of this event. The *entire* family. Dax, how about it? You want to sit in the fourth row?"

"Sure," I said, doing my best not to get excited. I know better than that. Getting excited just means more disappointment in the long run.

"Aldan, be reasonable," my mother said, exasperated. "Bill, tell him to be reasonable." She turned to my dad, who was once again absorbed in his book and ignoring everyone around him. Nothing shocking there.

"Hmm?" he asked, looking up. "What's that?"

"Aldan's got some preposterous idea of seating Dax with the rest of the family tonight. Could you please talk some sense into him?"

"Actually," Link interrupted, "I've got a better idea."

We turned to him in one motion.

"Why don't you take my seat, Dax? In the Box."

My mother was speechless. It was unheard of for someone like me to sit in the Box. I just stared at Link, dumbfounded. It might have been the only time my mother and I have ever had the same reaction to anything. It didn't last, though.

"Are you out of your mind, Link Harris?" my mother exploded. "Of course Dax isn't sitting in the Box. And she's not going to sit in the fourth row either, Aldan. I refuse to let our family turn into some kind of media spectacle. I can*not* believe we are having this conversation." She looked at me, her lips pressed together in a thin line. "Dax, do you want the entire country focused on you, or where the attention belongs—on your brother?"

For some reason, I wanted to laugh, but I knew that was the wrong response. I kind of specialize in saying the wrong things, especially where my mom's concerned, so instead I cleared my throat and waited.

"Dax? I'm asking you a serious question."

"Jacqueline." My dad interrupted my mom. He put his book down and looked at her in surprise. "Let's all calm down please."

"If it's my day," Aldan replied, "it should be my decision."

Before things could get any worse, I held up my hand. "I'll sit with the other Ashes. Mom's right. It'll turn into a thing if I sit with you all up front."

My mom glared around the table, head high in victory.

"But Dax," Aldan said.

"It's okay," I said. "Really." Even though it wasn't. But you get used to these things when you're a Blank. It wasn't like I had a choice.

"Then you'll wear this," Aldan said. He took off one of his cuffs and grabbed my arm, repositioning the stretchy material around my bicep. Where it had been, the naked skin now made a natural white band against his suntanned arm. He squeezed my hand before letting it go. "If you're not going to sit with us, then you can at least wear my colors today."

I studied the band of purple circling my arm. It's not like I hadn't tried the color on before. At home. In the privacy of my bedroom. Without anyone else knowing about it. But this was different.

My mother stood, her chair screeching against the floor. "Boys, really, enough. The way you two are carrying on you'd think your sister was Madden Sumner." She turned to me and crossed her arms in front of her chest. "You and I both know you are not wearing that band out of this house. The fine would be exorbitant."

My mom stalked off, leaving my dad to smooth things over. "Oh, sweetheart," he said, his tone apologetic. "Your mom doesn't realize how her words sound sometimes, and today she's especially anxious." He stood and walked around to me, kissing the top of my head. "I wish you could sit with us, but we'll celebrate at the after-party as a family, okay?" I could see the concern etched over his face.

"Sure," I replied.

"Okay, then," he said. "We really all do need to get moving now. Time waits for no man." He squeezed my shoulder before walking down the hall.

"Dax, I'm sorry," Link said.

"What is wrong with her?" Aldan muttered. "Don't let her get to you, okay? She doesn't know anything."

One of the things I hate about being a Blank is that I'm constantly forced to lie about how it feels to actually *be* a Blank. "It's okay, guys. Really. It would be fun to sit up front, but you know she's right." And she was. I could count on my mom for two things—the unsweetened truth and general annoyance at my existence.

"Dax, it's not alright. There's no reason she should treat you like that," Link said. "I'm going to talk to her."

"No," I said. "Let's just get ready, okay? It's Aldan's day, and we all need to get to the race." I laughed. "Seriously, you guys. I don't care, and if I don't care then why should you?"

Link looked unsure and I punched him in the shoulder. "Knock it off. Our brother's got a race to win, alright?"

He grinned back at me. "Fine," he said.

That's the other thing I hate about being a Blank. People feel so sorry for me that I'm always having to cheer them up. Well, people in my family at least.

"And you should probably take this back," I said, pulling off Aldan's cuff.

He stopped me. "It's yours."

"You know I can't wear it out of the house, Aldan."

"Sure you can," he replied. "Wear long sleeves. Who'll know the difference?"

I smiled. A real smile. The dress I had borrowed from Laira had three quarter length sleeves. I *could* actually wear his cuff and no one would know.

"Thanks," I said, trying not to choke up. I wouldn't trade my brothers for any destiny, no matter how big.

Aldan stood up. "Good," he said. "Now let's get ready." He and Link got up to leave, but Aldan stopped at the doorway. "For the record, you're better than Madden Sumner."

SIX

Madden

Cameras snapped as I sailed down the purple carpet, arm linked in Bastin's. We kept a tasteful amount of space between us as we made our way toward the private entrance leading to the Box.

Overhead, videos of tonight's eight racers were being projected onto the arena walls. I recognized footage of Aldan from a race I'd attended last summer with Link. He and I might be history, but I still had a soft spot for his brother. Aldan's enthusiasm could fill up a room. Or arena for that matter, I thought, as I looked around at the thousands of people who'd come to witness the Championship. Many wore his signature "1" somehow patched to their clothing. I loved how this kind of occasion could bring people together.

"Madden, look over here," a voice called from the crowd. I turned and smiled, not breaking my stride.

"Madden, anything you'd like to say to the audience?"

Seconds later a hovercam reached me and I stopped, looking directly into the lens. My face was projected onto the walls, interrupting the racing footage, and I casually adjusted a strand of hair I could see was out of place. "Tonight's race is about fulfilling a dream," I began, my voice echoing. "A dream each of today's athletes share. They've worked long and hard to be a part of this year's Loop Championship, and I wish them all the very best." I lowered my voice and let just a hint of mischief punctuate my words. "Though, to be clear—"

A hush fell over the arena as the crowd awaited my words.

"It's still about winning." I smiled brilliantly and yelled, "Go Aldan!" The crowd screamed and clapped, taking up the chant of "Go Aldan" as Bastin and I continued through the stadium and onto the lift. He pressed the top floor and within moments we exited into the Box.

As soon as we entered I could feel Brine Chandler looking me up and down, his eyes resting too long where they shouldn't. It took every ounce of willpower to resist telling him off, but I didn't need a scene. Brine was a member of the PAE and involved in all local security infractions. If there was a New City problem, you could count on Brine to be there. More importantly, he was also Bas's closest friend. I considered asking him about the earlier incident, but I knew now wasn't the time.

"Brine," Bas shouted, giving his buddy a slap on the back. I gave a tightlipped smile, in case the cameras were still broadcasting me, and began to wander, leaving the guys to themselves.

I loved being up this high. It was better away from the crowds, and the panoramic view through the glass walls was endless. Not only did the Box have the best seats in the stadium to see every twist and turn of the giant loop coaster, but it also had cold drinks. A Yellow server held out a tray of berry spritzers, and I took a glass. A straw with two loops jutted from the liquid. It was a nice touch.

Beyond the Box seats was a tiny soundbooth. Inside stood one of my oldest friends. His mess of reddish-brown hair had been tamed for the night, and I was surprised to see that he was wearing a suit. It wasn't often that Theron made an effort. It looked good on him.

At the moment, he was ruining the effect by cracking up with the Green sound technicians. No doubt in the middle of a joke. A moment later they all burst out laughing. That was Theron for you. He'd swap stories with anyone—even those he shouldn't. He glanced up, almost as if he felt me watching, and his face broke into an even broader smile. He waved before heading my way.

"Hello, Theron," I greeted him.

"Hey, Madden. You look ultra," he said, taking a drink from the server's tray as she passed again.

"Thank you. You ready for tonight?" I asked. Theron was the evening's emcee.

"Of course," he said, giving me an easy grin that rearranged the freckles across his cheeks. "I get to announce Aldan's coast to victory. What could be better?"

Theron always tried to act upbeat, especially around me, but I could tell he was tense. While tonight's race was a formality, the world would still be watching. And in Theron's case, listening. That took some getting used to—even for someone who was always the center of attention. I knew that firsthand.

I raised my glass toward him. "To an action-packed race."

"To not flubbing my lines," he said, clinking his glass to mine.

"Well, I'm excited to hear what you have in store," I told him and took a sip of my drink.

"It should get a few laughs," he said. "Hopefully some from you." He did a quick pan of the Box. "Where's your leech?"

I gave him a disapproving sigh but nodded toward the

entrance all the same.

"Ahh," Theron laughed. "So you finally admit your boyfriend is a freeloader. I knew you'd come around to my way of thinking."

"Shhh." I looked around to make sure no one heard what he was saying. Theron had a tendency to push too far when it came to Bas. I knew he was joking, but the right sound clip in the hands of the wrong reporter could be devastating. I threw my voice a little louder. "I said no such thing. Bastin is a remarkable man with a remarkable destiny."

"Yeah. 'To build.' How much do you want to bet that if he wasn't the grandson of a minister, he'd be on the crew building new air rails or containment units instead of in charge of it all? I can picture Mr. Manicure hauling beams around."

"Keep your voice down," I warned him. "You know very well a Destiny Specialist evaluated what Bas should be doing." There was no way a Specialist would give special treatment—deciphering accurate callings at birth is what made our system work. So I just smiled and reminded Theron what he already knew. "They wouldn't arbitrarily assign something, unless it was meant to be."

"Lucky for you," he replied, pointing at a stony-faced PAE officer across the room. "Can you imagine having to laugh at that guy's jokes instead of mine?"

The officer glared back at Theron, and I swallowed back my laughter.

"See, I'm already doing my job. I heard you laugh," Theron said.

"Try a grunt of annoyance," Bas said as he joined us, draping his arm around my shoulder. "Is he bothering you?'

I was used to the bickering between Bas and Theron. They hated each other. And not just because of Theron's destiny, but because Bas was a by-the-book type of guy and Theron, well, he liked to have fun.

I patted Bas's arm. "Give him a break. This is almost as big of a day for him as it is for Aldan. And you know he'll do anything to make me smile." He would, at that. Theron's destiny was to make me laugh—or, if you wanted the specifics, to make the Minister of the Seven closest to his age laugh, which amounted to the same thing. As a result, we'd practically grown up together. And since there was no time stamp on his destiny, we would be bound for life.

"Don't you have somewhere else to be? Sound check or something?" Bas asked him coolly.

Theron raised an eyebrow. "Are you suggesting I shirk my destiny? What would Granddaddy say?"

I felt Bas's arm tighten around me as he went on the defensive. "You know that's not what I meant."

"Okay, boys, enough." I said. "Today isn't about us. We're here to watch the championship, and support Aldan's Destiny Day while we're at it. Not to fight with one another."

Theron nodded and got a faraway look on his face. I could tell his mind had moved back to the race and his upcoming role.

"You'll be great," I assured him and nudged Bas.

"Yeah," my boyfriend muttered.

"Besides," I said, "It's Aldan up there. It's only right that you're part of his big day." The two were best friends. Theron had been there to see every record that Aldan had broken—which was all of them. "Remember how amazing he was at the track last summer?"

I almost hit myself for bringing it up. The last thing I wanted to think about was last summer, hand in hand with Link, sitting together at the practice track watching Aldan do impossible trick after trick. Back then we'd even talked about coming to the championship together. But that was before Link's stubborn streak had ruined everything.

I pushed away the memories. "Anyway," I said before Theron could respond. "I know you have to get ready, so we'll let you go. Good luck tonight."

As Theron headed back to the booth, my eyes scanned the others in the Box. There was no sign of Link yet, and I took a deep breath, willing the tight knot in my stomach to release. I wanted to sit before he and his parents showed up. Maybe I'd be able to avoid them that way. "Want to sit down?" I asked Bas.

"Sure," he said, grabbing my hand again.

We walked through several rows of purple-clad spectators, many of whom I knew through various charities or fundraisers. I waved hello to a few acquaintances as Bas led me to the front of the Box. The Seven took up most of the front row seats, of course. All but Dr. Og, the inventor of the destiny system. He rarely made it out anymore. When he did, it was for meetings, and he was always accompanied by his caretaker.

Minister Edward Worthington, my boyfriend's grandfather, stood as we approached. He wore a deep purple suit and matching pinstripe tie. A multicolored pin was attached to his lapel, representing the seven rings. His gray hair and matching beard were perfectly groomed, as always. Minister Worthington was tall and thin, where Bastin was broad and muscled. But he and Bastin shared the same cool, blue eyes. He turned them on me, nodding politely.

"Hi Granddad," Bas greeted him. The two shook hands.

"A good day to you both," he replied. He turned to me and pumped my hand as well. "I saw the broadcast of your speech to the Industry Employers over in AnaKurtz. Motivating yet firm," he said, giving me an approving nod. "Well done."

"Thank you, Minister," I replied. I had spoken to three hundred employees in the manufacturing sector named for our former president. It took me two days to write and prepare my speech, and then I ended up scrapping it, instead speaking off the cuff. I received a standing ovation.

"And I've heard your inauguration date is set," he continued. "Next summer, is it?"

"That's my girl," Bastin said, slinging an arm around me.

I smiled broadly at both of them. "I'm very much looking forward to it."

Which was an understatement. There had been complications during my birth. My destiny had been extracted with no problems, but its time stamp was another story. Everyone knew how quickly details about one's destiny faded after birth—the specifics were completely lost within the hour. In my case, immediately after my destiny was recorded, my mother had a seizure. She recovered just fine, but as a result, the Specialist wasn't able to continue the extraction and my time stamp was lost. It had never really been a problem for me. It just meant the date of my rise to council was "to be determined." Or had been until last week when the council announced I would be inducted next summer. I took it as a huge vote of confidence they felt I was almost ready.

Minister Worthington rubbed the hair on his chin thoughtfully. "You'll be the youngest minister in history," he said. He didn't have to say the next part. It was implied. Being the youngest meant that everyone would be watching—closely.

"I won't let you, or any of the other ministers down, sir," I said. "And I'm honored."

He chuckled as he turned back to Bas. "I'll see you this Sunday for dinner?"

Bas nodded. "Looking forward to it. And maybe afterward I can show you the new schematics I'm working on for ring security."

As Bas and his grandfather continued to talk I made my way down the line of the remaining Seven, stopping to shake each of their hands and exchange a few words. The only one who made me feel at ease was Minister Tagon Corbin. He was by far the youngest of the Seven, and a major loop enthusiast.

"Madden," he greeted me.

I shook his hand and smiled. "Are you excited for the race, Minister?" I asked.

"Oh, absolutely." He shook his head enthusiastically, and gestured toward the giant loop coaster rising in front of us. "I'll be interested to see how the players will navigate this orientation."

We both turned to appraise the course. From this vantage I could fully appreciate just how many modifications had been made for the championship. The track itself was built out of the same clear material used for the light rail, complete with the magnetic surface for the racers to hover over. But that's where the similarities ended. There were eight loops to pass through before a player could reach the end, with some sections wider, and others narrower so that only one racer could get through at a time. Colored lights pulsed through the structure in quick bursts. I'd never seen anything like it.

"Get a load of that drop." Minister Corbin pointed to the end of the track. "There's never been one that steep. It almost goes straight down."

My eyes widened. It was hundreds of feet. It looked impossible to maneuver safely.

A young girl's voice interjected from behind us. "Aldan could still coast that thing with his eyes closed," she said.

I turned around. An earnest little girl peeked up at me through a cloud of dark ringlets. She looked even smaller sandwiched between her security detail. "I bet you're right, Aya," I replied.

The girl gave me a shy smile. "I always pretend I'm Aldan when I play Loop Racer. Have you tried it?"

I shook my head no, and she punched a few buttons on her

wrist tracker. A small hologram appeared before us. "It's kind of like the real race. You have to guide your board to the bottom of the track without getting knocked off by the other players. Only in the game you also have to dodge falling stars and lightning. I'm on level 147. I bet you'd like it."

"I'm sure I would," I agreed. "Maybe you can teach me sometime?"

A smile lit up Aya's face, and she nodded furiously. "Definitely," she said.

I returned her smile. I was seeing more and more of the little Purple of late, and I had a feeling I would continue to. She was the only person on record to have a classified destiny—it was even above my Violet clearance—and every time we spoke I had to stop myself from begging her to tell me about it. I hated unsolved puzzles. I'd find out once I joined the Seven, of course, but in the meantime I'd just have to trust that she would play an important part of our future.

The first bell rang through the stadium, letting us know the competition would be starting shortly. "I guess I should find my seat," I said to Aya. "Enjoy the race." I nodded to Minister Corbin as I turned. And that's when I saw him.

I felt the bubbles from my drink twist through my stomach as I examined my ex. Link looked even better than when last I'd seen him. His dark blond hair was cropped close to his head. It was shorter than it had been when we'd dated. More befitting of his status as a Destiny Specialist. Although he still wore the faded lavender shirt I never liked. It was even more faded now—to the point that it had a tinge of ash. The handcrafted royal purple shirt I'd had Willa make him to replace it was still wrapped in my closet. Link had never spent money on clothes, or on anything really. Instead he donated his salary to his family. Even then, it was barely enough to counteract the tax Dax's status cost them. I sighed. He wasn't even bothered by having a Blank in the family. It was a good reminder of one of the many reasons we'd have never worked out. It didn't bring me any comfort, though.

Link looked up at that moment and locked eyes with mine. It took every ounce of willpower I had not to turn away, but instead I gave him a courteous nod. There were cameras everywhere, and I refused to have an awkward moment on record.

"Madden," Bas called, still standing next to his grandfather. "Come sit." He combed his hair back with his hand and adjusted his purple tie. Not that there was any need. Bas was always immaculately dressed for any occasion.

I made my way to my seat. Bas and his grandfather had moved from pleasant conversation to a heated debate on the latest Blank legislation that was held up in the Delegation—a group of appointed politicians chosen to represent each ring from New City and the other territories of the States. The Seven could eventually move the bill forward, but the Delegation might stall it for at least a few more months, or even years if they didn't plan carefully.

"Just overrule them," Bas said, exasperated by what I assumed his grandfather's explanation of policy was.

Minister Worthington gestured to me. "I'm sure Madden could explain the political intricacies. At least someone here is up on their studies."

I hated when Minister Worthington put me in the middle of their family squabbles. Bas was always desperately trying to win his grandfather's approval, and it didn't help our relationship to be pitted against one another.

"Gentlemen, today is about racing, not policy. Look at that track."

Minister Worthington gave a hardy laugh. "Right as usual, Madden. But my grandson here could use a lesson on the finer points of government. Do you mind switching places with me so Bas and I may continue our conversation?"

I looked down the front row, careful to keep my anxiety from showing. Minister Worthington's vacant seat was next to three additional empty ones, and I had a feeling I knew who would be taking them. "Of course not," I said, and moved to my new seat, where I feigned interest in the screens floating outside the Box. They broadcast snippets from last year's race.

"Madden Sumner, is that you?"

I did my best to keep the dismay from my face, instead twisting my lips into something I hoped would pass for a smile.

"Mrs. Harris, how delightful to see you," I responded to Link's mother. My words sounded flat, and I couldn't help but notice her yellow gown had two thin stripes of purple crossing one shoulder—a stripe for Aldan and another for Link. A little tacky, I thought, but by rights she had earned them.

"You dear girl," Link's mom gushed. "We have absolutely missed you to bits. Isn't that right, Bill?" Link's father leaned around his wife.

"Greetings my dear," he said. "As the bard says, 'How far that little candle throws his beams! So shines a good deed in a weary world.'"

I'd never cared for Shakespeare and wasn't interested in starting now. I nodded politely to Link's father. "Very nice to see you again, Mr. Harris," I replied.

"Link?" Mrs. Harris called. "Link, come and tell Madden hello."

Link turned from the conversation he'd been caught up in. Our eyes met again, and I froze, caught up in his perfect face. No one had features like him. His eyes, his jaw, his… I felt myself growing red and yanked my gaze away from his. Crilas, I thought. Why did I look away first?

"Hi," he said simply.

I looked back up. "Hello, Link. How pleasant to see you. Are you looking forward to the race today? Lovely weather we're having, don't you think?"

It was as though I was on autopilot, mouthing words that didn't belong to me. Lots of words that I couldn't seem to stop. Why did he have to look so good?

"I bet you can't wait to see what Aldan will do on the loops," I continued. "Because, you know, the loops are really ultra." My heart was racing as quickly as my words, and I couldn't stop the last few from tumbling out. "I mean, what an incredible Destiny Day, and what a wonderful chance for all of us to share it. You must be pretty excited." This wasn't happening. I'd spent the last year planning what I would say to Link when we next spoke. In all of these imaginary conversations, I'd been satisfied by the regret I knew my words would spark.

Link nodded his head somberly. "Pretty excited," he agreed, echoing my inane words. He didn't take his eyes off of me, and my heart was going faster than Aldan on a track. I used to love the way Link looked at me—like I was special, like I was all that mattered, like I was his destiny. But that was before. Now his eyes were filled with disappointment and a trace of betrayal. Our lives were no longer in sync.

The second bell rang, and I sunk down into my seat. Link would sit on the other side of his parents and everything would be fine, I reassured myself. I wouldn't have to look at him anyway. I wouldn't have to wonder what if…

"Oh, I have a marvelous idea," Mrs. Harris said, clapping her hands. "Honey, why don't you come sit next to Madden?" She grabbed Link's hand and pulled him toward me. "Take my seat. Quick now, the race is about to begin!"

And with that I was seated next to Link Harris.

SEVEN

—

Dax

"Come on, Laira," I said, dragging her closer to the entrance of the arena, and doing my best not to wrinkle the gray cotton dress I'd borrowed from her for the occasion. Its sleeves hid Aldan's cuff perfectly, but I hadn't counted on just how delicate it would be. I reached under the fabric and rubbed the cuff for luck. If we didn't get through the crowd soon, we might not make it into the arena. Everyone in New City was there, and Ashes weren't exactly a priority for seating.

Laira had stopped for the moment, transfixed by the images of Madden Sumner projected across the overhead screens. Our country's future leader was quite literally larger than life as she took a sip from her drink. Unless that drink was dribbling down her perfectly powdered chin, I had no interest in watching. I grabbed Laira's arm and dragged her after me, elbowing my way through the crowd with the others. It was still taking way too long, so I cut through the refreshment stands, collecting glares from the people working there.

"Sorry, sorry, sorry," I repeated like a broken voice cube as we snuck through their workspace.

Klay Kemp, who was manning the water stand, just shrugged. "Water?" he asked, holding out a bottle.

I shook my head no, right as Sol Josephson rounded the corner.

"Aww, come on," Sol said, flinging himself into our conversation. "You can't support your own classmate in his tireless pursuit of destiny? Isn't that the whole crux of our society? Our whole reason for living? What kind of person are you, anyway?"

"He does have a point," Laira said, totally missing the glint in Sol's eyes and the smile he was fighting to keep off of his face. "Klay's destiny is to give water."

"I always have a point, Laira," he answered, taking a bottle from Klay. "Aldan Harris, Loop Champion," Sol read from the label. "Well, Klay, I'm impressed with your professionalism. So much that I'd like to help the cause even further." He grabbed a second bottle from him and tossed it in his bag.

"Get lost, Sol," Klay said, as he continued to pass out bottles, never missing a beat. Not that that surprised me. Klay never stopped handing out water. Part of having a destiny that was extracted too late for a time stamp was that he didn't know when he was supposed to give water or who he was supposed to give it to. As a result, his Destiny Specialist, someone just like Link, had decided he should do it all the time. It got pretty bad for him in school—especially when we were younger. The Purples would say they were thirsty, just to watch him race up and get them something to drink. It didn't help that he was the only Slate at Spectrum. The higher rings were pretty merciless.

"I'm hurt," Sol said, slapping his hand over his heart. "But I'll forgive you. I know destiny is at stake."

Klay rolled his eyes. He knew Sol didn't mean anything by the ribbing, but it was clear he had enough for one day.

"Let's go," I said.

"Are you asking me to join you for the race? Like, a date? How forward of you, Dax." Sol matched my stride as we approached the entrance and gave me an appreciative look. "You didn't need to dress up for me, but I have to say I like it. So shall we make it official? Want to hold my hand?"

"What? No!" I said, smacking his outreached hand from mine.

"Oh Dax, didn't your dad tell you about the lady and protesting too much."

If Sol wasn't an equal opportunity flirt I might have read something into his words, but it was just his way, so I rolled my eyes. "You can't trust Hamlet, Sol. I hear he was nuts." But I admit I was secretly happy he noticed my dress. Hopefully that meant Theron would too when I saw him at the after party.

"Let's go in, *Laira*," I said and pulled out my ticket.

"You'll be back," Sol called after us. "You'll see. You won't be able to resist me."

"Keep dreaming," I said, handing my ticket to Eather Vanley, a sophomore Green from school, who was collecting them.

"Sorry," she said, giving it back. "The Ash area is full."

"But I have a ticket. I have to get inside."

She didn't even bother giving me a response, instead turning to another Green handing her a ticket.

"You don't understand. I have to get in. Aldan is my brother!" Eather shrugged. "Sorry, we're full," she repeated.

"It's okay," Laira said, putting her hand on my arm. I shook it off.

"No, it's not," I replied. My whole body began to shake. "I have to watch him race."

"There are the screens. We can watch it here."

"That's not the same." My words caught in my throat, as I witnessed Sol handing Eather his ticket.

He winked at me. "Ms. Vanley, these ladies are with me. Do you mind?"

Eather shrugged again, but stepped aside for the three of us to slip into the arena.

"Told you I was irresistible," he said smugly.

"How did you do that?" I asked, following him through the crowd. Sol had no pull. He was an Ash, just like me. He might have had a destiny—but the worst kind.

"My little secret," he said, as we squeezed ourselves onto one of the bleachers.

"What did you do?" Laira asked. "Give her better odds in your *gambling* ring?" She whispered the word gambling as if she was afraid that someone from the PAE would come and detain her just for saying it out loud.

"Let's just say," Sol began, "that the C-minus Ms. Vanley received in World History last year somehow got switched to an A." He gave me one of his lopsided grins. "You're welcome."

"Thank you," I said, and I meant it. While I may not have had romantic feelings for Sol, I did like him. And if he was a little blunt sometimes, I could hardly blame him. Sol was destined to die. His Destiny Specialist hadn't been able to pinpoint his time stamp to the exact date, but they did know he would die by his eighteenth birthday. That left him just under a year. Maybe. I couldn't imagine what it was like, living each day knowing that it might be your last. It wasn't something Sol really talked about.

Around us the benches were mostly filled and separated by color. The back rows, where we'd squeezed in, were occupied by Ashes. The Ash ring was the largest, and the row upon row of light gray-clad bodies filling the back of the stadium reflected that. A dozen rows in front of us, the color began to darken where Ash met Slate. Slate was the second largest ring, and at least another dozen rows of charcoal clothing passed before the colors flowed to brown, then yellow, then brightened to green, then crimson. The front row was exclusively purple. It was a perfect representation of our society.

Another image flashed on one of the screens overhead. It was Madden again. Only this time she was sitting next to my brother. "Poor Link," I groaned.

"Are you kidding me?" Laira shrieked. "It would be ultra if your brother got back together with her. If they got married, you'd be Madden's sister-in-law. That's almost better than a destiny."

"Careful, Laira," Sol warned. "Keep saying stuff like that and the Removers may come and take you away."

Laira looked at him in horror. "How could you joke about something like that?" she said, shocked. "I just completed my destiny this morning. You were there!"

"Relax," I reassured her. "Sol's just messing with you. *Everyone* knows how important the destiny system is to you. Right, Sol?"

"Mmhmmm," he answered, barely listening to me. I looked over at him. He was mesmerized by the screen.

Really? Even him? "Don't tell me you're a Madden fan too?"

He ripped his eyes away. "Jealous?"

"Hardly. I just think you can do better."

Laira snorted, and I elbowed her.

"Yeah," he said. "Who wouldn't want a guy with an automatic expiration date? She'd barely have a chance to get sick of me."

Once again, Sol left me not knowing how to answer.

"Shhhh," Laira told us. "It's starting."

An image of Dr. Og appeared on the screens. The minister was as old as the destiny system, and he looked it. No one was surprised to see his image projected in from a cozy living room instead of from the Box. He'd been sick for years. Still, it was too bad. He was the only minister who seemed to care about all people. From all rings. Madden would take his place when he retired next year. Poor trade, if you asked me.

Dr. Og smiled, making the folds of skin around his eyes ripple. "I want to take a moment to congratulate the athletes standing before you," he began, a slight wheeze accenting his voice. "Take a long look at these young men and women. They represent the best Loop Racers of our time. And I'm sure I don't need to remind any of you that one of tonight's racers is here by way of destiny."

A cheer rang out, and I chanted Aldan's name along with the crowd. Dr. Og smiled patiently until we quieted.

"But it's important to remember that every single athlete tonight is a role model. A champion. A beacon of hope as we continue to rebuild after the great pandemic. These men and women are heroes who have touched our lives, and inspired us with their unfailing dedication to the game, and to our way of life." He paused to cough into a handkerchief before continuing. "So to all of tonight's competitors, congratulations. And thank you. To all of those watching the game—from those seated in the stands, to those tuning in from home like myself—prepare to be amazed. Let the games begin!"

A roar went through the stadium. The projections changed from that of Dr. Og to the competitors taking their places at the start of the loop track. The screen in the center, along with several more on the side, was devoted to my brother.

"Go, Aldan!" I yelled out, with just about everyone else.

"If I can have your attention, please." Theron's voice filled the arena, and I shook my head in disbelief. I still couldn't believe that he'd managed to talk his way into announcing the race. Having a destiny like 'make the minister closest to your age laugh' came with privileges I couldn't begin to fathom. "Before we begin, we have a special message. So if I can have a moment of silence."

Theron sounded serious, and he was never serious when there was an audience around. Laira gave me a questioning look, but I just shrugged. I was as confused as she was.

"As many of you know," Theron began, "Aldan Harris's whole life has been leading up to this moment. As a result, his brothers would like to share a special tribute with the audience today."

The cameras turned to show five of my older brothers, Carlen, Shay, Strom, Pel, and Kai. A large purple "1" was painted on each of their faces, for Aldan's jersey number. They were laughing so hard that they could barely hold up their individual signs, which read together: BEEP BEEP. LOOP RACER. COMING THROUGH. WHOA! WHOA!

"Oh no," I said, starting to laugh. "Poor Aldan."

Laira and Sol both turned to me in confusion.

"What does it mean?" Laira asked.

"You'll find out," I said between giggles. "Look," I pointed to the screens overhead.

They showed a projection of Aldan at four-years-old, splashing in the bathtub. He sang enthusiastically through the soapy beard that bubbled from his chin. "Beep, beep," he crooned, honking an imaginary horn. "I'm a loop racer, and I'm coming through, whoa whoa. Beep beep," he began again, singing another round.

A second camera zoomed in for a close-up of Aldan, who was laughing hysterically from the track. He began singing along with his younger, wetter self and the crowd joined his laughter.

I couldn't believe Theron had gotten this broadcast approved. I looked up toward the Box with a grin, and a tiny flutter of the heart. Knowing Theron, he probably hadn't. My mother must be seething. The after-party would be interesting. I could almost hear her now. *How could you disgrace such a noble and prestigious event?* I laughed again.

When Aldan's song came to an end he pressed an imaginary horn and hollered out a final "beep beep." The audience howled with laughter, chanting my brother's name.

Everything quieted down when the clock tower chimed five o'clock. The race was set to begin and we all gave a moment of silence to mark the occasion. Then the eight competitors took their places.

"Eight, seven, six, five, four, " Theron counted down, his voice increasing in excitement. "three, two, one!" He sounded the horn and the racers rocketed off of the ramp. They were on the first leg of the track, trying to gain whatever speed they could for the first incline. It was the smallest, only fifty feet, but that was plenty of room to still get hurt. If one of the players fell from the tracks, their board would repel against the stadium's metal flooring to stop their fall. But if they didn't brace themselves properly, they could still get seriously injured. No matter how many times I watched Aldan race, I still found myself holding my breath from the moment he took off until the moment he crossed the finish line.

"Ladies and gentlemen, there's no surprise here," Theron announced over the speakers. "Aldan Harris is already in the lead. Followed closely—although not too closely—by Tred Nier and Lemad Loring. The other five, come on guys, speed it up. I'm looking at you Reiner Walley. Some people have you as a shoo-in for second, though my bets are on Lemad. That is if I were a betting man. Which, of course, I'm not. Though to be clear, if I *was*, I'd have Aldan finishing the race in three minutes, fifty-two seconds."

The middle screen displayed Theron giving the ministers a huge grin and thumbs up sign. Minister Worthington scowled at him. That is until he realized a hovercam was on him. Then he shook his head and gave a hearty laugh. "Boys will be boys," he said.

"Yeah," Sol said, his eyes glued to his plexi. He was tracking all eight racers with eight grids on the screen. "That's why he said anyone caught gambling would pay severe fines. A minimum of one thousand ostows."

I looked at him in shock. That was a crazy amount of money. Almost the amount of my Blank tax for a full month. "What will you do if you get caught?"

"I won't."

"Yeah, because you're so inconspicuous sitting there keeping track of all your bets."

He looked up. "Like anyone is paying attention to me. And even if they did, what are they going to do? Send me to prison? Remove me? My destiny will take care of that soon enough. It's not like the ministry would let anything get in the way."

Sol didn't talk about his destiny that much. I was surprised he was bringing it up again. And sorry there weren't words to give him that would make it any easier. Instead I kept my sympathy to myself. I knew from experience it was easier to deal with an empty future when people weren't dousing you with pity.

Laira grabbed my arm and squeezed, distracting me from my thoughts. "Dax, this is so exciting. That's your *brother* out there! Look how fast he is!"

I watched as Aldan easily pulled ahead of the pack. No surprise there. He'd broken every time on record for loop racing.

"The track looks weird," Laira shouted over the cheering. "Are there more loops than usual?"

"Customized for the race," I shouted back. "Usually there's an odd number of loops and twists, but they added an extra to this one." I pointed up to the biggest loop, the third on the track. "See, the loops are designed for racers to be able to pass one another. More loops create extra chances for stealing a position."

Theron interrupted my loop lesson. "Ladies and gentlemen, here's Aldan about to take the first loop. And if I'm not mistaken... Yes! He did it. He broke the record. He's out of there and onto the first twist in under a minute. Cha ching! Kidding, ministers."

The crowd cheered, but I could still make out Sol's mumbles. "He's so not kidding," he said in irritation, and quickly punched new numbers into his game screen.

I wasn't exactly surprised. It was just like Theron to bet that my brother could beat the odds. He believed in my brother just as much as I did. And Aldan wasn't letting anyone down. He was racing at top speed. He didn't bother to stop for any fancy tricks— not yet anyway. The winner would be the first to cross the finish line. Still, it wouldn't be like Aldan if he didn't win the secondary score for technique, too.

I didn't want to take my eyes off of my brother as he approached the second loop, but the action behind him was pretty ultra.

Reiner had caught up to Tred and Lemad as they were about to take the first loop. There was only room for them to go through one at a time, but none of them was about to give an inch. They headed for the loop together. Reiner on the left, Tred in the middle, and Lemad on the right. With everyone refusing to move, the body-slamming started. Tred shoved out his elbows to knock into the two men at his side, while Reiner thrust his body toward his opponents. The move threw Tred off-balance sending him into Lemad, who tried to stand firm. But Reiner wouldn't let up.

"Someone's going to have to give in or go over. Who will it be?" Theron asked. "No, he's not! But he is!" The excitement in Theron's voice was rising. "Lemad Loring is trying the flamingo. It's only been done successfully once in competition, and I bet you can all guess by who. Good luck, man you're going to need it!" Lemad crouched down and demagnetized his left shoe. It was no longer attached to the board. It would give him more flexibility to maneuver but a lot less stability. With the inclines and pushing, it was a brash move for any racer to not keep both feet planted on their board. Lemad switched his body so his left foot was now leading the way and he was able pull out in front of Tred, but his momentary victory didn't last long. Reiner surged forward, his board knocking into Lemad's, then with a shove, Reiner sent the "flamingo" over the side of the track. Lemad braced himself, ricocheting off the magnetized floor of the track with nothing more serious than a scowl on his face.

"Man down," Theron called.

Aldan was just about to go down the third loop but came to a halt right before the decline. I'd stopped asking how Aldan did the tricks he did. He'd made me try a bunny coaster once, and I never went back. Those loops are freaky. Racers are attached to their boards through magnets and that same tech work keeps the boards in line with the track. The magnets pull the board along, so stopping is anything but easy. It's a skill, and if you don't have it, you either crash, fall over the side, or miraculously get pulled to the end of the track. But my brother's gifted. He's always been able to stop on a hair. And this time as he did it, he saluted Lemad and then dove down the incline of the loop.

"A classy move by Aldan Harris," Theron said, "even if it did cost him five seconds. But a good attempt by Lemad Loring. And we're down to seven."

Reiner had pulled ahead of Tred for the second loop, but by this point they were three loops behind Aldan. Still, none of them were about to give up. Second place was a big deal—especially when you already knew who was guaranteed to take first. And these guys were taking it seriously.

Theron kept everyone up on the play by play. "Aldan is on his sixth loop. While Tred and Reiner are pulling out of their third. And what about Wybalt Morley, Analise Chorter, Zuma

Pipin, and Nelo Hebert? No, they didn't fall over the side. They're chugging along about to take the second loop. But the real action is going on with our second place frontrunners. Reiner is still in the lead, but Tred is getting ready for a move. Look at the way he's rocking his body. That can only mean one thing. He's going for the leap!"

And just as Theron said it, Tred jumped into the air, over Reiner's head, and landed directly in front of him. The crowd broke out in applause.

Theron let out a whistle. "Impressive move by Tred! Hear that crowd, Aldan? They're cheering, clapping, yelling, and it's not for you. I say you need to do something about it!"

Aldan gave a thumbs-up to the hovercam following his every move. He had that glint in his eye. The one that meant he was going to do something stupid. Or what he and Theron called an ultra rush. I gripped my arm, squeezing the purple cuff under my sleeve hard.

My brother, not to be outdone by Tred Nier, waved at the crowd, then jumped off the side of the track. A gasp went out through the stadium, and my heart almost stopped. Was he crazy? If the fall didn't kill him, the Removers would. You couldn't fail at your destiny. Not in today's society. But it was just one of his tricks. Aldan's hands caught onto the track in the nick of time, he swung his legs, and flipped back to his starting position. Then without missing a beat, he back flipped his way through the whole seventh loop. It cost him some time, and almost gave me a mini-stroke, but Aldan was sure to get extra points for a successful trick.

The crowd was going insane. Even Laira was yelling Aldan's name, and Laira never yelled.

"Look at him go," Theron said. "Alright, you can stop trying to impress the ladies, Aldan. We've all heard the rumors that you're off the market. But don't worry, while Aldan may be taken,

I would be more than happy to fill in for him." A screen above the track made a quick cut to show Theron giving us all a jaunty grin.

Just what I needed. More competition.

As Aldan continued on to the last loop, Tred and Reiner headed for number six. Tred was still in the lead since the jump, but Reiner wasn't having it. He lunged forward, clipping Tred's board. But instead of moving aside, Tred did something surprising. He did a 180, turning to face Reiner, and started going down the up incline, gearing up for a head-on-collision with his competitor.

Reiner's eyes filled the screen. They were petrified, and he started backing up toward the fifth loop. But unlike Tred, he wasn't facing the track. As he came to a dip in the metal, Reiner went over the edge, ending his part in the race.

"Then there were six!" Theron called out. "Tred took out the second place frontrunner, pretty much guaranteeing him a victory. That is unless Wybalt can gain a little gusto."

It didn't seem likely. Wybalt and the rest were still back near the beginning of the fourth loop.

"And look at this ladies and gentlemen. Mr. Aldan Harris has completed the eighth loop and is ready for the big finish. The drop!"

I couldn't even look at the last leg of the race without getting dizzy. It was a straight drop hundreds of feet that led into a narrow finish line. And Aldan was about to take it. Or at least I thought he was. But right as he should have gone over, he came to a quick halt and started dancing a jig.

"What is he doing?" Laira asked, giggling. People all around us were asking the same thing, including me.

"Messing with my betting pool," Sol complained, as he scribbled on his plexi.

But Aldan didn't stop with the dancing, he started making

fishy faces at the hovercam, then plopped himself down on the track and pretended to take a nap.

The audience really started laughing. It seemed like I was the only one who wasn't joining in, but I just didn't understand what he was doing. Or why. The ministers would be furious.

Still, Aldan didn't seem to care about that. The more laughter he got, the more he played it up for the hovercam. He threw in a few snores, made it seem like he was going to roll over the side of the track, stood up with his arms straight out and pretended to sleep walk.

I'd probably laugh about it too, once it was over, but I just wanted Aldan safely on the ground. I know he liked the rush, and letting Tred get closer was probably part of that, but I didn't care. I just wanted him to hurry up and win.

Sol looked at Aldan's screen. The numbers read six minutes thirty-two seconds. "I can't believe this. I thought the twelve minute finish time someone guessed for Aldan was a fool's bet, but I guess I was the fool."

"Someone bet twelve minutes on Aldan?" That was hard to believe. "Who?"

"Someone named Noreth Nadla," Sol said.

It all made sense now, and I burst out laughing.

"It's not funny," Sol grumbled. "I was supposed to make at least six hundred ostows off of this race. Even with my UV job, my family can barely cover our bills. Now I'll be lucky if I break even."

"Something tells me *Noreth Nadla* might cut you a deal," I said.

"Yeah, right," Sol said.

"Think about it. *Noreth Nadla.*"

Sol looked at me like I just stood up and yelled 'Blanks rule' at the top of my lungs. For a tech genius who decoded puzzles all the time, he could be really dense. "Look at it backwards," I told him.

"No way," he said. "Aldan Theron. They had this planned all along. The cheats. I'm keeping the money."

"They wouldn't rip you off. They're not like that." I couldn't help but get defensive. Aldan and Theron would never cheat someone. Sure, they like to joke around, but they always did the right thing in the end. "They were just being funny."

And Aldan certainly had the crowd in stitches now. He was egging Tred on, ushering him in, like it was a bullfight, and Tred was the bull. They were just steps before the drop, but Aldan didn't seem to care. He knew what would happen. We all did.

Tred came to a screeching halt, lining up behind Aldan. A destiny was a destiny. Aldan was destined to win, and no one would dare take that from him. Even if that meant every racer had to wait around all day until my brother felt like going down the drop.

"Wait, ladies and gentleman, what's this?" Theron called out. "It looks like Aldan Harris and Tred Nier are doing the... cancan!"

Although Tred looked a little confused, he still participated in Aldan's kick line. Pretty soon the two were jumping around, arm in arm, kicking to the claps of the crowd. They were so absorbed that they barely noticed Wybalt and Analise.

I got a weird feeling in my stomach. "Aldan," I shouted out. "Aldan." My voice was drowned out by the crowd.

The other racers were getting close, and they didn't look like they were stopping.

"Aldan," I screamed again, but this time I wasn't alone.

Theron's voice pierced through the laughter and cheers. It was filled with panic. "Aldan, go! They can't stop. Now."

Everything got silent. Aldan watched, the crowd watched, I watched as Wybalt Morley dove off the side of the track to avoid taking the final drop of the race. But right on his tail was Analise

Chorter. She tried to dive over the side too, but didn't have enough strength to fight the magnetic pull of the track. With his free hand, the one not wrapped around Aldan's shoulder, Tred tried to grab hold of Analise. But it was too late. She had worked up speed and had momentum on her side. Stopping was a science. One that Analise didn't have the skill or build for. And just like that, she took the drop and won the race.

"No," I screamed.

My brother didn't fulfill his destiny.

"No. NO. NO."

The sirens started blaring, drowning out my cries. Both were meant for Aldan.

EIGHT

Madden

The wail of the destiny siren blasted through the arena. I'd only heard the sirens a few times in my life, and they'd never been in my own zone. I sat frozen with the horrible knowledge of what was about to unfold, unable to rip my eyes from Aldan, who still teetered on the edge of the finish line.

To my left, Mrs. Harris's screams eclipsed the siren. She pushed past me blindly, reaching for one minster, then another. "Please, it was a mistake. He's just a boy." She finally collapsed at Bastin's grandfather's feet. "Minister Worthington, I'm begging you. It was an accident. He's a good boy. He deserves a pardon. Please."

Behind me, Aya's mother ushered her away. I took some comfort in knowing the little girl wouldn't witness the next few minutes. I wished I had a mother to do the same for me.

Below chaos swept through the crowds. The laughter and applause from moments before had been replaced by pandemonium. Screams and cries floated up into the Box, pushing at my growing panic.

"Madden." I heard my name slip through the chaos. Link shook my arm. "Madden, you can do something. Please. You can't let this happen. You'll be a minister soon. You can stop this."

I couldn't answer. I'd somehow lost my voice.

Out on the loop track Aldan had dropped to a crouch. His hair hung over his eyes, hiding his expression from the cameras. I frantically went through the list of pardons that might work.

"Madden," Link said again, his grip tightening on me. "Madden, they'll remove him. Please."

"Link, I—there's nothing, I, I—the law is clear," I stammered. There was nothing I could do. It was my job to defend the system from attack, no matter the cost. I'd felt the weight of my own destiny for my entire life, but I'd never felt strangled by it until now.

The opening chords of the national pledge started then.

"I'm sorry," I whispered.

I didn't know if Link heard me, but his hand went slack, and fell away from mine. Around us, the crowd's panic increased. Aldan's name was screamed over and over again, but even those voices couldn't mute the words. I'd started every school day with them for fourteen years, and couldn't help but follow along in my head.

We remember one man's refusal of destiny.

I closed my eyes, doing my best to breathe. This couldn't be happening. Not to someone I actually knew. Not like this.

We remember the aftermath. The sick, the helpless, the fallen.

Please, I thought. Please let someone do something. It can't be me. I don't know how to stop this.

We remember our seven billion brothers and sisters taken by the Event.

I swallowed, willing away the hysteria that was threatening to overtake me.

We remember our pledge to the system.

The drums and cymbals grew louder as the anthem reached the climax.

We remember that those who deny their personal destiny do so at our peril.

Aldan stood from his crouch, squaring his shoulders off and facing the camera.

We remember that to not work within the system is to work against us all.

As the last note trailed off, Aldan opened his mouth, and the entire stadium went quiet, waiting to hear what he would say. "I–" he began. The removal squad acted before he could finish his thought. A dull pop punched through the crowd's silence.

The front of Aldan's shirt disintegrated into a perfect circle where the "1" had been stitched, and a bright red flow of blood gushed from his heart. His legs collapsed, and he fell to the loop track. As convulsions ripped through his body, Mrs. Harris's high-pitched scream rang in my ears.

Bastin stood and motioned for me to come with him. Brine stood at his side, ready to escort us from the Box. I rose to my feet sluggishly and walked toward them in a daze.

"We need to get out of here," Bas said. "The lower rings are trampling each other to get out."

I nodded, still too shocked to form any comprehensible words, and let him lead me to the lift.

As I walked away, I could hear Link comforting his mother. I wanted to press my palms over my ears. I wanted to press rewind and somehow fix what had happened. More than anything, I wanted to run to Link. I knew I couldn't have done any more than delay Aldan's execution, but I would do anything to ease the pain

I heard in his voice.

Instead I watched him from the back of the Box as we waited for the lift. He helped his mother up from the floor, where she still quietly sobbed, and guided her back to her seat. His father clasped her hand as Link returned her to her seat. Instead of joining them, he stalked back to the ministers.

"How could you?" he said, his voice slick with emotion. "It was just a joke. A stupid joke."

Bas's grandfather replied, a note of warning in his tone. "A joke that denied destiny. It's not your place to question the ministry, boy."

"You just killed my brother," Link spat back, his voice getting louder. "I'll question whatever I want." He paused, glaring over the Box, eyes pausing to meet mine.

I gave a slight shake of my head. Had he lost his mind? This was the ministry he was talking to.

"You know the real joke? Us. Every single one of us, sitting in the Box because someone decided our destinies were more important than the people down below. This system is broken."

"Link, stop it," I yelled. I couldn't let him do this. He obviously wasn't in his right mind, but the ministry wouldn't know that—or care.

His gaze pressed into me, and I took a half step back from the sheer strength of it. "They killed Aldan for not winning a race, Madden. Do *you* think the system is working?"

I was mute. No one questioned the system. It was unthinkable to do so in front of the ministry. I gasped as Link yanked off his wrist tracker and flung it to the ground.

"I renounce the system," he said. "And I renounce all of you too."

"Arrest him," Minister Worthington said.

In seconds the Destiny Keepers who had blended into the

Box's background circled Link.

Minister Worthington stood and brushed off his hands as though they'd somehow been soiled by the conversation. "Perhaps the holding cells will help remind you of your obligations."

Mrs. Harris's wails began anew as the lift doors opened behind me. Bas took me by my elbow and escorted me in. The last thing I saw as the doors shut was a stun stick being punched into Link's shoulder, and him falling to the ground.

NINE

Dax

"Dax!"

I heard Laira calling my name as I ran through the mob of people, but there was no stopping. I had to get to Aldan. I pushed my way past the crowds, sometimes going up just to go down, but always moving. If I could just get to my brother then I would... I couldn't fill in the rest of the thought. It didn't matter. Nothing mattered, other than being at Aldan's side.

"I can't believe he's dead," one girl wailed as I flew past. I wanted to stop. Scream at her. Shake her until it wasn't true. But I couldn't stop. I had to get to Aldan, whatever the cost. I ran endlessly, through the crowd's tears and shouts, past the zone fights breaking out, past the people rushing to any exit available, up and down and around until I reached the loop perimeter.

I slipped past security onto the grass under the course. Destiny Keepers had already brought Aldan's body down from the upper track, and I sprinted after them as fast as I could.

"Let him go," I screamed, flinging myself toward one of the Keepers.

He pushed me back, knocking me to the ground. I didn't care. I got up, the tears now falling thick enough to blur my vision, and lunged again. This time someone grabbed my arm and pulled me back.

"No," I yelled. "Let me go." I swung wildly. I had to get to my brother. Every second put me further away from him.

Arms circled around me, pulling me tighter. I kicked as hard as I could.

"Dax, stop," a voice said.

The arms released me and I spun to find Theron. "We have to get to him," I said, a sob stopping further words. It didn't matter. I didn't need to talk. I just needed to get to Aldan. I turned, frantic to reach him.

Theron grabbed my hand. "Dax, you can't," he said. "Those are Keepers. They'll just as soon remove you." Theron's face tightened, and he pulled me toward him tightly. "You're not going anywhere. He wouldn't want you running after him."

I tried to push away from Theron, but he wouldn't let me go. "I have to get to Aldan," I said, swallowing down my sobs before they could surface. "I can't let them take him. I can't, Theron. They'll do something to him. They'll..."

Theron pulled me closer and spoke softly in my ear. "There's nothing they can do to him now that matters. He's gone, Dax. And I'm not going to let you get yourself in trouble too."

I stopped struggling and let Theron hold me. My brother was dead. It couldn't be true, it just couldn't. Because if Aldan was gone... my thoughts came to a screeching halt. I couldn't process anything past that thought. Aldan couldn't be gone. We'd sat at our kitchen table three hours before, laughing.

Other fans had joined us on the field. Their murmurs and cries mingled to create the soundtrack to my thoughts. Why? It was the only coherent question I could ask, and it pounded through my mind. Why had my brother done this? I remembered back to our earlier conversation. I would never forgive myself if his pause at the finish line had been because of me.

The Destiny Keepers—the Removers—stopped to cover Aldan's body with an ash-colored sheet. It was a final insult to his status, and I clutched onto Theron tighter as I saw Aldan's arm fall down from the sheet. It dangled, rocking back and forth. A pale circle around his arm gleamed against the tanned skin on either side. I held my arm to my chest, circling my hand around the purple cuff hidden under the sleeve. Had he known this would happen, I wondered, when he'd given it to me?

Next to us I heard a girl's whisper. "He wasn't supposed to do that."

I looked over at her. Brown curls framed her face. Shock still gripped her features.

"No," Theron agreed. I could feel his body shaking next to mine. "He wasn't. This is all my fault."

"It was his plan," the girl said. "Not yours."

"But *I* was the one who laughed when he told me. I was the one who placed a bet in our names."

I wanted to tell Theron that he couldn't have known what the end result would be, but I couldn't speak through my sobs.

Across the field, the Keepers once again began their steady walk. The sight forced me to find my voice. "Where are they taking him?"

"I'm not sure," Theron said. He paused, his own voice choking. "I'm not sure where Removals are taken."

"They can't have him, Theron," the girl to my left said. Her tone was fierce, and I looked at her again, trying to place her from

Aldan's friends. I'd never seen her before.

"Dax," I heard my name from the crowd. Strom, Pel, and Kai ran over to us. The face paint that had written Aldan's number was smeared over their cheeks, but still legible, and I couldn't stop the tears this time from pouring down my face. Strom pulled me to him and I buried my face in his shoulder. "Strom, why?" I asked. "I don't understand. Did you know he was going to do that?"

Strom stroked my hair. "None of us had any idea. I don't know what he was thinking."

I looked up at him. Tears were streaking down his face now too, cutting through what was left of the "1" on his cheek. Pel and Kai stood on either side of us as the crowd grew in size. We all watched as Aldan was taken from the stadium.

I wiped my sleeves over my face, drying my tears as best I could. None of it made any sense. It was Aldan's destiny to win the race. Laira and I should be headed toward the light rail, and on to Aldan's after-party. We'd laugh when Aldan would show up late, because he was always late. And when Aldan was involved, we always laughed. Except not this time.

I closed my eyes.

"We need to go," I heard Pel say.

"I know," Kai agreed. "Dad said he would meet us there."

"Where are you going?" I asked, looking at him in confusion.

"Dax, listen to me," Strom said gently. "I'm going to stay here and find out where they've taken Aldan. Carlen and Shay are going to help me. They're already talking to some of the guards. You need to go with Kai and Pel to the UV building."

"I don't understand," I said. "If you think they'll take Aldan there then why aren't we all going?"

"It's not Aldan." Strom paused. "Link's been taken to the holding cells."

I looked at my brother in disbelief. "What do you mean?" I

said. "Why would anyone take Link to a holding cell?"

"He renounced his destiny."

I sucked in my breath. This couldn't be happening. Nothing made any sense. Not Aldan. Not Link. I looked from one of my brothers to the next through blurring vision, trying to form some sort of rational question. My tongue suddenly felt too thick. And my throat too dry. I opened my mouth, then closed it, unable to make a sound.

"It's going to be okay," Pel said. "But we need to talk some sense into him. We should go now, Dax."

Overhead I could see the holographs of Aldan projected. The one closest to us was on repeat. I watched for a second time as my brother balanced on the finish line, the Destiny Keeper's blast, his body falling, convulsing. I gagged, trying not to throw up.

"Look away," Kai said, tilting my face toward his. "Come on, now. We have to go before Link does anything else."

"Theron?" I said, turning back to him. He was still deep in conversation with the girl. She wore a green dress. Odd, I thought dazedly, that he would know someone so far outside of his ring who didn't go to our school.

"It's okay, Dax. Your brothers and I will take care of things here, I promise."

I nodded as Kai took my hand in his, and pulled me through the chaos of the crowd, away from a dead brother, toward the living one in jail. As the tears started to slip down my face again, all I could think again was… why?

TEN

Madden

My car was waiting below when I stepped out of the lift, and Brine ushered Bas and me inside. People surrounded the car as far as I could see through the tinted windows. They were running, crying, screaming. Some stood in confusion, unmoving even when the driver honked at them. I was thankful that no one could see inside—that no cameras could record the tears trickling down my cheeks. Aldan had gone to my school. We ran in similar circles. He was my boyfri—my ex's brother. Link... I shook my head in disbelief. I had to do something. There was no way I was going to leave him, alone, in a holding cell. If I could speak to him I knew I could convince him to apologize to the ministry. It had been a rash conversation fueled by grief. I'd make the ministry understand.

Bas and Brine sat to my right, riled up about the race. Bas absently stroked my knee, and I pressed my forehead against the window, wishing I were anywhere else.

"I can't believe that happened," Bas said. "What a fool. Why didn't he just go down the stupid incline?"

"Had to prove a point," Brine muttered. "I can't believe he wasn't on the PAE's radar. He wasn't even flagged as a risk."

"Well, it cost me three hundred ostows. I bet on his time."

Anger welled up in me. "You're worried about ostows when Aldan is dead?" I didn't dare turn from the window. I didn't want them to see my tear streaked face.

"He was obviously an extremist," Brine answered. "Having to live with non-believers is bad enough, but when they act on it, and try to destroy our system, they have to pay. I have no sympathy, and as a future minister neither should you." He paused a beat, his passion growing. "Do you want another Event? I haven't forgotten our history, but it seems like you may have."

I wiped my face and swiveled my head toward them in anger, my hair flipping out around my shoulders as I did so. The Event may have happened thirty-nine years ago but it influenced everything we did today. How dare Brine question my loyalty? "Of course I know what happened. And you know I would never support a destiny breaker. But that doesn't mean I can't feel compassion." Bas patted my knee as if he was placating a child. "Any good leader should," I continued. "Nobody wants to look up to someone who'd dismiss a death, and the circumstances surrounding it, as an annoyance. It's a serious issue. Ask your grandfather, Bas. I'm sure he'll agree." Bas's hand froze in place. "Besides, Aldan…" My voice caught as I said his name, and I took another breath. "Aldan wasn't a bad person. I don't believe he meant to defy the system. I think it was an accident."

"An accident he could have prevented," Bas said.

"Exactly." Brine looked angry, like he wished he could have been the one to shoot Aldan. "If he wasn't fighting his destiny he would have succeeded in it," Brine said. "He obviously wanted to fail, to take a stab at our system."

"But why?" I countered. "He had everything going for him."

"You saw what his sister did to me today," Bas answered, as if that solved it. "She probably corrupted him somehow. You know how unstable and criminally inclined Blanks can be. There's a reason most of them are placed in the Ward."

Dax. I'd wanted to kill Link's little sister earlier that day. It seemed so long ago. Now I just hoped his family—all of his family—was okay.

I turned my focus back out the window, thankful that the car was pulling away from the crowd and onto the open road. It didn't matter why Aldan did what he did. Not anymore. What mattered was stopping Link from throwing his life away, too. I closed my eyes as we picked up speed. I didn't want to talk about the Harris's anymore. Not with Bas and Brine, anyway. I knew what I had to do.

"You may be right," I said. "My head is whirling after what happened. I need a distraction, something to get my mind off of it. Can you have the driver drop me off at the UV building? I'm going to try and get a little work done." I didn't have a formal office yet – it would come next year when I took my place in the ministry – but there was always a conference room available for me, and Bas knew I liked to put in face time when possible.

"Sure," Bas said, and squeezed my knee.

A few minutes later we arrived at the UV building. Its sleek, glass sides sparkled in the fading sunlight. It was the tallest building in the Purple zone, which meant it was the tallest in New City. Seven flags representing the seven rings waved out front, and even though I couldn't see it from my vantage point, I knew the spire would be glowing on top. Usually it displayed all of the colors, but today it had been changed to pure purple to signify the championship. And Aldan. I wondered if they'd changed it back already. I jumped out of the car before the driver could come around to open the door for me.

"Hey," Bas called after me. "We didn't mean to upset you. You know Brine was born 'to punish wrongdoers,' so sometimes he gets a little amped up, and I get sucked into it. We're okay, though, right?"

I stepped back to the car and gave him a light kiss on the lips. "We're okay." I felt a little bad. Here Bas was trying to make things right, and I wasn't exactly being truthful. But I couldn't tell him I wasn't at the UV building to work, but rather to help my ex. He wouldn't understand. So instead, I gave him a little wave and turned toward the building.

The steps leading up to the general entrance were already teaming with media. Several crews had also set up around the circular reflection pool out front. I'd hoped that Link's performance wouldn't have hit the news yet, but it clearly had. Not that I was surprised. Cameras and paparazzi had recorded the Box throughout the race. One of them would have captured Link's meltdown.

Rather than deal with the growing frenzy, I skirted the entrance, following a tree-lined pathway to one of the side doors for high-ranking officials. It was a simple, unassuming entrance that required a quick swipe of my tracker and retina scan to get through.

Inside the building was hushed—there were few people working this time of night, for which I was thankful. As I made my way through the empty hallways, my gown brushed against the carpeting with a dull hiss. I bypassed several security points on the ground floor before I reached the elevator that went down to the holding cells. I held my breath as I walked in, exhaling in relief when I saw that none of Link's family had arrived yet.

"Ms. Sumner," the booking officer said, standing as I

approached her desk. Her blonde hair was cut into a severe bob and she peered at me through black-rimmed bifocals. "What a pleasure to have a future minister visit our office."

I gave her a strained smile. "Could you tell me if Link Harris arrived yet?"

"He was hoverlifted in and booked five minutes ago." She shook her head. "Terrible thing, what happened at the race today."

"Yes," I agreed. "Truly terrible. I actually need to speak with Mr. Harris. There's been a misunderstanding I want to discuss with him."

"Oh, I'm afraid I can't do that," she said.

"Excuse me?" I said, letting a twinge of displeasure enter my voice. I didn't have time for this.

"I'm sorry, Ms. Sumner, but that's not proper procedure. According to Article 7, no persons other than family, or those expressly approved by the ministering board or Delegation are allowed to visit inmates of the holding cells." She tapped the screen next to her desk and a wall of tiny print sprang to life.

I was not about to be slowed down by bureaucracy. "And do you not consider me part of the ministering board?"

Her mouth fell open a little. She didn't know what to say, and I wasn't going to let up.

"Do the rules specifically say active ministers?"

"No, no they don't," she replied.

"Then please show me to Mr. Harris's cell." I looked down at the name plaque on her desk. "Officer McCarrick, the last thing I want is to tell the other ministers I've had a problem here due to your insubordination."

"Of course," she said, taken aback. "Please follow me."

She escorted me toward a heavy steel door, unlocking a series of bolts with her right hand, while pressing her left palm against a security pad.

She punched in a final code and the door slid open. "Mr. Harris's cell is down the hallway on the left. Just buzz when you're finished."

I walked through and she closed the door behind me. I heard the bolts slide into place with a kind of finality.

I'd never been to the holding cells before. The hallway was glaringly bright, and the ceiling and concrete floor were all painted the same dull gray. There was a long strip of tiny glass rooms on either side. Only two were lit, one on the right, one on the left. After passing several empty cells, I reached the first occupied one. I stiffened as I walked past, making sure not to glance in.

"Boo," a voice rang out from the cell, causing me to jump. Instinctively, I looked toward the sound. A man sat on the corner of his cot. He had dark hair and stubble covered his face. One leg was crossed over the other and he jiggled it furiously. Our eyes met, and he grinned.

It was the driver I'd caught impersonating the PAE officer in front of Spectrum. I stood frozen for a moment, staring.

"Hello, again," he said, and laughed uproariously. This man was crazy. I couldn't help but wonder what he had in the truck. I looked away.

He continued laughing as I walked down the hallway. It made me sick that Link was being held in a place like this.

I passed another four empty cells before I reached Link, and the thoughts of the PAE impersonator disappeared. He sat on the floor in front of his cot. His shirt was torn in several places and a dark bruise colored one eye. Despite everything that had happened today, my heart still leapt to see him. I knocked lightly, wondering if the sound would make it through the heavy glass wall—it was at least three inches thick. I hoped Link would hear me. Then I noticed the air holes in the wall and moved closer to them.

"Link?" I called.

His shoulders tightened at the sound of my voice, but he didn't look up.

"Link," I said louder this time. "Please, talk to me." I pressed my palms against the glass, wishing I could put my arms around him, stroke his hair, comfort him. "Are you okay? Let me help get you out of here."

I watched Link's chest rise and fall. His breathing was fast, labored. I waited a moment, hoping he'd come to me, that he just needed a second to compose himself. Only he didn't get up. He didn't even glance in my direction. He just continued to sit there, his fists pushing into the ground so hard that I could see the veins and muscles protruding from his arms.

"Link," I repeated, struggling not to yell. "Do not ignore me!" I needed to get him to listen, to take back what he said at the race, and to have everything go back to normal.

He finally looked in my direction. His eyes were bloodshot and swollen, his voice restrained, distant. "Go home, Madden. You don't belong here."

"Go home? And what, let you make some sort of martyr of yourself? That is not happening."

"Finally," the other prisoner called out. "I needed some entertainment. Nothing like Purple drama to pass the time."

Anger raged through me. "Mind your place," I hissed before turning back to Link. "I'm not letting you rot in here. We... you... can still fix this."

He wasn't listening. I leaned my forehead on the glass and closed my eyes. Before today, there was still a little part of me that hoped we'd wind up together. This wasn't how it was supposed to end. "Please, Link," I said, my voice almost a whisper. "I can't just leave you here."

I felt him there before he spoke. "It's not your decision to make." His voice was like a slap. My eyes flew open at the tone.

Despite his anger, I could see the emotion in his eyes as he looked at me. There had to be a way to get through to him.

"Link..." I tried to come up with the right thing to say. There just weren't any words. "I'm so sorry about Aldan. I really am," I began, keeping my voice low. "I don't know why he made the decision he did, but you can't let his actions destroy your life too."

"Don't you see," he said, his eyes longing for me to understand. "It wasn't a decision. It was a prank. Aldan got killed for a stupid prank. This entire system is a farce. His performance today proved that."

I was almost too stunned to speak. "Link, you can't talk like that." He was obviously out of his mind. If the ministers heard him, they'd keep him locked up forever. "Keep your voice down," I warned him. "Today was horrible, it truly was. But the rules are in place for a reason. Destiny has to be protected. You *know* that."

He gave a hoarse laugh that sounded more like a sob. "Aldan didn't believe that. And I don't, either. I'm done, Madden."

I stared at him in shock. "What do you mean, you're done?

"I'm not going back to work to support the same government that just killed my brother."

"That's grief talking," I said, horrified. I couldn't believe what he was saying. Did he want another Event to take place? Millions of lives lost out of revenge for Aldan's death? "Your job as a Specialist makes the world a better place, Link. It was your destiny to become one and destiny is never wrong."

"I'm making things worse, not better, Madden. I'm not going to be a part of it any more."

He sounded so confident, so sure of himself. Link had always struggled with some of the harsher sides of our government, but just like everyone else, accepted the reality of the situation.

"You know that things are better since the destiny enforcement began," I said. "Crime. Unemployment. Homelessness. Starvation." I ticked them off on my fingers one by one. "They're all problems from the past. You've read how it was before Og harvested the first destiny. It was dangerous when people were unfocused."

"You're missing the point," Link said.

I crossed my arms in front of me. "Well then maybe you should enlighten me," I said, temper flaring. Arguing with him had always been like beating my head against a wall.

"I spend my days ruining lives, Madden. You realize that only one percent of the babies I designate are Purples? Do you know how many are Ashes?"

I shook my head no. "What does that have to do with anything?"

He continued to spew statistics. "Thirty-two percent. Another twenty-four percent are Slate. Can you imagine what it would feel like to have your child designated to one of the outer rings?" He looked at me. "Can you?"

"I hardly think that would happen," I shot back. "If it did, I would accept it. That's the system we live with. It's not perfect, but it works better than the alternative."

"People used to have the freedom to define their own lives, Madden. They had a choice. The future was undefined. It could be anything. *They* could be anything."

I'd had enough of this. I had to remind him of the stakes.

"Choice is a luxury we no longer have," I snapped. "It's a small price to pay for safety. Billions of people died during the Event. Ninety percent of our world—gone within one week. Because John Crilas decided to ignore his destiny. All he had to do was close a door. He didn't. And so here we are. Our government is barely keeping things on track as it is. Your job is a big part of what maintains our safety. All of us."

"And what if it was Crilas's destiny to let those billions die?"

Link rounded. "What if he was supposed to open the door to that laboratory? Let the disease out. Then would it have been okay?"

We'd all studied the destiny system in school, and I'd heard variations of the arguments Link was making before. It didn't matter though. I knew what it was like before. And I knew we allowed the unthinkable to happen. By not monitoring destinies more closely, by not establishing a proper system, the Event had taken place. "You're being ridiculous," I said. "Would you rather go back to the old days when people were at war, or starving, or killing each other for one petty thing after another."

Link shook his head. "You say that, Madden, but *you* have all those petty little things. Like a home, food, clothing."

"Exactly. Everyone has those things now. Everyone is provided for."

"It's not the same. We place someone into a lower ring, and they never have a chance. They're forced into a certain kind of job, a certain kind of lifestyle, and their children follow, then their children's children. It's an endless cycle."

I tried to respond, but Link kept talking, unwilling to let me get a word in.

"Ash and Slate are growing faster than any of us can keep up with. Those families are playing the odds, hoping to have children born into an upper ring. It happens a few times a year in the entire city, Madden. But they keep trying, hoping for a miracle. Instead they wind up with even more mouths to feed." He gave me a haunted look. "Don't you see? The whole system is a broken cycle. And I'm responsible for it. I've extracted hundreds of destinies, and most of those kids I've had to place into Ash or Slate."

I took a deep breath, willing myself to stay calm. I could still turn this conversation around. "There's nothing wrong with the outer rings. Their people are fulfilling their destinies, just like we are."

Link snorted. "Didn't your parents want more? They were what? Crimsons? And yet they still moved to the Purple ring when they had you. They didn't gamble on a second child, either. A child that could have moved them back down to Crimson. Or worse."

I slammed my hand against the glass of his cell. The sound echoed and I raised my voice, unable to keep the anger at bay any longer. "Don't you *dare* bring my parents into this. That's not what this is about. It's about a successful government working to make things better for everyone."

Link's tone changed. His words sounded strained, tighter somehow. "Have you even been out there, Madden? Have you walked through the Ash zone? Because I have. I've gone with Dax. One day, she may have to live there, and she wants to be ready. It's horrible. Miles of crumbling concrete buildings and cracked pavement. Trash baking on the street. The buildings are falling down on themselves from disrepair. And do you really think there's no crime there—or that it's just not being reported?" He stopped, thinking to himself before speaking again. "'Destiny is the art of shepherding used by wolves.'"

I was starting to shake from anger and I balled my hands into fists, trying to remain steady. I looked deep into Link's green eyes, trying to find some remnant of my ex-boyfriend. "You sound like a conspiracy theorist," I said.

He turned from me, looking off into space, as if the answer was there, floating just out of his grasp. "You know where I read that line?" he asked.

"It doesn't matter," I murmured. "You shouldn't be reading propaganda."

"Last summer I took an Advanced Theoretical Destiny course. I was doing some research when I found that quote. It was hidden in the library, in a scrapbook of old *New World Times* articles. The byline was Mila Lantner."

It took a minute for the name to sink in.

"That was your mom, right?" he asked.

"She wouldn't have written something like that." I shook my head. I didn't know much about my mom's career, other than that she'd worked for the *Times* before I was born. My dad didn't like to talk about her, but I'd read many of her articles over the years. I knew she was an upstanding, destiny-abiding woman. "You're wrong."

"Your mother stood up for what's right. She didn't just let the ministry feed her things to say. She had a voice, opinions—controversial ones at that."

"You have no idea what you're talking about."

"Believe what you like." He turned away from me and walked back to his cot. "I'm done pretending."

"But, Link…" I began.

He refused to look my direction, instead staring up at the ceiling.

"Let me help you," I said.

"Any help I wanted from you died with my brother."

"Link," I began, tears stinging my eyes. "There was nothing I could do."

"You didn't even try."

I stood there for a moment, unsure of what to say, surrounded by his silence.

"Please go," he finally said. "Aldan's dead and there's nothing you can do to fix that."

ELEVEN

—

Dax

When I was little I remember looking with wonder at the seven colors that comprise the spire on the UV building. Each represented a color from the rings and, at night, their individual colors gleamed in harmony. Back then I still believed in the equality of the rings. Of course, even then I'd known that Ashes were further down the food chain. It was right there in descending order for anyone to see—purple, crimson, green, yellow, brown, slate, ash. But my brothers had never treated me differently, and unbeknownst to me at the time, they tried to make sure no one at school did either. It wasn't until a fieldtrip that I understood the true symbolism of the building. "UV stands for Ultra Violet," my first grade teacher explained. And that's when it hit me. This was a building for Purples. With ultra destinies. It was right there in the name. Add to that I didn't see a single Ash worker (believe me, I looked), and my lot in life became pretty clear.

Since that day I'd avoided this place. Everyone knows that

Blank destinies and government don't mesh. Walking up to the UV building entrance, my hand clenched in Kai's, I felt as confused and helpless as my six-year-old self. Reporters and hovercams surrounded us, and the lights from their flashes blinded me. Kai's hand holding mine was the only thing that kept me steady against the onslaught. Voices called out as we passed, all asking the same questions.

Why'd Aldan do it?

Was Aldan's performance an accident, or a statement against the destiny system?

Was Link in on Aldan's plan all along—and did they plan this together?

Does the entire family share the anti-destiny sentiments of Aldan and Link?

Was Aldan influenced by the under rings?

As I turned to tell them where they could put their cameras, Pel put his arm around me from the other side.

"Steady, Dax," he said in my ear. "Saying something now will give them more to talk about later."

He was right, and as quickly as the anger had flared, it left. I slipped back into numbness as we waded through the last hundred feet to the doorway. Security guards checked our trackers, and then the doors were opened. Inside was cool, and as the doors swung closed behind us, quiet. Light streamed in through pockets of glass mixed into the crystal walls, highlighting the purple-colored carpet and furniture in the lobby. We passed through four security checkpoints before we made our way to the elevator going down to the holding cells.

My parents were already at the sign-in desk, arguing with the booking officer as we approached.

"It's our son," my father said. "It's our right to see him."

The officer tapped her pencil impatiently against the desk,

looking down her nose through thick glasses. "Sir, I'm going to have to ask you to sit down and wait your turn. We stick to protocol in this department."

My mother turned as we approached, and began to cry. Pel went to her immediately, hugging her tightly. "She won't let us in," she said between sobs. "I just want to see your brother." As my mother's cries got louder, my father reached into her purse and handed her half of a pill. It was a pretty safe bet that she'd already taken the first half. She swallowed it and sat back down.

"Officer, there must be some kind of misunderstanding," Pel explained. "We're Link Harris's family. We need to see him. Please."

"I understand that," the officer said, sighing. "But protocol says I can't let you in right now."

"And what is the protocol, exactly?" Pel asked.

The officer tapped the screen next to her desk, pulling up a numbered list. "Article 47 Clause 3.1.7. Inmates may not, in accordance with policy, see more than one visitor at a time during authorized hours of designated visiting days."

I looked at her in confusion. "You mean that someone is already with Link?" I asked.

"I'm not at liberty to say," she replied.

"What do you mean you're not at liberty to say?" I pressed. The woman wasn't making any sense.

She gave me a stern look through her glasses, pointedly ignoring the question. "I suggest you sign in, and I'll call your name at the soonest availability."

We each scanned our wrist trackers. As my name and status appeared on the screen, the officer looked up at me, her eyes narrowing suspiciously. "You're a Blank?"

I nodded.

She sniffed. "Then I'm afraid you can't go in. Blanks are

not allowed to see prisoners unless permission is granted by the warden or higher authority. I can't allow it unless you have documented consent."

I shouldn't have been surprised, but it still hurt. After everything that had happened, I just wanted to see Link. To hear his voice. And to tell him to take back what he'd said. I knew if I could just talk to him, he'd listen. I'd lost one brother today. I couldn't lose another.

I turned from her to follow my family into the waiting area, passing portraits of the Seven along the way. I hated the ministers. After today, I even hated Dr. Og. Seventy years ago, before Og had discovered the first destinies, Aldan might have just been a regular athlete. Link wouldn't be in jail. And I'd be a normal sixteen-year-old girl. With an unknown future to shape any way I chose. I didn't care what anyone said. The system might have changed the larger world for the better, but it had made the lives of anyone not born into the upper rings miserable. I blinked back a fresh round of tears as I sat down next to my father. Behind us, a screen showed clips from the race, and I did my best to tune it out.

"How are you, Dax?" my father asked.

"Okay," I lied. What else could I say? Aldan was dead. Link was in jail. And I was a Blank, with no power to fix anything. "Dad?" I asked, "Do you know why he did it?"

"I don't know, honey," he answered.

"And Link…"

"Hey," he said, cutting me off. "We're going to get Link back. Don't worry, okay?"

"Okay," I agreed.

From behind us I heard Link's voice, and I turned excitedly before realizing it was just a broadcast. The camera was zoomed in on his face. It was red and tense with anger as he spoke. "You know the real joke?" my brother asked. "Us. Every single one of us, sitting in the Box because someone decided our destinies were better than the people down below. This system is broken."

I sucked in my breath. I couldn't believe Link would say such a thing. Out loud. In front of the ministers.

The broadcast cut back to the newsroom, to a Purple anchorman. "It was a stunt no one saw coming. One that left one brother dead—and the other in jail. Tonight we examine Aldan Harris's misguided suicide, and Link Harris's subsequent spiral into madness."

Aldan's cuff was still concealed under my sleeve, and I gripped it furiously. "How can they say that?"

My dad just shook his head. "The media is going to spin this for their own agenda." He leaned in toward me, lowering his voice. "Nobody stands against the ministry, honey, but your brothers just did in front of the entire world." He glanced at the officer behind the desk pointedly. "Everyone is going to be watching the rest of the family now, so we'll talk for real when we get home. For now, just try and hang in there, okay?"

I couldn't help but turn back to the screen as the anchorman continued. "What I think we all want to know is just how deep this thing goes. Did Link know about his brother's anti-destiny conspiracy? And were others involved as well?" He paused. "Breaking news to tell you about. I'm getting word there's a full-blown riot in the New City Blank Ward. Three Keepers were killed trying to subdue the violence. In a time when Blank legislation is heating up, this can't be a good sign. Our crews are on the way, and we'll have a live report after we speak to some of Aldan Harris's former fans."

I turned away as the scene cut back to the track, even more shaken. I'd never actually met another Blank. Most were institutionalized at birth. We were too expensive to keep. Most families couldn't afford the annual forty-percent income tax that was attached to us. It was the ministry's way to ensure the majority of my kind were handed over to the state. The government feared we posed a serious danger to the public, especially if we were allowed to roam freely and band together. Blanks were considered highly volatile. The thought was, a lack of destiny meant we were capable of anything. Only it wasn't meant in a good way. I'd been monitored my entire life, but living without a destiny had never made me feel violent. Angry, sure. Sad, sometimes. But never violent. If the ministers upped the Blank tax again we'd be in serious trouble. Even with my brothers' Purple credits, we could barely afford the Yellow ring. I stopped, remembering all over again that Aldan was gone. Without his credit, there was no way we'd be able to stay in Yellow. Not with me living free anyway.

I slumped down in my seat, glancing at my wrist tracker. There were dozens of pings from Laira, but I let them go unanswered. Instead, I let my thoughts drift, trying to build up walls around my emotions. My family would still be living in the Crimson ring right now if I'd never been born. And while my brothers didn't seem to care, nor my dad for that matter, my mom did. She hated the Yellow ring. She'd hate the Brown even more. I closed my eyes, focusing on building a wall all over again. I don't know how much time passed before my mother's shriek pierced my thoughts.

"Madden!" she cried.

I sat up, whirling around just as Madden Sumner exited the holding cells. She was the last person I expected to see. She plastered on a smile when she realized she had an audience, but I could tell something was wrong.

"Mr. and Mrs. Harris," she said, nodding to my parents. "Hello," she continued, nodding to my brothers. She paused, then turned to me. "Dax," she acknowledged. "I'm so sorry for your loss."

"Wait a minute," I said. "You're the reason we couldn't get in to see Link?"

"I was trying to help," she answered.

"You realize while you've been inside, we've all had to sit here," I replied in disbelief. "None of us could get in to see him."

My mother interrupted. "What Dax means to say is that was very kind of you." Her words were punctuated by a weird mix of energy. It was the pills. She didn't take them that often, but when she did, they made her jittery. Still, it was better than the alternative. I remembered the wild panic attacks she'd had throughout my childhood. None of us would be able to handle it if she had an episode tonight. My mom's voice grew even more uneven as she continued. "You're always so thoughtful, Madden. Thank you."

I rolled my eyes. Our future minister wasn't trying to help Link. She was managing her PR. It couldn't be good for her image having an ex-boyfriend in the cells.

"If there's anything I can do," Madden continued, "please let me know. Link needs time to process everything. I'm happy to come back."

"Thank you, dear," my father said. "We appreciate that."

My brothers echoed his thanks, but I stayed quiet. As far as I was concerned, Madden Sumner represented everything that was wrong with the system. By next year, her smiling portrait would be on the wall next to me, proving it.

Madden said goodbye and sashayed out the door, her purple gown swinging as she walked. I pressed my lips together, not trusting myself to talk. Saying anything about Madden was likely to get me thrown into my own cell. Instead I returned to my seat, getting comfortable. I knew my parents and brothers would want to spend some time with Link, and if I couldn't get in to see him myself, at least I could wait for the rest of my brothers to arrive.

Except even this wasn't to be.

"Visiting hours are ending soon," the officer said. "One of you may go in now." She made a point of excluding me as she glanced at the rest of my family. "If you are brief another can go in after. That's it for today."

"That would have been helpful information to have earlier, officer," my father said.

"The hours are listed on the door," the officer replied, sounding offended.

My father turned to us, defeated. "Why don't you all head home. Your mom and I will check on Link today, and we can all come back tomorrow and see him."

Thanks to the rules, I knew "all" didn't include me.

TWELVE

—

Madden

Link was mistaken. About everything. My heels echoed through the empty hallway as I made my way from the holding cells, from Link, from his family. He was obviously out of his mind with grief, whether he realized it or not. He took an oath to protect and serve our system, and he believed in what it stood for. Before the system, we'd been on the brink of world war. People were hungry. Clean water was difficult to come by. And everywhere there was a sense of apathy. We'd had no meaning back then. Link knew all of that. He was one of the most rational, logical, intelligent people I'd ever met. It wasn't like him to romanticize the past. The spontaneity it had offered came with a huge price. Collective destiny gave everyone a common goal, a reason to work together. It went past religion and culture and background. It was a different kind of faith that was grounded in science—one that everyone could ascribe to.

Yes, what happened to Aldan was devastating. But Brine had

a point, Aldan brought it on himself. He wasn't a fool. He knew there were consequences to disobeying destiny. Consequences that were now extending to Link.

I knew all too well how fiercely loyal Link was to his family, but that didn't mean he had to throw away his life for his brother's ridiculous cause—a cause Link didn't even believe in.

The more I thought about it, the more upset it made me. Why did Link have to be so stubborn? Did he realize what he was doing? He wasn't just ruining himself, but was trying to put a hole in our system. A system that protected us all. And then bringing my mother up in all of this? Suggesting that she'd been a non-believer? How dare he?

I made it back to my wing of the building and collapsed into one of the large chairs located in the reception area outside of the ministers' offices. No one was around—everyone had gone to the race—and the silence was deafening. Why had Link said those things about my mom? It wasn't like him to lie. But it wasn't like him to make mistakes either.

No, he must have just been trying to get me worked up—to see his point. But the whole idea was ridiculous. Everyone knew Mila Lantner Sumner was a great woman. A writer, an advocate, the mother of a future Minister of the Seven. She worked hard, sought the truth, fought for our system, and was devoted to her family. Everything written about her said the same thing. There was nothing about her being a conspiracy theorist or having anti-destiny leanings. If there was, I would have seen it. I'd read some of her articles. An interview with Dr. Og about how he discovered destiny harvesting and the advancements made in the process. A detailed look at the life of John Crilas. There was even a transcript of the interview she conducted with his family a few months before her death. Everything supported our way of life. Was there something I missed? Was there any chance Link was right?

I pulled out my plexi and plugged Mila Lantner and *New World Times* into the search. Thousands of hits came up. I swiped across the plexi's surface, clearing away the ones of no interest to focus on actual articles written for the *Times*. I grouped titles that focused on the destiny system, and ran a search for similar articles. Some I was familiar with. Others I had never seen. I tapped on a *Times* article entitled "Destiny's Future Looks Bright." It was about the light installed in the clock tower, so the time could be seen at all hours. I read another one about a woman whose destiny was to take the light rail to the East Crimson stop on April fourteenth at 5:15pm. She did, and ended up saving a child who was choking on a hard candy. A sense of relief washed over me. These articles were fine. I clicked on the next. It was called "Destined" but it redirected me to a "Restricted Access" page. I flipped back and tried the next article, but it also dead-ended me to the same government-flagged "Restricted Access" message. I clicked on a dozen more. Two of them were flagged. I felt my stomach tighten.

I placed my plexi on the chair beside me, willing myself to calm down. There was no way my mother had written the words Link quoted, I reminded myself. The government had restricted access to plenty of things over the years, not just anti-destiny propaganda. There was a perfectly reasonable explanation—I just needed the access to find it.

I picked my plexi back up, logged into the ministry records, and called up my mother's file—everyone in New City had one. At the top of the list was her obituary. I quickly swiped past that and skimmed through my birth announcement, my mother's destiny certification and marriage license. I stopped when I came to her *Times* articles. I put them in order by title and punched up "Destined," but it wouldn't load. Instead I got the "Restricted Access" message again. It didn't make any sense. I had just about the highest clearance there was. I should have been able to read these articles.

I stared at the screen, racking my brain for a solution. Then it came to me. I probably had to use a mainframe computer to open protected documents. They had stronger security than the plexis. Three of the ministers had the computers in their offices which, of course, were locked. And then there was the one in the Records Room. I checked my wrist tracker. At this hour that would be locked too, but I couldn't wait. I had to get in. Only I didn't know how. Everyone with access was gone, even the janitors. Minister Corbin had given everyone the night off to attend the loop race.

I didn't know who to ask. It wasn't like I could just call in one of the ministers. Not for personal business, and not without explaining myself. And it would certainly get around if I called in one of the janitors. The whole staff would be buzzing about what was so important that I forced someone to come in on their evening off.

Then it came to me. That infuriating Ash from Spectrum. Sol. He worked in the Records Room, which meant he'd have access. He'd also be able to help if I hit another wall. He was some sort of tech geek. It's why, despite his ring, he was employed at the UV. Officially, he was just there to sort files, but his skill set had even the highest Purples using him to fix computers, plexis, you name it. I'd even heard he helped with encryption. Not that anyone would admit it. And it wasn't just at work. He'd managed to hack our school system to fix test scores for a few of my friends over the years (for a price, of course). He'd changed Portia's mathematics grade from a pass to an excellent rating last year now that I thought about it.

Although I had never sunk that low. Was I really going to ask 'the dead guy' for help now? If people found out, they'd talk. Still, ostows had kept him quiet after Portia's test fix. Hopefully a small donation would do the same for me.

I went back and forth with the decision. This was way bigger than a grade change. And Sol was destined to die by his eighteenth birthday. What if he wanted to go out with a bang? No, I reasoned with myself. He wouldn't risk putting his family in jeopardy by messing with a future minister. I'd be fine. And if anyone questioned my talking to him, I could cover it up by saying my plexi was acting up, and I was afraid some non-believer was trying to get into the mainframe. It sounded reasonable. I did a quick search and found his name and information, then pinged him despite my better judgment. A Purple, especially one of my standing, shouldn't be contacting an Ash. But I had to. The things Link had said had gotten to me, and I was determined to find out the truth. I kept my eyes glued to my tracker. Why hadn't Sol responded?

The race had been over for two hours now, and I stopped, thinking again of Aldan Harris standing on the finish line. I shuddered, unable to stop my mind from replaying the scene of his removal. I sent a quick note to Nora and requested she send flowers. It was the appropriate thing to do under the circumstances. Then I pinged Sol again. Five minutes passed and still no answer. I looked at his address. No. 15½ , Ave D, Ash Ring. It was so far out. I didn't dare go—not alone. Then Link's words rang through my head. *Have you even been out there, Madden? Have you walked through the Ash zone?*

He made it sound downright awful, but I knew better. Link was spewing craziness. The Ash ring was fine. That's what I told him, and it was time to put words into action—to prove that I was right. About the outer circles, about destiny… about my mother. I took a deep breath.

The Ash ring was about to get a visit from Madden Sumner.

THIRTEEN

—

Dax

Nothing about home felt real. It was like walking into a memory that had been perfectly preserved. There was the box of Rice Puffs, still sitting out on the kitchen counter, and my dad's glass next to the sink. The cube screen brightened as my brothers and I entered the kitchen, one side showing Aldan's inbox of unopened fan mail, the other flashing headlines. I didn't read them. I wasn't interested in hearing more. I looked at the clock with blurred vision. Could it really have been only hours earlier that I'd sat right here, Aldan on one side, Link on the other?

We walked past the kitchen into the living room. Carlen, Shay, and Strom were already home. I didn't have the heart to ask them if they were able to get Aldan's body for burial. Their faces answered for me. They sat in a kind of daze. Shay tabbed through something on his plexi, but I knew he wasn't concentrating. The other two barely moved. Traces of paint were still smeared over their cheeks. I wanted to scrub it off, remove the evidence, pretend that Aldan would be walking through the door in a few hours, that he was still out celebrating. I'd always been a realist—my status saw to that. But tonight I couldn't bare it.

I listened as Kai and Pel updated my other brothers up with the trip to the holding cells, answered their questions, and made plans to visit the next day. The talk soon turned to the race. No one understood what had happened any better than I did. When the musings became too much, I said goodnight and shuffled up the stairs leading to our bedrooms. I walked slowly, stopping to stare at our high school portraits. They were lined up in chronological age. Carlen, at the foot of the stairs, then Shay, Strom, Kai, Pel, Link, Aldan, and finally me at the top. Everyone looked so happy. Except for Link. His was the only photo that wasn't smiling. But that was Link in a nutshell. He was the serious one. How could he just throw away his life? I studied his photo. All of my brothers were handsome, but Link was the one with the classic features. Square jaw, defined cheekbones, wide green eyes, straight nose, dark blond hair that was always combed to one side. He looked like the poster boy for the Purple ring. They wouldn't keep him in jail forever. Would they?

The thought made my eyes move to Aldan's photo. His status didn't save him. My boisterous, loud-mouthed brother, whose sun-kissed hair hung in his eyes and huge grin leapt off the wall. Blond stubble covered his face and he wore his purple jersey. The top half of the number "1," given to him by his first coach on account of his destiny, peeked into the photo. I closed my eyes, picturing the number as it disintegrated, the blood spilling from his chest, and Aldan falling to the track. He couldn't be gone. He just couldn't. I bolted up the remaining stairs and down the hallway, stopping when I was inside Aldan's room. I slammed the door shut behind me, leaning against it as I looked around.

Clothes and gear were covering the floor, his desk, and sticking out from his dresser drawers. His collection of loop boards hung in a line on the wall with one noticeable gap. I wondered if we'd get the board back. I doubted it. His purple bedspread was in a heap on the floor, and he'd forgotten to turn his photo cube off. It was on projector mode, and a stream of pictures rotated over the ceiling. I climbed onto his bed and lay down, watching the photos fade in and out. His pillow smelled like him. Like wind and sweat and shampoo. I curled into a ball and cried.

I'm not sure how long I stayed that way. Grief shifts time, I think, and at some point I must have dozed off. When I woke the moon was beginning to rise, and its faint light trickled through Aldan's window. The photos still played overhead—smiling faces swapped with other smiling faces—some were friends of Aldan's I had known, some weren't. I wondered what they were all doing now. I wondered if they understood the race any better than I did.

There had to be some explanation for Aldan throwing his destiny. It wasn't like him. My brother didn't have anti-destiny leanings. It had to be a mistake. Aldan would have told me if he was up to something. There would have been signs.

That was it. I got out of Aldan's bed and raced to his desk. There had to be a clue somewhere in his room. Something to give me, to give everyone, an answer. I started tearing through his things, looking at papers for some sort of hidden message, scrutinizing knick-knacks and gadgets for hidden compartments, but I wasn't coming up with anything. One after another, I'd look, throw it on the floor and move on. When the desk proved of no help, I moved to the dresser, flinging out every piece of clothing until I could remove the shelves, hoping he taped something on the back of one of them.

But he didn't.

Not finding anything sent me into a frantic craze. I pulled his loop boards from the wall, praying that he wrote something on one of them. When all eight were piled onto the floor, I moved on to the closet, yanking everything out. I didn't care what kind of mess I was making. I needed answers. But there weren't any to find.

I sunk down onto a rumpled pile of clothes, shoes, and loop pads. If I just had his wrist tracker. But that was gone with Aldan. I threw my head back against his bed. Pictures were still being projected on the ceiling. I got a sharp pang in my stomach. Had the answer been above me the whole time? I grabbed the cube from the bed and put it into album mode. Everything looked normal, one marked 'championships' that had subfolders filled with snaps of Aldan at each of his races across the country—places I'd never been. Southsphere. The Middle Territories. Even New Vegas. I'd never left New City. Then again, most hadn't.

There was a main folder for 'family.' I tapped on the album marked 'Shay's Destiny Day.' It was from three years ago, at Shay's celebration party, after he'd fulfilled his destiny of forming New City Park. He still worked there as the public parks administrator. Everyone was happy in the photos. Especially Aldan. He didn't look like a guy who was anti-destiny. I stopped on the last photo. One of Aldan and me laughing, covered in cake. Aldan had accidentally dropped a piece on my lap. So I flung some icing at him. And he threw some back. It escalated until we were both covered. Shay snapped the photo. When my mother tried to send me home for messing up the cake, Aldan was the one who changed her mind. He had that affect on people. I pushed past the photo. I couldn't get weepy now. I needed to keep looking—find something that might answer my questions.

The last album was marked 'Other.' It had subfolders marked 'UV tour,' 'loop views,' 'tricks,' but the one that caught my attention was marked 'OM.' I had no idea what that stood for, and when I tried to open it, it was password protected. None of Aldan's albums were locked. My breathing picked up. For a split second, I considered pinging Sol and asking for help. He could hack anything. But it didn't feel right. If anyone was going to get a glimpse of my brother's hidden secrets, it wasn't going to be an outsider. It was going to be family.

I studied the cube. The password was only four numbers long. I could figure it out. First I tried 1-1-1-1, hoping my brother had been lazy and went with his shirt number four times. But it didn't work. I closed my eyes and focused. *What would Aldan pick?* His birthday, March seventeenth. I tried typing in 0-3-1-7. Still no luck. Then it hit me, the only day more important than Aldan's birthday was the one he had been prepping for his whole life. September nineteenth—his Destiny Day. I typed in 0-9-1-9, and the album opened.

A close up of a girl's face appeared on the screen. She was about my age, with brown curls framing her face. Pretty, but even relaxed she had a kind of fierceness to her expression. Her head was leaning back like she was taking in the sun. She looked so familiar. I'd seen her before but couldn't place her face. There were no other photos of her. Why, I wondered, had Aldan locked this one? Was this his secret girlfriend? I stared at the image, trying to place her. And then I remembered. She'd been talking to Theron after the race. What was it she had said?

Aldan's door opened slowly, and I flipped the cube off. My mom stood in the door. She seemed broken, stooped over, like a much older version of herself. Her eyes widened as she looked around the room.

"Oh crilas, what have you done?" she asked. Her voice was hoarse and scratched, as though she'd just found it after a period of misuse.

I didn't know how to answer. Any normal day Aldan kept his

space messy, but never this bad. This was a disaster.

My mother fell to her knees, picked up one of Aldan's jerseys and held it to her face. "You ruined it. It's like he was never—" her voice cracked, "never here."

I stood up, coming out of my own fog. "I didn't mean to mess anything up."

"Why Dax? Why?" Her eyes were sunken and her skin looked gray. It was obvious from the tremor shaking her hands that she was flying on Xalan. This conversation was going to spiral if I didn't stop it fast.

"I don't know," I said gently. "I just thought I could find some answers."

"And did you?" she asked, gripping the jersey tight.

I shook my head no.

Tears streamed down her face. "You destroyed his room. This was all that was left of him, and now it doesn't even look like his."

"I'm sorry."

"You're always sorry, Dax." Her voice shook. "And you've always got some kind of reason, don't you? So why don't you answer this. What kind of world takes one son, then the other?"

I should have kept my mouth shut, but she was staring at me—waiting. I had to say something, anything to make it better, for both of us. "Destiny can be unfair sometimes," I said, hoping they would be the right words.

They weren't.

She stared at me. "You want to talk about unfair destiny?" she said, her voice growing louder. "Unfair destiny is being told that having a daughter is your destiny. To have baby after baby—all boys. And to finally have the girl, only to be told she's a Blank."

Anger spiked through me, but I pushed it back down. To keep talking would invite a fight that I didn't have the energy for. I swallowed anything else I could have said and walked over to where she was still crouched on the floor. I reached out to help her to her feet, "Come on, Mom." She stumbled up, and I steered her out of Aldan's room, down the hall to her own. "It's time for bed. We can talk about this tomorrow when you're feeling better."

"Better?" she whispered. "Tell me how can it get better? All of my boys grown up and moved on. Aldan dead. Link in jail."

I didn't have an answer for her. I didn't even try. "Goodnight," I said instead. I walked away, stopping off in my room to change out of Laira's dress and into my usual pants and shirt, then slipped out the front door and into the night.

FOURTEEN

—

Madden

I caught the next train east from the UV station and settled into a private compartment in the Purple car. It had been almost a year since I took a connector zone ride. Sure, I had jumped on the Purple line to get from NoPur, the northern border between the Purple and Crimson ring, or to SoPur, the southern border—but going from Purple to a bottom ring was a whole different animal. This was a real commute, not just a shuttle ride, and called for the proper amenities. Fortunately, the Purple car was well equipped. I ordered an energy fizz from the porter and gave him a generous tip to ensure my privacy. I then activated my tracker's sound cloud. Immediately the background noises of the train were muted, and I was surrounded by a protective layer of Beethoven.

We pulled away from the Center Lake, and my home beside it. Below the streets were lit brightly enough to imagine the sun was still overhead. The shining skyscrapers soaring up from both sides of the rail only added to the effect. I watched them go by in an aggravated stupor. It was incomprehensible that Link would think *my mother* was a non-believer. I'd get to the bottom of the restricted articles soon enough, and when I did, I'd march right back into the holding cells and explain. Maybe that would help him shed his disillusions.

A few minutes later the buildings began to lose height as we sped past the eastern border of the Purple zone and into Crimson. I turned the geolocator on my wrist tracker off as we approached the East 2 stop, wondering if I would receive a fine. It was illegal to disable the locator feature, but Purples were generally given a pass, and I could afford the fine if it happened. It wouldn't do for my father to find out where I was going tonight.

The rail sliced directly through the bustling center of the Crimson zone, but tonight, the usually raucous bars and clubs were subdued, and the bright lights seemed somehow harsh instead of energized. Had the race turned out differently I'd be here now with Bas and the rest of our friends celebrating. Say what you would about Crimsons, but they definitely knew how to throw a good party.

Another stop later we were in the Green zone. The buildings were closer to the ground in this ring—most not higher than ten stories—and I could see the moon now, round and bloated, resting on their tops. The area surrounding the rail was mostly residential, and the apartments were made from recycled plastic and solar roofs. They weren't particularly pretty, but Greens hadn't paid for energy since the ministry created the homes during the rebuilding. It was one of the many reasons post-Event zoning had been so efficient.

The next stop, East 4, brought us to a residential section of the Yellow zone. There was no one on the streets, but I could see the lights on in some of the buildings we passed. The ministry planned to renovate this area soon, but for now, most of the architecture still relied on aluminum and solar panels. Link's home was out there somewhere, but I'd never visited. One of the many issues in our relationship. Past relationship, I reminded myself. I shook my head, growing angry all over again. No one could make me lose my temper as quickly as Link Harris. He had a soft spot for the lower rings that could become downright absurd if his family was brought into it. I understood he came from a mixed ring home, but he was a Destiny Specialist. He, of all people, should have understood that certain individuals were destined for certain paths.

I looked out the window as we approached the Brown zone, still fuming. The other thing about Link was that he could never be wrong. Today's conversation was a perfect example. He'd brought my mother into it to prove a point, and once I had the truth I'd squash the discussion once and for all. I took a sip of my energy drink, then returned it to the windowsill ledge, noting how close we were to the East River. The Brown zone was the last on the main island of New City. It looked about the same as Yellow, though lower to the ground, and darker. The zone was mostly populated by minor Trigger destinies, the kind of destinies that weren't great by themselves, but could cause something to happen. A ripple in a pond. I'd been trained to give the Browns some respect. Even the best Destiny Specialists could occasionally misdiagnose the importance of a Brown. It was a rare occurrence, but I'd seen the stories on the news. Like Argo Eta who was destined to pull a lever. During a maintenance call to the New City Blank Ward he witnessed 'the uprising.' The Blanks had overtaken the guards, demagnetized the gates, and were about to make it out, when Argo managed to pull the emergency security lever. The alarms were sounded and the force field reactivated. If it wasn't for Argo, the Blanks would have headed straight for the UV and who knows what might have happened then. Despite his unfortunate death, he was made a post-mortem Purple, allowing him to die with the utmost dignity and respect. I let out a sigh. The exact opposite of Aldan.

As we neared East 5, I once again pinged Sol. This was the last stop before the overpass, and I still hadn't heard back from him. I pressed my lips together and considered getting off the train and turning around. But I didn't. I needed to find out about my mother, I reminded myself, and this was the quickest way. The train came to a stop, and an overhead sign flashed that we'd reached a transfer to the agricultural or AnaKurtz sector. There were transfers involved to get there? When I gave my speech, I was driven to AnaKurtz. I couldn't imagine taking this commute every day. How time consuming.

As the rail zipped over the water we seemed to float in the darkness. I looked back toward the island we'd left, my reflection superimposed over the twinkling buildings. It was beautiful from the distance, like a steep, glittering mountainside, rising quickly from the banks of the Brown zone to the crests of the gleaming skyscrapers of the Purple. I focused back on my own reflection. I fluffed my hair a bit and looked at my face with satisfaction. My cheekbones were still perfectly defined, my lips still red. Nora's work would remain intact for another three days if I chose to leave it on. The marvels of modern science, I thought.

We soon crossed the water and entered the Slate zone. I knew this area was enormous, though I'd only visited once before. The factory lights in AnaKurtz gleamed in the distance. Beyond that were farms, though you couldn't see them at this time of night. A memory came to me unbidden. I'd been seven when we'd gone to an orchard in the north on a class trip. We'd picked apples. I'd always been competitive and had quickly gathered the largest quantity. I reported my success to my father that night, begging him to take me back the next day. But instead of congratulating me, he threw the fruit in the trash. He told me the area was no place for a Purple, and I couldn't go back. There'd been a new teacher when I'd returned to school the next day. In retrospect, I understood, if somewhat reluctantly. The sector wasn't a play zone, it was where work was done. Taking a group of Purple children so far out of their ring, especially without a proper chaperone and explanation, just wasn't appropriate. I looked down at my wrist, triple checking that my geolocator was disabled. I was no longer a child, and I didn't need my father to treat me like one if he found out about my trip.

It would be three minutes until I'd arrive at the Ash stop. I took down my sound cloud and enabled the atlas feature of my tracker, making sure to keep my placement hidden. I then opened my hand and projected a tiny holographic map onto my palm. I set my purple dot to begin at the Ash train station, then forwarded through the directions that would lead me to Sol's doorstep. It would take eight minutes from door to door. Easy enough. Though walking in four-inch heels would never do. I adjusted my heels down to the ground level mark. I hated being this short, but I hated sore feet even more. The porter was nowhere to be seen as I exited my compartment, and I whisked out the sliding doors of the train, the holographic map now flattened into a bird's eye view. I opened my palm again, checking the directions. Straight onto Park Street, right onto Downing Way, left on Ashton, right on Avenue D.

The Ash platform was deserted as I walked out. A holograph of a much younger Dr. Og smiled as I approached. "Welcome to the Ash ring, one of the most important, hard working areas in our system today. As you know, all rings are vital to the success of our world, and all people are vital to..." The holograph cut out for a second, then began the loop again. 'Vital to the rings,' I filled in. It was one of Og's most famous quotes. I made my way down the stairs and onto the street. Though street, I thought, was being charitable.

I wrinkled my nose and lifted my dress from the dirt covering the cracked and broken concrete underfoot. A steady breeze blew from the west, from the river. I shuddered involuntarily, looking down at the ground more closely. The tragedy of the Event had been drilled into us at Spectrum. The surrounding area that had existed before New City formed had lost nine million people alone, and the majority of the bodies had been transported by underground subway—now known as the Tombs—to Sinderlock Island for cremation. Due to some trick of the coastal wind coming up the river, the residue from the fires skipped over most of Slate, instead dusting the Ash ring. *Quiet, Madden,* I told myself in annoyance. The dirt on the ground was just dirt, not the ashes of my ancestors.

The thin pools cast by overhead streetlights did little to ward off the darkness, and I walked down Park Street with care, doing my best not to trip over the broken pavement. The buildings to either side of me were made from the same dismal gray concrete as the street, and they all appeared to have been constructed from a two-story, rectangular mold. The business signs in front were their only distinguishing features. Despite the hour—only 8:37— most lights were off and doors and windows barred. There were few people on the streets, and all turned to stare as I walked by. I felt my heartbeat beginning to increase, and I realized for the first time that this might have been a bad idea. My purple dress was a burst of color through the gray and although its cut had been perfect for the championship, I now felt like a moving target. I held my head up and did my best to appear indifferent. It was one of the earliest lessons I'd learned. People only reacted when you gave them something to react to.

I felt a buzz in my palm, indicating it was time to turn right.

I could barely make out the "D" and "WN" and final "G" of Downing Way. The rest of the sign had faded, or fallen off out of disrepair. I'd known the Ash ring was poor, but really, clear signage was the cornerstone of civilization. When I joined the ministry, I'd see that the streets were clearly marked.

I turned and paused. It appeared the streetlights were unique to Park Street. In front of me was only moonlit darkness. And more endless concrete buildings. Everything in this zone was made of hard angles. I sniffed the air. Hard angles, and pockets of bad smells, one of which I was now standing in. The rot of garbage filled the air and I hazarded a glance at my palm, instinctually not wanting anyone to see my map. I considered calling Sol's house, but something stopped me. I didn't want anyone to know how lost I was beginning to feel. Show no weakness. That was another early lesson. And anyway, I was so close there was really little point. A left turn at Ashton, and a right onto Avenue D and I would be there. Still, I looked back over my shoulder. In a place like this, I could almost believe that Revenants existed.

The stories always had them emerging from the Tombs to steal from New City. Now that I was surrounded by the shadows of the Ash zone, it didn't seem so farfetched. Of course, everyone knew that Revenants were just old wives tales told to keep children in line. Even the name was ridiculous. The definition of Revenants was animated corpses that returned from the grave to terrorize the living.

But there was a kernel of truth to the tale, like all myths, I supposed. The Tombs had received their name following the Event, when the old underground subway had been used to carry the dead away. Afterward, the Tombs had been sealed to keep us safe from any toxins that might have remained there from the decomposition and rot. Anything beyond that was just a silly story.

Still, thoughts of the walking dead were enough to spook me, and I made my way even more carefully, walking as quickly as I dared. Across the street I noticed a lump on a bench and I stared at it, trying to imagine what it might be. I stifled a scream as it moved. Someone was sleeping there. I swallowed, hurrying even faster. The Ash zone was poor, I reminded myself. And no one would hurt me. I was a Purple. Except, what if Aldan's death had stirred something up? The thought bloomed in my mind, and I considered my options as I slid through the darkness. It was a short walk back to the train. But I was so close to Sol's house.

My palm buzzed as if responding, and I turned left, crossing the street to put more distance between myself and the sleeping Ash. I walked through the gloom, taking comfort in the occasional dim light within the buildings surrounding me. These looked exactly the same as the storefronts, but were missing the business signs. Residences, I assumed.

There was a man on the sidewalk ahead of me, and I stopped myself from crossing to the other side. I'd just passed what I assumed was Avenue C, and in half a block I'd be turning to the right. I couldn't cross to one side and then back again. I marched on, raising my head even higher. The man stopped as I approached, staring at me. I chided myself. I really should have changed out of my dress. What was I thinking coming out here in a gown? I could feel my heart pounding in my chest. I realized for the first time that no one knew where I was. Bastin thought I was at work. My father thought I was with Bastin. And my geolocator was off.

Keep moving, I urged myself. I kept my eyes carefully forward, noting how tall the man in front of me was. He was a giant. At least a head taller than Bastin. I wanted to scream. As I walked past his eyes followed me. I took a full five steps past before I remembered to exhale.

I ignored the need to look over my shoulder. And I ignored the voice shrieking in my head to run. While it was extremely rare, there had been cases of Ashes striking out against the upper rings. Two years ago, Edium Grale, a member of the PAE, vanished in the Ash Zone. The only thing that was ever found of him was his wrist tracker and the sleeve of his purple shirt. Link had known him. Edium had been a senior at Spectrum when Link was a sophomore.

I pressed my lips together hard enough that I could feel the ridges of my teeth. I was being silly. There was nothing to be afraid of in the Ash ring. Link was wrong. There was no crime here. The Edium disappearance was an exception. It was like I told him. This ring was an important part of our society—it was perfectly safe and livable. Still, I breathed a sigh of relief as I turned onto Avenue D. I was almost at Sol's. And that's when I heard the footsteps behind me.

FIFTEEN

Dax

My mind raced as I took off from my house. I had no idea where I was going, I just needed to get away from my mother. The city curfew would sound in a little while. It didn't matter. There was no way I was going back home.

I tried to clear my head as I ran down the deserted streets. I didn't want to think about anything. Not Aldan. Not Link. Not my mother. Instead I focused on my feet hitting the ground, the wind rushing past me. Before I knew it I had run miles. I was back in the Purple Zone. Back to the Loop Arena. Back to where Aldan was shot.

The arena was locked. I considered scaling the wall, but I knew I'd only get a couple of jabs from a stun stick and a fine for my troubles. The truth was I didn't really want to go back in there anyway. The thought made me feel hollow. Besides the arena didn't represent Aldan, not the way I wanted to remember him—smiling, happy, goofing around. I wanted to be someplace he loved.

My feet knew where I was going before I did—Aldan's loop practice area. It was a quick jog away, in a quiet patch of land located off of the park. Halfway there I noticed a pregnant Crimson woman kneeling on the ground.

"Are you okay?" I asked as I rushed over.

She looked at me like I was from another planet. "Of course. I'm making a wish."

I looked around and realized where I was. We were at the wishing tree at Center Park. It was the only tree left standing in New City Center after the riots and fires that followed the Event. More were grown and others transplanted in, and plenty of trees surrounded the trails, but the large oak was the only original in the park. People from every ring trekked to the tree to share their dreams. It wasn't busy now, but during daytime hours you could find dozens of people tying their wishes to the branches, stuffing them in the trunk of the tree, burying them in the ground. The slips on the tree were pretty in their own way—if you ignored the fact that the whole concept was a sham. Most people who came here were expectant parents. Pregnant women and their husbands, hoping for ultra destinies for their kids. My family doesn't believe in the tree. My mom says it's a custom for fools. She says it gets people's hopes up just to slash them down. In other words, she came here when she was pregnant with me.

The pregnant lady was making a production of breathing in the air around the tree, probably hoping it would create some extra good karma.

"Good luck," I said.

"I don't need luck," she said, "I have destiny."

I kept quiet. I wasn't going to be the one to debate her dreams—not tonight. I nodded and walked until I passed the looming metal fence that surrounded the practice area outside of City Center. It was dark out, but the lights around the track were on. So was the one highlighting the sign at the main entrance. For the past twelve months the white backdrop read the same, "Practice track of future Loop Race Champion XXV Aldan Harris." Underneath the words a holograph showed an almost life-sized Aldan coasting through the finish line during last year's race. I used to love looking at the sign. The expression on my brother's face was one of pure exhilaration, like nothing could touch him. Only now I couldn't focus on the image, I could only see the giant words written on the backdrop in dark purple marker: DESTINY BREAKERS DESERVE TO DIE. It stopped me in my tracks. How could somebody do this? I walked toward the sign, emotion rising. I used the arm of my sleeve to scrub at the hateful words, but they wouldn't come off.

"Crilas," I muttered. I couldn't just leave it there, I'd come back tomorrow with cleaning supplies I promised myself.

I headed over to the fence. No one was around and the quiet and emptiness came as a relief. The gate door wasn't locked, but that didn't surprise me—Aldan spent most of his time here, even getting special nighttime access to the track. He often stayed out practicing 'til just before curfew, particularly during the weeks leading up to the championship. He was probably the last one to use the track, and he never bothered to lock anything. "If someone not authorized wants to give loop racing a try, let them," he'd always say. Maybe I should have seen that as a clue to how he saw the system. I walked inside, the memory of Aldan giving me a slight chill. I lay down on the grass, in the shadow of one of the loops, and stared up at the steep inclines and crazy turns, remembering the way my brother flew through them, taking each loop with such skill.

If I closed my eyes I could almost hear the sound of his board against the track, the yell of adrenaline he let out after finishing the course. My memory was interrupted by a buzz on my wrist. I glanced at my tracker to see a ping from Theron. *Hope you're doing okay, Dax. Thinking about you.*

My stomach flipped to see his message. I knew he was just being nice, but I still couldn't help think back to the last time we'd been here together.

We'd stood in our usual spot on the sidelines, both of us yelling and cheering as Aldan swished over our heads. When we sat down, Theron's hand landed right on top of mine. At first I thought it was an accident, but then he left it there. When I glanced over at him, he was looking right back at me. For a second, I actually thought he was going to kiss me. Then Aldan came barreling down the final loop, whooping at the top of his lungs. Theron pulled back, and after that we just pretended like it never happened—but the memory kind of lingered.

I always wondered what Aldan would think if his best friend and I got together. Now I'd never know. Not that it would have mattered anyway. Theron was a Purple. I might have been fine to hang out with, but I wasn't dateable. I was just his buddy's little sister. After today's race, I'd not only lost my brother, but Theron too. Upper rings hanging out with non-relative Ashes just wasn't done.

I shook my head, disgusted with myself. How could I be thinking about this when my brother was dead? That empty, hollow feeling washed over me again.

The sound of a stick breaking, followed by a "shh" made my whole body freeze. Was the PAE already out? Curfew wasn't for another half hour, but if they found me, they'd send me home. The Yellow ring was more than a thirty-minute run from here.

I didn't know if I should make a bolt for the bushes or stay hidden in the grass. One was less visible, but the other quieter.

I decided to stay put. I was hidden by the shadows. Unless they shined a light on me, I'd be okay.

A minute passed and no guards. Had I imagined the whole thing? I moved to sit up but froze when I heard a voice.

"I told you no one was here." A man's deep voice bobbed through the night, sounding ghostly without a visible owner.

"Well, we can't take any chances. Just be quiet. And move. We don't have all night," a woman rasped in reply.

I squinted into the darkness until I could make out a silhouette of two people mostly obscured by the trees. I watched as they crept along a row of bushes against the surrounding fence and pushed one aside. "You first," the larger figure said. A moment later both had disappeared.

I exhaled, racking my brain to understand what I'd just seen. Who were they? I doubted they were PAE. Not sneaking around like that.

My heartbeat picked up as a new idea popped into my head. Stories of the Tombs and Revenants were a kind of New City mythology. The details changed by storyteller, but everyone agreed on the basics— a group of anti-destiny fanatics who'd run off to build a secret army in the subway tunnels below the city. Except that no one in their right mind would go down there. The subway had been decommissioned after it was used to cart out the dead post-Event. Everyone knew it was still contaminated. I shuddered. More likely the two people were a couple, sneaking around to find some alone time. If so, where had they gone?

I couldn't shake the feeling that they might know something— something about why my brother did what he did. Aldan had spent a lot of time at this track. Sometimes he'd even sit up on the top loop for hours, just thinking. No one would have noticed him there, but he would have seen everything. And everyone. I jumped up and trailed after them, pushing apart the bushes where they had slipped through. There was nothing. Just a few more trees and then the fence surrounding the track.

That's when I noticed a strange ripple distort the metal of the fence in front of my feet. I stared at the now smooth surface, wondering if my eyes were playing tricks on me. But once again, a glitch sent a tiny ripple through the metal. I reached toward the fence and gasped as my hand passed right through it. It was a holograph. I waved my hand back and forth, finding where the real fence met the edge of the projection. It was big enough to crawl through.

My heart pounded against my ribcage hard enough that I could barely breathe. I stuck my head through the holograph and peered down into the darkness. A tangle of shadows concealed all but the platform at the very top of a descending staircase. I had no idea what was below or if it was even safe. But I couldn't stop now.

I felt for Aldan's cuff beneath my sleeve, then disabled my locator, knowing full well I'd be slapped with a fifty ostow fine for it. I didn't care. Let my mom yell. I took one last look around before crawling through the hole in the fence to stand on the platform. The darkness pushed in from around me, and I reached to turn on the light on my tracker. Except I didn't get the chance.

An arm, muscular and hairy, darted out and grabbed me. I was knocked off of my feet, and I fell back into my attacker. I tried to scream, but his other arm circled around me, pulling me into his chest. His hand clamped over my mouth, muffling my cries.

"Quiet," he said. His voice was deep, the word unraveling like the slow rumble of thunder.

A gag quickly replaced his hand, followed by a large piece of fabric draped over my head. Seconds later he threw me over his shoulder and pinched my wrists between one of his giant hands. My body jerked as he pounded down the steps, away from the surface.

I'm going to die. The thought hit me like a tranquilizer, and for a moment I was too stunned to do anything. Whoever this man was, he was strong enough that my weight presented no hindrance.

And then the full realization of the thought took shape. *I'M GOING TO DIE.*

My body surged to life, kicking and flailing desperately, but his arms just crushed me tighter. I thrashed with even more energy, thrusting my elbows with all of my weight. I wasn't going to go down without a fight. But it was no use. My jabs and squirms were met with no response at all, just an unconcerned, unaltered jog. We moved on for several minutes, and I became more frantic with each heavy step.

"Stop moving," the man commanded.

I did nothing of the sort, continuing to kick as hard as I could, struggling to yell despite the gag in my mouth. I could tell we were going down a decline by the air, which was getting colder. Damper. And as I listened, I realized that there was another set of running steps beside my kidnapper. There was someone else with us. I had to get away. I renewed my efforts, determined to get out of his grip.

"I mean it," the man said in his rumbling voice. He squeezed my body to his even more tightly.

A woman's voice hissed next to me. "Let's just kill her already. This is a waste of time."

The man stopped, and I froze, expecting the worst. I heard the squeak of a hinge. "That's not your call," he replied, stepping through what I thought must be a door.

"Yours either," the woman spat back.

I could tell the man was distracted, and I finally managed to get one kick in. I was rewarded with a grunt, and then a toss to the floor. My whole side throbbed in response, but I ignored it, scrambling in one direction, then the other, only to run into walls. I was backed into a corner.

"You know your problem, Thom?" the woman continued. "You've always been too nice." I heard footsteps walking toward me and then small, cold hands pinned my wrists behind me. The woman bound something around them before kneeing me in the stomach.

I curled over in pain, gasping for the breath that had just been knocked out of me.

"Fortunately," the woman continued, "being nice is a weakness we don't share. Shall I demonstrate?"

SIXTEEN

—

Madden

I should never have come to the Ash ring, I thought. The footsteps from behind now pounded toward me, and I stood frozen for a moment, unsure of what to do. Then instinct overwhelmed my nerves, and I began to run. I had three blocks to go. I could get there. I *would* get there. There was no way that anyone was going to… and then my shoe caught on a piece of rubble, and I fell onto the sidewalk. I turned back, hearing the footsteps behind me growing louder. The dark shape of two people approached. Right as I was about to scream, I heard a faint voice call out in the night.

"Oh no, she's fallen. Should we call Mom?"

The moonlight revealed two children approaching—a boy and a girl—neither could possibly be over the age of ten. A wave of embarrassment washed over me, and I did my best to gracefully climb back to my feet.

"Are you okay?" the girl asked with obvious concern.

I patted my dress and examined my hands. No cuts, thankfully, but I suspected I'd have bruises on my knees. "I'm fine," I assured them.

"Is it her?" the boy whispered.

"She wouldn't be here," the girl said, shaking her head.

"It looks like her. And she's wearing purple. Just ask her," he said, ushering the girl on.

The girl studied my dress and then gave me a timid smile. "You're not Madden Sumner, are you?" she questioned.

I nodded. "Yes, I'm Madden."

Her eyes got wide. "I can't believe you're really here!"

"Told you," the boy said. "Why *are* you here?"

"I just thought I would take a tour of the Ash ring."

His face scrunched up in disbelief.

"A tour, now?" he asked. "Why would—"

The girl elbowed him in the side. "Who cares why she's here." A giant grin spread over her face. "She is!"

"It was nice meeting you both," I told them. "But I should get going."

"Wait. Please." She reached into her bag, pulling out a scrap of wrinkled paper. "Would you..." she trailed off and handed me a pen and a photo. Of myself. "Would you sign it?"

She must have seen the perplexed look on my face because she looked down and began speaking again, her voice stammering. "We were learning about the ministers in class. And my teacher promised that anyone who got a perfect score on the test would get a picture of their favorite minister. We all chose you, even though you're not a minister yet."

"That's so nice," I said with a fresh wave of embarrassment. I asked for their names and wrote out a quick inscription. *To Kerla and Vanco, make your ring proud. Madden.*

It was strange seeing my picture on paper instead of a cube or electronic poster, but I suppose that was part of the Ash ring. They still kept some of the old traditions. I'd have to point that out to Link—if he was so big on the old days, then he should appreciate this zone. I waved goodbye to the young Ashes and left them whispering on the sidewalk.

I walked the last two blocks until my wrist vibrated again, and found myself facing Avenue D, No 15. A smaller sign next to it read 15½ and pointed to a path wrapping around the concrete block. I followed it to an aluminum door. The windows to either side were barred, but there was a light on inside. I knocked, wondering what I had possibly been thinking by coming here. Never again, I vowed.

I heard footsteps approaching, followed by a sudden light overhead. A curtain swayed to one side, and moments later the door swung open. A tall, gaunt woman stood there, her eyebrows raised into two arches of astonishment.

"Oh my," she said. "Why you're... well, you know who you are, now don't you, dear? Please come in."

She stepped to one side, and I entered into a narrow hallway. Several pairs of small, dirty tennis shoes were in a pile next to the door. The woman nudged them to one side so I could pass.

"But are you sure you're at the right home?" she continued. A spasm twitched one of her eyelids up and down, and she blinked at me rapidly. "We don't normally get your kind here. Not that I'm complaining. A Purple is a glimmer of sunshine in a bleak world, and you're the brightest Purple I've ever seen. Why you just glow, now don't you?" She smiled, showing a row of pale pink teeth. "Are you one of Sol's schoolmates? He certainly is a popular boy. People contact him all hours of the night. Gets that from his father. My husband was an exceptional man. Brilliant, really, but he never really did recover from the Event..." She trailed off and looked through the open front door, as though she could see a happier past unfolding through the darkness.

I recognized her twitches, stained teeth, and frailty. She was one of the afflicted—one of the many in our society who had witnessed the Event and never fully recovered. The government had given out Xalan pills to help people cope with the trauma when it first happened. It was supposed to calm nerves, dull the senses. Back in the day, most people took a dosage. It was the only way to do what needed to be done—move the bodies, regroup, rebuild.

Except that prolonged use caused weight loss, anxiety, indifference, giddiness and, in the worst cases, extreme paranoia. It also stained the teeth a telltale shade of pink. Those who could afford it bleached their teeth to disguise their habit, but even so, Xalan addicts were easy to spot. The government had tried to offer them help— withdrawal patches, therapy, counseling—but some people refused to give up the medication. At one point, the ministry had even outlawed it, but that only resulted in disaster. The AnaKurtz sector practically shut down. Too many people had become dependent on Xalan. The ministers had no choice but to legalize it again. But as an added incentive for people to get help, they upped the taxes on the pills.

It was supposed to motivate people to quit using. But it seemed no matter how poor a family, they still managed to find enough ostows for pills. This was clearly the case with Sol's mother.

"Is Sol home?" I asked softly.

She turned her gaze back to me, looking at me in confusion. "Oh, I'm sorry. I didn't realize we had company. Why you're Madden Sumner!"

I gave her a warm smile. Dealing with the afflicted always made me sad. "Yes, I go to school with your son."

"Well come in, let's find him, shall we?" she asked, and turned to walk down the hallway. I closed the still open front door, and followed her into a tiny kitchen, my shoes clicking against the concrete floor. The remnants from a meal were still on the dining room table. It looked like soup of some kind and smelled horrible. I tried not to wrinkle my nose. Above the table hung a picture of a man in his late twenties to early thirties who looked like Sol. It must have been his father. Next to it was the only other adornment in the room—a black-framed, old-fashioned clock. The sound of the second hand bounced off of the empty walls surrounding us, amplifying the steady tick.

"Sol, Sol," she yelled. "Come here quick. Get your brothers and sisters too. You are not going to believe who is visiting us!"

Sol appeared at the top of the stairs. He paused briefly, surprise clouding his expression. "Mom," he said, making his way down to her and putting a hand on her arm, "can you give me a few minutes alone?"

"But we have company," she said. "Important company. Let me make some tea." She turned back toward to me. "Where are my manners? Have you eaten? Would you like some dinner?"

She motioned to the table, and I shook my head. "No, thank you," I said. "I just need to speak to Sol."

"It's okay, Mom," he said. "Why don't you go upstairs. Lucia wants a bedtime story. Maybe the one about the night star?"

"Ooh, I love that one," she said, clapping her hands.

Sol led her from the room while I silently thanked destiny that I hadn't grown up with an afflicted. My father was difficult enough.

A minute later Sol breezed back into the room. I assumed he would say something about his mom's behavior. I was even prepared with my 'there's no shame in being an afflicted speech. It's a disease,' but it wasn't necessary.

"It appears that patience isn't your strong suit," he said,

completely catching me off guard.

"Excuse me?" I asked.

"Usually when someone ignores a ping, you don't expect that person to show up on your doorstep."

"You mean you got my pings and didn't answer?" I asked. I couldn't believe it. The nerve of him, letting me come all the way out here.

"Busy night," he said, as if this was some kind of explanation. He motioned for me to take a seat as he scooped up the bowls from the dinner table, dropping them with a clang into the sink. I wiped a few crumbs away before sitting.

Sol yanked a chair out next to me, scraping it noisily over the floor, before draping his lanky body over it. He raised his eyebrows, "So princess, tell me what brings you to the Ash zone?" He leaned back on two legs of his chair, and flipped his dark hair out of his eyes, fixing me with a curious look. "After everything that happened today I doubt you're here for the answers to Professor Fellers' Modern English exam." He gave me a forced grin and a single dimple dented his left cheek.

"I just need access to some information," I replied. "It's restricted access. It's a personal project." Seeing the sudden burst of interest on his face I hastened on. "Family history is all."

"You came to the Ash Zone after dark, despite everything that happened at the championship today, for a—" Sol paused, his eyebrows shooting even higher if that was even possible. "Family history project?"

"Not that I should have to justify anything to you," I replied testily, "but it's about my mother. She was a writer for the *Times*, and I want to read some of her articles, but they're blocked." I smiled. I was asking for a favor, I reminded myself. "I need to get into the Records Room so I can access them, and I know you have a code. That's all." Sol leaned forward on the table, looking at me quietly. His dark eyes were thoughtful, and held mine for several seconds. I refused to look away.

"Why not just ask the secretary?" he asked.

"I don't want her to know my business. And I know you've handled a lot of classified information."

He nodded. "Okay, I'll get you in tomorrow."

Tomorrow? I needed to get in tonight. "Can't you just give me your code?"

He shook his head no. "You need my handprint too."

I groaned to myself. I should have realized the records were sealed with touch pad security as well. I was going to have to walk back through the Ash zone, alone, having accomplished nothing. This trip had certainly taught me a lesson. No more rash actions. I was going to be a minister soon. I needed to act like it. But maybe there was still a way to salvage the trip.

"Can't you come with me tonight? I'll pay for your transportation, of course," I offered, trying to sound more businesslike.

He laughed. "It's not the train fare." He looked up at the clock. "It's after nine o'clock. Curfew's at ten. There's no way I'd make it back by then."

"So I'll pay the fine."

He shook his head. "Too risky. You saw my mom. With the price of her pills and our taxes, we can barely make ends meet. No offense, but I can't trust my family's home on your word."

"Fine," I said. "But tomorrow?"

"Sure," he agreed. "I'll help. My shift starts at three. Why don't you meet me at 2:30 outside of the Records Room. No one is ever there but me."

"Thank you," I said, giving him a real smile. "That's very nice of you."

"Who said anything about nice?" he replied. "Services

provided will come to—" He did a quick mental calculation, making a show of counting the total out on his fingers. "Three hundred ostows, even. I accept cash or e-transfer."

That was probably more money than his family made in a week, but I wasn't about to quibble over price. It was low enough that my father wouldn't even notice it missing. "Deal," I said.

"I would have taken one-hundred-fifty," he replied, the dimple appearing again with his grin. He stood up, pushing his chair back with a screech. "Now come on. I'll walk you back to the station."

I stood, relieved by the offer, but determined not to show it.

"And, princess," he said. "Word of advice. Next time you visit the Ash zone, you might consider wearing something a little less," he paused, groping for the right word.

"Elegant?" I offered.

He shook his head. "Scandalously purple," he replied. "The resell value of that dress alone could feed a family for a month." He winked before turning and walking down the hallway and out the front door.

I followed after him, unsure if he was joking or not. I wasn't about to ask.

SEVENTEEN

—

Dax

My thoughts spiraled. Who were these people? And where was I? If I got away, would I even know which way to run? I couldn't move my hands well enough to reach my wrist tracker to call for help. And my locator was off, not that it would work this far below ground anyway. This was it. No one in my family knew I was gone. Except my mother, of course. But she'd been halfway to crazy when I'd left her. I'd have to get out of this alone.

My captors were arguing to one side, and I heard footsteps approach me. I tightened into a ball, expecting a kick, or worse. Small hands clenched around my shoulders. It was the woman again. "Fight me and I swear I will knock you unconscious." She yanked me to my feet and led me about ten paces, then pressed me down to my knees. She grabbed my wrists and cut off my restraints. For a second I thought maybe she was letting me go, but then she twisted my arms and tied me back up around something cold and metallic. A pole, I thought.

I tried to say something, to talk myself out of whatever insanity I'd just gotten caught up in, but it came off as a jumble of sounds through the gag.

"Shut up," the woman said, smacking me over the head for my troubles. A moment later she moved away from me. Two pairs of footsteps sounded in the air, then a door slid open and slammed closed. The man and woman argued on the other side, their voices a muted, angry buzz.

I sat in shock, breathing through my panic. *Think, Dax,* I commanded myself. I began to take stock of my surroundings. Somewhere a steady drip splashed against the ground. Its echo made me realize I was in what must have been a small space. The air itself was damp, and heavy. It smelled of mildew, though that could have been from the fabric over my head. Next to me, I heard something scratching and running around on what seemed like small, clawed feet. There were rats in the Tombs. That's what everyone said anyway. Contaminated rats that could kill you with a single bite. If I made it out of here, no way was I going to be taken out by a rat. I stumbled up to my knees, wincing in pain, then pulled myself up to stand and stifled a groan.

My side still hurt, but at least I was on my feet. It was something. Now I just had to get myself free. I tested the binds around my wrist. With every tug I felt the bands dig into my skin. I was going to need something to cut through them. I decided to focus on the gag first. If I could at least speak, I'd have a chance to explain myself. I turned my head from side to side frantically, loosening the fabric.

From there I rolled the gag back and forth between my teeth and finally used my tongue to push it out of my mouth, over my chin.

I tried shaking off the bag covering my head, but I didn't have enough freedom to move, so it wouldn't budge. Instead I redoubled my efforts, biting down on the material and tugging up. It gave, and I felt a twinge of hope.

The next few minutes were excruciating. I bit the material, nodded my head up, and then clamped it between my chin and shoulder before I began the whole process again. Outside, the argument continued to heat up, and I knew it was only a matter of time before the man and woman returned. The cover moved inch by painstaking inch, and I almost shouted with relief when I pulled the fabric up over one eye. My elation was short-lived. As my eyes adjusted to the gloom, I took in the broken windows, the filthy benches on either side of me, and the metal poles evenly spaced through the narrow room. I'd seen the photos. There was no denying it. I was in a pre-Event subway car.

I turned back and forth in horror, looking around for lingering bodies. These were the cars responsible for removing the dead from the city. I was surrounded by contamination. Oh crilas. Forget the rats. If I made it out of here, I doubted I'd last the night after exposure to the toxins. The longer I stayed, the worse my chances were. I had to get out.

I crouched down, using my foot to kick over a piece of shattered glass about the size of my palm. I got it close enough to where I could just reach it, when I saw my captors turn toward the door. My fingertips wrapped around the shard, and I managed to grasp onto it and stand back up before the door slid open. I hid the piece in my hand as they walked toward me.

The man was huge—well over six feet. His arms were massive, and his head shaved. Stubble covered his face and he frowned down when he saw I'd gotten rid of the bag. "Great," he said, crossing his arms in front of his chest. His biceps bulged through his black shirt.

The woman looked tiny when paired beside him. She ran a hand through uneven, cropped brown hair and glared at me.

"That was quick work," she said. "Told you she was trouble."

Were they PAE soldiers? Only, what would they be doing down here? I took in the woman's black shirt, pants, boots, and the absence around her wrist where a tracker should have been. Not wearing a tracker was illegal. Dressing in pure black was unsanctioned. You were allowed some white or black, but you had to prominently display your ring's color at all times. Whatever I had just stumbled into I needed to get out of. Fast.

"This is a big mistake," I said. "I just came here looking for answers that have nothing to do with you. I don't know who you are. Honestly, I don't care. Just let me go, and we can all forget this ever happened, okay?"

The woman ignored my words, striding toward me. She reached for my arm and I flinched, gripping the glass shard I was holding tighter. I'd use it if I got the chance.

"Why don't you tell us about this?" she said. Aldan's wristband had fallen down from where I'd concealed it. She pulled it away from my skin and let it snap back into place. "Only a Purple would be vain enough to ruin a perfectly good Ash disguise like yours."

"I'm not a Purple," I said. "I'm an Ash. This was my brother's— it was a gift."

The woman snorted. "*That's* your story? You've got a Purple brother who likes to share accessories?"

I glared back at her, battling anger and terror. "It's true. Aldan used to practice above ground on the track. He died today in the loop championship, and when I saw you come down here I thought you might know something about why he did what he did. My mistake."

The woman's expression changed, her anger shifting to a look of worry. She glanced over at the man uneasily.

"Wait, do you know him?" I asked. "Do you know something about what happened today?"

"I'll get Oena," the woman muttered, striding out the door.

"Wait," I called. "Don't just leave. I asked you a question!" I turned back to the man. He was staring at me like he wanted to say something but was holding back. "Please, you have to tell me. I need to understand what happened." I pulled against my restraints.

"Stop," the man said. "I'll untie you. Talk to Oena when she gets here. It's not my place."

"Who's Oena? Are you guys PAE? Is this some kind of training facility?"

The man grunted. "We're not PAE."

"Then who are you, and what are you doing in the Tombs? Aren't you afraid of getting infected?"

"It's not true what they tell you about the contamination," he said, walking behind me. I heard a laser crackle to life and a moment later the binds fell from my wrists. "There hasn't been a documented case in ten years," he continued. "That's not what gets you killed down here."

I took a few steps back from him, wary. "Then what *does*?"

He didn't answer, and after a long pause the door slid open again. I slipped the glass shard into my pocket, waiting. Two women stood by the entrance. One was my original captor. The second one took a step forward, watching me. Like the others, she was dressed in black—black tank top, work pants tucked into tall boots. A cap was pulled down over her eyes, shadowing her face. She wore a knife strapped to her belt. Everything about her looked dangerous.

"Why are you here?" she asked. Her voice was quiet, but it carried.

"For information," I replied, trying to sound confident. I'd made it this far. These people knew something about Aldan and I was going to find out what. "My brother, Aldan Harris, threw his destiny today. He used to practice above ground on the loop track. I noticed your—" I paused, unsure what to call them. "Your friends while I was there tonight. I thought they might know something."

She walked closer, and I realized she wasn't that much older than me. We were about the same height. Dark curls jutted out from under her hat and, as she stopped beside me, our eyes met. Hers were swollen and red. It seemed impossible that someone who carried a knife on her belt would cry, and yet the evidence was right there. In that instance I recognized her. She'd worn green last I'd seen her. It was the girl from the race. The girl from Aldan's photo cube.

"We don't have the answers you're looking for," she said. There was a kind of exhausted finality to her pronouncement. "You're lucky Thom was the one who found you. Others would have shot first, asked questions later if they saw you with that cuff." She turned back to the man. "Take her back to the surface, please. I'm not in the mood to rescue lost children right now." With that, she turned and walked away.

I glared at her retreating back. "Wait," I called. "I'm not some child."

She kept walking.

"I saw you," I continued. "At the race. You were there, with Theron. You knew my brother."

She stopped.

"He has a picture of you," I said.

She turned, staring back at me.

"You were the one he was always talking to, weren't you?" I asked. "The mystery girl."

"I don't know what you're talking about," Oena said.

But there was something. A catch in her voice that told me I was right. It made sense. Aldan hadn't kept her identity a secret because he'd wanted to. He'd done it because he had to.

Oena shook her head. "Whatever you think you know is wrong," she said. "You need to go home." She marched back up to me, her eyes flashing. "Curfew is coming. "

"I'm not leaving until you tell me what happened," I pressed. "Why didn't Aldan complete his destiny? Does it have something to do with all of this?" I waved my hand, gesturing around the gloom.

"We would never have asked Aldan to risk his life," she snapped back at me. "It was his decision. His destiny."

I sucked in my breath. She did know what had happened. "You mean he threw his destiny on purpose?"

Oena rocked back on her boots, her eyes closed for a moment and she winced as if my words had physically hurt her. "Of course not," she finally said. "It was an accident. He was going to wait at the finish line until some of the other athletes caught up. He knew they'd never pass him. He planned to stand there and wait, show how ridiculous predetermining the race was. He kept saying the system was a joke. That it was time to make people laugh so they'd see it too. He'd expected a huge fine. Maybe some time in the holding cells. Not… what happened. Aldan didn't have a death wish."

It took me a minute to process what she was saying. Aldan and I had always been close, but we'd rarely talked about the system. He'd openly disagreed with some of it. I'd listened to him debate the rings with my mom. I'd even joined in. But that was in the privacy of our home. When had that changed? Had it been this girl? I sank down into a nearby subway bench. Had it been because of me?

Oena sat down on the bench across from me. She leaned forward, resting her elbows on her thighs, gazing off into space. "I've gone over it a thousand times in my mind. It was just an accident. A stupid, horrible accident. From what I could see, his board somehow froze. Then that girl came flying down the incline." She stopped, her voice going hoarse. "I still can't believe it."

So that was it. An accident. One mystery solved. Another sat in front of me.

"But how did you even know him?" I said. "Who are you? All of you. Thom said you're not PAE. But if not that, then what?"

"We're just people living as best we can outside the system."

"Revenants?" The word was out of my mouth before I realized it.

"Some call us that," she said.

The stories were actually true. My head was swimming with the revelation and what it meant. "And my brother? How did he fit in?"

"He didn't," Oena said. "He was my friend outside of this world. End of story."

From far above the distant sound of bells began to toll from New City Center's clock tower. It was ten o'clock. Curfew.

Oena's tone changed abruptly. "It's time for you to go."

"But I have more questions."

"I've told you everything I know," she replied. She turned to Thom. "Drop her in the Yellow zone, as close as you can get to her home."

She knew where I lived. Aldan was more wrapped up in this than she was letting on. I opened my mouth to protest, but she interrupted me.

"Dax," she warned.

"What?"

"You can't come back here—it will put us all in danger. You'll be watched after this. Your entire family, but especially you. Your status makes you a bigger target."

"You know about me—what I am?" I asked.

"Aldan mentioned it," she said.

"Yeah, well, Blanks are scary," I muttered sarcastically.

"Blanks create their own path," she replied. "I should know. My brother's one."

I looked at her, shocked. "Seriously?" I asked. I'd always been curious to meet another Blank—to see what they were like.

"Seriously," she said. "Now I'm sorry, but there's nothing more I can do for you. Go home. Forget you met any of us. It's the best thing for everyone." She turned to the man once again. "Thom?"

"On it," he replied and nodded at me. "Let's go."

So that was it. I knew more than I had. Not as much as I wanted to. But they were right, curfew had come. I had to get home. I followed Thom out of the train car onto the tracks.

He stood in front of me shining a pinprick of light. "Watch your footing. There's a lot of debris around."

"Thom," I asked, once we were alone. "What are the Revenants really trying to do?"

"Survive," he answered.

He knew that wasn't what I meant. "Beyond that," I pressed.

"Give people a choice about the life they lead, not just accept what's dictated to them." He paused and put a hand on my shoulder. "None of us wanted your brother involved, but you should know his death wasn't for nothing. Someday he'll be looked at as a hero. Things are changing, and Aldan reminded millions of people that the system isn't absolute. That you can alter what you're fated for. If a Purple like your brother was willing to take a stand, imagine what else could happen."

"Yeah, and look where it got him," I said.

"Not everyone sees it like that. Come on," he said ushering me ahead. "We need to be quiet as we make our way through. There's others down here who I'd rather avoid tonight, alright?"

I nodded but there was so much I wanted to talk about.

We wound through the tunnels for what had to have been an hour. Even watching where I was going, it was hard to see anything, and I stumbled over broken track in places. In others it was just large rocks and metal scrap. I tried to memorize all of the turns we were taking, but my sense of direction became muddled within minutes. As we made our way, I kept playing my conversations with Oena and Thom over and over. More and more questions bubbled up in my mind.

"This is it," Thom said, stopping below a rusted ladder leading up a dark hole. "You climb that and you'll be a few blocks from your house. The PAE doesn't usually do residential sweeps, but keep out of the lights all the same."

"Thank you," I said.

"It's Oena you should thank, not me," he replied.

"Is she the leader of your group?" I asked, unsure.

"Oena's not the boss. Her brother is.""Oh," I said. "Where is he?"

"Captured by the PAE today."

"I'm sorry," I replied, unsure of what else to say.

Thom shrugged. "Too soon to be sorry," he said. "It was a public arrest—means he wasn't shot on sight." I remembered the man who'd been caught at Spectrum. It seemed a lifetime ago. Had that man been Oena's brother? The one with a Blank destiny? "Zane's slippery as they come," Thom continued. "I reckon he'll make it home eventually. Which is where you should be heading too." He gave me a pointed look. "We're on the eastern Yellow/ Brown border so be careful on your way. Don't want you to wind up in the cells too."

He crossed his arms, and I wondered if his muscles ever ripped his shirts. Suitably impressed, I began to climb. When I looked down to say goodbye, he was already gone.

EIGHTEEN

Madden

I caught the last train leaving the Ash zone for the night. With the exception of the conductor and me, it was vacant. No one from the outer rings traveled that close to curfew—the fine was too expensive. It was a relief to not have to deal with the public. But the silence didn't stop the clamoring of thoughts in my head. Aldan, Link, the Ash ring, hiring Sol—it was all overwhelming. Although none of it was going to be worse than dealing with my father when I got home.

I opened the front door to my house at ten minutes past curfew, expecting my father to be waiting with that look on his face. No doubt, PAE officers would be out searching and I'd get another lecture on responsibility.

As it turned out, it wasn't my dad waiting, but Nora, looking sick with worry.

"Madden, you scared me half to death. I was getting ready to call your father."

Of course my dad was still at work. After a public destiny breaking, the Chief of Security would be working around the clock. I looked at the lines on Nora's face and immediately felt terrible. "I'm so sorry, I just lost track of time. Today was so horrible, and I, well…"

She shook her head in disbelief, but then I saw her face soften. I think she knew there was something I wasn't telling her, but she didn't push it. Instead, she put her arm around me and gave me a hug.

"I know this must have been a hard day for you," she said. "Go get some sleep. We'll keep this between us." I thanked her and tried to take her advice, but I only managed to get a couple of hours in before it was time for school.

The next day at Spectrum was pandemonium. Everyone was talking about Aldan. The teachers tried to quell it. I guess they figured that if we didn't talk about it, we could all pretend it didn't happen. Only it was the craziest thing to happen in New City in years. There was no way people were going to keep quiet. I looked around for Dax; I didn't see her. She must have decided to stay home. Not that I blamed her. I didn't see Theron either. I reminded myself to check in on him. Aldan was his best friend, he had to be taking this hard.

I spent most of the day in my own sleep-deprived daze, ignoring the gossip, and trying not to think about the previous day. That was until Sol passed me in the hallway. The Ash actually winked at me. *Winked.* In public! Portia and Lavendar witnessed the whole thing. I thought I was going to die.

"You aren't having him change one of your grades for you, are you?" Lavendar asked, her dark eyes widening.

My cheeks burned as I tried to decide how to answer.

"Don't get all preachy," Portia chided her. "There's nothing wrong with buying a little help if you can afford it." She turned to me and whispered. "Although I swear if I didn't need him, I'd have him reported. He totally thinks he's above his standing. That alias he uses for his business—the tech king? Who does he think he is?"

He was the guy who was going to help me figure out my family history, I thought. But I knew better than to say it. "I'm not changing a grade," I assured them. I couldn't have people—even my friends—think their future minister was a cheat. "He took a virus off a computer I was using at the UV, that's all."

They seemed to buy it, and I managed to avoid Sol the rest of the school day. When the last class ended, I made a beeline for the door before anyone could stop me to talk. It wasn't exactly odd that I was racing off to the UV building. I went there regularly after school to do homework. But the last thing I needed was one of my friends inviting themselves along for a study session.

I found myself standing in front of the Records Room with time to spare, wishing Sol would hurry up and arrive. I tried so hard to avoid him at Spectrum and here I was waiting for him to show up already. The air conditioner hummed around me—the UV was always chilly. All things considered, the cool temperature was probably a blessing. It was the only thing keeping me alert. I tightened my cashmere wrap around my shoulders and blinked rapidly to keep the exhaustion at bay. I don't know how anyone functioned on less than eight hours of sleep a night.

With nothing better to do, I pulled out my plexi and reviewed my class notes from the last week, trying for nonchalance. The last thing I needed was to draw any suspicion from Elba Drewn. She was the receptionist for the minister's wing of the UV and sat just around the bend from records. The woman had a keen sense for finding out other people's business, and was not above sharing it if it worked to her advantage.

I checked my tracker. 2:25pm. Sol wasn't technically late, but he certainly wasn't early. I couldn't believe I was stuck waiting for an Ash. Lavendar, Portia, and the rest of the world would have a field day if they ever found out. The thought alone made me consider asking Elba to swipe me into the room, but she'd just offer to find whatever file I needed and put a hologram copy on my desk. There was no way I was confiding in her about what I was looking for. I had no choice but to wait for Sol.

Each second felt like hours. Finally at 2:29 he strode toward me. "Look at this," he said. "The princess herself, waiting for little old me."

"Shh," I said raising my finger to my lips and gesturing my head in the direction of Elba. "Just open the door," I mouthed.

Sol put his palm up against the sensor then entered a few numbers in the keypad and the door slid open. I pushed past him and walked inside.

I'd never been to the Records Room before. It was emptier than I'd expected. The walls made a perfect circle around me, and looked as though they'd been sculpted from a pane of white glass. The ground was made from a sheet of the same glass, though had a tint of purple shining through. A dull white circle punctuated the middle of the floor.

Sol followed me in and slid the door shut behind us. "Why, thank you, Sol," he mocked. "Thank you for taking time out of your schedule to do me a *personal* favor. I really appreciate someone as smart and good looking as you helping me out."

I rolled my eyes at him. "You're being compensated." I reached into my pocket and pulled out three hundred ostows.

Sol's eyebrows shot up in surprise. "I never thought a Purple would lower themselves to…" his voice grew hushed, "paper money. Least of all you."

"Well, obviously you don't know me very well," I said, crossing my arms over my chest. Although, my indignation was for show. Sol was right. I never touched ostows if I could help it. I supposed they were pretty in their own way—slips of paper that gradiated through all of the colors in the rings. But they were also dirty. I much preferred the e-transfer. Just a quick tap on your tracker and you were done. The thought of thousands of hands touching each ostow, spreading germs, was sickening. But it was a necessity today. I wasn't planning on leaving a digital trail for someone to stumble across. I certainly didn't need any linkage to Sol Josephson.

"Okay," Sol said. "So what are we looking for?" he asked.

I ignored the smile that twitched the corners of his mouth. "*We* are not looking for anything. *I'm* looking for some files."

"I know," he said. "It's just—"

"I appreciate your assistance with getting me in, Sol," I said in my most minister-like tone, "but I'll take it from here."

Sol put up his hands in defeat, took a few steps back, and leaned against the door.

My voice came out harsher than I had meant it to, but I was on edge. I was about to find the truth about my mother. And just because Sol helped me get into the Records Room, didn't mean I wanted him to know I had questions about my family. I hired him for a job—not to learn the secrets of the future Minister of the Seven.

I took a deep, steadying breath, clearing the last remnants of sluggishness from my mind. It was time to get to work. I looked around the room. Where were the records controls to activate the files? I could feel Sol watching my every blink. I grit my teeth in annoyance. I knew I needed to keep control of the situation. Any plan was better than no plan, I decided, and marched to the wall. I grazed my hand over its smooth surface and walked in a circle around the room, hoping I might trigger some sort of sensor to make the files appear. Before today, I'd always gotten any records

I needed on my plexi or had Elba take care of it. I had no idea the room was so advanced.

As I passed Sol, he had a smirk on his face.

"Fine," I said in defeat. "How does it work?"

He shoved his hands in his pockets and shrugged. He was enjoying this.

"Come on, Sol. Just tell me."

"I thought you were going to take it from here." He parroted my words back to me.

I could feel my face growing hot. I grasped onto my zone bracelets. I hated asking an Ash for help. Again. Although each ring had its relevance and every person their importance. I knew that. And Sol clearly had knowledge that I needed.

"Are you," Sol began incredulously, "blushing?" His smirk split into a full-blown grin.

I didn't know what to say. Or do. I needed his help. "Please, Sol."

"How could I refuse a damsel in distress?"

I smiled politely, despite my discomfiture. I couldn't believe I'd actually blushed. And I was hardly in distress.

"What I was trying to say earlier," he began, "is that the records use state of the art technology—upgraded by yours truly." He walked to the center of the room and tapped on the white circle with his foot. A hologram of a keyboard instantly popped up in front of him.

I pressed my lips together in annoyance. Not with Sol, but with myself. I should have realized the circle would be the system's trigger. I joined Sol in front of the hologram.

"You type in what you want here," he said gesturing to the board. "You can use the entire wall as your monitor. It makes it a lot easier to search when you have this much space."

I typed in my mother's name. Documents spread themselves

out over the walls of the room. Pictures, articles, videos, sound clips—her entire life and life's work surrounded me.

"This is where it gets really ultra," Sol said. "You can narrow down the documents through a word search," he explained. "Or, if you see a document that you like, just point and swipe."

He pointed to my parent's wedding announcement, guided it to a spot on the wall directly in front of us, and with a flick of two fingers expanded it to triple its original size. "You can make it as big or small as you want. And if you want to take a hologram copy with you, just gesture it toward you and it will appear here next to the keyboard."

I was impressed. "You created all of this?"

"The initial software was there, but I created the motion touch sensor and sorting software."

"That's incredible."

He looked down. "Thanks."

Maybe there was more to him than I had thought.

"Give it a try," he said.

I pointed at the document right next to my mom's marriage document, titled Mila Sumner data sheet. I gestured for it to come to me. And just like Sol promised, it landed neatly beside me.

I picked it up and studied the hologram. It listed all the major facts about my mother. Her married and maiden name, her birthday, the day she died, her destiny, which was 'to uncover the truth.' There was no timing listed for when she would do this. Which wasn't surprising. Time stamps hadn't been discovered until several years after she was born, and in some way, not having a time stamp of my own made me feel closer to her.

Most of my classmates had a specific time associated with their destiny that told them when their calling would come to fruition. Specialists made a point of making extractions within the first few minutes from birth. The whole procedure had to be performed quickly. An injection, monitoring, tissue extraction, and analysis. But in the end, it ensured a crystal clear future for all. The longer the process took, the blurrier the details, and no one wanted that. Still, not having a time wasn't the end of the world. I was proof of that. It just added a little more mystery.

I continued looking through my mother's records. I glanced over her university degree, her employment history. A complete listing of her newspaper articles was available, and I tapped it open to spill the documents over the walls. I noticed some of the same articles that had been restricted from my plexi. Nothing here was flagged, I realized with relief. Although, I wasn't about to read through them in front of Sol.

"Is there a way I can take these with me?" I asked.

"Sure," he said. "Drag everything you want over here and I can download it for you."

I closed the articles and moved them all to the spot Sol had indicated. If he thought this was odd, he didn't push it. Fortunately.

I glanced back at my mother's primary record. It even included information about her marriage to my father and, of course, my own birth and destiny.

I pulled the hologram closer. That was strange. Next to my destiny was a time stamp. It was for this year on December eleventh at 5:30pm. But that was impossible. The Specialist hadn't extracted my destiny early enough to get a date, let alone the hour and minute. An error had obviously been made. Sol must have seen the shocked look on my face because he gave me his own quizzical look in response.

"You okay?"

"Of course," I answered. There had to be a simple answer. It was probably just a data entry issue.

"You sure?" he asked. "You don't look so good."

"I'm fine," I assured him. "I bet people file things incorrectly all the time in here, don't they?"

"Not really, it's computerized," he answered. "Not much room for human error. The computer reads the name on a document and puts it in the corresponding folder. I guess a mistake could happen, but it'd be pretty unlikely."

"But what about the documents themselves?" I pressed. "Someone could input the wrong data?"

"Yeah, that could happen," he agreed.

I let out a small sigh of relief. It was a clerical error, just as I'd imagined. My relief was followed with a flare of outrage. I couldn't believe someone would mess up when it came to destiny. Especially the destiny of a future Minister of the Seven. Having a time and not knowing it would have been huge—especially if it came out too late. It would have caused chaos. My minister inauguration was scheduled for right after graduation when Minister Og stepped down—not this December. If I missed my destiny time, every non-believer would have used it as proof the system didn't work—that destiny could be changed, controlled. I shook my head. "People who input the incorrect destiny information should be fired instantly."

"No one ever messes that up," he said.

"What?" I felt my stomach drop.

"The Destiny Specialists input the information three separate times. Once on the baby's file and once on each parent's file. If there's no parent of record, they put that information on a separate sheet and input the destiny and time stamp again there. If any of the data varies an alert is sent out. Then a second Specialist looks over the records and signs off on them."

I readjusted my wrap around my shoulder as a shiver crept over my body. I could handle this. It wasn't the end of the world. If the records were accurate, then I had a destiny time after all. It was actually excellent news. It just meant that I'd need to push my inauguration date up and advance my studies. It was all doable. In fact, it was probably destiny that brought me to check out my mother's data sheet in the first place. That way I'd successfully complete my calling when I was supposed to. It was an incredible story, if you thought about it. I'd tell Link when we spoke next. It was just the sort of personal anecdote to help remind him why our system worked.

I looked at the hologram again. It was strange seeing a time stamp there. And then I looked at the smaller print. My time of birth read 6:52am. The destiny extraction—7:46. For a minute, I thought my heart stopped. Fifty-four minutes for extraction. That couldn't be right. After thirty minutes it was impossible to extract a time stamp. An hour after birth you couldn't even extract a destiny. At that point it was too far-gone into the recesses of the brain. Something was obviously wrong here.

"Pull up my file, please," I said through quick breaths. "I want my data sheet. My father's too."

Sol did as requested and handed them over.

These were different. They matched what I'd always been told—that my extraction had happened too late for a time stamp. Then why was my mother's file different? Somehow, someone had made a mistake. They must have. And I was going to get to the bottom of it.

NINETEEN

Dax

I opened my eyes. Sunlight poured through my window, and I realized it was well into the afternoon. I rolled to one side and groaned as a stab of pain traveled up my side. I squeezed my eyes closed once more trying to stall the inevitable, but it was useless. I was awake and yesterday's horrors were already stampeding through my mind. Aldan was dead. Link was in jail. And I'd broken curfew in the Tombs with a group of Revenants.

My walk home after leaving Thom had been uneventful, and my house silent as I'd snuck up the trellis and into my room. I'd never climbed it before, but I'd seen Aldan do it all the time. I always thought he was coming and going from late night loop race practices, but maybe he'd been doing a lot more than he'd let on. I'd lain in bed for hours thinking through everything that had happened. Oena had told me she'd answered all the questions she could, but she obviously knew more than she was saying. I wanted to kick myself for not asking her more when I had the chance.

I forced myself to get out of bed and go through the motions of starting my day. I knew I wouldn't be any help at the cells, but I'd go crazy sitting at home. There was no way I was going to school, not even for the tail end, but I needed to do something. I thought back to the graffiti at the practice tracks and knew what to do.

I grabbed the oldest, rattiest t-shirt and shorts I could find – both Aldan's hand me downs. The shirt was on the small side—he'd probably last worn it a decade ago. I pulled it on over my head, ignoring the giant hole in the sleeve. The shorts were from that era as well and a little too short, but my wardrobe was limited, and I was going to be cleaning. I couldn't afford to mess up my better outfits. I slipped on a pair of sneakers and pulled my hair back into a ponytail. Then I stopped off in the kitchen to dig through the mess under the sink. I grabbed some cleaner, a water spray bottle, a bristle sponge and a couple of rags and threw them in my backpack.

As I turned to go I noticed a large bouquet of purple tulips sitting on the end table by the door. It was a nice, unexpected gesture. I was surprised anyone would have thought to send something to a destiny breaker's family. I leaned over the flowers and inhaled deeply. A sweet, slightly fruity scent filled my nose— the flowers somehow even smelled purple. I tapped the card and read the inscription: My thoughts are with you in this difficult time. Sincerely, Madden Sumner.

Seriously? What was she trying to prove? The last thing any of us needed was Madden's pity. I picked the vase up and marched over to the trash compactor. I paused as I held the vase over it. Knowing my mom, she'd probably want to dry the flowers for posterity. I didn't care. I dropped the arrangement in and kicked the lid closed, smiling as the compactor did what it did best—smashed things.

I rushed to shut off the machine as my dad walked in. "Um, I was just—"

"It's okay." He came over and kissed the top of my head. "The smell was driving me nuts, too."

I let my head rest on his shoulder for a moment.

"How are you holding up?" he asked.

I wasn't sure how to answer the question. "Okay, I guess."

"I heard you and your mom had a pretty big fight last night," he said, leaning back against the kitchen counter. "Do you want to talk about it?"

"There's nothing to talk about," I said. "She took too much Xalan. It's not like it hasn't happened before." I turned from him, rummaging through the cabinet to find a breakfast bar. I so didn't feel like talking about this.

"Just do me a favor and go easy on her, okay?" My dad furrowed his brow. "Losing Aldan brought back some hard memories from the Event. She snapped last night. She didn't mean to take it out on you."

I sighed. "The Event was thirty-nine years ago, Dad. I get that it was a really horrible time, but it's not fair to blame everything on that."

"I know, but what she went through..." He took off his glasses and rubbed the lenses onto his shirt. "That time haunts everyone who lived through it. But your mom had it worse than most. Both my parents survived. They kept me safe during the riots, they protected me from what was going on outside. But your Mom..." His voice caught in his throat. "She saw it all. She watched her whole family die in front of her. Her parents. Her sisters. She was seven, Dax. She stayed at home for days hoping one of them would wake up. Finally she left, wandering through the streets for weeks on her own before an orphanage took her in. You can't imagine what it was like. Death in every direction. The smell of decay so thick in the air that you could barely breath. It took years for all of the bodies to get removed from the city."

I shivered. I studied the Event in school, but we rarely talked about it at home. Especially not my mother's history. It had always been hard to picture, but my dad's description seemed somehow more real now that I'd actually been to the Tombs. "I really am sorry about that," I said.

"Me too. What your mother went through is part of why she reacted so violently last night. You know how strict she is about the system. The orphanage preached complete dedication to the Seven. Enforced destiny was the only way to avoid another Event in their minds." My dad gave me a sad smile. "Not only did your mom see yet another family member—her son—die right in front of her yesterday, but she was raised—like all of us—to believe that destiny breakers should be removed. Only, this time the destiny breaker was Aldan. He's our son, but to your mother, he's also a traitor. She can't bridge those two ideas."

"Do you think he's a traitor?"

My dad paused. "No. I don't. My destiny is to study Shakespeare. I grew up on books, many that are no longer available, that talked about what life was like before the Event. A time when people shaped their own future. If nothing else, it's taught me that human nature is about asking questions and challenging beliefs. Aldan was true to his nature. And Link is doing the same. It doesn't mean I'm not heading back to the cells to talk him into doing it in a healthier way."

I nodded, relieved. But there was something I still wanted to know.

"Dad, do you still believe in the system?" I knew it was a question that could get us both in trouble, but the more I was learning, the more unsure I was becoming. I wondered if I was the only one.

My father's face twisted, a world of emotions flickering in his eyes. "It keeps us safe. But that safety comes at a high cost... too high, maybe." His voice faltered and lowered to almost a whisper. "'Men at some times are masters of their fates. The fault, dear Brutus, is not in our stars, But in ourselves...'"

"What?"

"Just more Shakespeare." He clapped his hands together. "Okay, enough talk. Why don't you come with me to see Link?" he asked. "Your mom and brothers are all there."

I thought about it, but the idea of being cooped up in the waiting room knowing I wouldn't be able to go in and see my brother sounded horrible. "If it's okay with you, I'd like to be alone," I said. "I'll meet you guys back here later, okay?"

"Of course," he said. "You know where we'll be if you need anything."

We said our goodbyes, and I headed out into the afternoon, adding our conversation to the growing list of impossible things that had happened over the last twenty-four hours.

The air was warm, but still crisp. I kept my head down as I walked, zigzagging my way through the rings, trying to avoid as many people as I could. I stopped when I finally reached the practice loop. The graffiti on the sign was still there, even more harsh in the afternoon sun.

The gate on the fence was open. I knew I shut it last night, which meant I probably had company now. I peeked inside. There was one person lying across the yard in the grass, his hands behind his head, staring up at the track.

Theron.

He was in our usual spot. I felt myself start to blush, thinking about what I must look like in my ratty hand me downs. I almost bolted, but Theron looked up at that moment, almost as if he could sense me standing there.

"Dax?" he called out. He scrambled to his feet and jogged across the lawn.

I tugged on my shorts, trying to pull them down. Why, I wondered, had I not at least brushed my hair, or something. Laira was going to love lecturing me about this when I told her.

"Um, hey," I said as he stopped in front of me.

"Hey."

He stepped forward to give me a hug, but I, ever so suave when it came to Theron, stiffened and looked down at my shoes, causing him to pause in his tracks.

"I've been worried about you," he said, breaking the awkwardness. "How are you doing?"

"Well, you know..." I trailed off.

"Yeah," he said. Then softer. "Yeah, I do." Then he reached out, this time not stopping, and pulled me toward him, enveloping me in his arms. I let myself hug him back for a few seconds, resting my head against his chest as I inhaled his scent—it was his own peculiar mix of sunshine and New City and boy.

"I'm sorry, Dax."

I pulled away and looked at Theron. Really looked at him. He was pale, and his usual flop of red hair stood up in a disheveled disaster. His eyes were puffy, and dark circles smudged half moons underneath them. Theron—eternal comedian, prankster, and lover of fun—looked horrible. I thought about reaching out for him again, burying myself inside of his arms and staying there for a good long while. Instead I took my backpack off and unzipped it. We both needed something else to focus on.

"You saw the graffiti outside?" I asked.

"Yeah," he said, voice turning sour. "Hard to miss."

I pulled out my cleaning supplies. "I thought I'd get rid of it.

Want to help?"

He flashed me that disarming grin of his, the one that you couldn't help but smile back at. "Definitely."

I held out a rag toward him and he took it, grazing my fingers as he did so. He let them linger for a second and then took my hand. "Come on," he said and led me to the sign. I was relieved my feet still remembered how to move, because I certainly couldn't think of anything to say at the moment. Theron Oliver was holding my hand. I tried to act casual, like it was no big deal.

"Looks like we have our work cut out for us," he said, eyeing the sign. To my disappointment he dropped my hand. He was just being friendly, I reminded myself. The gesture didn't mean anything. He was Theron, he made everybody feel important. "I guess we should get started."

The afternoon sun shone down on us as we began to clean. On most days, the area would have been packed. The track brought plenty of other racers, and whenever Aldan practiced, there were always fans that would gather. I guessed it would take a little time before people came back, and for that, I was strangely happy. For the time being, this space belonged to Theron and me. And Aldan. The hologram of him cresting the final loop and sailing past the finish line played over and over between us.

I could feel my muscles working as I pressed into the sign, rubbing away at the letters. It felt good to remove some of the hate. I fell into a kind of rhythm. Spray, scrub up, down, up, down, repeat. Theron and I didn't talk, but it was a comfortable silence. The kind that didn't need to be filled with meaningless chitchat. Behind us I could hear the swish of the monorail in the distance. Wind rustled through the leaves overhead, birds chattered, and soon Theron joined them, whistling an odd little song. It wasn't happy, exactly. But it wasn't sad, either. Bittersweet, I guessed, just like this afternoon. This would probably be last time the two of us would see each other outside of Spectrum.

It took about thirty minutes until I'd almost finished my section of the sign. There was just a small portion over my head that I couldn't quite reach.

"Let me help you," Theron said and reached up over my head. "See, it's a good thing you ran into me."

"I could have gotten it," I said, and then cursed myself for not making my tone flirtier.

"Yeah?"

"Yeah, it's simple. Watch," I wound up my arm and threw the rag at the sign. It hit it all right, but then bounced off, falling right onto Theron's head. "I didn't do that on purpose, I swear," I said, trying to hold back a laugh.

"Well, that might not have been," he said, "but this is." He then took the water bottle and sprayed it at me.

"No you didn't! This is war, Mr. Oliver. Get ready," I said, and went to grab my weapon of choice—the rag closest to me. Only as I stepped back, I tripped over my backpack and fell, hitting the ground with a thump.

So much for being cute and flirty. Pure mortification rippled through my body.

He stepped closer in concern. "Dax, are you okay?"

Then I surprised myself. I started cracking up. Uncontrollably. I just fell on my butt in front of Theron. A week ago, nothing would have seemed worse. But now, after everything I'd been through, this was nothing. This could be fixed. I picked up the rag and snapped it at him. "Gotcha!" I yelled and sprung to my feet.

He looked at me, incredulous, and then started cracking up too, trying to snap me back with his own rag. I jumped out of the way just in time.

For the next few minutes we were running around and laughing and forgetting everything, until I backed up into the hologram. The image of Aldan literally hit me in the face. And with that, the moment was lost.

I stepped away, the rag now hanging limply from my hand. Our early, easier silence was replaced with a kind of heaviness until Theron spoke. "I should have talked him out of it, Dax," he said. "You don't mess around with your destiny. Not with the whole world watching. It was supposed to be the ultimate prank. It was just so stupid." He rubbed a hand through his hair. "I was going to come by your house today. Apologize to you and your family. I feel like," he paused, "like I'm partially responsible."

"Theron, no one blames you," I replied, startled. "Really, I promise. If anything I feel like it's my fault."

"What are you talking about?" he asked. "Of course it's not."

"Half the time that Aldan argues politics it's on my behalf, Theron. You really think if his kid sister wasn't a Blank any of this would have happened?"

Theron shook his head. "Dax, it wasn't because of you. Your situation may have opened his eyes further, but he always saw the world in a different way. He thought the system should be colorblind." He let out a sigh. "I probably shouldn't be telling you this, but he'd been seeing this girl. I only met her a couple of times, but she was a Green."

He was talking about Oena. I wondered how much he knew about her. "His mystery girl," I said. "She was the one you were talking to at the race?"

"That's her. They hadn't known each other for long, but he really liked her. He kept saying how he didn't care about the policies. That he'd found the girl for him and that was all that mattered."

"Kind of like one of the stories my dad is always talking about. Romeo and Juliet."

"Yeah," he said. "Just like that."

"But it would never have worked between them," I said. I looked into Theron's eyes, holding his gaze. Gold flecked the green of his irises. "You know how it would have been. They were from such different rings."

"You're probably right," he said, looking away. "But Aldan didn't care about that. He wanted to take a stand. He wanted to, I don't know, do something dramatic. I just know I could have done more to stop him from doing what he did."

"There wasn't anything you could have done, Theron."

"You don't know that," he said, his voice going tight.

"Yes, I do," I said. "Aldan always does exactly—" I paused, realizing my brother was now in the past. "Aldan always did exactly what he thought was right. No one else figured into that. You could have argued with him as much as you wanted. If he wanted to mock the system, he was going to do it, one way or another. If it hadn't been the race, it would have been something else. A week later. A month later. It would have happened."

Theron chewed on that for a few minutes. I wasn't sure if he believed me or not, and before he could say one way of the other, the clock tower began to chime. It was five o'clock. Theron glanced at his tracker with a groan.

"I'm late," he said. "I told my parents I'd be home over an hour ago. Let me walk you home."

I thought about the empty house that was waiting for me. Or worse, my mom already there.

"Thanks, but it's okay," I said. "You're already late. And I want to stay here a little longer. It's nice to just have some quiet, you know."

"Yeah," he agreed. "See you at school?"

I nodded. As I looked at him I realized this was a real goodbye. When Theron left things would be different for us. They would have to be. There wasn't an Aldan to connect us any longer.

I think he sensed it too. His eyes lingered on me, and he reached toward my face. "Hold still," he said.

I froze, wondering if this was it, if he was about to finally kiss me.

He rubbed his thumb over my cheek. "A little bit of dirt," he explained. "I got it."

"Oh, uh, thanks." I felt myself blushing, and I turned around to reach for my backpack, hoping he hadn't seen my face go red. Stupid, idiotic crush.

"And thanks, Dax," he said.

"For what?"

"When your destiny—your job—is to make someone laugh, the world expects you to be "on" all the time, lighten the mood, no matter what. Even when your best friend dies. That's why I didn't go to school today. It was bad enough pretending in front of my family and their friends. I've had to put on a fake smile around everyone. You're the only one who actually got me to do it for real. You even got me to laugh."

"Well I guess it's a little easier when it's not your job, when you just care about the person," I said. I wanted to kick myself when the words were out of my mouth. I was certainly on a roll today.

"You may be right," he said and kissed me on the cheek. "Though if that's the case, I should have you cracking up all the time."

Theron waved goodbye and left me standing there wondering what on earth had just happened.

TWENTY

—

Madden

The Records Room seemed to shrink around me. Everything felt like it was closing in. I looked away from the hologram documents in front of me, unsure of what to think. I stalled, studying my nails while I tried to remain calm. I'd left them unpolished, and the skin underneath was turning a dark purple from the cold of the room. It was somehow appropriate. I stared back at the documents again. On one document I had a time stamp. The rest—none.

"Madden?" Sol asked. "You look like John Crilas just showed up at your door and asked you out on a date. What's wrong?"

I just stared at the hologram documents in front of me. There was something wrong with my destiny. Mistakes like this didn't happen. Not on purpose. I didn't answer Sol. I couldn't. I needed answers before I could do anything, but I had no idea where to get them. I couldn't very well talk to the ministers. It could put my destiny at risk, cause some sort of scandal, and the ministry did not look highly upon scandals. My reign as a leader of the country would be a joke. The other ministers would push me out days after I was appointed.

There was always my father, but I knew him too well. If I told him, he'd just say it was a mistake in my mother's file. Then he'd tell me not to mention it again. Right after a lecture about snooping and subsequent grounding.

I looked up. Sol was still watching me. He understood the complexities of the records. He'd even modified the technology. But could I trust him with something this huge?

I studied his eyes. Brown, almost as dark as his pupils. They looked kind.

"Madden, what is it?"

Maybe it was because he didn't call me princess this time, or because he actually sounded concerned, or just because he was there, but I decided to tell him the truth.

"I need you to swear you won't tell a soul," I said.

He nodded.

"On your family's lives—on their destinies?" I questioned.

"Yes," he said. For some reason, I trusted him.

"There's a discrepancy with my time stamp," I blurted out, shoving the documents toward him. "I have no idea what it means." His eyes widened as he looked them over. "Can you figure out why? I'll give you another three hundred ostows."

"No," he said, shaking his head.

"Fine, six hundred. Please, I have to know." I was desperate enough to beg if that's what he wanted. It didn't matter that he was an Ash. He had answers I needed.

"I mean, no, you don't have to pay me." He held my gaze. "I'll help you."

For a flicker of a second I had the impulse to hug him, but I quickly composed myself. "Thank you."

Sol held my gaze for long enough that I began to feel uncomfortable, and I finally looked away not knowing what to say. He'd surprised me today. If he had been a Purple, we might have even been friends. But he wasn't, I reminded myself. Being a Purple was something you were born with. He was just a lower rung doing me a favor. And for that, I'd repay him one way or another. I couldn't get myself into a position where I was indebted to anyone—especially an Ash. It would be a disaster when I took my place as a minister. No doubt he knew that too, and was smart enough to know that by helping me, he would help himself.

Sol went to work typing away at the keyboard. I fidgeted, adjusting my weight from one foot, back to the other, wrapping and rewrapping myself in my cashmere shawl. Each second felt like hours.

"Did you find anything?" I asked.

"Not yet."

We played out different versions of the conversation about a dozen times over the next five minutes.

"Madden, you've got to give me a little time. This isn't easy."

I realized I was being overbearing. Stressing out Sol would just make it harder for him to get anything done. I knew that. Leadership training taught me that remaining calm and approaching problems with a sense of humor helped motivate people. Staring over Sol's shoulders was only going to slow his productivity, so I changed tactics. "I'm sure it's nothing for the tech king of New City," I said with a smile. "You don't get that title for nothing."

He pushed his black hair out of his eyes and cocked his head. "Are you flirting with me?"

"You wish."

Sol's cheeks reddened a little, and I stifled a laugh. "Now come on, figure this out."

"Anything you say, princess," he said, his voice playful.

I wasn't sure how I felt about him calling me a princess after I'd dubbed him a king, but I let it go. I didn't need verbal sparring, I needed him to work. I lowered myself to the ground and put my back up against the wall. Sitting on the floor was not very Purple-like behavior, but neither was trying to decrypt old files. Fortunately, no one was around to see either.

For the next fifty-three minutes, I sat in silence watching Sol. Once I stopped bothering him, he entered some sort of trance. As if nothing existed but his work. He typed away at the keyboard, his eyes glued to the data popping up on the wall in front of him. None of it made sense to me. A lot of gibberish, random numbers, symbols, and commands. I'd received good marks in my comp sci classes, but this was way above my studies.

He finally stopped typing and turned to face me, rubbing his hands over his face. "I've never seen anything like this. The encryption was incredible. You'd never find it if you weren't looking for it, and even then most wouldn't spot it. It was thirteen layers deep. The first few algorithms were based on a symmetric key encryption model, but I had to get creative when I hit the fifth. They tried to trick me with a dummy multiplier, which also used an invertible affine transformation. Then—"

"Sol!" I yelled. "English. What does it all mean?"

"It means that someone worked very hard to hide the fact that they tampered with your information."

I wanted to stand, but I couldn't. "On which file? The data stamp on my mother's? Or removing it from my father's and mine?"

He got very quiet.

"Sol."

He wouldn't look at me, instead he studied a spot on the ceiling.

"Sol, answer me."

He brought his eyes down to meet mine. "All of them, Madden. Someone changed your destiny."

TWENTY-ONE

—

Dax

I sat in the grass in the same spot I'd found Theron. I felt energized and happy and sad and confused all at once. My brother was dead, and there I'd been playing and laughing. It seemed wrong… only, part of it didn't. Aldan loved life. He wanted me to live it. He wanted me to live it in a colorblind society.

Those words sent a slight shiver down my spine. I never imagined that could be a possibility. But apparently Aldan did. In a way, he died for it. Wasn't that what the Revenants were about? Defying the system. Letting people live the way they wanted? Having options?

Options that weren't available to people like me, no matter what we did. I got better grades than most of the Purples at Spectrum, and that was without the tutors and privileges that came with status. But it wouldn't change my future, because I was an Ash. A Blank Ash. But it didn't have to be that way. Just because the system hadn't provided me with a destiny at birth didn't mean I couldn't define one for myself.

I closed my eyes and breathed in the dirt and grass and faint smell of salt from the sweat in my damp t-shirt. I felt the blades of grass sticking into my body, pressing into my palms. And then I opened my eyes and sat up, knowing exactly what I had to do. The entrance to the Tombs was thirty yards from me. And there wasn't a soul around.

Aldan wasn't the only one who could help the Revenants.

I double-checked the area to make sure no one was around and turned off my locator. I felt a pang of guilt knowing this would cost my family another fifty ostows in fines, but it was worth it.

After one last careful look around, I snuck over to the bushes near the fence. I pushed them aside and ran my palms over the metal where I knew the holographic covering was projected. My fingers found the edge where metal met air. Without a second thought, I ducked through the hole and found myself back on the same platform where I'd stood the night before. I darted down the stairs. When I hit the bottom, I paused. There was enough daylight seeping in from the entrance to the Tombs that I could tell I was in a large tunnel. I couldn't see more than a few feet in either direction, and I had no idea how I would find my way back to the subway train car where I'd met Oena.

I flicked my tracker light on, and off just as quickly. Even on its dimmest setting, it was still a bright light in the darkness. I covered it with my sleeve as an added dimmer, and turned it back on. Its subdued light did little to disturb the darkness. That was fine by me. I'd learned my lesson last night. No need to get caught and captured by another crew of Revenants. Assuming that there was another crew down here somewhere. Just one more question I'd ask Oena when I found her. I did a quick survey of the ground until I found what I was looking for—loose scrap metal. I picked up a piece about a foot long. It wasn't much, but after my scare last night, I figured some kind of weapon was better than nothing. On a whim, I turned to the right and began to walk.

It was hard going. Last night's walk through the Tombs had been rocky, but not like this. There was enough rubble underfoot that I had to tread carefully, and my light did little to help. The tunnel was slanted steeply downhill, and the angle combined with the rocks and beams covering the path made it treacherous. I tripped repeatedly over the next several minutes, barely catching myself each time. This couldn't be right. There was no way Thom, even with all of his muscles, could have carried me over this kind of ground while I was squirming and fighting. I turned around, retracing my steps until I found the stairs, then followed the tunnel in the other direction. The ground slanted downhill in this direction as well, but was easier to walk over. I made my way along the path until it split in two directions. I chose the larger one and continued.

I followed this path for a much shorter period before it split once again. Which is when I started to worry. My sense of direction had always been dependable, but this was an underground labyrinth. The darkness made any visual markers impossible to spot. I knelt down and roughly arranged some of the debris into an arrow formation showing the way of my next turn. It wasn't perfect, but at least it was something in case I needed to retrace my steps.

I wandered on for some time, marking my twists and turns with whatever I could find underfoot. The air was stale and dusty, and with every step I kicked up clouds of filth. No matter how hard I listened, the only thing I could hear was the sound of my feet crunching over the uneven ground—no reassuring swish of the light rail or hum of voices—even the rats had deserted this section of the Tombs. Thom had said we were safe from contamination, but goose bumps crawled over my skin anyway. Did that mean everywhere in the Tombs was okay?

I was almost ready to turn back when my path dead-ended at a battered, decaying rail track. A phosphorous yellow line followed the wall next to the track and stretched in both directions until it curved out of sight. This was a good sign. I'd met Oena in a train car, and it stood to reason that a train car would be found on a train track. I fashioned some rubble underfoot into an arrow leading to the right, and followed my new projected course.

I'd only walked a few minutes until I reached an impasse. It looked as if the tunnel had collapsed in on itself. A wall of boulders cut across my path. I turned, preparing to retrace my steps when I noticed a bobbing light coming down the track toward me. I clicked off my light, cursing under my breath. I was trapped. What if the person headed toward me was dangerous?

I clutched the metal in my hand tight. Whoever it was didn't know any more about me than I did about them. I needed to convince them that I was the dangerous one. "Don't come any closer," I warned, trying to make my voice sound as gruff as possible. "I don't want to have to kill you."

The bobbing light grew closer, and a second stream of light shot out toward me, hitting me full in the face.

"I'm warning you," I said, shielding my eyes with one hand and holding out my weapon with the other.

"Idiot," a raspy voice said.

I recognized it immediately. I had listened to it trying to convince Thom to get rid of me. "You're Oena's friend." What was her name?

The brighter stream of light clicked off and the smaller light resumed its bobbing approach. The girl planted herself in front of me, her hands firmly anchored to each hip. Her face spoke volumes. I was the annoying intruder who was warned not to return. And she wanted me gone.

"The name's Raze," she said. "I thought Thom took you home last night. What are you doing back down here?"

"I want to join your crew." Out of the three Revenants I knew, Raze was the one I was the least excited to see. She obviously wasn't one of my bigger fans. I hoped that wouldn't stop her from helping me find Oena.

Raze gave me a sour milk expression. "You're joking, I hope."

I shook my head no. "I want to help."

She rubbed her palm against her cropped hair making it stick up in spikes. "No," she finally said.

"Give me a chance," I made sure to sound authoritative. Raze wasn't the type who would respond to pleading.

"No," she repeated.

"I'll do whatever it takes," I pressed.

"Are you deaf?" she asked.

"This is my fight too," I said. "They killed my brother, Raze. The government has done nothing but hurt me and the people I care about." I motioned upward. "Everything that goes on above ground was created for the upper rings. I want to do my part to help change that."

She snorted.

"I'm serious."

"And what about your family?" she asked.

"What do you mean?"

"Your other Purple brother is being held in the cells for dissent. What do you think the ministry would do to him if you disappeared and they figured out it was because you defected to us? Not to mention the rest your family. The government would probably take it out on all of them."

But I'd already thought about this. "I wouldn't disappear," I reasoned. "I would help you from above, like Aldan did."

"Too risky," Raze replied. "Oena told you last night—you and your family will be under more surveillance now."

"Then at least take me to Oena. Let me ask her."

"Oena doesn't make the decisions for our crew. Her brother does."

I cocked my head to one side in confusion. "But isn't he in the holding cells?"

Raze gave me a ghost of a smile. "For now, yes. Cages rarely keep Zane long."

I wondered what other type of cage he'd been in, but I knew better than to ask. "Then I'll come back when Zane gets free and ask *him*."

Raze crossed her arms in front of her.

"I'm not going to give up," I said.

"Fine," she said. "I'll take you to Oena and let her tell you no. But be quiet as we head that direction. There was word we might get some company today. I was out scouting when I found you." She dimmed her light and gave me one last stony glare. "Keep up," she advised. And then we were off.

I moved as silently as possible. Company? What did that mean? Was it a group of Revenants she didn't get along with? Was it the PAE? Neither felt particularly reassuring, but I swallowed my fear and kept moving. This was what it meant to be a Revenant. We walked for about twenty minutes, turning here and there. I wondered if I'd ever be able to learn my way through this maze. We'd just climbed a ladder and entered into another, smaller tunnel, when we heard something. It sounded like the rustling of fabric. Raze immediately clicked off her light and grabbed my arm. She took a step back, and another, pulling me toward the ladder in retreat. Her fingers dug into my flesh, warning me to keep quiet and follow. We crept down the ladder, and I did my best to keep my breathing regular and silent, even though my nerves were rerouting my body into overdrive.

Raze continued to pull me along behind her. When we had moved a little ways away from the ladder, I heard another sound from above. There was a click, and then a crackle as a laser came to life.

Raze yanked me toward her and breathed into my ear. "Stay with me no matter what." She tightened her grip on my arm and then we began to run.

From behind I heard a second laser, and a light flooded the upper tunnel the ladder had taken us to.

"Stop," I heard a man's voice yell after us. "This is the PAE— we've got you surrounded."

We ran faster, flying through the Tombs. I didn't have time to worry about losing my footing, I just kept going. Shouts followed from behind, and when I glanced over my shoulder, multiple lights followed.

Raze pulled me down another ladder, which lead to a smaller tunnel. Soon we were forced to crawl. From the distance, I could hear the sound of water. "Can you swim?" she whispered frantically.

"Yes."

"Let's hope they can't," she said. "Come on."

The sound of the water grew louder until it surrounded us— rushing somehow in front of us and below us at the same time. "The tunnel dead ends over the water," Raze said over the sound. "Follow the flow and it will dump you into the East River. If we get separated, be at the East 8 stop in the Ash zone at nine tonight." Raze pushed me ahead of her. "Hurry. I'll be right behind you."

I didn't need any encouragement. The tunnel had opened up enough that I could manage a crouched run. From behind I could see the lights again, and I propelled myself forward with every ounce of energy I had. Shouts filled the air as my eyes adjusted enough to see an opening in front of me.

"Jump!" Raze bellowed.

My foot hit the edge of the tunnel, and I flung myself off. From behind, the darkness lit up and I heard Raze scream as my body dunked down into the cold. I struggled to swim up through the rushing water. When I surfaced, I looked back, choking on the water I'd swallowed. The tunnel I'd jumped from was bursting with light, and I could see the shadows of a struggle going on, then the unquestionable snap of a laser being fired. I heard Raze scream again. I struggled against the rush of water, trying to swim back to her, but I was no match for the current. Soon I was dragged around the bend, Raze's screams ringing in my ears.

TWENTY-TWO

—

Madden

"What do you mean someone changed my destiny?" I asked, barely recognizing my own voice. It was low, angry, desperate. "That's not possible. I'm a future Minister of the Seven. It's who I am."

"It's okay, calm down," Sol said. He kneeled down to where I was sitting on the floor. "I don't mean they rewrote your destiny, I don't know what they did. I just know somebody tampered with it on all three files."

My head seemed somehow thicker, denser—his words were taking longer to seep through and I looked up at him in confusion, trying to understand what he was saying. "How? What did they change?"

He shook his head. "I told you, I don't know."

"What do you mean you don't know? You need to find out." I grabbed his hands, clutching them in mine. "Sol, please, I have to figure out what's going on."

He looked at me, at our hands, then around the room. "Okay, but I need higher access."

"You can have mine."

"It's not that easy," he said, struggling for words. "You have access to find and take out files. So do I, since I work here. But inputting is different. There's a system to keep people from accidentally entering or overriding information. People only have access to input if their job calls for it."

"You can hack that. Just override it."

"To find what you're looking for, I need to write new code, introduce a new program into the system. If that doesn't have minister approval, it will send out security alerts. I might be able to cover my tracks initially, but it would only be only a matter of time before I was caught. I couldn't do that to my family. And I know you want this to stay quiet too."

He was right. Government class covered Article 31 in depth. Anyone caught penetrating and tampering with secure information from the ministry would suffer the full extent of the law. Sol would be locked up and possibly put to death even sooner than his destiny called for. And his family forced to endure an investigation into what they knew. Their whole lives would be turned upside down. "I understand. Thank you anyway," I said, dropping his hands and gathering myself up off of the ground.

"Wait," he said. "I didn't say I wasn't going to help you. I just said I need higher access." He took a deep breath. "If you can get me into one of the ministers' offices, I'll be able to access the system as one of them."

I didn't know what to say. Part of me wanted to talk Sol out of what he was suggesting. Getting caught using a minister's computer was just as treasonous as breaking into the mainframe in the file room. But I was desperate to understand what was happening to me. The time stamp had changed everything. My destiny had been tampered with. I needed to know the truth.

My conscience won out in the end. "Sol, I can't ask you to do that."

"You're not. I'm offering."

I couldn't believe he was willing to do this for me. "But what if someone sees you?"

"I don't plan on getting caught. Do you?"

I shook my head no.

"Good, then Sealy, Worthington, and Kurtz all have mainframes in their offices. Any of them out of the office?"

"Worthington is speaking to the Delegation today." I checked my wrist tracker. "He should be starting any minute."

"Perfect," he said. "Next step, get rid of Elba." He pulled out his plexi, and began typing. "Done. In a few seconds, we should have a ten minute window."

"What? How?"

"I just sent her a message, saying she needs to bring a hard copy of Minister Worthington's notes to the forum room. It's a five-minute walk each way."

"And you don't think she'll be a little suspicious when she sees the ping came from you?"

"Please, give me some credit. I hacked Worthington's aide's account. It came from there."

I couldn't help but smile at his quick thinking.

"Now let's clean up in here." Sol made a sweeping gesture with his arms and took the files, all of them still posted on the walls—the articles I had selected to copy as well as my mother's additional files, mine, and my father's. He swiped them to his plexi where they instantly downloaded.

"What are you doing?" I cried. "Are you crazy?"

With another sweep of his arms, he cleared away the

holograms. "You came looking for something other than your destiny, right?" he asked.

I nodded slowly.

He shrugged. "Then you may want to see that information later. This way you can have it whenever you want. Everything is saved on my plexi."

"Don't you think someone will notice that hundreds of files were downloaded?" The last thing I needed was attention on my family issues.

"Nope. I'm synced with the mainframe. No one can tell if I move anything."

I hedged. Everything was happening too fast. I didn't want all that information about my family on his plexi. "What if you lose it? You don't want to be connected with stolen data."

He stepped on the center circle on the floor and the keyboard disappeared. "Not an issue. First of all, I can access it remotely. So I can always track it down, or if need be, erase everything on the drive. Second, I wrote a program. It's ingenious really in its simplicity. It just takes the first letter and the last letter of each word and condenses it. If anyone were to stumble on my plexi they'd just think it was gibberish from the dead guy." He grinned and then launched into another lesson on encryption codes, but I couldn't focus on what he was saying.

"Elba's probably gone by now," I said. "We should go."

"Hold on," he said studying something on his plexi. "I called up the security cameras. There's a hover cam circling by now. We should be clear in twenty seconds."

Sol poked his head out the door and when he saw it was all clear we both exited. We repeated the process as we approached the corner near Elba's desk.

From there we darted to Minister Worthington's office. It was a large room, with a heavy wooden desk and oversized visitors chairs to match. Plants bloomed in the windows and the Ministry seal hung on one wall. It was a comfortable, stately place that Sol and I were violating. I locked the door behind us with shaking hands. "We need to hurry. Elba will be back soon, and she comes in here all the time."

"You don't need to tell me twice," Sol said, and sat himself down in Minister Worthington's leather chair. He seemed nervous. Not that I blamed him, I was too. But this must have been even more nerve wracking for Sol. He was in the seat of one of our country's greatest leaders. Behind him a wall of windows showed the peaks of New City skyscrapers jutting up around us.

Under any other circumstance, I'd be appalled to see an Ash sitting there. I'd have written out the fine for ring violation myself, if I had stumbled upon the sight. But while the contrast of Sol's dingy ash clothing against the plush, royal purple chair still seemed surreal, right now I didn't care.

Sol didn't waste any time. He was typing so fast, everything seemed to blur. Codes and files raced at his command. A photo cube sat next to the screen, flashing pictures. I felt my entire body seize as Bastin's smiling face rotated through. What would my boyfriend say if he could see me now? My mouth felt suddenly dry, and I swallowed.

I kept looking from my wrist tracker to the door. Ten minutes passed. I didn't dare check to see if Elba was back, but odds were good that if she wasn't, it would only be a matter of moments.

Another ten minutes passed. Then another eight. Then finally Sol spoke up. "Here we go. Let's see what your original destiny said."

I held my breath, and he tapped one last key.

"Well," I said, moving closer to him, trying to read the screen myself.

"That's strange," he said. "It's blank. They must have erased it completely."

I was at a loss. "What do we do now?"

"I don't know," he said. "I guess I can check if there were any other overrides or tampering, but there are billions of files. That could take days."

"How long would it take to just check birth records from New City, the year I was born?" I asked.

"A few minutes," he said.

"Then let's do it."

A moment later, he declared, "Done. There's just one other destiny override."

I looked at the name on the screen. Dax Harris.

"Open it," I instructed him.

"That's strange," he said. "Did you know she was born on November eleventh too? Right around the same time as you."

I hadn't. November eleventh was always my big day. I'd never really considered who I might share it with.

"You guys had the same Destiny Specialist too. Karina Palcove."

"Do you think she did this? Maybe she made some errors and went back to fix them," I suggested. If it was just the case of trying to correct a spelling mistake or two, I could handle it. And maybe in her confusion she added a time stamp to my destiny in my mom's file. It was all pretty reasonable.

"Doubt it," Sol said, crushing my explanation. "You'd need some serious access to make that kind of change and have no one notice it. You can't get that at the hospital. And the changes were made about an hour after you were born. Not enough time to get from the hospital to here, and encrypt the files."

Part of my body was overheating, the other part shivering. I knew my next question, but I wasn't sure I wanted the answer.

I took a deep breath. I came this far, I had to find out.

"Can you tell how the Specialist changed Dax's destiny?"

"I'll try," Sol said. He played around for a few minutes on the computer, and then his face paled as Dax's original fate appeared on the screen.

I had my answer.

"Madden," he said, his voice a whisper, "your file had the word Blank written on it when I decrypted it. I just thought that meant they didn't fill it in. But it looks like—"

"Don't," I said. I knew what it meant.

My destiny had been swapped at birth.

Dax Harris was the future Minister of the Seven.

And, I, Madden Sumner, was a Blank.

TWENTY-THREE

—

Dax

"Raze," I yelled out. The PAE had her, I had to get back to her, I had to help, but the current was too powerful. It carried me along like a piece of debris, and I wasn't strong enough to fight back. I tried to call out to her again, but the waves pulled me under, flinging me into the tunnel's slimy walls. Dirty water caught in my lungs.

I grabbed hold of a nearby rock to catch my breath, to ease the coughing. The spot where I got separated from Raze was barely visible. I strained to make out if she was there, but I couldn't tell. My body froze as a narrow beam of light hit right below my right shoulder. I might not have been able to see the PAE, but they clearly saw me. It would only be seconds until they fired the pulse. I had no choice, I took a quick, deep breath and dove.

For the next thirty minutes it was all I could do to keep my head above the water. The rushing waves made it impossible to see anything. I thought about kicking my shoes off, but after slamming against several sharp rocks, I knew I had to keep them on. My energy was waning, my body felt numb from the cold, and I kept swallowing water. I didn't know how much more I could take. The current would pull me down soon.

No, I told myself, I wasn't giving up. I kept my arms and legs out around me as much as I could, compelling myself to keep my head above the frigid water. I would make it out of here. I would survive.

Eventually I could see a lighter smudge against the darkness. It was the tunnel's end. The water picked up the pace as it exited, and it took everything I had to stay afloat as I was flung into the East River. My body felt like putty as I crossed one arm in front of the other, kicking back toward the land. Exhausted, I dragged myself onto shore.

In the distance, a crack of lightning sliced through the night. I felt a drop hit my nose, then another as I rose to my feet. I looked at my tracker, still working despite the water—trackers were virtually indestructible. The numbers glowed faintly: 8:23. If I hurried I could make it to the Ash Zone on time. I took a step and winced as the water squished in my shoes. I paused to wring my shirt. I was tired, more than tired, and my muscles sore, but I couldn't stop. I had to find the Revenants. I closed my eyes, took a deep breath, and set off on my path, scrambling up the rocky bank, and into the Brown zone.

Rain began to fall in earnest as I left the shore. I kept my head down, racing toward the Brown rail station. I wasn't the only other wet traveler standing on the platform. It was a lucky break. No one would think twice about my soggy clothing.

Soon enough, the train arrived. I stepped into the Ash car on the train and, despite the absence of any other passengers, was immediately hit by the smell of wet feet. It was a short trip, and soon enough we pulled into the Ash zone. While I knew I should have been scared (what I was doing was certainly punishable by death), I felt energized, like I was on the right path.

I kept an eye out for other people as I walked out of the station's main entrance, and around the corner. The streets were deserted, and I quickly found the storage doorway that Raze had described. My heartbeat quickened as I reached out and rapped my knuckles again the metal door. When there was no answer, I turned the handle and pulled. My excitement turned to confusion. The room was little more than a closet. A few hazard cones were stacked in the corner next to a box of metal pipes. Beside this was a splintered mop stuffed into a bucket, a pile of discarded rags, and various other cleaning supplies. Several grease-streaked Ash jumpsuits hung from pegs on the wall. This couldn't be right. Even alone, I was cramped inside of this space. Forget about a rabble of covert destiny defectors. Had I somehow misunderstood Raze's directions?

I shined the light of my tracker around the room, trying to see if I had missed anything. There were several wet footprints. Someone *had* been here recently.

I knelt down next to the clearest print, looking at the tracks more closely. One disappeared behind the uniforms. It looked as though the wall had cut it right in half. I hesitantly reached out and moved the uniforms to one side. My fingers pressed right through the holographic surface and inside I cheered—I'd found the entrance.

I stood up, cautiously stepping into a dark, narrow hallway. At the end was another door. I knocked, then pushed the door open.

On the other side, six people sat around a circular table. Most jumped from their seats as I entered. Their clothing and trackers announced they came from various rings. Each of them pointed a weapon at me. Guns, lasers, knives, all ready to take me down.

I stood rigid, half in, half out of the doorway, numb with fear. Was I supposed to run, jump for cover, try to explain who I was?

"Hold," Oena yelled before I could say anything.

No one lowered their weapon.

She leapt around the table toward me, graceful, yet still agile despite her ankle length green dress. "Dax, what in crilas are you doing here?" she asked.

Thom stood at the far side of the table. His green blazer looked surprisingly polished. He shook his head in exasperation, slowly lowering his gun. "You have got to be kidding," he muttered before sitting back down. "She's safe," he said. "It's Aldan Harris's kid sister."

Around me the other weapons began to lower.

"Hey," I said weakly. "I'm Dax."

One girl—a Yellow who couldn't have been more than a few years older than me—still held her gun on me. She squinted her large almond eyes at me in surprise. "Then that means your other brother is Link? The one who renounced the system?"

"That's him," I agreed.

"Huh," she said, looking me over. She too lowered her weapon, giving me a look that I rarely saw. One of interest. And respect.

Oena took me by the arm and pulled me further into the room. "How did you find us?" she asked, ushering me toward a seat.

I sat down at the table and cleared my throat nervously, eyeing the group surrounding me. There was the Yellow who had asked about Link, two Browns with unusually large noses who looked like brothers, Thom in Green, and a Slate girl in a baggy factory dress. I wondered if these were disguises, or if these people came from the rings they represented. I never imagined Thom as a Green before he turned Revenant, but I guess it was possible.

"Dax?" Oena prodded.

"Right," I said, trying to sound confident as I began telling them my story. I sounded awkward at first, stopping and starting as Oena prodded for details, but soon I reached my stride, and the words poured out. The Revenants interrupted several times to ask questions—about how I had found Raze, where the PAE had been positioned, and how many there had been. Otherwise, everyone was silent. I ended the story, explaining how I had jumped, and how Raze hadn't followed. "I'm not sure what happened," I said. "The PAE was there. I'm not sure if Raze is…" my voice caught, and I struggled to sound calm. "I'm not sure if she's alive or dead," I finished. I glanced at the weapons laid out over the table, and then back to the grim expressions of their owners. I hoped I had done the right thing by coming here.

The quiet was broken by Oena. "Raze is a fighter," she said. "Let's hope she managed to get away." She looked around, pausing to hold every Revenant's gaze for a moment. She then knocked twice on the tabletop. "All lost souls find their way home," she said. The others knocked twice in unison, repeating the phrase. I thought about the words, trying to keep my expression blank. Was this some kind of Revenant ceremony?

When no one spoke, I said the only other thing that was still on my mind. I tried to sound brave, but the truth was that my insides were churning. "I'm sorry, Oena. Really. Maybe if I stayed away like you said, Raze would be here right now." I squirmed in my seat, unsure of what else to say.

Oena shrugged. "I'm sorry too," she said. "But this isn't your fault. Raze's mission was to scout that part of the tunnels. Scouting missions are always dangerous. PAE patrols have been out with a vengeance since Zane was captured. Raze knows that. She took you right through an area we'd identified as potentially compromised. She shouldn't have done that. Had she been alone and not come back, we'd have sent in a backup team, and they might have been caught too. The fact that you made it here means we can warn others on similar missions."

Thom nodded beside her. "If we move quickly, we may even be able to set up traps in that section of the tunnel. We could capture some of their patrols for a change."

Around the table the other Revenants were nodding and talking. One of the Browns pulled up a map from his tracker and pointed out the location of the tunnel I'd been in with Raze.

"Would you say this is about where you were when you first heard them?" he asked.

"It's actually a little more this way," I said, I pointing out where I had been and explaining the terrain to him.

He turned to the other Brown with a sly smile. "Are you thinking what I'm thinking?"

"Let's go say hello to the PAE, shall we, brother?"

"Thanks, Dax," the first said.

"No problem," I replied. So they *were* brothers. And they had accepted me just as readily as mine had always done, despite my Ash status. I felt my nervous energy begin to dissipate. At school, we might attend ring-blended classes and be forced to use the same cafeteria and common space, but our place in the system still governed all interactions. I would always be an Ash. But at this table, no one had so much as glanced at my clothing. I hadn't been scrutinized in any way. They were treating me as an equal.

"Actually," the second Brown asked, "Do you want to come with us?"

I felt my heart soar. "Really?" I asked.

But Oena answered before he could. "No," she said. She shot the Browns a look. "Absolutely not."

The conversation immediately stopped, which made my response that much louder. "But that's why I'm here," I said. "I want to be a Revenant." If these people were going to try and fix the system, I wanted to be a part of it.

Oena sighed. "Let's take a walk, Dax," she said, standing.

"See you," the first Brown said as I stood to follow. The others nodded and Thom raised his hand as I followed Oena out the door.

We walked back down the hallway, stopping near the exit. "Dax, I understand why you're here. I'll do everything I can to avenge Aldan's death. But it's going to take time."

"Then let me help you," I said.

She ignored me, continuing as if I hadn't spoken. "Look at what happened to Raze today. We go on scouting missions, and we don't come back. Do you understand? The PAE kill on sight. Aldan died because he got too close to me, to this group. My brother was captured a few days ago. It's possible he's dead by now as well. If he's not dead, he may wish he was by the time the PAE finish with him."

Oena's voice was detached. Completely matter-of-fact. A crop of goosebumps raised over my arms as she continued.

"The only thing I can still do for Aldan is honor what I know he would have wanted. Or not wanted. He wouldn't have wanted you in harm's way. You have to understand that it may be me the PAE takes tomorrow. Or Thom. Or any of the rest of the crew back there. That's our choice. Aldan would have never agreed to it for you."

"But Aldan's not here anymore," I argued. "He made his choice, and now I'm making mine. I've thought a lot about this, Oena. People have been telling me what I can't do for as long as I can remember. I can't live like that anymore. I need to make my own choices. I need to do what I think is right. Please. Let me be a part of this, let me choose my own path."

Oena's voice grew a little softer around the edges. "You sound just like him," she said. Her face sagged, making her look like someone much older, then she sighed, seeming to come to some sort of agreement with herself. "I'm not agreeing to anything, Dax. But I'll make you a deal. If you want to talk again, you can reach me through your tracker. I can modify the program. You'll be able to override your location signal if you need to. And you'll be able to reach me directly. For emergencies only, though, is that clear?"

A thrill jolted through me. "Of course," I agreed immediately. I had changed her mind. Or at least nudged her in a new direction. It was a start. "How does it work?" I asked.

"Let me see your tracker."

I held my arm up and Oena bumped her wrist against my own. She tapped a few times onto her own tracker, showing me how to reprogram my position on my geolocator. Then she showed me how to contact her.

"Don't make me regret this," she said, her earlier tone coming back.

"I won't," I promised.

"Good," she replied. "Now get home before anyone wonders where you are."

I'd taken a few steps away before she called after me.

"Hey," she said.

"Yeah?"

"Good work today. Aldan would have been proud of you."

"Thanks," I said, happiness and sadness flooding my emotions at the same time. I turned before she could notice the tears pricking my eyes. "You won't regret this," I said, and walked back out into the rain.

TWENTY-FOUR

Madden

It had to be a mistake. It needed to be a mistake. But I knew it wasn't. Mistakes like that didn't happen accidentally. Someone went to a lot of trouble to cover up the switch. But why? Why would they swap my destiny? Nothing about this made sense. Blanks were impetuous, reckless, violent even. I was none of those things. I was the future leader of my country. Or at least I used to be.

I stared at the records. Dax had been born at 7:44am. It fit with the extraction time on my mother's file—7:46am.

"Crilas," I never swore, but this certainly called for it. "What, what if…" I couldn't bring myself to say it.

"What?" Sol asked gently.

"What if it wasn't our destinies that got switched? What if it was us? What if Dax is really a Sumner, and *I'm* really a Harris." The thought made me feel faint. That would mean Link and I… I grasped onto the desk to steady myself.

Sol shook his head violently. "No, the DNA tests are here. They put them in place decades ago to ensure no one tries to steal a Purple baby. Yours haven't been tampered with. You're definitely a Sumner. Besides, look at you. You look like your parents. So does Dax." He pulled photos of my parents and photos of Dax's to the bottom of the screen. Dax had her mother's hair, eyes, even nose.

I let out a sigh of relief, but it didn't last long. It didn't change the fact that my destiny was wrong. I had no idea what to do. I couldn't keep it a secret, could I? Not following destiny could cause the whole world to fall apart, but mine already was collapsing. I needed time to think.

"Shh," Sol warned me, putting a finger up to his lips then pointing at the door.

I strained to hear. There was definitely someone out there. I made out a voice; it was Worthington, which meant I had to act quickly. "Cover everything back up," I whispered to Sol. "Don't leave any digital tracks. No one can know what you found. This is our secret."

"Madden—" Sol started.

"You swore on your family." I looked him square in the eyes until he nodded, then I headed for the door. I opened it just enough for me to slip out.

"Minister Worthington," I said, shutting the door behind me. "I thought I heard you."

The minister turned to me, his face stern. He'd obviously just come from the Delegation. He was wearing his formal speaker's attire—a floor-length purple robe with multicolored tassels hanging from each shoulder, representing the seven rings. "What were you doing in my office?"

"I was just about to leave you a note about your legislation when I realized you'd returned. I naturally thought it would be better for us to discuss the matter in person."

Elba stood up at her desk. "I didn't see you go in there."

"You may need another cup of coffee," I told her, mustering my best fake smile—the one I always used at meet and greets for the lower rings. "I walked right past you. We said hello, and I asked about your husband. You joked you're the one in pain, having to deal with his broken foot." I had heard her say that line above fifty times the past week.

Her face scrunched up, confused, "Oh, right, right. So silly of me."

She was a Crimson and wouldn't dare contradict a Purple. Not that I qualified anymore. No, I told myself. Now was not the time to feel panicked or sorry for myself. I had the rest of my life for that. Right now, I had Sol—and my secret—to protect.

"Anyway, Minister," I said. "The reason I stopped by was that I watched the stream of your talk to the Delegation. I could not agree more wholeheartedly with what you said. It's about time someone tried to get this legislation passed, and I want to be a part of it. I want to help you however I can." The truth was I had no idea what he was talking about today, but it didn't matter. Worthington ate it up when people agreed with him, and if that's what it took to make him not care that I was in his office and get him into another part of the building, then I'd work on whatever law he was trying to pass.

He put his hand on my shoulder. "I'm glad to hear you say that. I've been getting some opposition on this one. It's nice to know someone feels as strongly about it as I do. And now is the perfect time to strike. With what happened with the Harris brothers, we just may get this passed. It's clear that Blank sister of theirs must have been the influence. If she had just been committed at birth we could have avoided all this trouble. Compulsory Warding is going to make for a safer New City, both for its citizens, and for the Blanks who need more assistance than their families can give. And we'll make the Ward safer too. We can't have these uprisings. Any Blank caught in the act will be taken care of. Permanently."

His hand felt like an eight-hundred pound weight. A weight that would crush me if the truth came out. Of all the legislation he had in the works, why did *this* have to be the one he spoke about today?

"Tell you what," he said. "Why don't you get me some notes in the next couple of weeks? And don't forget to highlight the current situation." He lowered his voice, like he was letting me in on a secret. "I wish we could find a more *permanent* solution to the Blank troubles. Nip the problem right in the bud." He gave a hearty laugh. "But one step at a time, right?"

I laughed right along with him. "Right."

What had I gotten myself into? And what did he mean by permanent?

Worthington looked down at his wrist tracker. "Will you excuse me, Madden? Minister Sealy needs me in the South Wing. Hmm," he said, studying the message. "That's strange. It doesn't say who the ping came from. I didn't know you could do that."

You couldn't—unless you knew how to hack the building's messaging system.

"They're always coming up with new technology," I said, forcing my voice to stay steady. There was no time for nerves. I could do this. After giving hundreds of speeches I was a pro at hiding my emotions.

"That they are," he said, fixing his attention back on me. "Glad to have you on board, Madden."

"Glad to help," I said.

As Worthington walked off, Elba got up to bring some hologram files into his office. I might have been able to convince her and Worthington that I had reason to be in there, but there was no way I'd be able to pull that off for Sol. I couldn't let her go inside.

"Oh no!" I exclaimed holding my wrist up and tapping a few buttons on my tracker. "I hope it's not another fight," I said as Elba continued toward the door.

"What?" she asked, her interest piqued.

"I don't know if I should say anything. It's probably nothing."

"You can tell me, I won't tell anyone, cross my heart and swear to destiny." But we both knew that was a lie. Elba was the biggest gossip in the building.

"Okay," I said. "I heard something was going down in the break room. Last time that happened there was food and dishes flying everywhere."

"That's right," she said. "Everyone was talking about it for weeks. Maybe I should go check it out. You know, to help rein everything in."

"Of course," I said, as she scurried off.

After checking that there were no hover cams nearby, I opened the door to Worthington's office. "You done?" I asked Sol.

He nodded.

"Then come on."

He looked around and then leaned toward me. "Everything—"

"Not here," I said. "Go to your office, I'll follow."

I stayed a few paces behind Sol so no one would think we were together. Purples and Ashes didn't walk the halls together. I closed my eyes tightly. The memory of what we found in Worthington's office punched me in the gut. I *was* an Ash. Not just an Ash, but a Blank. The lowest of the Ashes. *Get a grip, Madden.* I opened my eyes and forged ahead. Now was not the time to break down. Now was the time to keep up appearances. If anyone asked why I was with Sol, I'd just say he was helping me gather data for Worthington's legislation. We arrived at what looked like a closet at the end of the hall. Sol opened the door and waited for me to enter. It was a tiny room with a several computer monitors squeezed onto a desk in the corner.

"Welcome to my world," he said.

He must have seen me wince, because his eyes widened in alarm. "I'm sorry, I didn't mean it the way it sounded. I just meant my office. Not the Ash world."

"It's fine," I said, plastering on my camera-made smile. "Good job making Worthington think he was needed somewhere."

"Good job getting Elba out of there," he countered.

But I knew it wasn't Elba or even Worthington he wanted to talk about. We were dancing around the two-ton clock tower in the room.

"Madden, what are you going to do?" he finally asked.

I couldn't answer him, because I had absolutely no idea.

TWENTY-FIVE

Dax

The next few days blurred together. Moments of grieving. Moments of frustration. Even the odd moments of laughter. When my family wasn't trying to talk some sense into Link at the cells, they spent most of their time at the house. We swapped stories of Aldan—the safe ones, the funny ones—no one mentioned the race or what he did or why he did it.

But I couldn't stop thinking about it. I tried to piece together the part of my brother I didn't know—the part that was a Revenant—or at least aligned with them. There were still so many questions. Not just about Aldan, but the Revenants themselves. How did they find one another? How many were there? Where were they from? How did they plan to change the system? Could they really do it? I wanted to ping Oena, but I didn't. I'd told her I would only contact her for emergencies, and I would keep my word.

That didn't mean I wasn't bursting to talk to someone about

it. My brothers. My father. Theron. Even Laira. Only I kept my mouth shut. The information was probably more than they could handle, and it wasn't like Laira could keep a secret. Besides I knew better than to bring my friends and loved ones into something dangerous.

After a few missed school days I returned to Spectrum. I did my best to ignore the whispers and stares as I walked up the front lawn. I could feel my classmates' eyes on me. Some were hostile, I thought. Others pitying, which was almost worse. Before I could make it to the building I heard someone yelling my name.

I pretended not to hear anything, picking up my pace.

"Dax, hey Dax," an out of breath voice hollered.

I stopped, realizing it was Theron. I gave him a hesitant wave. Act normal, I reminded myself. After what happened at the practice track, I wasn't sure how to be around him. We had pinged a few times over the past days, but not about anything to do with us. Not that there was an us.

"Wait up," he yelled, jogging across the lawn.

I collected even more stares as Theron reached me a moment later. No one expected us to be hanging out together without Aldan—not even me.

"Have a few minutes?" he asked.

"Sure."

We walked until we found an empty bench, and in silent agreement sat down. "I'm glad you're back," he said.

"Thanks," I answered. I wanted to say something clever or witty or even just conversational, but my brain wasn't cooperating. So much for making him laugh.

"I was thinking about how you can get in to see Link," he continued, not seeming to notice any awkwardness.

In one of my pings I told him I thought I could convince Link to retract his statements. It was sweet that he was trying to come up with solution for me, but it was a pretty hopeless cause. "They'd never let a Blank in," I said.

"They might if a future minister put the request in."

"Madden?" I couldn't help the look of annoyance that immediately plastered my face. She was the last person who would do me any favors.

"No, seriously, Dax," Theron said. "Think about it. I bet she can get you clearance."

"There's no way she would do that," I scoffed.

"You might be surprised. I know you have your differences, but Madden cares about Link. She'll help if she can. Anyway, it can't hurt to ask. Let me talk to her."

"Really?" I asked, buoyed by his confidence.

"Really," he said, "I think you should start planning what you're going to say to Link."

"Oh, I know exactly what I'm going to tell him. It's stupid to fight the system head on. There are other ways. It's not like he's alone."

Theron's eyes got wide. "What are you talking about?"

I'd said too much. "Nothing," I replied, trying to sound nonchalant. "He just doesn't need to fight Aldan's battles for him."

Theron leaned back against the bench like he was trying to look casual, but I could see his muscles tense. "Dax," he said, his voice low. "What exactly do you know about Aldan's battles?"

I wasn't sure how to answer. Did Theron know about the Revenants? Was it safe to talk to him about it? I decided to play it cool. "Probably as much as you."

He was studying my face. "I know things he wouldn't tell his sister."

"Well, maybe his sister did some investigating on her own," I said, hoping to push him into giving something away.

He looked worried. "What did you do, Dax?"

"I tracked his girlfriend down. We had a conversation is all."
I figured that was safe to say. If Theron didn't know the truth, he
would think I chatted up a Green. If he did, then maybe I'd finally
have someone to talk too.

"You found Oena." He shook his head. "Dax, you have to be
careful."

"You know who she is, don't you?" I asked.

He looked around to make sure no one was in listening
distance, then came clean. "Yes. She doesn't know I know the
truth, but Aldan told me about her. And about her people."

"Well, I'm going to help her. Help all of them. I'm going to
pick up where Aldan left off."

"You can't."

"Of course I can."

He shifted on the bench, turning to face me. "Please Dax. I
didn't stop Aldan and he wound up dead because of it. I can't lose
you too." He reached out and put his hand on top of mine.

My whole body felt warm at his touch.

"Theron…" I was so focused on him that I actually jumped
when Laira plunked down on the bench to my other side.

"Dax!" she said, her voice just a little bit plaintive. "Finally.
I've been calling and pinging you for days." She pulled me into a
hug and gave me a sympathetic squeeze. "I'm really, really sorry
about your brothers. I've been so worried about you." She leaned
forward to look past me at Theron. "Hi Theron. It's so nice of you
to make sure Dax is okay. I mean, seriously, really nice." She gave
a self-conscious laugh. "Right, Dax?"

"Right," I answered. Could she not see we were in the middle
of something?

"What are you guys talking about?" she pressed on. "Is it
about… *Aldan?*" She glanced around nervously, as though the act
of saying my brother's name could somehow get us in trouble.

"No," I said. I let the single word sit there, and the silence stretched out around us. I hoped by not saying anything more she'd leave us alone, but she didn't take the hint. She just looked back and forth between us until Theron finally stood.

"I should go. Dax, think about what I said, okay?" He held my gaze until I nodded, then he headed back toward the school.

When he was out of hearing range, Laira turned to me, her eyes about to pop out of their sockets. "Theron. And you. Together?"

I gave her a look, and she shrugged, suddenly sheepish. "Right, that's probably the last thing you're thinking about right now. Sorry." Her brow crinkled up in worry as she continued. "Seriously, are you doing okay? Did you get my pings? I thought about just coming over, but I didn't want to bother your family."

"Yeah," I said. "Sorry I didn't get back to you. I just wasn't in the mood to talk to anyone."

She looked down at the bench, biting her bottom lip. "It's okay. I understand. It'll get easier. I know how hard it must be, but just don't listen to what anyone has to say. It's not your fault your brother is," she lowered her voice as if she didn't even want to say the words, "*a destiny breaker*. You couldn't have known."

That's why she thought I was upset? "Laira, I don't care what people are saying about me or what Aldan did; what I care about is my brother." I tried to remind myself that Laira's heart was in the right place. To her a broken destiny was worse than death.

"Oh…" she stammered. "Of course."

I could tell she was searching for the right words. "The whole thing is just so horrible," she said. "But you know, it's still possible there may be a purple lining. Like maybe you and Theron getting closer. What if this triggered something no one ever saw coming? Destiny works in mysterious ways."

She saw the stricken look on my face and stopped short.

"That didn't come out right," she stumbled, looking unsure of what to say next.

Part of me wanted to scream and shake her. The other part knew she was just saying what she had been taught to believe. What I had been taught as well. Only the lessons no longer fit me the way they used to.

"It's fine, Laira," I said. She wouldn't understand. She couldn't. She had blind acceptance of everything the Ministry said. But I knew better. And if I had my way, one day, she—and the rest of the world—would too.

TWENTY-SIX

—

Madden

The conversation with Theron played over and over in my head.

"I need a favor, Madden. Well, actually, it's not for me. It's for Dax Harris."

My voice must have shot up an octave. "Dax Harris? What does she want?"

"She needs your help," he said.

"Why? What did she say?" My heart hammered in my chest. This had to be it. Dax knew—somehow she'd figured out the truth.

"She wants to see Link. I thought maybe you could help her."

"Is that all you talked about?" I asked.

Theron raised an eyebrow at me, and I quickly looked away. Clearly, he didn't know my secret, but that didn't mean Dax wasn't on to me. Maybe she was just using Theron to get to me, manipulating him into setting up a meeting where she could confront me before cracking the truth wide open.

"I thought you could get her into the cells," he said, interrupting my spiraling thoughts. "They won't let her in because of her status. She may be able to get through to him."

That took me for surprise, and I mulled it over. I wanted to say no. It wouldn't look good for me to be associated with a Blank. Or the Harris's. But I couldn't. I owed it to Dax, and I still—if I was honest with myself—cared for Link. A lot. I wouldn't put appearance before his life.

"That's really all she wants to talk about?" I asked, just to make sure.

He gave me a strange look. "Of course that's all she wants to talk about." A hint of impatience threaded his voice. "Would you please just help her? For me? Her family has been through a lot lately."

That did it. Theron's tone snapped me back to my senses. If Dax thought she could help Link, I would make it happen. "Of course," I said. "Tell her to meet me after school."

Only, as the minutes ticked down to the end of the day, my nerves started to get the better of me. A tiny voice kept reminding me that Dax and Sol were both Ashes, and thus practically bound together by ring loyalty. What if, despite his promises, Sol said something about the destiny switch? Yes, he'd sworn on his family. And more than just that, he seemed to genuinely care about what was happening to me. But I had to prepare for the worst. There was a chance Dax knew everything. But if she did, it was better to find out now. That way I could manage the story as it broke, and maybe even salvage the situation. Spin it in my direction, somehow. And if she didn't know, then I had a reprieve for a little longer.

"Uhhh, hello, Madden." Portia waved her hand in front of my face.

"What?" I asked, bringing my thoughts back to my

surroundings. Everyone was getting up. Trig class was over. I hadn't even really remembered it starting.

"You're usually the first one up when the bell rings, now you're acting like you're coming down from Xalan," she said.

"I would never take Xalan," I snapped back at her. "You know better than that." The last thing I needed was for people to think I had a drug problem. They'd start looking for any reason to get me out of the ministry—and they'd find one.

"I…" Portia bit at one of her fuchsia painted nails. "I didn't mean—"

"Then what did you mean?" I stood up and glared at her.

"Nothing, I was just making a joke."

"You might want to work on that." I shoved my plexi into my bag. "If you think defaming one of your future leaders is funny, you and I may have some problems moving forward."

"There's no problem. I'm sorry."

"You should be."

Lavendar approached us slowly. "Hey," she said, her head bowed and voice soft. "Please don't be mad at her. Or me. We're just worried about you. You haven't been yourself the last couple of days. You didn't even say anything about Portia's hair."

I looked over at Portia. A streak of color that matched her nails ran down the right side. It was such a lower ring thing to do. I was about to tell her so too, when I caught myself. It wasn't Portia and Lavendar I was mad at—it was me.

How could I keep hiding my true destiny? I knew the history. I knew the possible repercussions. John Crilas didn't shut a door and billions of people died. Who knew what would happen if the proper minister wasn't appointed. I was risking lives because I didn't want to give up my standing. Because I was afraid of what would happen to me? That wasn't good enough. What was I thinking?

"I'm sorry," I told them. Part of me wanted to just tell them everything, to get the truth out in the open. But the other part—the part that wanted to fight for my survival—wouldn't let me. "I shouldn't have snapped. It's just this whole Link thing."

"We understand," Lavendar said, putting her hand on my arm. "You think you know someone and then they go and do something like disavow their destiny. But it's not your fault you went out with him. You couldn't have known. No one blames you."

"Yeah," Portia said, wrapping a strand of her dyed hair around her finger. "Everyone knows you'd never support a destiny denier."

Little did they know. "Thanks," I told them. "You guys go ahead. I just need to clear my head. I'll see you tomorrow."

Lavendar and Portia each gave me a quick squeeze before packing up their things and leaving. I watched them go. If Dax knew my secret that would be the last time my friends would be my friends.

The class continued to thin out and after a few minutes it was just Dax and me. It was the moment of truth. I closed the door to the classroom and turned to face her.

She didn't speak. She just looked right at me. This was it. She knew. Was she waiting for me to say it? Would she just blurt it out? Would she make me suffer?

"Theron said you might be able to get me in to see Link," she finally said.

I let out a breath. Dax really didn't know. This truly was just about Link.

"I can convince him to change his mind. I know I can," she continued. "Will you help me?"

Normally when a person from the lower rungs—even some from my zone—asked me for something they looked down. But not Dax. She kept her head level, her eyes focused on mine. It was a strong move. A move of a leader. It was me who looked away. She shouldn't be asking me for anything. She was the true Purple.

"You really think he'll listen to you?" I asked.

"He might. I want a chance to try," she replied. But it wasn't delivered in her usual tone of anger and pride. She just sounded thoughtful as she continued. "He's my brother, Madden. I love him. Maybe he needs to hear from me, from an Ash. That's the group he's fighting for most. If I could get him to see there are other ways to influence the system, that I'd rather live in the Ash zone than lose a brother, it might help him see things in a new way."

I let her words sink in. I knew I should be trying to keep my life as separate from Dax as I could, but if there was a chance she could get through to Link, I had to say yes. "Fine," I said. "Head over first and I'll meet you there." Just because I was willing to help didn't mean I wanted people to see us walking there together.

She looked like she had something else to say, but instead nodded and gave me a quick thanks.

She left the classroom, closing the door behind her, and I sunk into one of the chairs. Why was this happening to me? Why couldn't I go back to not knowing the truth? Or maybe it was just a test! Maybe the ministers were trying to see how I would handle this situation, to see how honorable I was. If that was the case, I was flunking. For a moment I had a glimmer of hope, like an Ash mother going to the wishing tree praying for a Purple baby. But just like the mother's odds, the chances of it being some elaborate exam were next to none. The ministers weren't testing me. They'd know there was no way I could have uncovered the hack on my own, and no Purple test would require the aide of an Ash. This was real. Which meant I knew what I was supposed to do—what I needed to do. I needed to tell the truth. Yet… that didn't feel right either. I'd trained my whole life to be a minister. I knew I could do it. I was smart, I was a gifted speaker, I was resourceful. I wasn't a Blank. I just didn't fit the profile. But it didn't matter. Destiny was destiny. It wasn't fair to deny Dax hers. There was too much at stake. Still, could there really be any harm in waiting a little longer? Dax's time stamp wasn't until December.

The door to the class opened, and I sat up straight. I still had an image to maintain. At least for now. I relaxed when I saw Sol. I should never have doubted he'd keep my secret.

"For such a public figure," Sol said, walking toward me, "you may want to up your tracker security. It was pretty easy to find you."

"Not everyone's a genius," I said, trying to sound upbeat. It sounded strangled instead.

Sol saw right threw my charade. He sat down next to me, worry plain in his face. "What happened?"

"Oh, you mean other than my whole world moments away from shattering in front of me?"

"Yeah, other than that," he said, one side of his mouth rising into a smile.

"I just agreed to do Dax Harris a favor. Now maybe she'll owe me one, and when the truth comes out, she won't have me executed."

"Nah, Dax won't have you killed. Though she might throw you in the Ward. High probability, now that I think about it."

He winked. Even though the idea of being in the Ward sounded like a fate worse than death, I couldn't help but laugh. Somehow Sol always managed to make me feel better.

"In that case," I said, "I better get moving. Wouldn't want to anger the future minister." The laugher left my voice as I said those last few words. She was going to steal my life. But I guess it was fair. I had stolen hers.

When I arrived at the UV building Dax was surrounded by

a group of reporters. She was trying to get away but they weren't letting her through.

I walked straight up to them; if they wanted a quote I'd give them one. That way Dax could get inside, I could say words of comfort to the nation, and everyone would be happy. Only the reporters ignored my presence. They were more concerned with Dax. If this was a glimpse of my future, I didn't like it one bit.

"Enough," I yelled out to the crowd. "This is a government building. People have work to do and business to conduct. If you continue to harass *any* citizen, you'll find yourself with a steep fine. Now clear the walkway."

They parted, and I stormed through, Dax quick on my heels. I pretended not to notice her. Not until we reached the first stop point. My tracker allowed me to get straight through, but Dax would have to wade through a lot of security before making it to Link. "I'll sign for her," I told the guard. "I'm bringing her to the cells. I'm hoping she'll be able to convince the prisoner to do the right thing," I explained.

He scanned her tracker and allowed her through the Purple halls. A few minutes later we were at the cells. At the desk was the same guard as the last time I'd been there.

"Officer McCarrick," I said, nodding my head at her. "I trust we will not have the same problems we had before. I'm here to see Link Harris. And I'm authorizing Dax Harris to go inside as well."

"Ms. Sumner," the guard said, "No Blanks are allowed inside."

"We've already been through this, Officer. I have override approval, and I am using it. I'm hoping to get that man in there to fulfill his destiny. Are you trying to hamper that?"

"No, Ms. Sumner, It's just—"

"There's no just. We all know what can happen when someone doesn't complete a destiny. Do you want to be responsible for another Event?"

She shook her head no.

"Good, neither do I." I felt my pulse quicken as I spoke those words. Wasn't that exactly what I was doing by keeping silent? "Now let us in."

Officer McCarrick raced to the security access panel. She wasn't going to risk causing another catastrophe. The question, I kept struggling with though, was I?

TWENTY-SEVEN

—

Dax

Theron had come through. Madden Sumner, New City royalty and general pain in the you-know-what, was doing me a favor. Sure, she had an angle. Madden always had an angle. Link was an ex-boyfriend of hers, and in some ways I knew this was political housekeeping. But there were lots of ways to clean house, and the easiest would have been to detach herself from my brother completely. She hadn't. Instead she'd done something I never would have guessed in a million years. She'd agreed to help me. Of course, she'd done it in a typical Madden fashion, but still. She'd gotten me through the crowd of reporters outside the UV before I could shoot off any choice one-liners. No one ever crossed Madden Sumner. I wondered fleetingly if that ever got old. Doubtful.

She then somehow bedazzled Officer McCarrick into letting me into the cells. Say what you wanted about the girl—I certainly had over the years—but when it came down to it, it turned out she wasn't quite the monster I'd taken her for.

"I guess we won't be seeing you down here again," the officer was telling Madden.

"Why is that?" Madden replied.

Officer McCarrick pushed her glasses up on her nose before pressing her hand over the palm pad. "The news just hit. If Mr. Harris doesn't come to his senses, he'll be removed in three days in a public execution."

Madden and I sucked in our breath at the same time.

"What do you mean?" I said. "They can't do that. He's... he's just confused. He's a Purple." This couldn't be happening. Somehow this had gotten blown all out of proportion. They couldn't just remove Link.

The officer nodded her head briskly. "That's exactly it," she said, talking to Madden even though I was the one who had spoken to her. "There've been a few too many ripples happening of late. Mr. Harris's execution will get major coverage. A bit of a reminder to respect their places in our system." She shook her head and glared at me. "I'm not sure what your brother is trying to prove, young lady, but I hope for destiny's sake you can talk more sense into him than the rest of your family." When she opened the door, a blast of cool, stale air whooshed out.

I felt sick, like I might throw up or pass out or both. I couldn't seem to move as the woman's words settled over me. This couldn't be happening. Not again. I startled as I felt Madden's hand brush against my arm.

"Are you ready?" she asked. She met my eyes for a beat before busying herself with digging around in her bag. Her face was unreadable, but two red blotches now covered her usually flawless skin. She pulled a shawl out of her bag and draped it over her shoulders. "Let's talk some sense into your idiot brother, shall we?" she asked, then marched away from me. Her heels clicked over the polished floors, echoing in the hallway. I gave one last look at Officer McCarrick, then hurried after Madden.

It was a long, gray hallway. Fluorescent lights glared down from above. The cells were more like individual glass cubes. The first couple were empty, but when I passed the third on the right, my steps faltered. A rush of relief filled me as I realized the woman sitting on the bed was Raze. We locked eyes and I caught myself as a smile split over my face, immediately covering it with a fake cough. Raze was alive. One of her eyes was swollen and there were several bruises on her arms, but she was right there in front of me.

"What are you looking at, kid," she snapped. "Mind your own business."

"Sorry," I said, catching on that she didn't want anyone to know that I recognized her.

Madden had paused ahead of me. Her arms were crossed as she glowered at the man inside. He was chuckling to himself— deep-throated belts of laughter. He must have said something to her. She seemed on the verge of telling him off before buttoning up her irritation and turning on one heel, once again marching down the hallway.

As I moved toward Link's cell, I stopped in front of the other prisoner and glanced in. Was it someone Madden knew? It wasn't just anyone who could get past the future minister's game face. He looked vaguely familiar. He was older than me, though not by too many years. He had dark hair and the beginning of a beard. Then it hit me. It was the man captured outside of Spectrum. Oena's brother. The Blank.

"An Ash with a Purple," he called to me. His voice was deep. "Careful of the company you keep, love. The upper rings don't treat their toys very well."

"Come on, Dax," Madden yelled back. "Let's go."

I picked up the pace, but risked another look back at him. I had never seen another Blank before, not in person. He grinned at me, and tipped his head. I was dying to talk to him, to find out what growing up as a Blank had been like. And more importantly, how he'd become a Revenant. But I had something more important to do. I had to stop my brother from becoming the ministry's next target. I quickly rushed over to Madden who was standing in front of Link's cell. He sat on an unmade bed. His scowl turned into a smile when he saw me and he jumped up, rushing toward the glass barrier separating us.

"Dax," he said, looking from me to Madden, and back to me, obviously surprised. "What are you doing here? How'd you get in?"

"Madden helped me."

His eyebrows shot up even further. "It's really good to see you."

I hoped that meant he'd listen me to. I looked my big brother over, anxious to make sure he was okay. He appeared exhausted and his usual groomed head of hair stood on end, but otherwise he seemed no worse for wear. All I wanted was to fling my arms around him. Since there must have been a foot of glass between us I settled on a smile.

"Good to see you too," I said. "Are you okay?"

"Sure," he said. "I'm fine."

"You know you've got Mom in hysterics."

"Mom is always in hysterics."

"Everybody else is pretty upset too."

"I know. I'm sorry, but I have to do what I think is right."

Anger flashed through me. "No, you don't. Link. This is insane, you being here. The woman who let us in here, she just said they were going to execute you in three days."

Link closed his eyes for a minute and hung his head. When

he looked up his expression was resolute. "I expected something like that would happen sooner or later."

"I just told you the government is planning to remove you, and you're going to accept it? What's wrong with you?" I felt like punching the glass between us. "Just tell them what they want to hear and let's go home. There are other ways to make a point." I had to somehow explain the Revenants to Link. I turned to Madden. "Could you give us a minute?"

She nodded before moving down the hall.

I wasn't sure what to say to him. I didn't know if Madden could hear or if anyone else was monitoring our conversation.

"Dax," Link began, "I know it seems crazy to you. To everyone. But I have to stand by my beliefs."

"There's another way," I said, my voice low. "I've met people, Link. Others who want to change the system. Aldan's mystery girl, she's one of them."

That stopped him in his tracks. "Then it's happening already. That means it's even more important to see this through. Aldan and I talked a lot before the race, Dax. He hated how the rings segregated people just as much as I do. He started something. People are talking. As long as I'm in here, the conversation is continuing. It's getting louder. If I recant, it's going to fade back to a whisper. Sometimes people need to be pushed too far." He swallowed and his eyes got a far away look. "Aldan's death started a backlash. If I need to give my life too, then that's what I'll do."

"Would you just wait a minute? You aren't listening. I'm telling you there's another option."

"Not for me. Not if something is going to actually happen."

"But—"

"I'm sorry, Dax, this is too important to let it go. People need to know that others are willing to fight, no matter the cost. Anything less than that won't make an impact."

My face flushed with anger, and I slapped my palm against the glass wall separating us. It hit hard and the sound slammed through the hallway. "Link, knock off the martyr act, okay?" I realized I was shouting. I didn't care. "Just stop. Come home."

He held his palm up against the glass, a reflection of my own.

"I can't, Dax." I stared at him. My handsome, quiet, serious big brother. I could see how much our conversation was hurting him in the tightness of his eyes, the clench of his jaw.

"No," I said. I pressed harder on the glass, willing it to crash down. "Please, Link."

"Dax, I'd do almost anything I could not to hurt you. But I can't give on this. You have to understand, okay?"

"It's not okay," I shot back, my voice frantic. "There is nothing about this that is okay. Link, I am begging you—"

"I love you, Dax. I'm sorry." He turned and walked back to his bed, stretched out and closed his eyes.

After that there was nothing else to really say. I'd said my piece. He hadn't listened. He didn't want to listen. Rage and terror boiled through me, but I kept my anger in check as I stalked back down the hallway. I still had three days. This wasn't over yet.

TWENTY-EIGHT

—

Madden

Dax blew out of the cells, and I felt my stomach clenching in what was starting to become a familiar coil of knots. I had hoped she would talk some reason into Link, but it looked like her words had made no difference.

I marched back to his cell, fuming. When I got there, he was laying down again. "Get up, Link Harris," I ordered. Surprisingly, he actually listened, sitting up to meet my gaze with startled, unblinking green eyes.

"You may think you know everything, but you don't. What you're doing isn't going to help anyone. It's going to do the opposite—remind them what happens when you break the rules."

"I don't see it that way," he said.

He was so irritatingly stubborn.

"Then how about this way—you are going to destroy your family, the people who love you, if you go through with this. Have you thought about how they'll fare? Between Dax's Blank tax, losing Aldan *and* you? They'll probably wind up in one of those Ash complexes, the ones you say are horrible. Is that what you want for them?"

He shook his head no. "I don't, but they'll understand, I'm doing this for our country. They're fighters. They'll be okay."

I glared back. "You're taking the easy way out. You want to do something for our country, fine. Propose legislation, write an article." I lowered my voice. "Be more liberal in your designations. Instead of Ash, assign Slate or Yellow."

"That's not something I ever thought I'd hear you say."

Neither did I. "As long as people are still completing their destinies, I don't care where they live if it means you stay alive."

That stopped him for a moment, but finally he just shook his head, his voice softening. "It's not that simple, Madden. You know that. My ring appointments are scrutinized, just like any Destiny Specialist."

"Then make a better case for a higher ring designation."

"It still doesn't fix it. Look at Dax. She's a Blank. There's no improving her standing. She's smart, she has the ability to be anything, but she can't, because our system has cast her aside as worthless. And there are others just like her."

Others including me. But I couldn't think about whether he was right or not, I just had to get him out of here.

My voice was quieter than a whisper. "I don't want you to die."

"I know." He reached his fingers through the air holes so they were touching mine. "You've changed. The Madden I knew wouldn't be here. Wouldn't have helped Dax come to see me."

"I care about you, Link. I never stopped caring."

He hung his head down, and when he looked back up at me I saw his eyes were starting to well up. "I never did get over you, Madden."

We just stood there, looking at each other. I wanted to say

more, I wanted to tell him everything—about my destiny, about Dax, about my feelings for him. But then he turned away from me and his voice got distant again. "You should go."

"Please, just think about what I said," I told him. He didn't turn back around. I took one last look at Link and headed toward the door.

"Got a thing for prisoners, do you?" The man from the other cell yelled out to me, "Want to come play in my cell?" he asked before erupting in a ridiculous laugh. I rushed out of the holding area, past Officer McCarrick into the lobby.

Dax was standing there, her face looked empty. On another person that might have been normal, but Dax went through expressions like Portia went through gowns. They were noticeable and extreme, and you couldn't help but take note. I didn't know what to do with that look.

It was just the two of us. I did my best to keep my expression in check. "I couldn't get through to him," I said.

"This... he... I hate this."

"Yeah."

We stood there awkwardly. Dax scuffed a sneaker over the floor. Her shoes were filthy, and a hole was starting to form in one toe.

She looked at me again with those hollow eyes. "There has to be something you can do. Isn't there some kind of loophole? Or protocol? Or government legislature that can be enacted?" She was starting to wake up now. "Madden, there's got to be something no one's thought of. Just tell me where to look. I'll go through old archives. My dad works at the library—he and I can both look. If we could just buy him some more time. Maybe we can get him to come around."

I was racking my brain as she spoke, trying to think of anything I might have overlooked. "Unfortunately the law is very clear on anything related to destiny like this. There's no room for interpretation. I've done everything I can think of."

Her face fell again. I took in a deep breath, knowing full well I'd probably regret it later. "If there is anything I can do to help, I'll do it. Maybe there's an angle I haven't thought of. At the very least, I'll petition for an extension."

Hope flickered across her face, and I immediately dashed it. "I wouldn't count on it, though." I held up my hands helplessly. "Like I said, the law is very clear on destiny breakers. I'm sorry. I wish there was more I could do."

"We have three days," she said.

"That's right." I wasn't sure if she was reminding herself or me.

"You'll work on an extension?"

"Of course. But it's a long shot. More than a long shot," I amended.

"Then we'll just have to increase the odds," she said. "I'm going to get my brother out of that cell, one way or another." She flipped her blonde ponytail back over one shoulder. "And Madden, thanks. Really. I appreciate it."

"Anything for Link," I said. And the truth was, I meant it.

TWENTY-NINE

—

Dax

My head was swimming as I parted ways with Madden. There had to be a way to save my brother.

I felt a small vibration on my wrist. Theron was pinging me. "What happened? How'd it go?" he asked. I could barely think straight, let alone write out an answer. Especially to questions like that.

"I didn't get anywhere," I tapped back. "He just ignored me."

I felt another buzz, followed by a request for a full connection. I accepted and a second later Theron was standing before me. Well, a tiny, holographic version of him anyway.

"Are you okay?" he asked.

"Yeah," I lied. "I'm fine."

"Dax," he said, "what's going on? How are you really?"

That was the thing about holo-talking—it made it a lot harder to hide how you were feeling. "I'm… I don't know. Angry. Sad. Frustrated. I have to get Link out of there." I told him everything that happened.

"Maybe he just needs some time to think about what you said," Theron offered.

"He doesn't have time."

"Then go back again tomorrow. Wear him down. Convince him there are other ways," Theron said.

The knot in my stomach started to uncoil. Theron was right, there were other ways. I might be able to get my brother out. With some help. "Thanks, Theron," I said. "I know exactly what I have to do. I've got to go. Talk to you soon, okay?"

I saw the confused expression on his face as I disconnected the holo-talk. But I couldn't tell him that he just triggered an idea. One that he would in no way support.

The more I thought about what I was going to do, the more right it felt. I pinged Oena. "We need to talk. Urgent."

She said to only contact her if it was important—and this certainly qualified.

Seconds later, through no doing of my own, a map opened up on my tracker with a black dot situated near the East 2 stop in the Crimson zone. It was a meeting spot, I assumed, and it was close by. I hopped the train and was there within minutes.

My tracker led me to an alleyway behind a bar. I ran my hand over the back of the building, hoping to find a hidden hologram, but no luck. The dot on my map was exactly where I was standing, but I couldn't find the entrance. There was just dirt, some dried up leaves, and an old manhole cover. Was that it?

I got my answer soon enough. I jumped as the metal under my feet began to move, and the top of Oena's head appeared "Come on," she whispered, "before someone wanders back here and sees us."

She didn't have to tell me twice. I darted after her onto a narrow ladder and slid the lid back in place overhead. Once we hit ground, she immediately got down to business. "I saw the feed of you going into the UV building," she said. "What happened? Did you find out any news?"

I told her about Raze and Zane, happy to finally share some good news. A look of relief wash over Oena's face. "I hadn't heard anything about Zane in the past few days, and nothing on Raze, period. I'd thought they'd been killed."

"They're okay for now. But the ministry *is* going to kill Link," I told her.

"I know," she said, her voice grave.

"What? How?"

She paused, as if debating on what to divulge. "We have a couple of people on the inside at the UV. Purples," she finally said.

I was taken back. I knew Aldan was helping the Revenants, but I never expected that they'd have other higher ups on their side.

"They do what they can," she continued. "Information, supplies, things like that. But they had a hard time getting intel on Raze and Zane. The insides of the cells don't have cameras. The ministry doesn't want proof of what's going on. It doesn't help with the illusion that New City is crime-free and that Revenants don't exist."

"Then how did they know about Link?"

"His lock-up is common knowledge, so information on him is available to those with clearance."

"Oena, I can't let him die. And who knows how long Raze and Zane have? We have to get them all out of there. These contacts of yours, can't they do something?"

Her eyes clouded for a second. "Not enough. A breakout is impossible."

"You're a Revenant," I shot back. "Not too long ago I thought your existence was impossible. There *has* to be a way."

Her expression hardened at my tone, and for a moment she looked dangerous. "You're not the only one who has a brother in there. You don't think I would have tried anything I could to get him out?"

"I didn't mean it like that," I said. "I know you want to rescue him. I was just hoping we could come up with something no one's thought of yet."

Her expression relaxed. "I know, I'm sorry. I didn't mean to take out my frustration on you. We thought we had a way to break them out. Our people got us the UV floor plans and most of the security overrides. But it wasn't enough. We didn't have anyone with high enough clearance to do what we needed."

"What level of clearance?" I asked.

"The highest," she said.

A glimmer of an idea started taking root.

The Revenants didn't have someone who could help, but it was possible that I did.

THIRTY

Madden

I asked Dax to meet me at the Kurtz Memorial Bench on the lawn of Spectrum after classes ended. I knew the area would be empty. Lavendar, Portia, and just about everyone was at the wishing tree. There was an honorary pinning ceremony for three of our Purple classmates who had completed their destinies over the last year. I couldn't bring myself to go and told my friends to send my regards, but that I had too much on my plate.

I sat on a bench as I waited. It wasn't often that the grounds at Spectrum were deserted. The emptiness fit my mood. In a moment I was going to have to tell Dax that I had failed. I'd gotten final word last night that my bid for a stay of execution was denied. Afterward I'd done the only other thing I could think of. I'd gone to my father. If anyone could influence Link's sentence, he could. It was a short conversation.

"Please, Dad. It's Link we're talking about. He's a good person. You know that. He just needs a little more time to get his priorities straight."

"He's a traitor, Madden. There's not a separate rulebook for ex-boyfriends."

"I'm begging you. He doesn't deserve—"

"He deserves exactly what he's getting. Consider this a lesson. Emotions have no place in leadership, and the sooner you realize it, the sooner you'll be ready to take your place on the ministry. End of conversation."

I was out of options. In two days Link would be put to death. Part of me wanted to let Theron be the bearer of the news, but I felt I owed it to Dax. To let her know I tried, that she wouldn't be alone in grieving Link.

Not that I could truly talk to Dax. She wouldn't want to hear how thinking about Link's fate gutted me. She saw me as a privileged Purple who never deserved her brother. At least she had her family for support. There was no one I could share my thoughts with. I couldn't talk to my friends—they thought of Link as a traitor now and would expect the same from me. Theron would listen, but then he'd try to make me laugh. It was the opposite of what I needed. And forget about Bas. He'd probably celebrate Link's death. The thought made me cringe. I hadn't seen or talked to Bas since our last fight. I hadn't had the heart, but I'd have to face him soon enough. He'd been pinging me for days at this point. I'd just gotten another one asking why I wasn't at the ceremony. "Buried in work," I sent back, hoping he'd leave me alone. I could only use schoolwork and ministry duties as an excuse for so long. For now I had no choice but to put my problems behind me, and live like a Purple. At least until I figured things out. I didn't want to think about what Bas would do if he knew he was really dating someone who belonged in the Ash ring. I twirled my zone bracelets, knowing that soon I would have to give up all but one. The one that lacked any color. Any power.

My whole body stiffened as Dax finally arrived and sat on the other end of the bench from me. "Did it work? Were you able to get a postponement?"

I shuddered at the hope in her voice, shaking my head slowly. "I'm sorry, Dax. I did everything I could. I tried to convince the ministry that prolonging the execution would give Link the time to change his mind and fulfill his destiny. But they're set on making an example of him. I even suggesting killing him could cause another Event, but they see it as preventing one."

Her face fell, and I continued on softly, as if my tone could somehow cushion my words. "Since Link didn't have a time stamp, they said he might have already completed his destiny, but having him disgrace the system could cause others to follow suit. They said executing him was the best way to stop others from jeopardizing the system—and our lives."

She let out a small breath. "So that's it?"

"I'm afraid so. I wish there was something else I could do." Right then I would have done just about anything to help Link. I looked away, unable to handle the feelings that were rushing through me.

"Madden?" she asked. "What if I told you I may have a way to get Link out?"

I gripped the arm of the bench. "What? How?" If I couldn't pull any strings, there was no way she could.

"Okay, I'm going to tell you something," she continued, "but you have to promise you won't get looped out. Alright?"

It wasn't like I had much of a choice. "Alright."

"I have a group of friends. They're, well, they're hard to explain." She paused, thinking through her next words. "They live off of the grid. They're people who don't function in the system."

"You know people off the grid?" I asked, shocked. I'd heard rumors, of course. People who'd gone into the woods after the Event. It was even possible my aunt was one of them. But those people were the exception and it happened ages ago. The government kept a list of who they were—there weren't many as far as I knew. How would Dax know any of them? Of course there were other stories. Mole people living underground. That kind of thing. But the Ministry made it clear that it was fiction. "Who are they?"

"They're just people who escaped the system. People who had a bad lot, a horrible destiny, or like Aldan, who felt there needed to be a change."

I was about to tell her that there was no such thing as a bad destiny. That every human being was a piece of fabric that wove together into a collective tapestry. That Ashes served a purpose, just as Purples did, and what could be more important than that? Only the theories, the quotes that had been ingrained in my head weren't cutting it as I thought about giving my future up to preserve destiny. "How do you know them?" I asked instead.

"They were actually friends of Aldan's. I met them… you know. After."

She didn't have to say after what. "Okay," I said. I was starting to get a bad feeling about this conversation. "So what do they have to do with this?"

"We came up with a plan. The thing is that we need your help to pull it off."

Curiosity conquered my worry for the moment. "What kind of help?"

She fiddled with the end of her ponytail, coiling it backwards, then forwards around her fingers. "I know you've gone out of your way to help Link already."

She met my eyes with an intensity that made me want to scoot away from her. I didn't move a muscle though.

"I don't know if we should even be having this conversation,

Madden. You're a future minister and the plan isn't exactly legal. Can I trust you to keep this to yourself?"

"I can keep a secret," I said, cringing inside. I'd never been one to hide something from the ministry, yet here I was getting ready to do it again.

She tugged on the end of her ponytail before releasing it. "Okay then. We're going to break Link out of the cells," she said.

I almost laughed until I realized how serious she was. "Dax, that's crazy. There's surveillance throughout the UV building. There are multiple alarms and clearance points getting into the cells. And assuming you're able to get in, how do you get Link out undetected? You may as well sign your own removal sentence."

"I know all of that. But my friends are good with technology. They have a way to circumvent the cameras. We know how to avoid the security guards once we get into the building. We even know how to get into the cells. All we need is for you to let us in the building. That's it. There are the special government entrances I know you have clearance to use. They use eye scanners; we can't hack those."

I held up a hand. "No way, Dax."

"We need you to open a door, Madden. Open a door, save Link's life. It's a minute of your time. No one will know you were part of it."

"Do you know what you're asking? My life for Link's if they realize I'm involved. It won't just be me, my father will be punished too."

"If anyone sees anything, we'll make it look like we grabbed you on your way out and forced you to use your clearance to let us in. No one will ever know that you were in on it. I swear to you. I'll even tie you up at the door to make it look real. You can sound the alarm after you give us a head start. This can work, Madden."

Only I knew it wasn't that simple. She couldn't guarantee the outcome. Even if Dax and her friends could pull off their escape mission and save Link, it could just as easily make me a prisoner for life. I didn't know what to do.

We'd talked our way in circles by the time I noticed someone walking toward us. I looked up as the figure approached, realizing too late it was Bas. His entire body screamed annoyance as he loomed over us. "What is going on here?" he demanded, grabbing my wrist and pulling me off of the bench. "I haven't heard from you in days, and when I come to rescue you from work, I find you here, passing the time with an Ash?"

I yanked my arm away from him. "Stop it, Bas," I said. I made a production of smoothing down my skirt as I thought of what to say next.

"I'll stop when you tell me why you are associating with *that*."

"I don't owe you any explanations," I told him. "But if you must know we were discussing ways to convince Link to continue on his destiny path."

The vein on Bas's forehead started to pulse. "That Ash sympathizer deserves death. A brutal one."

"What he needs," I said, my own anger flaring, "is to complete his destiny. If he doesn't, our whole world is in danger, isn't it?"

"He already served as a Specialist. Destiny complete. He needs to be put down. He's probably been unstable his whole life. It stands to reason," he snarled at Dax, "that Blank insanity would be genetic."

"Stop it," I yelled at him. "How dare you talk about the people, *any* of the people of New City like that?"

"I'm not having this conversation in front of a Blank." He grabbed me again. "Maybe her craziness has rubbed off on you."

"You're hurting me," I said, as he pulled me toward him. "Let me go."

That only made him yank harder. "Not until you learn some

respect. I may not be a future minister, but I am a Worthington. You'd be smart to remember that. Now let's go, Madden." He dragged me after him.

"You heard her," Dax said, standing. "Let her go."

But I didn't need Dax's help. Before I knew it my left foot stomped down on Bas's, my right arm curled into a fist, and I punched him right in the Adam's apple. He sputtered back, grasping his throat. My hands flew to my face. What had I done? Yes, he deserved it, yes I needed to get away, but I wasn't a fighter. Or was I? Was it true? Were all Blanks violent?

Bas looked from me to Dax in disbelief, then back to me. "We are over," he sputtered, contempt dripping from his words. "You should mind the company you keep, Madden. It's obviously tainting you." With that he stalked off.

"Not as much as hanging around with the likes of you," I called after him.

As Bas retreated I stayed standing, rigid with anger. How had I put up with his moods for this long? Maybe Theron was right. Maybe the system was rigged. If Bas had been born to an Ash family instead of a Purple, his destiny "to build" would have had him doing menial chores. But then again wasn't it destiny that he was born to a Purple?

"Madden?" Dax said. She still stood next to the bench. "Are you okay?"

"Yes," I said, trying to quell my temper. "I'm fine."

Sol raced toward us from across the lawn. "What's going on?" he asked. "I was up in the computer lab, I saw him grab you. I got down here as fast as I could."

I could see Dax watching the interaction between me and Sol with interest, so I made sure to keep my distance. "It's not a big deal," I said, trying to downplay the situation.

Sol's face twisted in concern. For a split second I imagined going to him, letting him wrap me in his arms. "Seriously, I'm fine," I said, pushing the thought from my mind.

Only I wasn't. This was too much. The entire situation was surreal. I'd just punched my boyfriend. I was daydreaming about embracing an Ash. My ex was going to be removed in two days. I could stop it if I helped his sister, whose identity I'd stolen, break him out of prison. And I'd been living a lie my whole life. Rage and confusion and disbelief whirled inside of me. I'd never felt this out of control. As if to prove it, I looked over at Dax and heard myself say, "Count me in."

I couldn't quite read her expression as she nodded. "Thank you," she said. "I'll be in touch." She left then. I guess she wasn't going to stick around to have me change my mind.

As soon as she was gone, I sat back down on the bench.

"May I?" Sol asked, gesturing to the seat next to me.

I nodded. It was sweet that he was still thinking about my reputation. I certainly wasn't doing a good job with it at the moment. I needed to get a grip, but having Sol there wouldn't hurt anything. If anyone showed up, I'd just tell them he was helping me on the new Blank legislation. The legislation to do away with people like me.

"What's going on?" he asked.

I told him everything—about Bastin, the group Dax knew who lived off of the grid, their plan to rescue Link. He listened intently, not interrupting me once.

"It sounds dangerous," he said, when I finished talking.

"I have to do it. My clearance is really *Dax's* clearance. How can I not help her save her brother?"

"Then you'll probably need some backup," he said. "I'm coming too."

"No, Sol, I couldn't let you do that."

"You're not *letting* me do anything. I want to. Look, I trust

Dax, but we don't know these friends of hers. You need at least one person you know is on your side. I'd go in your place if I could. I know the UV building inside and out, and how the security works. I just can't hack the eye scanners. What I *can* do is help you pull this off and make sure you don't get caught."

"But Sol—"

"No buts. If you're in, I'm in, okay?"

I couldn't help it. I reached out and squeezed his hand. Just for a second. "Thanks," I said. His hand was warm and steady.

"Don't mention it," he said, squeezing back.

THIRTY-ONE

—

Dax

My tracker glowed up at me softly: 7:25. I rubbed my sweating palms over the cloth of my pant legs and glanced over at Oena and Thom whispering beside me. Clouds blocked what little light the crescent moon overhead could muster. A good omen, I thought, doing my best to stay calm and focused.

The three of us knelt in the shadows outside of the back entrance of the UV Building. The plans had been drawn and my inner monologue was doing its best to stay positive. *Nothing will go wrong tonight. We'll get in and out with no one the wiser. This is going to work.* It had to work. Oena, Thom, me… and Madden… were the only thing standing between my brother's execution. He was scheduled to be removed in a little over twelve hours.

7:26. I adjusted my cap, making sure my blonde hair was securely tucked underneath. I then shoved the dark-rimmed glasses I was wearing further up my nose. They were my mother's reading glasses, though I'd popped the actual glass out so I could see. It wasn't much of a disguise, but anything more might have been noticeable. We were all dressed as maintenance workers from Slate. Oena had brought the clothing. "Just don't do anything to cause a second look," she'd warned. "I doubt it will stand up to scrutiny." I didn't plan to test her theory.

7:28. "Two minutes," Thom murmured.

Oena tapped into her tracker. "Stationary cameras are looping," she replied, then turned to me. "You ready?"

I nodded. I didn't trust myself to speak.

She gave me a knowing look back. "You'll do great. Just keep your head down, no matter what. The main cameras are taken care of, but the hovercams are impossible to loop. We shouldn't run into any of them as long as we stick to the schedule."

At 7:29 we walked across the pavement toward the UV. I kept my gaze down, focusing on following Oena's footsteps. Adrenaline poured through me, and I balled my fists to keep my hands from shaking with nervous energy. Sweat dripped down my back. In one minute I would be an official criminal. I ticked my offenses off in my head as we approached the door. Forcing my way into the UV building. Subduing a minister. Impersonating a Slate. Breaking out convicted criminals.

There was less than a minute until Madden had to do her part. If she backed out, Link was dead. When I had gone over the details of the plan with her this morning, she looked like she was going to be sick. She held it together, but the uncertainty in her expression was clear. It had me worried she'd chicken out, but I tried to push those feelings away. I had to trust Madden would come through.

After the UV closed its public doors, the only way in was either through the guarded main entrance or by using one of the high-clearance entryways. Those could only be opened from the inside or through an eye scanner. Very few had access, but Madden did. Her part was simple. She just needed to open two doors for us. It was the rest of us that had to do the impossible.

Relief flooded through me as a crack of light spilled onto the pavement. Madden stood at the door, blinking into the night, right on schedule. She moved to one side as Oena, Thom and I slipped inside. Sol waited right behind her. I wondered once again at their relationship of late. It made no sense that she'd confide in him about our plan. The future minister was proving to be continuously full of surprises. It made me think about Theron. He'd been asking about Link and if there was anything else he could do. If I had told him about the plan would he have wanted to come? I let the thought go just as quickly. There were enough people in my life who were in danger. There was no way I would have risked him too.

We all followed Madden down the hallway to a second steel door. "Let's get this over with," she said. Her voice sounded strained.

"Hold a moment," Oena said. She tapped her fingers over what looked like a modified plexi. Sol glanced at it and whistled. "Is that a Holo Extreme display? How'd you get that?" he asked.

She made several adjustments to the sheet then nodded. "We have our ways," she replied. She turned her attention back to Thom and me. "I've added our locations to the map, you'll find it on your trackers. We'll be able to see where everyone is if we somehow get separated. Dax, stay close behind me. Thom, you bring up the rear." She addressed Madden. "You're up."

Madden pressed her eye to the scanner and tapped her tracker to the pad next to the door. It slid open to reveal an empty hallway.

"Here we go," Oena said, stepping through the door. "Remember, we just have to get to the East Wing. From there it's a few doors to unlock and we're in. Let's cuff them and be on the way." She looked at Madden and Sol, her voice all business. "Thank you for your help. We'll make sure this doesn't come back on you."

I pulled the cuffs from my backpack and held them up. Madden looked like she was going to pass out. This had to be hard for her; it went against everything she believed in. I found myself feeling just a little guilty. "I won't make them too tight, don't worry," I told her.

"Wait," she said in a small voice. "Did you say you were going in through the East Wing?"

Oena glanced at her tracker. "Yes, and we have to hurry to beat the hovercams. Their next loop is in three minutes."

Madden muttered something under her breath softly enough that I couldn't make out the words. "Stop," she said. "You can't go that way."

"Of course we can," Thom rumbled back. "The West Wing is crawling with PAE. We've got handprint holographs for the security checkpoints, and there won't be guards manning this route."

Madden looked like she was about to panic. "They just tightened security." She glanced at me. "Ever since that driver interrupted Laira's destiny they've been taking extra precautions. I heard my dad talking about it. They've installed retina scans at the unmanned entrances."

I felt my stomach turning inside out. Next to me, Oena groaned softly.

"I could redirect the guards from the West Wing," Sol offered. "Hopefully that would clear enough out of there that you can get through."

"Too risky," Thom replied. "An alarm will put everyone on high alert throughout the building. The only way it works is if it's done quietly."

"Then I guess that settles it," Madden said. "I'll have to come with you."

I had to hand it to her. Gone were the nerves. She was back to cool and collected. Of course that was where the resemblance to the Madden I knew ended. I couldn't believe she was willing to take this much of a risk. I knew she cared about my brother, I just never realized just how much.

"I suppose this means you're coming too?" Oena asked Sol, as he moved to be by Madden's side.

"I am," he answered.

"Let's go then," Oena said. "Quietly. And quickly. We're behind schedule. The two of you stay behind Dax," she instructed Madden and Sol

Before I followed Oena out, I quickly turned to Madden. "Thank you. You didn't have to do this, but you did. I owe you."

"I hope you remember that," she whispered. There was a certain gravity to her response that made me pause.

"Of course I will." Although I wondered what I could possibly do for Madden Sumner that would be of value. But now wasn't the time to think of payback. I rushed after Oena, with the others right behind.

Thick carpet muted our footfall as we flew down several purple-walled hallways. I held onto my cap as we ran, covering the route Oena had planned with no problems. I found myself starting to breath a little bit easier when she stopped, holding up a hand and waving at us to wait.

A man's voice drifted from around the corner. Fear lurched through the pit of my stomach. We'd made it this far. We couldn't be caught. Thom inched closer toward the hallway, his giant hands curled into fists. I tensed, ready to charge if the guard rounded the corner. Instead I heard him laugh at something and his voice fade as he walked away from us. A moment later Oena motioned us to follow and we resumed our sprint.

Another left took us to the first locked door. It was a nondescript shining steel, marked with a simple placard that read "East Wing." In addition to a palm and tracker pad at the door, there was a retina scanner as well. Madden had been right. She got us through the door in seconds.

We went down a flight of stairs, and soon after reached a second door, this one marked "Holding Cells, Monday through Saturday, 8am-6pm; Sunday, 11am-5pm." We were well after visiting hours. I hoped Oena had been right and there was no one inside. Once again Madden held her palm, tracker and eye to the door. It slid open to reveal the empty waiting room. I let out a breath. There was no officer behind the desk. Oena had timed this part of the plan to correspond with the guard's scheduled break. The one good thing about the system was that everyone took time very seriously. The downside meant that the guard would be back on time too. We had fifteen minutes max.

"That's as far as I can get you," Madden said. She was slightly winded as she spoke. "Only a sanctioned officer can get into the cells themselves."

"It won't be a problem," Oena said, once again pulling out her plexi. "I'll need someone to stay out here as lookout." She met Sol's eyes, and he nodded. "Let us know immediately if you hear anyone coming."

He held his tracker to her plexi and tapped in some commands. "You'll all have an alert in seconds," he said and headed back toward the door we'd entered through.

"I'll go with him," Madden said.

"You can't," I said. "If the guards come, it needs to look like we have you hostage and are forcing Sol to do what we say. It's the only way to keep both of your covers."

Oena frowned, but she didn't contradict me. If Madden was going out on a limb for us, the least we could do was keep her from getting arrested. From beside me, Thom was pulling out various supplies from his pack. Most noticeably were the three laser wands we'd use to cut through the glass and the discs we'd detonate it with. As he was unloading the gear, Oena approached the final door leading into the actual cells cautiously.

"Dax, I need your help over here," she continued.

I quickly joined her. Link and the others were behind this door. We'd almost done it. "Keep Madden quiet when we get in," she said in a low voice. "Her sympathy won't stretch past your brother, and we can't have her jeopardizing anything."

"Of course," I replied. A shudder of excitement passed through me as she turned a series of bolts, then gripped her palm around a small ball she took out of her pocket. It rippled and transformed around her hand, creating an almost glove-like effect. "It's a palm simulator," she explained. "We pulled one of the officer's prints from a pole on the light rail a few days ago, then recalibrated it for this." She pressed her encased palm against the pad while she punched in a string of numbers into the keypad next to us. The door slid open to fluorescent lights and a long gray corridor.

Thom gave me a wand and small disc and the four of us charged down the hall together. I made a beeline toward my brother, Madden hot on my heels. Link was lying on his bed, bleary eyed when I got there. "Dax?" he said. "What are you doing here?" He rose from the bed as Madden joined me. "Madden?" He sounded even more confused.

"We're breaking you out," I said.

"What?" he said, horrified. He jumped up from his bed to stand just on the other side of the cell. "Do you two have a death wish? Get out of here."

"No time to argue," I said.

"Dax, seriously," he said. "You have to leave." He was growing frantic. "Both of you. Now. This is a wasted trip. I'm not coming with you."

I had a feeling he was going to say something like that, but I wasn't about to give him a say in the matter. From behind me I could hear the sizzle of Oena and Thom's laser wands. I saw Madden look in their direction, her mouth settling into an O. "We need to get Link out. Fast," I told her, hoping it would keep her from doing anything to interfere with the others. I didn't wait for her response. I activated my wand. It glowed crimson at the tip. Oena had told me I just needed to trace a big enough circle over Link's cell that he could squeeze through.

"You're coming," I told my brother in my best no nonsense tone. "If you don't, Madden and I are going to climb inside of that cell and keep you company until the guard comes back."

Link just stared at me, mouth open, stunned into silence.

I touched the tip of the wand against the glass wall. A high-pitched whine responded as I traced it over the surface.

From down the hall I heard the sound of loud pop, then the consequent shattering glass. Madden swirled toward the noise. "Dax," she said, shaking her head in disbelief, "this wasn't part of the plan."

"We can't leave the other prisoners here."

She gave me a look that could have cut glass all by itself. "Let's just get this over with, okay?" I said. "Oena knows them. It was the only way she'd help."

Madden put her hands on her hips and jutted her chin out. I interrupted her before she could start the argument I knew was coming. "We don't have time to debate. Now get out of the way if you don't want to get cut. Both of you."

She and Link stepped away from the circle I had formed as I placed the tiny detonator in the center. I pressed it down onto the glass and took several steps back, wishing the glasses I wore actually contained lenses. Instead, I squeezed my eyes shut until I heard the now familiar pop. The circle I had cut free shattered, leaving a hole just big enough for my brother to climb through.

"Time's up," Oena shouted from down the hallway. "We need to move." She and Thom stood with Raze, the latter two speaking in hushed tones. Zane was off to one side, a little worse for wear, but his look of euphoria eclipsed any bruises. The fluorescent light ricocheted off of the glass littered at his feet, sending tiny slivers of light to dance around him. He caught me looking and nodded his head in my direction, tipping an imaginary hat. I could see why the Revenants followed him—he had a presence about him that commanded attention. But he wasn't the only one.

My focus was drawn back to my brother, who was emerging from his cell.

"Thought I was going to have to come in there and get you," I told him. "Glad to see you came around."

"Someone has to make sure you and Madden get out of here safely," he growled. "This is unbelievable. I couldn't even get the two of you to watch a loop race together, but committing treason, no problem."

"Guess your life is a little more important than a game," I said.

"Come on," Oena called again.

I grinned at my brother, relieved, exhausted, so happy I could burst. Link was out. "But fine, whatever. Link, you want me to watch a race? Okay. I already owe Madden for life. Anything you guys want. *After* we finish this whole prison break thing."

I bolted before either could answer.

THIRTY-TWO

Madden

I was so going to kill Dax, I promised myself, even as I ran after her. Glass covered the ground, and I did my best to avoid it as Link and I followed the rest of the group out. This just could not be happening. Two extra prisoners were escaping. One of whom *I* had helped capture. I could feel my resolve starting to unravel and panic began to claw at my stomach. "Keep it together, Madden," I whispered to myself. A few extra members in the escape party didn't change the plan.

We all regrouped in the waiting area. Sol caught my eyes, glancing toward the two unexpected prisoners, confusion plain on his face. I shrugged helplessly. This night was spiraling out of control. How could I have allowed myself to be talked into something so dangerous?

"Took you long enough," the male prisoner they called Zane was saying, although his voice was almost exuberant. He was the one who crashed Laira's Destiny Day and had given me the creeps when I had gone to visit Link. Now he was my co-conspirator.

"You're lucky I came at all," she replied, and punched him in the shoulder.

He rubbed it dramatically. "Is that any way to treat your brother?"

Brother?

"When *you're* my brother, yeah." Oena's tone actually sounded warm for a moment.

This was getting overwhelming. Dax's friend was related to this lunatic? Who were these people?

Oena swept her gaze over all of us, her typical aloofness returning at once. "We have eight minutes before the next rotation of guards. We'll need every minute to get out of here."

She looked around and I felt myself nodding.

"Make sure you all keep up," Oena said and slipped out the door, followed by her brother, Thom and the third prisoner—a woman, maybe five years older than me, dirty and tattered. I cringed when she glanced my way. One of her eyes was swollen shut, but the functional one glared hard enough for both. I couldn't believe I'd broken these people out of jail.

A hand pressed against my back and I jumped. It was Link, pushing both me and Dax forward. "Go," he said. "I'll bring up the rear."

I didn't wait to be told twice. I yanked my long skirt up around my knees, feeling for a split second irrationally pleased with my choice of sturdy lace-up shoes, before running for all I was worth. We ran in packs. Me, Link, Sol, and Dax in the back. The others in the front with Oena and Thom in the lead. We sprinted upstairs, through the hallways, taking a left followed by a quick right. My breath was coming in deep rasps, and I promised myself that if I made it out of this unscathed I would take up something sporty. We continued on for several minutes until I saw Thom leap at something around the corner. I stopped, paralyzed. I heard a crash, and then something smashed to bits. Thom cursed before poking his head back around the corner. "Hovercams," he said. "Come on."

If the guards didn't know about the escape yet, a broken hovercam would tell them something was up. We ran even faster. A few twists and turns later and Oena scrambled to a stop ahead. "Back," she hissed. "Guards."

We bolted back the way we came. But we couldn't run forever, the guards were about to catch up. Dax seemed to realize that. I saw her try the handle of the closest door. It didn't open, but the next one did. "Everyone inside," she said, ushering us into an office. "Hide." I couldn't believe how calm she was. Minister-like, I realized as my stomach dropped.

Moonlight streamed in through a tiny window, enough to see everyone scattering. I wished it were big enough to squeeze through and get out of this mess. Dax and Sol ducked behind floor length curtains. Raze crouched behind a potted tree and Thom behind an overstuffed chair. I stood there, unable to move, until Link grabbed my wrist and pulled me behind the desk.

"Stay down," he whispered. I crouched there, panting, as Link ducked down beside me. Whoever's office we'd landed in kept a row of well-shined shoes under his desk. I wanted to scream at the mundaneness of it all, but fear kept me silent. Link kept his hand in mine and my heart swelled even as it crashed in terror of being caught. I peeked around the desk. Where were Oena and Zane?

A moment later I heard one of the guards call out, "This way." They were close.

Link tightened his grip on my hand.

From there I heard two rapid thumps followed by a startled yell. The commotion ended with a sickening crack.

Oena flung the door open. "Come on," she ordered.

We piled out of the room, and I almost choked when I saw the three guards crumpled on the ground. Zane knelt between them, confiscating their guns. He tossed one to Raze, but kept the other two, shoving one in the back of his pants. The third guard began to stir. He pinched the man's neck and he immediately stilled.

"Are they... is he..." I began.

He looked up at me with eyes that seemed to dance, then turned toward the guards with smug satisfaction. I felt like throwing up. "Thom has a thing against killing people. I humor him when I can. These three will wake to nasty headaches, nothing more." I got the sense that it disappointed him.

A man's voice blasted through the third guard's tracker. "Report, Officer Suresh."

Zane grabbed the man's limp wrist, raising it toward his mouth. "Quiet," he said to us, then activated the audio function. "Suresh here. All clear."

"Any sign of disturbance, Suresh?"

"No, sir. Maybe a glitch in the system." His voice oozed confidence. Oena made a noise in the back of her throat— impatience paired with a waving of her hands. Zane gave her a wolf's grin in return.

"Hold, Suresh. We've got two more troops coming to join you," the voice replied.

"Negative," Zane replied. "Everything is under control. No need to send backup."

There was silence and then another voice, this time a woman's, came through. "State your clearance code, Officer."

Zane shrugged. "Of course. It's tschhhhhh er come in grktzttzztt chh chh. Do you read me? I think something is wrong with my krsssshhhhzzzztttk interference tschhhhh." Zane clicked the tracker off.

An alarm blazed from unseen speakers. I looked around the group, wondering if this was it. What would I say when we were caught? Would the kidnapping rouse work, or would the PAE know Sol and I were willing participants? I wouldn't let him go down for this. If it came to it, I'd tell them that I pulled rank and forced him to take part.

"I'll reroute the alarms," Sol hollered over the din. A moment later the ringing could be heard faintly in the distance. "Give me your plexi," he instructed Oena. She didn't question him, she just handed it over. Sol held the glass to one of the officer's trackers and started coding. "There," he said. "Now we'll know where the guards are, their locations are added to your maps."

I was impressed. If Oena was too, she didn't show it. She just ordered everyone to get a move on. Once again we raced down the corridors. I ran as fast as I could, pushing my legs even faster. A few more minutes and we'd hit the exit. Ahead of me I saw Oena and Thom slam into something and bounce backwards, both landing in a tangle on the floor. I almost tripped over my skirts trying to stop myself from crashing into them.

"Establish the perimeter," Thom bellowed, stumbling to his feet.

"What's happening?" I said, looking around as Thom, Oena, Zane, and Raze all scattered. Link joined them, standing between the other convicts. Half of them were pushing against the walls, others appeared to be miming against thin air.

Link was using both hands to press against what appeared to be a wall of air. "It's a holograph trap," he said, answering my question over his shoulder. "It makes walls appear like open space and vice versa." I wondered how he knew about them as he continued palming over the surface. All of a sudden a surge of electricity crackled around us. Link fell to the ground, followed by Oena, Thom, and Raze, all dropping like ragdolls. I bit the inside of my cheeks, stifling a scream.

"Electric field, " Zane said, already pulling Oena away from it. "Get them away from the walls. Hurry," he commanded.

Dax and I ran to Link, dragging him several feet away. Next to me Sol helped Zane pull the others from the current. Holograph traps, electric fields? My father never mentioned any of this. I never even considered that the UV would need something like this—not since right after the Event.

Dax looked near hysterical. "Wake up," she said, shaking Link. "Come on, Link. Please."

I could feel my own panic rising and I reached over her, pressing two fingers onto his neck. "He's got a pulse," I said, relieved.

"Just a bad zap," Zane said. "I've seen worse." He stood over Thom and nudged him with a boot. The big man groaned without opening his eyes.

"They'll wake up soon?" I faltered. I stood up from Link, facing Zane. Dax was still crouched over her brother. If they didn't get out of here, they'd both be sent to the cells, maybe even removed.

"Soon enough," he replied. With a flourish, he pulled off one shoe, then the next. "Hopefully before the guards come round. Rather not have to take them all out on my own." He looked around us, eyes gleaming. "Not that I couldn't." He slashed his shoe through the air at a pretend adversary. "Quite the misadventure, isn't it?"

"Is this some kind of joke to you?" I asked, angrily.

Zane just waved me off. "When you've got nothing to lose, you find comedy in the strangest of places. A philosophy your kind will never understand."

I glared back. "How about you worry less about my kind, and focus on getting us out of here," I said.

"Fair point," Zane responded, snapping his head toward Sol, who was frantically working with his tracker. "Siren boy," Zane called. "How goes the computing?"

"Working on it," Sol said between gritted teeth. "I'm trying to bypass some pretty intense security right now."

Zane seemed unperturbed. "In that case, I should get back to what I was doing." He shoved his hands into his shoes and began to thump them against the walls, humming along to the crackles of electricity each smack of his shoes made.

"Back to your foolishness," I said half to him, half to myself.

"Just because you don't understand something, doesn't mean it's foolishness. Not that I expect you to comprehend a Revenant's ways."

The Revenants? I tried to hide my surprise but it didn't work.

"She left out a few details, did she?" He looked over at Dax, his approval obvious. "What exactly did she say to get you to come along?"

"I knew what I was getting into," I lied. I wasn't about to tell this madman that I had no idea the Revenants were anything more than scary stories, that Dax made it sound like her friends were harmless nobodies, and that everything I thought was true and real was getting turned on its head. "Don't let me distract you from your *important* work," I told him instead.

"You're not." He jumped up, then down, counting under his breath as he circled the space. "About fifteen-by-fifteen feet I'd say, with two false walls." He pointed to the hallway that appeared to stretch out in front of us. "*That* is actually a wall, which is why Oena and Thom took a tumble." He pointed in the other direction, toward the wall. "And *this* is actually a hallway. Tricky things, holographs. At least it's roomier than my last box." He looked over at Dax, practically leering at her. "And the company is infinitely better."

He was so crude. At least Dax didn't notice him eyeing her.

"Guards are coming down corridor C," Sol interrupted. "I'm setting off alarms throughout the building to buy us more time. There's not much more I can do though. If I could just access that box I could get into the mainframe." Sol pointed to a small outlet on the other side of the current.

"Rubber can hold the current off, right?" Dax asked. "We can use shoes to make you an opening. It'll be small, but it should let you reach the box."

"Smart," Zane said, and then turned to Sol. "How much time do you need?"

"A minute, maybe," Sol replied.

"I'll give you thirty seconds." Zane turned to me. "Hand over your shoes. Yours look to be the best made in the rabble."

I didn't bother to argue. I gave him my shoes. He stuffed them inside his own shoes, and once again shoved his hands inside. "Ready?" he asked Sol.

"As ready as I'm going to be," Sol answered, moving to stand beside Zane. I wasn't quite sure what they were up to, but they seemed to understand one another.

"These won't last long. You're going to have to hurry." With that Zane shoved his covered hands toward the current, pushing through it, to create a small open tunnel. The shoes that were protecting his hands immediately began to blacken.

Sol reached through the opening and tapped his tracker to the outlet.

Smoke billowed up around Zane and Sol's faces. "Gonna hit flesh soon," Zane warned.

Beside me I heard Thom cough. He sat up blearily. "Something on fire?" he asked me.

"Ahh, Thomas," Zane called cheerfully. "I'll be the one on fire in a moment if the boy doesn't hurry it up."

"One more second," Sol said. I could see him tinkering with something, and then he shouted. "Got it!" He and Zane both tumbled back from the wall, Zane cradling an arm, Sol still tapping into his tracker. Then just like that, I heard the crackle silence. Zane threw a shoe—*my* shoe—toward a wall. It sailed right through.

"Gather the fallen and let's move," Zane said. He picked Oena up. I heard her groan. I ran over to Link, who had woken up, and seemed to be getting his strength back. Dax and I helped him to his feet. Next to us, Sol pulled Raze up. Thom, thankfully, was already walking on his own.

"Come on," Zane said, plunging through the holograph wall.

"We've got you," I told Link.

"I'm okay," he said. I helped him to his feet and, after a wobbly start, he stood on his own. Everyone seemed to be getting their strength back.

"You sure?" I asked.

"Yeah," he said, locking eyes. "Thanks."

I nodded. This was probably the last time I'd ever see Link. Once we got to the door, he'd run with the others into hiding. I had so much I wanted to say, but none of it really mattered anymore. He was about to be out of my life for good. I could feel the tears starting to form, so I just gave him a small smile and ran ahead to catch up with Sol and the others, making sure not to look back.

Just as the exit came into view, several guards stepped around the corner in front of us. Everything seemed to happen in slow motion. Zane slid to a stop ahead, pulling out both of his guns. He shot one guard, then the next. They jerked backward from the impact, blood splattering over one cream wall as they fell. I tried to look away, but I couldn't. I stood there frozen. I wanted to help, but I didn't know what to do. Zane dropped, rolling behind a corner, as a third guard pulled his gun. With Zane out of the way, he aimed at Sol.

My reflexes kicked back in. "No," I screamed, diving at Sol and pushing him to the floor. I heard a boom in response, and then a searing ache stabbed my side. I fell to the ground. Pain like nothing I had ever experienced ripped through my stomach. I struggled to get to my feet, but my legs no longer seemed to function. A rush of activity surrounded me, but it was all a haze, like watching an outdoor film under a cover of mist. There was Sol and Link running to me. Another loud boom. Raze holding a smoking gun. A third officer falling.

Blood was pooling around me. Someone held a cloth over my stomach. It dripped a brilliant crimson red.

I reached down and touched my side. It was wet and slick, but it didn't hurt anymore. It didn't feel like anything.

"Madden, Madden, stay with us." It was Sol. "Open your eyes. You'll be okay."

"Hang on, Maddy." This time it was Link's voice.

I opened my eyes to see them both crouched on either side of me. They were both so handsome, one light head, one dark. I wanted to keep looking at them, but my eyelids felt heavy.

"We need to get her to a hospital," Link continued.

"We don't have time for a hospital," Zane said, his voice growing further away. "They'll be more guards here any minute. We'll all be dead—not just her, if we stay."

Dead? Was I dying? My head felt cloudy, it was hard to stay awake. Maybe this was my punishment for defying the system. For hiding my destiny.

"I'm not leaving her," Sol said.

"Me either," Link said.

"Suit yourself," Zane said. "I'm not sticking around to be caught again."

"Dax, go with them," Link instructed his sister.

"Not without you," she replied, kneeling down next to him. She was so close I could touch her. "Madden, I'm so sorry," she whispered.

I didn't want them to risk their lives for me. I needed them to be safe. I struggled to keep my eyes open. I knew my voice was weak, but I had to find it. With all my strength I reached out for Dax, grasping her hand in my own. I couldn't die. Not without telling her the truth. It would save her. Hopefully it would save them all.

THIRTY-THREE

—

Dax

Zane and the others rushed out. Part of me wanted to follow, but I couldn't, and not just because Link was staying. It was my fault Madden had been shot. I was the one who talked her into this, who said it would be safe, that no one would get hurt. Now here she was dying in front of me.

"Hold on," I whispered as she grasped my hand harder. It was covered in blood. Everything around her was. *Stay strong,* I instructed myself. I didn't know what to do. Sol was cradling Madden, telling her it would be okay, but I wasn't so sure. The color was draining from her face as he pressed his jacket against her side. It was covered with blood. Link ripped off his shirt, balled it up, and swapped it out to cover the wound. Dark red saturated the gray material. "This isn't helping," Link muttered. "She needs surgery."

"Let's try to get her out of here," I suggested.

Link shook his head. "We can't move her. Dax, go. Make a run for it. I'll stay with Madden."

"I'm serious, Link. I won't leave if you're not with me."

"Stop," Sol said not taking his eyes off of Madden. "Both of you go. We need to stick to the plan. This was a botched kidnapping. I'll make sure she's taken to the hospital and that the right story gets out."

Link looked from me to Sol. I knew he didn't want to leave Madden, but I also knew he wouldn't risk me staying by his side. "Fine, but I'm not waiting for them to just stumble upon you." He raced over to where one of the officers had fallen. I closed my eyes as he punched something into the man's tracker. I had only seen one dead body before. Aldan's. Now I was in a room with three dead guards and a dying future minister. Oena had been right. There was nothing glamorous about the Revenants' life. It was dangerous. Link and I would be lucky if we were able to get out before the guards arrived. I checked my tracker. We had three, four minutes tops before the other officers arrived.

"We need medical attention, now," Link was saying. "Get ready to airlift to UV General. It's a gunshot victim."

I hoped they would get to Madden in time. Just a week ago I hated the future minister, thought she was the biggest hypocrite in all of Spectrum. I'd been wrong. "You'll make it," I told her. "You have to."

"Dax," Madden said, her voice so slight I had to put my head down to her lips just to hear her. "You need to know... if I don't make it. You're the minister. Not me."

She had to be delirious. "What?"

Madden strained to speak. "Our destinies were swapped."

"Dax come on," Link said, grabbing my arm and pulling me to my feet.

I stood motionless.

"Dax," Link yelled.

"Go," Sol said, giving me a pointed look. "You heard what she said, Dax. You have to make it out."

"What are you talking about? What was *she* talking about?" I had a million questions, but there was no time for answers. Guards were heading toward us, their footsteps growing louder. If I didn't move, Link was going to carry me out of there.

"Let's go," my brother ordered. "And keep your head down in case there are any hovercams."

I pulled down the brim of my cap and followed him out the door. Once we rounded the corner, it was a straight shot to the side entrance. Link and I sprinted side-by-side, our tread light over the carpeting. We reached the door and didn't stop, dashing out into the trees behind the building. My mind kept playing over what Madden had said, but I forced myself to push the thoughts aside. I needed to focus on making it to the Tombs alive.

Up ahead, Oena, Thom, and Zane slipped down the same entrance we'd arrived through. As they disappeared I ran even faster. "Come on," I yelled to Link. When we reached the entrance it was still propped up. I yanked it open, and Link and I climbed down into the Tombs.

Zane nodded as we joined them. "Good," he said. "Gang's all here. I was afraid you weren't coming. Let's go."

I yanked my glasses and cap off and stuffed them in my bag before following. We ran in silence for over an hour, winding one way, then another, but always heading more or less down. It was dark and I strained to hear anything beyond the sound of our feet pounding over the ground, but the tombs were silent. Zane called back several times with warnings of rubble or holes to avoid, his voice hushed but still carried. Eventually the tunnel stopped. A mound of rocks and beams barred our way—it looked as though the cave had collapsed going forward. I wondered if we had somehow taken a wrong turn along the way.

Zane didn't seem concerned, though, nor particularly winded. He leaned against a boulder, blending into the darkness. A moment later the others caught up, and Zane flicked on the dim light of his tracker.

"Secret entrance," he said softly, beckoning us to follow as he disappeared behind a boulder twice my height. "Come on and stay close. This part is tricky."

He flashed the light over the rock, revealing a thin black opening. Even in full light I'd have missed it. I squeezed in after him, trying to ignore the images of rockslides and cave-ins my imagination was conjuring. Link followed right behind, and a few minutes later we emerged into a large cavern. Several dark shapes filled the space. Subway cars, I realized, as Zane walked toward one.

He wrenched open a door and bounded inside. A blaze of light greeted me as I followed, and I was momentarily stunned. It looked like someone's house. A couch and round table sat at one end. Bunk beds were built into the other side of the room. Several metal poles ran from ceiling to floor throughout the space, one of which Zane grasped. "It's good to be home," he yelled, laughing freely as he spun himself around.

He stopped mid-rotation, his face maybe six inches from my own. Brown curls framed his face and his mouth stretched into a satisfied smile. "Now that's what I call a successful mission," he said. "Nice work on your part."

I stepped away from him, not sure what to make of the theatrics. "I don't think I'd call it a success," I said. "Madden was really hurt."

He shrugged. "A little blood loss is good for the soul. Builds character."

Link joined my side, crossing one arm in front of the other. He was bigger than Zane, but only just. "Madden helped us escape, and we left her in a pool of blood. You think that's something to joke about?" His voice was low, the warning obvious.

Zane held up his hands. "Peace, Link. No harm meant." He broke away from the pole, sliding open a drawer I hadn't noticed. "No one will let a future minister go untended. Still, if it makes you both feel better, I'll check." He pulled out a plexi, tapping his fingers over the surface. A moment later he nodded. "Airlifted, stable condition. She'll be fine. As will we, now that we're free."

He reached out a hand to Link. My brother hesitated, but finally nodded. I let out a breath of relief as the two shook. Zane grinned, then turned to his sister, sweeping Oena from the ground and twirling her around the room.

Oena shrieked with laughter, and like that, enthusiasm infected us all. Thom whooped from beside me and Oena squeezed my shoulders. "We did it," she said. Even Raze was smiling.

"Yes we did," I said, turning to Link to give him a fierce hug.

He hugged me back before pulling away. "I still can't believe this. How in crilas did any of this even happen?"

"I *told* you I knew people who could help," I said. "Are you angry?"

"Shocked more than anything. You saved my life. I'm grateful for that, I am. But Dax, what you did was crazy. You could have been caught. If you were, you'd have been warded at best. More likely removed." He looked down at his hands. They were still streaked with blood. "Madden was *shot*."

"I know," I replied. "But it sounds like she's okay. You know she'll have the best treatment they can provide."

He nodded slowly, hopefully. "How did you get involved in this. And how did *she*? It's," he paused, trying to find the right word. "It's not like her."

So I gave him the short story of everything that had happened, ending with Madden. "I was desperate," I explained, "so I asked her for help. I knew she cared about you. I took a gamble on how much. When she said yes… I guess, there's a lot more to Madden than I realized." Which was a colossal understatement if she'd been telling the truth in that last minute. "Our destinies switched," she had said. They were the ravings of someone seriously injured. They had to be. Right?

Before I could ask Link about it, a door on the far side of the subway car slid open. The two brothers I'd met at the rendezvous in the Ash zone walked in. This time they wore pure black, as did the four others—two men, two women—who followed them in. "Zane," the larger of the two brother's shouted. "Hail, captain," the other hollered. This was followed by a lot of complicated handshaking and backslapping between the whole group.

Oena walked over to us then. "Dax, I've got a team checking the route back to Yellow before we send you home. It shouldn't be much longer. Your tracker is showing you on a run right now through Green. It will be a hard path to trace if there are patrols out looking for you. Just stick to what your map says if anyone asks and you should be fine.

"Okay," I said. "Will I still be able to talk to Link when I get back?"

Oena paused, considering, then grabbed my wrist. She frowned as she tapped over it, then released my arm back to me. "I've added another channel in here to speak with Link. Don't worry, it's untraceable—all of our programs should be. We'll set Link up with a modified tracker too."

She saw my look of happiness and held up one hand in caution. "For emergencies only. We can't be too careful. Understood?"

"Sure," I agreed. "Thank you."

"Good. Now let me introduce you to the others."

For the next little while I actually found myself having fun.

There was the residual exhilaration of having gotten away with breaking three people out of prison. And then there was the simple happiness of standing next to my brother. What I hadn't counted on was what it would feel like to be surrounded by people who all wanted to talk to me. No wonder the Purples got to school early. More and more groups of people stopped in. Five here, ten there, until soon the space was packed. I noticed that all went to Zane first. Some were genuinely happy to see him. Others seemed more reserved, almost nervous. Their clothing varied. Most wore black, but there was still color in the mix from most of the rings. Whether their designations were true was another story. Despite Link's initial unease, he was soon talking to various groups. The conversations ranged from radical changes to the system to smaller ideas that I knew could make a difference. No one here cared about the destinies they'd been born with. They spoke like people in control of their futures, with choices to make. I found myself thinking they were right.

Soon enough I got the signal that it was time to go. I realized I had no idea when I would see Link again. "You'll be okay?" I asked.

He looked around at the people surrounding us, nodding. "Yeah, actually, I think I will," he said. We walked off to the side of the crowd gathered. "I still can't believe this is real. That Revenants actually exist. Or that Aldan was dating one." His face still had the shell-shocked look whenever he said Aldan's name. I recognized it from my own. "Maybe this is where I was meant to be. I might even be able to do some good here. I'll miss you though. All of you."

"I'll come down here when I can."

He shook his head. "You shouldn't get mixed up with this group. After this, the PAE will be looking for a reason to get back at our family."

I didn't want to argue, but I needed him to understand. "It's my fight too," I said. "You're not the only one who gets to take a stand for what you believe in."

He was silent for a moment, considering. "I just worry about you."

"I know. I worry about you too. I wish I could tell Mom, Dad, and everyone that you're okay."

"They're better off not knowing," he said. "I might not be able keep you out of this world, but we can keep them out of it. Okay?"

"Okay," I agreed.

"And try to stay low for awhile," he warned again. "As a Blank, you're going to be a prime suspect."

"I know," I said. "About that… Madden said something to me at the UV building." Even thinking about saying the words aloud felt surreal, but I needed to tell someone. "She said my destiny and hers were switched at birth. She said I was supposed to be the minister." I held up a hand, anticipating Link's response. "I know it sounds impossible. Of course destinies can't be switched, but, well, what do you think?"

Link looked at me, doubtful. "I don't know, Dax. She was hurt pretty badly. Chances are she was delirious."

"I know," I said. "I thought that too, but Sol heard us talking. He wasn't surprised. I could see it on his face. He believed what she told me. He thinks I'm the future minister, not Madden."

"Dax?" a voice interrupted. Zane stood there, an eyebrow raised. "The tunnel is clear. It's time to go."

"I'll be right there," I said.

"Meet me at the door when you're ready. I'll escort you myself." He nodded to Link before walking back into the gathering.

Link watched him walk away, his expression unreadable.

"So what do you think?" I said.

"I think you should be careful around that guy. Maybe we can have Oena or someone else take you."

"Stop, I'm not worried about Zane. Everyone here trusts him. I mean, he's their leader, right? I'm probably safer with him than anyone else. But I was talking about what Madden said. What do you think?" I pressed.

"Honestly, it sounds pretty looped out. I don't know." He looked lost in thought. "For now you just need to get home. Wait until Madden is better, then ask her. If it's true, she'll tell you."

Link reached out and crushed me into another hug, then held me out, both hands on my shoulders. "Be careful, Dax." He glanced over to where Zane was waiting for me. "And let's not trust these people completely. Not yet, okay?"

Typical big brother, I thought. He'd still be trying to protect me when we were old. If we made it that long. "Sure," I said. I gave him one last hug before I followed after Zane.

I said quick goodbyes to the others before leaving the car, then Zane and I walked back out into the tombs, heading the opposite way we'd come from.

We made our way in companionable silence. It didn't take long before we stood under a short ladder. I zipped out of my worker's uniform. Underneath I wore my typical t-shirt and pants. I handed the uniform back to him. Moonlight seeped in from a grate overhead casting long shadows over us both.

"Thanks for the escort," I said.

"It's *you* I should be thanking," Zane replied. I'd seen him exuberant, obnoxious, crazy even. This was the first time he'd been serious. "You saved my life," he continued. "I won't forget that."

I shrugged, suddenly awkward. "You're welcome. You should thank Oena, though. And Thom. They were the ones who organized everything."

"But you were the one who put the group together. Like calls to like. I recognize another leader when I meet one." He tilted his head to one side, his expression curious. "Oena tells me you're a Blank, like me."

I nodded.

"We're rare," he said. "Luckier than most. Others use destiny as an excuse. You and I don't have that problem. Nothing to drive us forward but ourselves."

"Oena mentioned something like that to me once before," I replied. "I think I'm starting to see your point."

He paused, studying me. "I have to admit that I overheard what you told your brother. About the switched destinies."

"Oh, that was—" I began.

Zane held a hand up. "I didn't mean to eavesdrop. But I did hear what you said."

"Then you know how unlikely it is. Madden was shot, she didn't know what she was saying."

He nodded. "Perhaps, but if I believed in the system, I'd believe you could be a minister. You'd be well suited for it. Minister or Blank, I'm equally happy to have you on our side."

I kept the smile from my face, but Zane's words warmed me. "Thanks," I said. "I appreciate that."

He gave me a thoughtful look. "If you want, I can look into it for you. I'm good at finding out what I want to know. And information is more powerful when you can trust it."

I couldn't see how Zane's help would hurt anything. "Okay," I agreed.

"It's settled then." He climbed up the ladder, moving the grate to one side. He poked his head above ground before coming back down. "Your tracker data should keep your story straight, just stick to the facts—you were out for a long run that took you through most of the city zones. Contact us if you need anything. Anything at all," he said.

I waved goodbye as I exited the Tombs. After the dark mustiness of the underground, the world felt endless and I swallowed fresh air in gulps. However unlikely they were to be true, I played Madden's words over and over in my mind. They kept me company as I sprinted through the empty streets toward home.

THIRTY-FOUR

—

Madden

I woke with a jolt, blinking open my eyes, straining to see past the fluorescent light overhead. For a brief second I wondered where I was, but then I saw them—the guards stationed outside of the door. I'd been captured, I was in the hospital. The PAE must have figured out I was part of the escape plan. The thought of what awaited forced me from my grogginess. I needed to be alert, I needed to think.

I was in a hospital bed, that part was obvious. I moved to roll to one side and pain sliced through my abdomen. There were no restraints, but perhaps no one had thought I needed them. It was unlikely I'd make it too far on my own in this condition. That, paired with the two PAE officers less than twenty feet away, guaranteed I'd stay put. I tried to ease myself up, wincing before I leaned back. I didn't have the strength. Just shifting caused a stabbing pain to sear through my body. So this is what being shot was like. I wondered how the others had fared.

It was only a matter of time before the inquisition would start. Then it would be the cells, or the Ward, or worse—they'd remove me. Maybe the ministers would have mercy and let me say goodbye to my father and Nora first. I squeezed my eyes shut. It wouldn't matter—my family wouldn't want to see me once they discovered the truth about my destiny and my recent actions. The thought was almost as painful as the gunshot wound.

Maybe I was better off pretending I was in a coma. It was probably a better fate than what I'd be facing. I quickly dismissed the idea—I'd been awake for a minute and was already antsy. There was no way I'd be able to stay like this much longer. Besides, the PAE weren't the only ones who wanted answers. I needed to know if Sol and Link and the rest of them got away.

I was no longer a future leader, but that didn't mean I couldn't behave like one. I pressed the call button next to me, and waited to face my punishment.

In a matter of seconds, two people were standing over me. One furiously checking my vitals, the other scanning my body with her handheld MRI machine.

"Get the minister in here," the one looking over my data spoke into his wrist tracker. "He wanted to know as soon as she was up."

Normally, doctors and nurses doted over me when I went to see them. These two wouldn't even look me in the eye. My drop in status was apparently already widespread. "How long have I been here?" I asked.

The male doctor looked at me, opened his mouth, then shut it, instead turning away.

"You can't even answer me?" I yelled. "You're my doctors. Didn't you take some sort of oath? Or does that not matter in the face of the government."

The door swung open, and Minister Worthington walked in. His expression was neutral as he loomed over me, stroking his gray beard in consideration. "I told them not to speak with you. I wanted to be the first, to make sure the story doesn't get tainted by outsiders." He gestured toward the doctors. "You two can go."

They left. It was just me and the minister. A hospital was not where I wanted to be questioned. The country rarely saw crime—who knew how it would handle the situation? We no longer had a need for juries or judges. Would he go back to pre-destiny times when they tortured criminals for answers? He probably thought I deserved it. Not only did I keep my true destiny a secret, but I'd helped three criminals escape.

Worthington angrily paced the room. "We lost three officers in the breakout," he said.

I closed my eyes letting the news sink in. I'd seen Zane shoot them, but everything had happened so fast that I'd still hoped that they'd pulled through. This so wasn't what I had intended to happen. I just wanted to help Link. No one was supposed to get hurt. Tears sprung to my eyes. I knew, or at least had seen, most of the officers in the building. I'd been to graduation and promotion ceremonies. I shook hands with spouses, children, of so many of those who served, and now I was partially responsible for their deaths. I might not have pulled the trigger, but if not for me they would still be alive. "I'm so sorry," I said.

"Me too," he said. "And then there was you..."

This was it, it was over. I readied myself for my punishment. The cells, the Ward, removal.

He took a few steps closer. "I thought they got you too."

What?

"Seeing you wounded like that," he continued. "I was afraid you wouldn't pull through. I'm so happy to see you're alright."

I sucked in a deep breath until my lungs felt like they would burst. He didn't know. He didn't know my secret or that I was a part of the escape.

My relief mixed with my guilt. I was free, at least for now, but did I deserve it? Three guards were gone.

"Madden, what I need to know from you, is how did that Ash fit into the escape?"

"Who?" I asked, the tears warm against my cheeks.

"The Josephson boy. We found him by your side," the minister explained.

I held back a scream. Why hadn't Sol run? He was supposed to leave me there, he was supposed to save himself, but he had stayed.

"He says the two of you were kidnapped by a group of intruders. Is he telling the truth, or was he one of them?"

"No," I said, my mind racing. Thank the rings. Sol had covered for me, now I just had to run with it. "He tried to save my life. These people dressed as maintenance workers, they called themselves Revenants, forced me to let them into the building. Sol was working late and saw them. He tried to help me, but then they caught him too. He tried to get word to the outside, that's how the guards were alerted." It was a lie, but the only people who knew that were either dead or in on the escape plan. "He's a hero. If anything, he should have his ring status elevated."

Worthington nodded. "I'll take that under advisement."

"What about the others?" I asked.

He shook his head. "They escaped. But we'll find them. They're dangerous people who will be removed, as will anyone protecting them. There's a manhunt in progress now. They won't be able to run long."

Link was safe. At least for the moment. The Revenants had stayed hidden for years, they'd be able to continue their invisibility streak. But then an awful thought occurred to me. Worthington wasn't shocked that the Revenants existed. He had known. But the cells were never full. Did that mean those with the highest military access—like he and my father—handled those cases quietly? Were they killing dissenters without giving them a chance to defend themselves or repent? Had the government waged war on the Revenants? Was Dax right?

I didn't have a chance to ask any more questions. The door to my room flung open and my father raced in, Nora right on his heels.

"You're awake," he said, wrapping his arms around me bringing his head down to mine. He was sobbing. The last time I'd seen my father cry was right after my mother died.

"I'll give you all some time alone." Minister Worthington moved toward the door. "Madden," he paused. "We're asking that you not discuss the details of what happened with anyone. We don't want to cause a public panic. You'll be briefed on what you can and cannot say. I'm glad you're okay. Vanders," he nodded at my father before slipping out of the room.

My dad didn't even acknowledge the minister, he just held onto me tightly. Before I knew it I was crying too.

"Okay, make room," Nora said. "I need to get in there too." My father didn't even object to having a Yellow give him an order. He just moved so she could come in.

Nora gave me a hug, careful to avoid my injured side. Then she put both hands on my face and looked me straight in the eyes. "Don't you ever do that to us again, you hear me?"

I nodded.

"Good," she said. "Now we packed up some things for you since the doctors say you'll be here while you recover."

My father handed her the bag she'd placed on the ground when she came in. In it was my cube with the pictures of my mother, some sugar cookies, my favorite pillowcase (it was a dark purple silk that smelled of lavender vanilla), and a book—the one Laira had given me to sign. I had left it on my dresser. Nora must have thought it was important to me.

Both she and my father were looking at me with such love on their faces. I shivered to think just how tentative that love might be. What would they do when they learned about my destiny? And what would Dax do now that she was armed with the truth?

The doctors had to force Nora and my father to leave my hospital room so I could rest. My father even tried to use his rank to stay, but the doctors insisted. They gave me something to help me sleep, but it didn't work—not with the way my mind was racing.

With nothing else to do I reached for the book that Nora had left. It felt odd to hold the bound pages in my hands. They smelled musty, and somehow ancient, but I liked it. I flipped through carefully. I hadn't really paid attention when Laira had given it to me. Now it seemed like some kind of cosmic joke. It was a book of destinies. From the lowliest triggers, to the most important ones that had reshaped our world after the Event. I felt the absence of my own to my core.

I read deep into the night, though must have fallen asleep eventually, because I was jolted awake by an alert on my tracker. I was sure I had it set to do not disturb, but it kept sending out a soft ping.

I rubbed my eyes and looked down at it. A message marked high importance kept blinking on the screen and sending out an audible alert. In all my years involved with the ministry, I'd never seen that—not even in the rare instance when a destiny was broken, and that had only happened twice.

I tapped the message, and it jolted me wide awake.

Happy to hear you're alive, it read. *Especially since I know your secret.*

I instinctively looked to the door. But no one was there, no one was watching me, not even the guards. Once they realized

I wasn't the intended target at the UV, they were dismissed. I grasped the rails on the hospital bed, and squeezed my eyes shut. This was all a bad dream. Maybe the sleeping medication was creating some kind of hallucination. I opened up my eyes and looked back at my tracker. The message was still there. I had to face facts, this was happening.

The worst part was that I didn't even know what secret they were referring to. That I helped three prisoners escape, that I was in cahoots with the Revenants—who weren't even supposed to exist—or that I that I was hiding my true destiny. Any of those would be enough to have me locked up, or worse, for life.

Was it from Dax? Doubtful. She was smart, but she wasn't a hacker. Whoever it was had broken into my tracker, overriding the settings. I studied the message, but there was no clear sender. It came from a proxy server that just gave me a list of numbers. Sol was the only person I knew who could do something like this, but he'd never try and blackmail me. Not after everything that had happened. Besides, if he had wanted to extort ostows from me, he would have done it ages ago. But he would be able to help me find the person responsible. I knew it was late and that he was probably asleep, but I pinged him to come see me as soon as he could. Then I replied to the note: *Don't know what you're talking about.*

Before I even had time to lower my wrist, there was a reply. *Sure you do future minister. Though I guess that name doesn't suit you any longer, does it?*

Who is this? I responded.

Someone who wants justice. And if you don't want the truth to come out about who you really are, you'll do as I say.

I wrote back, fingers trembling. *I'll do nothing of the kind.*

Of course you will.

I didn't respond, but that didn't stop the mystery sender from continuing. *Get me Minister Worthington's security clearance code and we can forget this ever happened.*

I would never do that, I replied.

You have thirty-six hours.

I waited, but no more messages came. This was crazy. There was no way I'd do what they asked. I wasn't a thief. Only I sort of was. I'd stolen Dax's destiny. Not only that, but I'd helped break criminals out of the cells. Was stealing a simple security code really that much worse?

I chided myself. I didn't take Dax's destiny. It was given to me, and I wasn't planning on keeping the truth a secret forever—just until I worked out a plan. And the jail break, well, I couldn't let Link die. I just couldn't.

There was a slight knock on my door, and Sol peeked his head in.

"Hurry," I said. "Come in and shut the door behind you." If my doctors saw anyone in my room, they'd send him away, possibly even punish him, and I needed to talk to Sol. "How did you get here so fast?" I asked once he was safely inside. "It's after curfew."

"They have me staying here overnight as a precaution. I wanted to come see you before, but they wouldn't let me. Are you okay?" he rushed over to my side. Panic and worry flickered over his face as he looked down at me.

"I'm okay," I said. "You?"

"Madden," he looked away from me, his voice growing hoarse. "You shouldn't have done that. The bullet was for me. You could have died."

"But I didn't."

He turned back to face me. "But *I* will. It's my destiny. If I'm not dead by my eighteenth birthday, the Specialists will take me out. I wouldn't have been able to live with myself if I knew I cost you your life."

"Well," I said, giving him a tiny smile. "You wouldn't have had to live with it that long. Eight months tops."

I could tell he didn't know whether to laugh or stay mad at me. He wound up with something in between. "Just don't go putting yourself in danger again. Especially not for me."

"Maybe I changed your destiny," I said. "Maybe it's possible."

"It's not…" he stopped himself. "You never know," he said instead. "And thanks to you, they may raise my ring. Even if it is posthumously, it will help my family. It will get them out of Ash."

"That's great, Sol. It really is." I hated thinking about what his fate held for him. Before I could continue, he changed the subject.

"You called me here for a reason. What's up?"

"Maybe I just wanted to see if you were okay," I said.

He knew I was more selfish than that. "Visiting hours are over, you wouldn't break the rules if it wasn't important."

"Well, I did want to see you, but yeah, there is another reason," I confessed. Then I showed him the messages.

"You shouldn't have responded to them from your tracker," he reprimanded me. "Not without me setting up a roundabout."

"If anyone sees it, my cover's blown anyway," I said. "Besides, if they were able to get it to override my settings, I could always say they sent the response messages."

"True," he said, pulling out his plexi. His fingers flew over the keys. "Whoever sent this knows what they're doing. It's bouncing off a dozen signal points. I can't pinpoint it."

Then it hit me. I knew who was behind this. Dax might not have been tech savvy, but the company she kept certainly was. "Not surprising. The Revenants seem to know how to do a lot of things," I said, and explained to Sol who Dax's friends really were.

"I thought it might be something like that," he said.

"Wait, you knew they were real?"

"I had a hunch." He must have seen the shock in my eyes. "I

see things I'm not supposed to," he explained. "Pulling files is my job, I fix the UV computer system, I hack sites on the side. I mean, I didn't know for sure, but it looked like there was some truth to the rumors."

"And now they want me to steal for them." Dax must have told the Revenants my secret. Not that I could blame her. If I was an Ash who found out I was a Purple, I'd have been screaming it to anyone who would listen. At least they hadn't spilled the news to the rest of the world. Not yet anyway.

"You know," Sol said, "I can get you that code if you want it."

"Who knows what they'll do with it though?"

"It will give them access to his files, but with their hacking skills they'd probably be able to get it without you. This just makes it easier for them," he said.

"And makes me… us… their accomplices."

"We already are."

"Don't remind me," I said.

On one hand, I wanted to tell Dax and her friends to take their threats and shove them, but on the other, I wanted to comply. It would buy me time. Dax's time stamp wasn't until December eleventh. That gave me more than two months to come up with a plan to let her fulfill her destiny without giving up my status, but that was only if I could get the Revenants to stay quiet.

That meant one thing—it was time to add 'thief' to my resume.

THIRTY-FIVE

—

Dax

Two PAE vehicles were outside my house when I arrived. I hoped Zane and Oena were right and that my tracker would hold up under inspection. I wasn't the strongest liar, but since I met the Revenants I'd had no choice but to come up with some clever alibis. Tonight was going to be no exception.

"What's going on?" I asked as I opened the front door, trying to look as confused as possible. Four officers were standing in our living room. Two by the door and two by my parents who were seated rigidly on the couch. They looked like prisoners in their own home.

"We'd like to know that ourselves," the female guard asked. "Where have you been this evening?"

"Out for a run."

"Since six o'clock?" she questioned, each word a jab.

"Off and on," I answered. "There's not much else for me to do."

"We've tried to track you down for the last hour," she said.

"You weren't in the spots your tracker indicated."

"I run fast." I tried not to cringe at my response. Even I knew that was lame. There was no outrunning a tracker.

The guard turned to her partner. "We should take her in for interrogation."

"You'll do no such thing," I heard my mother say.

I looked at her, shocked. We all did.

"She was out because I told her to get out of our house. I've been upset. Of course I have." Her eyes filled with tears. "Two sons gone in a week. It's more than a mother should have to bear."

"I don't see how this has anything to do with your daughter's whereabouts," the guard said, pulling out a pair of laser cuffs.

"It has everything to do with it. I sent her out at six. You can check the time on our trackers, 6pm. She was here, my husband too," my mother said.

I had been here at six, but I took off right after. I had no idea where my mother was going with this, but I nodded along as she spoke.

"I needed space, and I told her to leave. To not come back until curfew." My mom motioned to her own tracker. "And you see it's almost curfew. It's hardly any of our faults that you can't keep up with a teenage girl."

I couldn't believe it. My mother was actually trying to cover for me. I did my best to sound sincere as I added to her story. "I'm sorry if I caused any trouble." I held out my tracker. "Would you like to check? I did take some trails off the usual path, so it might have been hard to find me. I run a lot, so I try and mix up my route."

The guard grabbed my wrist. I thought she was going to cuff me. Instead she powered the handcuffs down and hooked up a small drive to my tracker. I felt my body stiffen. Would the Revenant's apps and information show up? Would they somehow be able to track Link down? She studied the results for a good four minutes and little beads of sweat began to form on my forehead. I did my best to stay calm.

"Everything okay?" I finally asked.

"Looks like it checks out," the guard said, but I could tell she wasn't convinced I was innocent. "Tell me, Miss Harris," she questioned, "what do you know about your brother's actions tonight?"

"Which brother?" I asked, careful not to give anything away.

"The outlaw," she said.

"Do you mean Link? He's in the cells." I let the real panic I felt fill my voice. "Wait, did something happen? Did they execute him already?"

"Your parents will fill you in. Those are all the questions we have for now."

I nodded. I was going to have to be extra careful about my dealings with the Revenants going forward. The guards turned and exited.

My father watched from the window. "They're gone."

"Great," I mumbled.

"Dax, where were you?" he asked.

"Just… out," I answered, avoiding his gaze.

"Dax…" He stopped himself and shook his head. "'It is a wise father that knows his own child.' I'll let you have your privacy, but you know you can always talk to me, right?"

"I know."

My mother remained silent. She was standing with her back to me, bracing herself on the sofa.

I moved toward her. "Thank you," I said.

She turned her head to me, and it looked like she was going to say something. Instead she left me standing there and went upstairs.

My dad put his hand on my shoulder. "She loves you, Dax."

Maybe. Or maybe she knew where I had been, that I helped save her son. Or maybe she just couldn't bear the thought of losing another child. Either way, my mother finally came through for me when it mattered.

"What did the PAE say happened?" I asked my father.

"That Link escaped from jail."

"But how?"

"They don't know. They say he must have had prior knowledge, that before he denounced his destiny, he knew he'd be thrown in the cells and devised a breakout plan."

"That's crazy."

My dad rubbed his temples. "That's not even the worst of it. They say he got a hold of a guard's gun, killed three people and shot Madden Sumner. They say, in an odd twist of fate, an Ash was the one who saved her."

"No," I yelled. "That's not what…" I caught myself. "Link would never shoot Madden. Or anybody. He would never put someone else's life in danger to save his own. They're lying. We can't let them say those things about Link."

My father pulled me in for a hug. "Let them say what they want. Whatever happened, he's alive, that's what matters."

At least for now, but there was sure to be a manhunt. And as far as the general public knew, Link was enemy number one.

"Go get some sleep," my father said. "It's going to be a long week." He had bags under his eyes himself but, despite it all, he looked happy. His son was free.

I flipped my bedside lamp on as I walked into my room. The space was exactly how I left it, yet it didn't feel the same. The knickknacks I'd collected over the years were still there. An old-fashioned paper fortuneteller sat on my dresser, compliments of Laira. We'd made them as kids so we could pretend to be Destiny

Specialists. My cube sat next to it. I was probably the only Ash with her own personal one—all of my brothers had chipped in to buy it for my last birthday. There was the quilt that usually covered my twin mattress in a crumpled heap where I'd tossed it that morning. A sock lay on my dresser, resting there until I could find its match. Laira's dress still hung on the rack in the corner, waiting to be returned. I used to think all of this mattered. Now it just seemed insubstantial. I didn't feel like the same girl who had grown up here. It was like I was splitting into two different Dax's. Maybe three. The Blank. The Revenant. And if Madden had been right, the Minister.

I wanted to ping her and get answers, but I stopped myself. She was in the hospital recovering. I could wait another day. Besides Zane said he'd look into in. My dad was right. I needed to sleep. I grabbed some clean clothes from my dresser when I heard a rap at my window.

I turned toward the sound. Someone was outside. It was too dark to see more than a shape, but that was enough. Fear gripped me, but I forced myself to relax. Intruders wouldn't knock. I had just left Zane, maybe he'd come to tell me something. To be safe, I reached into the pair of pants I'd worn when I'd first met the Revenants. The glass I grabbed from the subway car was still there. I picked it up and paused. "Who's there?" I said.

"Dax, it's just me," a frantic voice whispered.

The glare made it hard to see, but I could make out a shock of familiar coppery hair. I put down the glass and flipped off my bedside light to cut the reflection before sliding the window open.

I had to be seeing things.

"Theron?" I whispered.

"Hi, Dax," he said giving me a sheepish smile as he stood balanced on the trellis.

I opened my mouth to speak, then closed it, for once

absolutely stunned into silence. Theron. Was outside my window. In the middle of the night. I took a step back, finally settling on the obvious suggestion. "Come in before someone sees you."

I moved out of the way as he hoisted himself over the window frame and into my room. The space was small to start. With Theron standing next to me it suddenly felt tiny. I was basically pressed up against my bed with the boy I'd been dreaming about for as long as I could remember. "What... what... are you doing here?"

"I just wanted to make sure you're okay. I'm sorry if I scared you. I didn't mean to; I just had to know how you were. You didn't answer my ping. And I heard there was a breakout, and after our conversation the other day, I thought you might have been there," he said barely pausing for air. "Madden's in the hospital. I needed to know you weren't hurt too."

The look of concern on his face was overwhelming. "I'm fine, honest."

"But you were there, weren't you?"

I nodded. "I went with Oena. We got Link out. He's safe."

"Dax, what if you'd been caught?" he asked. "You have so many people who care about you..." His voice caught.

"But I wasn't."

His eyes searched mine. "I couldn't stop picturing you hurt. I didn't know what to do." I had never seen him look so intense.

"So you came all the way to the Yellow ring after curfew just to see if I was okay?"

"Yeah, it was stupid. I'm sorry. I shouldn't have—"

I could barely hear the rest of what he was saying, my heart and mind and lungs were all working on overdrive. The moonlight streamed through the window, turning his face into a complex series of valleys and planes. I caught his eyes and everything seemed to stop. "It wasn't stupid," I said and for a brief second my nerves were gone. I reached up and pulled him toward me, closing my eyes as his lips touched mine.

I was kissing Theron. I was kissing Theron! *I was kissing Theron?* A moment of panic set in. What if he had only come here as a friend? What if he didn't want to kiss me? What if I had just made a huge fool of myself? I quickly stepped aside, afraid to look at him.

I was about to apologize, when he gently lifted my chin back toward him. Theron's gaze was so strong I couldn't turn away. I didn't want to. It was like there was a magnetic pull drawing us together. Then Theron leaned down and kissed me. His lips, his tongue, hungrily exploring mine. He circled his arms around my waist, drawing me closer. I relaxed into him, like we were two pieces fitting together. For the next minute I think I left my body.

We were interrupted by the squeak of someone on the stairs. My dad, coming up to bed. I froze and Theron pulled away. I held a finger up to my lips and listened as my parents' bedroom door opened, then closed shut.

"Dax," he began.

"You should go," I said, panicked that my father would stop in to say goodnight.

Theron started to speak, then paused, nodding instead. He took a step back, grasping the windowsill with one hand. His face was full of emotions. "I hope, I mean—"

I closed the distance between us before he could say anything else, and gave him a quick kiss. "You really need to go," I said, looking back at my door.

"Okay," he said. "Just promise me you'll be careful, alright?" he said.

I nodded. There was so much I wanted to say. More than anything, I wanted to tell him what Madden said about our destinies. If it was true, Theron and I might actually have a real chance at a future together. But I couldn't say anything—not yet.

The next thing I knew he was climbing out of the window and down the trellis. He looked back up at me and our eyes locked one last time. He flashed a final smile at me before darting across the street.

I stood at the window long after he'd gone, grinning into the darkness. Who knew what my future held, but at this very minute, I didn't care. Link was safe. The Revenants had my back. And Theron Oliver had snuck into my room and given me my very first kiss.

THIRTY-SIX

—

Madden

Once I made the decision to give in to my blackmailer, my betrayal was surprisingly simple. Sol hacked the system and located Worthington's code within minutes. As an extra precaution he set up a new account for me to send the information through that was filtered through layers of encryptions and codes and false documentation that ultimately would keep my name out of it. The Revenants had given me a thirty-six-hour window to get them what they wanted. I waited to send the code until the very last moment, partly because I was hoping a better option would present itself and partly because I wanted to make things as difficult for them as possible. I shouldn't have been surprised by the ping I got back upon delivery, but it still had me steaming.

"Now was that so hard? Stay tuned for further instruction."

Of course they were going to demand more. They had me under their thumb now, we both knew that. I just had to come up with a solution to fix everything before things got too out of control. The problem was that nothing was coming to mind. Not in the hospital, and not at home.

I took five full days off of school to recover. My father even cut his hours short to be there with me for most of it. It was just him, Nora, and me. He didn't even allow visitors, he just wanted me to get better. It was the most time we'd spent together, really together—not at some briefing or formal event—since I was a small child. As much as I was horrified by everything that had happened over the last week, I was thankful for the time it gave me with my dad. I would hold on to that once the truth came out.

As much as I wanted to hide in my room for another week, I knew it wasn't feasible. People were getting antsy for my return. I'd collected a garden's worth of get-well foliage. The media had set up shop in our front lawn, despite my father's ongoing threats and more than one broken hovercam. Lavender and Portia pinged me constantly, and I had a nonstop influx of messages from my classmates. Even Bas got in on the action, sending me notes and coming to the door armed with five-dozen violets. I had Nora send him packing. Now that I was New City's favorite victimized hero, I suppose it was only natural that he would want to share the spotlight. But I was having none of it. I wasn't even seeing my best friends, I certainly wasn't seeing my obnoxious ex. It was strange to think about. Had my entire life not been a lie, I would have been pleased with all the attention.

The only other message that I really cared about came from Dax saying that she needed to talk to me. It wasn't a conversation I was looking forward to having, but I knew it was inevitable. So on the morning I returned to school, I told her to meet me after final period in Ms. Almodovar's classroom.

That morning, my father insisted on driving me to school even though I was perfectly fine to walk. I knew he was concerned about the media frenzy surrounding me, but there wasn't much either of us could do about that. Reporters and hovercams weren't allowed on school grounds, but that didn't mean I could avoid my classmate's scrutiny. I knew there were some who would share a snap of me within moments of my arrival.

With that in mind, I made sure to march, albeit with a slight limp, out of my father's car and onto the courtyard with my head held high. As far as everyone, well, almost everyone, was concerned, I was still the future minister, and that's how it needed to stay.

I made it barely five feet when I was bombarded by that irritating Ash. Laira, I corrected myself.

"Oh Madden. You're finally back. We were all so worried. How are you feeling? Can I help you?" she asked. She didn't wait for my response, instead barreling along. "I have all of the notes you missed from class if you want to borrow them. Just let me know. I'm happy to help." She got close. Too close. She clearly didn't know a thing about personal space. In fact, I thought she was actually going to try to hug me until Portia showed up.

"Don't you have a street to cross?" Portia snapped, pushing past her to stand by my side. "Why don't you go try *not* to get run over? Or do, it doesn't really matter."

"Portia," I warned.

"Oh, don't give me that," she said, clasping my hand in hers. "I haven't seen you in almost a week, and I'm supposed to let some *Ash* get to you first. I don't think so."

Lavendar joined us from the other side. "Hey, don't forget about me." She gave me a squeeze on the shoulders. "Give me that," she said taking my purse. "You don't need to carry anything today."

"Thanks, but I'm fine."

"Don't be silly. That's what friends are for," she said, and her eyes got a little misty. "When I heard you got shot, Madden. I mean, thinking about losing you. I..." Her words got caught in her throat.

"Hey," I said. "I'm still here." My eyes started to water too. I'd known Lavendar since we were three. She was the one who was there when Link ended things, the one who convinced me everything would be okay, the one who listened to me rehearse my first public speech dozens of times. She wouldn't lose me, but chances were when she found out what ring I really belonged too, I'd lose her.

"Welcome back, Madden," Theron said, joining us to complete the circle. A crowd of students hung back, whispering and staring at me. Theron cocked his head, sizing up the teary moment in a glance. He gave a loud groan. "You guys, seriously, don't make Madden cry. You know it makes it look like I'm not doing my job." He mock whispered. "Plus we've got an audience."

I smiled as he leaned down to hug me, but was really just trying not to heave. I had forgotten what my lie meant for Theron. His destiny was to make the future minister laugh. Had he missed his moment because of me? How many others would be affected because my destiny was swapped with Dax's?

I couldn't dwell on it too long. I was bombarded with well wishes from throngs of classmates who were now permeating our circle.

"Do you need space? I can get you space," Portia said.

"It's okay," I told her. "Class is only a couple of minutes away." And seeing the look of concern in everyone's eyes was nice. If my conversation with Dax later went the wrong way, it could be the last time I ever felt it.

"Well, we have you covered if you need anything," Lavendar assured me. She linked one of her elbows with mine and Portia did the same with the other. Crossing the courtyard was near impossible. Everyone was trying to talk to me at once. A kind word here. A sympathetic pat there. I'd never heard the courtyard so alive with voices. Sol sat at his usual place on the wall ledge, there but on the periphery. I thought about calling him over, introducing him as the Ash who saved me, but I knew better than to try and mix our worlds. My friends wouldn't understand and it would just make Sol uncomfortable. And soon enough a friendship with me would prove toxic. I'd call a formal event before the truth came out. I'd even ask Minister Worthington to preside, that way if… when… my status was revoked, it wouldn't affect him. Sol wasn't looking at me, he was staring at his plexi, but I couldn't help but smile when he peeked up to glance my way.

So many people were asking me for details about the night Link escaped. They all wanted to hear what happened. Only I couldn't tell them. Not the truth anyway.

The official word from the ministry was that the entire breakout and my shooting was Link's fault. That was what they wanted me to say. I tried to reason with Minister Worthington, but I'd gotten a curt response. "The public can't handle the truth, Madden. Link Harris is responsible, and that is all anyone needs to know." My father, whose position in the ministry made him privy to what the government actually knew about the escape, told me not to argue, but I couldn't believe they were going to spread a lie. If the breakout events weren't true and the Revenants were real, what else was the ministry hiding? When I tried to discuss it with my father he said I was being ridiculous, that everything was being done in the interest of public safety, and I'd understand when I was a minister. I wasn't so sure. But regardless, rather than towing the line, my public statement was "a complete lack of memory due to shock and trauma" and a "thanks to the Ash who stepped in to help." I wasn't going to further implicate Link for something he didn't do, and if I could help Sol's standing in the process, even better.

The sound of the crowd went quiet. I turned to see what—or rather whom— everyone was looking at. It was Dax.

I think it was the first time I ever really noticed her. I mean, truly took her in as a person. Her clothing was too big—she wore an oversized long sleeve shirt. The arms were rolled up and pinned to stay that way. The neck was beginning to fray. Her pants had been hemmed a little too short, and there was a hole in one knee. Her sneakers were streaked with dirt. Everything about her was colorless and threadbare, and yet is still somehow worked. Dax was pretty—very pretty—despite the ragged ensemble. She'd be downright beautiful in a purple gown. My future was standing in front of me, as clear as looking into a mirror.

"Seriously?" Portia said, interrupting my thoughts. "I can't believe they still let her go to school here. Hey," she yelled. She waved a hand toward Dax. "Hey you," she shouted again. "At least have the courtesy to go inside or something. No one wants you here."

"It's not her fault," I said.

"Madden, her brother shot you," Lavendar said in a way-too-loud whisper. "She's always hated you, I'm sure that played a part. She's a *Blank* after all. You know they're sneaky and dangerous."

Dax nodded in agreement, her eyes glittering. Her voice carried across the courtyard like a bullet. "Very sneaky, right Madden?"

This was not how I wanted my first interaction with Dax to go. If they kept egging her on, she might spit out the truth right there in the courtyard.

"Enough," I called out. "I don't need this today. Can someone please lighten the mood?"

"Sure," Portia said, coiling her finger around one of her ringlets. "In fact, since we have a total mutant in our midst, maybe someone should just remove it."

I saw Theron glance from Dax to Portia, weighing the situation. "On it," he said. Only he didn't go over to Dax. He lifted Portia, and looked at the crowd, "Where should I put her?"

Everyone started talking at once. The crowd was in disbelief. Portia was screaming and kicking her legs in outrage. And then there was Dax.

She was cracking up like it was the funniest thing she'd ever seen. When our eyes met again she just nodded, a smile plastered over her face. She didn't have to say anything. The message came through loud and clear. Theron's destiny was to make her laugh, not me.

The bell rang then and the student body dispersed, saving me from listening to more of Portia's hysterics. Temporarily anyway. It was all she talked about between classes until Lavendar finally told her to stop making the day about her. I even got Portia to forgive Theron, which she said she only did because I almost died. True friendship at its finest.

At the end of the day, I told everyone I was going to Ms. Almodovar's class to catch up on some missed assignments. She was my favorite teacher, and I had touched base with her when I was home. I told her I needed a place away from my family, friends, and work where I could just concentrate. She said I could use the room undisturbed all week. When I got there, Dax was already waiting.

I couldn't quite read the expression on her face. We stood there facing one another, each waiting for the other to begin.

I looked back at the door to make sure it was shut and that the shade on the window was closed. "Link?" I asked, breaking the silence.

"He's fine," she answered.

I looked down. I hadn't realized how much his escape had been weighing on me. "Good," I said. I wanted to say more, but it wasn't the time or the place. Link was gone from my world and needed to stay away. It was the only way he'd be safe.

"He was worried about you. I guess we both were."

"They had me walking the next day. Wonders of modern science and all that." I knew my health wasn't the topic Dax was interested in, and for that matter, I wasn't either. "You said you wanted to talk, so talk."

She looked at me incredulously. "I want to know the truth. What you said—am I really the future minister?"

She knew full well it was the truth. You don't go stealing codes for a lie. This had to be a trap.

"Madden?" she prompted.

"Why are you doing this?" I asked.

"What?"

"Are you recording our conversation?"

"No," she said, "Would I admit to knowing my brother's whereabouts if I was?"

She probably wouldn't, but you could do amazing things with editing. Although, I guess I could claim the whole thing was a fake. "Fine," I replied. "It's the truth. But you know that. I got your friends' blackmail request while I was in the hospital. I did their dirty work."

"What?"

"Please," I said. "Don't act innocent. I told you something that could save you, and you used it to hurt me."

"Madden, I have no idea what you're talking about."

"Right."

"No," she said, her voice rising. "I'm not letting you turn this around on me. You're the one who knew our destinies were swapped and didn't say anything until you thought you were going to die. You're the one who always wants to tell everyone how great the system is, and yet you were going to break it."

"I wasn't going to break it," I yelled back, before remembering to lower my voice. "I was going to tell you. I just needed time to think."

I felt my mouth go dry. I couldn't believe we were having this conversation.

"Go on," she said.

"I found a discrepancy in my birth records a few weeks ago when I was doing some family research. I hired Sol to dig into it. You and I were born on the same day."

She nodded. "I know. Your yearly birthday gala is all anyone can ever talk about that day."

That was going to change soon enough. I forced myself to keep talking. "Sol looked through my birth records, and he realized the switch happened with someone who was born on the same day. In the same hospital. That was you."

"Impossible."

"It should have been," I said.

"How could someone switch a Blank destiny with a minister's destiny? They triple check every birth. Link told me sometimes they even do a fourth check for good measure. There's no way to mix up something like that."

"Someone did," I said, trying to keep the bitterness from my tone. "Sol checked and rechecked, Dax. It's the truth. You're the future minister, not me."

Dax narrowed her eyes, still trying to process it. "So you're telling me that my entire life has been monitored, controlled, and preordained for a limited Ash existence. And it was all just, what? Some big misunderstanding?"

"Yes," I said. "But this can still be fixed. There was a time stamp. The future minister isn't scheduled for induction until December eleventh of this year. That's why I didn't say anything yet, I needed time to plan, to come up with something. I still do."

"You mean so you don't get stuck like me? At the bottom rung."

I didn't answer. We both knew it was true.

Dax paced back and forth, her hands covering her mouth. I was scared to ask the question, but I needed to know. "What are you going to do?"

She stopped pacing, and looked right at me. "I have no idea."

THIRTY-SEVEN

Dax

I walked out of the building in a daze. It was true. All of it. I was actually the future minister. Madden's secret could change everything. Part of me wanted to climb onto central fountain and scream the news for all of my classmates to hear. I could just imagine the reactions. Shock. Awe. Regret for the way they treated me over the years. Or more likely, they'd think I was trying to pull something. I needed hard proof before I opened my mouth. If word got back to the PAE that some Ash was claiming she was a member of the Seven, I didn't want to think about what would happen. My family was in enough trouble as it was. Still, the idea of everyone knowing was freeing, and I let myself slip back into the daydream as I walked across lawn in front of Spectrum. It took me a minute before I realized someone was yelling at me.

"Go back to your ring!"

"Leave her alone," another voice replied.

I looked up. Three of the school's top Purples stood there,

Theron included.

"What? It's not like we have to pretend anymore," Devon Latcher, a lanky senior who used to trail my brother around, said. "Aldan's gone."

"Even if he wasn't," Wen Steed butted in, "it's not like it would matter what he'd have to say now."

"Aldan was our friend," Theron said, frustration thick in his voice.

"Sure," Devon replied. "Before we knew what a Crilas-loving destiny breaker he was."

I couldn't listen anymore. I picked up my pace as I made my way across the courtyard. Devon and Wen had been two of Aldan's best friends, but since the race I'd watched them turn into animals. Everywhere I went I heard ugly variations of what they were saying—about Aldan and Link, or my family—more often than not, about me. If they knew the truth, they'd be groveling right now. Not that it would change my opinion about them. I didn't care how influential their families were, when I was minister I'd remember how they acted since Aldan was killed.

"Dax, wait," Theron called after me.

"You are not going after that thing," Wen told him.

"Let go of me," Theron said.

I turned back. Wen's hand was grasped around Theron's arm and they both looked ready to fight.

"I said 'let go,'" Theron repeated.

"Not if you're chasing an Ash. First it was that thing with Portia this morning, and now this? What's with you?"

Theron pushed him away, and Wen stumbled back. His nostrils flared, and he lunged at Theron. I didn't know what to do.

"You still think Aldan's so great?" Wen shouted, grabbing onto Theron's shirt, right near the throat. "Maybe I should call the PAE. Let them know we have a sympathizer among us." He tightened his grip. "Not so funny now, are you?"

"Okay," Devon said, coming between the two. "You made your point, Wen. Let him go."

He released Theron, but the two stood there staring at each other. For a second I thought they were going to go at it again, but Theron turned around and walked in my direction.

"Dax," he said, as he approached. His breathing was hard, his entire posture rigid. I could almost see the fury wafting off of him. Talking to me now in front of Devon and Wen was just going to make it worse. For both of us.

"Meet me behind the building," I whispered and headed away from him.

I'd been so excited about Theron coming to see me last night that I hadn't thought about the full implications of our… friendship? Relationship? Whatever this thing was growing between us. Our future would be impossible if our rings remained the same. It wouldn't just be the gossip and name calling we'd have to put up with, but actual threats. No one would stand to see a Purple and Ash together.

The thought lurked as I neared the back of the building. I looked around before approaching Theron. I didn't see anyone— not his friends or any PAE detail. I took a breath before I spoke. "Hey," I said, surprised at how nervous I felt. Other than a quick wink he gave me this morning, Theron and I hadn't spoken since he climbed out my window.

He took a step toward me, then stopped. I guess we were both unsure of what to do next. Some of the tension released in his eyes as he looked at me, and he smiled. I wanted to rush to him, put my arms around him, kiss him. But I didn't. I was still a Blank in the eyes of the world. Until the truth came out, I'd have to act like it.

"Dax, I'm so sorry," he said.

"It wasn't your fault."

"They'll come around," he said. "It will get easier."

I took a deep breath, stealing myself for what needed to happen. "No, it won't. You know that."

He got that serious look again. The one I'd been seeing a lot more of recently. "Then let them talk. I don't care what they say, Dax." He reached his hand out for mine.

Instead of grabbing it, I shook my head no, trying to ignore that my heart was breaking. Theron wanted to be with me. It was everything I ever wanted. But it couldn't happen. Not yet.

"But I care," I replied softly. Until everything was sorted out with my destiny, the two of us were better off alone, whether he realized it or not. "I'm sorry, Theron. I can't do this." I turned away before he could see my eyes tear up.

I wanted to tell him the truth. I wanted to tell him I was really a Purple and that his destiny was tied to mine. But I couldn't. I didn't know how he'd react. Would he try to tell people to defend me? Blurt it out to someone like Wen? Make some stand against the system the way Aldan did? I could risk it. I wouldn't put his life in jeopardy. My future—our future—would have to wait until the truth was wide open. I just wasn't sure how to make that happen.

I left Theron standing there and pinged the Revenants. I knew it was dangerous to contact them now with the amped up security surrounding my family, but I had to chance going to see them. I was desperate to talk about what happened. Beyond that, I wanted answers. Madden's ravings about blackmailers were eating at me. Zane had overheard my conversation with Link. I'd trusted him, but had he done something with that information? Had Oena?

I received a ping back in minutes. "Purple zone running trail, Marker 7, ten minutes."

I didn't have far to go. I cut away from the school and headed toward the wooded area that zigzagged to and from the shore. It was one of my favorite running paths and one that I took at least once a week. Smart thinking on whoever's part had orchestrated the meet. Marker 7 was within the most heavily wooded area and it would be unlikely that anyone would follow me. Unlikely, but not impossible. The PAE had made no mystery of their presence in my family's life. We were all being watched. There was a PAE van parked in front of my house for a good portion of the day. Officers would do sporadic check-ins on all of us. Sometimes they'd stop me on my way to and from school, other times a guard would pop up during my afternoon run. I was constantly looking over my shoulder. It felt like there were eyes on me even when there weren't.

When I hit the designated location I slowed down, anxiety sending my senses into overdrive. The birds were louder. The distant waves against the shore were denser. I could hear the animals in the trees around me. When Zane finally stepped out from the shadows I had to stifle a scream.

"Not quite the reaction I had hoped for," he said ruefully.

"Crilas, Zane," I said. "You scared me." I rubbed the back of my hand over my forehead, wiping the sweat from my face.

He seemed amused by my reaction. "I've been known to do that," he replied. "The crew's down below." He reached into the leaves next to his feet to lift up a trap door.

"Are you sure—" I began.

"Your tracker data will send the PAE on quite a chase if they follow. I've got you circling around Marker 7..." he looked down and punched something into his own tracker. "Starting *now*. We've got ten, maybe fifteen minutes before it occurs to them that something's off. That's me being charitable, really. The PAE's observation skills have never been one to brag about." He nodded at the black hole next to his feet. "Ladies first."

I climbed down the ladder and Zane followed. We made our

way through a short tunnel until we reached a doorway so grimy it blended into the wall. Behind it was a small, crowded room. My brother's arms immediately crushed me, lifting me off of the ground into a hug. I squeezed back, relieved to see him. Oena was there, as well as Thom and Raze. I greeted everyone quickly.

"We don't have much time," Oena said.

"I know," I said. "Do you all know about Madden's confession?"

Thom answered. "We do. We've all been discussing it since we found out."

"Okay," I said. "I spoke to her today. It's true, I really am the future minister." I filled them in on what Madden had told me after school. "But there are still some things I don't get," I concluded. "Like why Madden said she's being blackmailed. Is it true?"

"Blackmail is such a nasty word," Zane said. "Test is more accurate. I wanted to get to the bottom of your mystery, so I asked her to retrieve a code for me. It wouldn't have taken me long to find it on my own, but I knew if she agreed to help, then she'd told you the truth. Simple and effective."

I saw Link's face harden at Zane's words. I didn't blame him. I crossed my arms in front of me. "It was also sneaky. Why didn't you tell me what you were doing?"

"It wasn't the kind of information I wanted you to receive under observation. Oena and I have spent the last few days trying to find a place where one of us could tell you in person. Problem is, as you know, you've developed some nasty PAE tails," he said, raising his shoulders in an apologetic shrug. "It couldn't be helped."

I felt a knot of tension unravel as his words sunk in. Zane had just done what he'd promised—he'd found out the truth.

"But this leads to the next question," he continued. "What will you do now that you know?"

"I'm not sure," I said. "There's no way I can prove anything

Madden said. Until she's ready to tell people, there's not much I can do. Sol can get the proof, but he won't—not if Madden doesn't want him to. I saw the way he looked at her during the breakout. He's practically smitten." My brother's jaw tightened, and I felt a little bad for bringing up another guy liking Madden. "I know how you feel about her, Link. But I don't want to wait. Just imagine what I could do if people knew the truth. Everything would be put under a microscope—destinies reevaluated, decisions reconsidered. If I was minister, it would show people they shouldn't judge others by their ring. Everyone thought I was an Ash, but I'm not. It will make them look at things differently." My mind flashed to Theron. It would make it possible for us to be together, and that was just one of hundreds of reasons I needed to take office. I looked straight at my brother. "Maybe you could even come home."

Link ruined my fantasy with a shake of his head. "The minute I poke my head above ground someone will blow it off. We've been keeping track of the news. Outside of our family, there's not a person in New City who doesn't want to see me removed. Telling everyone your destiny won't change that."

"I agree with Link," Oena said. "As much as I want to see the truth come out, the PAE twists destinies to fit their plans. You'll be a pawn for them if you don't plan this carefully. That takes time. The ministers have spent their entire lives building alliances. Worthington and Sealy vote the same on every issue. Kurtz sides with Blythe on tracking legislation, except when it comes to territories outside of New City."

I knew Oena and Link were right. Everything they said made sense. But it was the last thing I wanted to hear. "So what, then?" I asked. "I just act like nothing is different?"

Zane answered. "Madden is trusted by the ministry. She can make more headway than you for our cause, and now that she knows the truth, she'll help you. She'll help *us*," he waved his hands to include everyone. "It boils down to timing. You tell the truth now, they'll induct you. At best you'll be a puppet for the rest of your life. At worst, you'll have an accident the morning after your Destiny Day, followed by a very nice memorial service. Lots of pretty speeches. Impressive purple bouquets."

I shuddered. "They wouldn't."

"They would," Zane said.

"They have," Oena agreed, her voice soft. "Zane and I know from experience."

I looked back and forth between them, waiting for either to elaborate. Oena looked sad. Zane grim. Both were silent as I mulled their words over.

"Think of it as training," Zane finally said. "The best leaders are patient. They play the long game to win and don't get tripped up by the details. The next few months are a gift. Watch. Study. Learn. We'll help you position yourself to take the ministry on your terms."

"Alright," I said. Although it didn't feel like a gift. It meant nothing would change in my life. The constant observation. The hatred. Keeping Theron at a distance. But there was a bigger picture to keep in mind. "Madden can stay minister for now." Which reminded me, "What was the code she got for you?" I asked.

A slow smile spread over Zane's face. "A good question," he said. "We've known for some time that there's a Purple with a destiny somehow attached to the Revenants. I've used the code to uncover the information."

I heard Oena catch her breath.

So this was news to everyone.

He nodded. "The destiny is to expose the Revenants. It's attached to a girl by the name of Aya Lee. Her time stamp is scheduled for this year."

I saw Link stiffen next to me. "You're talking about the child with the classified destiny, right? She's what—seven or eight?"

"What she lacks in size, she makes up for with threat," Zane said. "But this is for a later discussion."

"What are you planning?" I asked.

"Nothing to worry about, we're still figuring it all out. But we do have to get you out of here. The PAE will notice your absence."

I wanted to hear more about Aya Lee, but I knew he was right. "Okay," I said. "Keep me posted on what's next."

"On my honor." Zane pressed two fingers over his heart. "Link, you'll see Dax out?"

I left in a chorus of goodbyes and well wishes. As we walked out the door the conversation turned back to Aya Lee.

"Seriously Zane, what are we going to do?" Oena said.

"What we always do," he replied.

"She's a kid."

"She's a risk."

"There are other ways to contain a threat."

Their voices were lost as Link and I walked down the hall. "I don't like the way that conversation was going," he muttered. "Aya's a sweet kid. I've met her."

"What do you think will happen?" I hadn't liked the conversation any more than Link.

"I don't know, Dax. I've spent a week with these people now. I like them. They've got a bunch of good ideas. But they're radicals. They're just as bad as the ministry in some ways. Zane sees people as chips on a board to move, and I'm still trying to figure out what he's moving them toward. Destiny happens, and you never know how it's going to play out. Aya is a perfect example. Her destiny is to expose the Revenants, but it might be the Revenants getting involved that triggers her destiny to occur. Either way, using a child isn't the right way for the Revenants to get their point across."

"Are you saying I shouldn't listen to Zane?" I said. "Or to any of them?"

"I guess I'm just telling you to keep your own council first," he said. "We're still figuring them out. Until we do, the safest thing either of us can do is pay attention to ourselves. Do what we think is right."

"Sooooo," I said, stretching the word out. "You think I should head up and tell the world to bow down to my new status?"

He cuffed me on the top of the head. "That's not what I meant, Dax."

"Kidding," I said. "Mostly."

I gave him a quick hug and climbed back up the ladder, to the sun and the running trail, to the PAE surveillance and my classmates' hatred, and to my eventual future as Minister Dax Harris. I could be patient. My future would wait for me to catch up. And when I did, New City was going to change, whether the rest of the ministry liked it or not.

THIRTY-EIGHT

—

Madden

I told my father that I needed to walk to school the next day, that the fresh air would do me good. My injury was almost healed and it felt good to finally move around. More importantly, I just needed to have the time alone to clear my mind.

After yesterday, I was in no desire to get to Spectrum any faster than I had to. I slowed my pace, hoping to avoid extra time in the courtyard and another run-in with Dax. Would she tell my, *our,* secret before I had a chance to fix things? How could she not want to? A Purple life was worlds above Ash. I tugged at my Zone bracelets. I'd been lying to myself when I'd said there was nothing wrong with living in Ash. When it came down to it, I wasn't ready to give up the Purple life. But did that mean I was ready to do more of the Revenant's bidding?

I still couldn't believe Dax was helping them. Sure, she claimed she wasn't involved, but she had to be. I was scared to think what they'd ask for next, but I was going to find out soon.

I'd received another anonymous message last night saying that I should stand by for my next assignment.

I looked up at the clock tower. It was only 7:40, and I was already at the wishing tree, just a few minutes from school. I'd be stuck in the courtyard with everyone for at least fifteen minutes. I debated stopping and sitting by the tree for a bit, but I decided against it. I was still the future minister. At least for now. I was going to go to school and be the Madden everyone expected.

"That's a lovely shade you're wearing," a voice called out from behind me. I recognized it instantly. It was Zane. The one I helped break out of jail. "Really brings out your eyes." I turned around and there he was, leaning against the tree. His dark hair was combed back and he wore a smart green jacket. He looked like any other visitor to the wishing tree, nothing more, nothing less. "Too bad you'll be outlawed from wearing it soon."

I felt rooted to the ground. Had he been following me? Part of me wanted to run, part of me wanted to scream out for the PAE, part of me wanted to cry, and part of me just wanted to rip that smug look off of his face. I kept my composure. "Keep your voice down," I told him. "Someone might come by here any moment."

"Then you'd better look busy."

I pretended to study a note the color of amethyst, letting my fingers pass over the edges. Zane was right; if the truth was discovered, this color would be off-limits to me. "What do you want?"

He hung a lime slip of paper on a low branch. "My wish."

So did I. I wished that none of the events of last month had ever happened. That Aldan Harris never lost the race, that Link didn't denounce his destiny, that I didn't investigate my file, that I didn't tell Dax the truth. But wishes couldn't change the past, and now I had no future.

"Don't you want to know what it is?" He flicked the note he

hung with his finger.

I didn't respond, but that didn't stop him from telling me. "It's to try new things. Open my horizons. Make some new friends."

"Great," I said, the sarcasm practically dripping from my words. "I hope it all works out for you."

"The problem is," he continued unfazed, "The friends I'm looking to make are from the Purple ring. I'll need an introduction. That's where you come in."

I scowled at him. "My friends aren't really your type."

"Well let's be honest, if they find out the truth about you, they won't be *your* type any longer either. But that's a problem for another day. Assuming you cooperate."

It took every bit of self-control I possessed to stop myself from smacking the superior grin off of his face.

"You and I aren't that different, Madden," he said. "Both being Blanks and all."

I tried to keep the shock from my face. Zane was a Blank? Now that he'd said it, it made sense. He was what everyone always described Blanks as being—dangerous, unpredictable, insane. He deserved to be locked up. But not all Blanks were like Zane. Then again, it wasn't like I had ever met one before—other than myself. But I certainly wasn't like that. Was I?

As if sensing my thoughts, he continued. "It's not a bad designation, despite what others say. You may not have a place in New City when the truth comes out, but that doesn't mean you have no options. You're a diplomat, so I'm sure you understand how this works. Help me, and I'll help you in return."

I crossed my arms in front of me. "What do you want, Zane?"

"Delighted you asked," he said. "To begin with, I'd like to meet a charming young lady. I'm sure you know her. Rather small. Goes by the name of Aya Lee."

I sucked in my breath. "Aya? She's just a kid. What do you

want with her?"

"None of your concern."

"It is if you want me involved." I'd already heard enough to know I wasn't about to help him, but if he was suddenly interested in Aya, I wanted to know why.

He shrugged a shoulder. "Just a little chat."

This was ridiculous, there was no way I was a scheduling a meeting. "So you just want me to waltz you on over to her house so you can say hello? It would never work."

"That's why you're going to set up a private meeting, where you'll bring her—just her—to me. Little Aya and I have much to discuss."

Of all the things I imagined the Revenants would ask me to do, something like this had never crossed my mind. This wasn't just stealing some minister's code. This was about the fate of a little girl. "I'm not bringing Aya to you. I'm not bringing anyone," I said. "This stops now."

He leaned toward me, his eyes shining. "Future Minister Sumner, we both know that's not true."

His breath was hot on my face, and I flinched back. "Think what you like," I said. "*Do* what you like. I'm not one of your minions to order around."

Zane clapped. "A fine performance. Now if you're done, let's get down to business."

An Ash woman approached to hang up a wish. Zane and I pretended we were making our own. I could barely tie the slip of purple paper onto the tree, my hands were shaking so badly. From anger or fear, I wasn't sure. I used to love standing by the wishing tree. I'd had dozens of photo ops here, meet and greets with the public, speeches about new reforms. It made a beautiful backdrop. It was hopeful, optimistic, a place of possibilities—but not today. Today it was a reminder of the importance of destiny and how not following it could lead to catastrophes. Had I just told the truth, had I accepted my true destiny, Zane wouldn't have any power over me now. The Ash touched her fingers to her lips and then placed them on the paper, sealing it with a kiss before she left.

I had hoped the interruption would help me come up with a solution to dealing with Zane, but I had nothing. Of all the people the Revenants could have sent, this one seemed the least likely to understand reason. "Why Aya?" I asked. My voice sounded small, and Zane seemed to delight in my discomfort.

"Well, if you must know, I used that code you gave me to unlock the child's destiny. Between you and me, I don't care for it. Not one bit."

Aya's destiny had always been a mystery. Only a select few were privy to the details. At least that was the case until I handed over Worthington's code. But from the way Zane was acting, it clearly spelled trouble for him. "What's her destiny?"

"You just concentrate on getting me the girl," he said.

"So you can what? Hurt her? Kill her?" My fists were balled up at my side, one hand clutching the amethyst slip of paper. I hadn't even realized I tore it down. "I won't be a part of that."

"I already told you, you are going to do what I say." The amusement was gone from his eyes. They were cold and staring straight at me. "If you don't, not only will I expose you, but I will destroy the rest of your world, starting with that Ash you are so fond of. I can see to it that his destiny comes to pass sooner than later. I probably don't need to remind you, but death can be such a painful affair. From there I'll move onto Link. Then your father. He's been a huge inconvenience over the years. And after that, I suppose I'll simply go down the list and kill anyone you've ever known or cared about. Believe me when I say that this is no idle threat." He smiled. "Stay tuned. I'll send coordinates for the meet in the next few days. The choice is yours, future minister. But I don't think you want to disappoint me on this one."

THIRTY-NINE

—

Dax

I couldn't sleep all night. All I could think about was the conversation I overheard about Aya Lee. Would the Revenants hurt her? I wanted to believe that they wouldn't, but I knew the lengths they were willing to go for what they believed in. Would they justify killing one child to save thousands of others? No, I told myself. They'd find another way. Besides Zane had promised to fill me in on the group's next steps, and it was in his best interests to keep his word. The Revenants needed me. My destiny would be able to further their cause. They wouldn't do anything to jeopardize that. Yet, as much as I tried to reassure myself that Aya would be fine, something still gnawed at me.

When I woke up I knew what I had to do. I got ready for school like any other day, but instead of heading straight to Spectrum I waited about a block from the main building. Madden would be coming this way. Our last conversation hadn't ended well, but I knew this was something she'd want to hear about.

She was later than usual, which was good and bad. It meant that no one else was walking in now, but also that we'd have less time. Madden was so lost in thought as she passed me, she didn't even look in my direction.

"Hey," I called out softly.

She swirled in my direction, ready to ream someone out until she saw that it was me. I hadn't expected a welcome committee, but was surprised when I saw her nostrils flare and eyes turn to slits. I had thought she'd be all minister-like and diplomatic, but instead anger shone through. I ignored her look and gestured for her to meet me across the road at the sports facility. She was definitely annoyed but crossed the street and waited for me inside. At this hour it would be empty.

"What now?" She flung the words at me angrily before I even had a chance to step inside the door.

I wanted to tell her to knock it off with the attitude, that she was the one who stole *my* identity. But we only had a few minutes before first period, and I had to make Aya my priority. "Listen," I said. "I can't tell you how I know this, but there's this Purple kid, her name is Aya Lee, I think something might happen to her. Can you maybe see about getting her extra security?"

Madden's face went through a rainbow of emotions. "You don't know, do you?" she said.

"Know what?"

"What your *friends* asked me to do?"

As Madden recounted her meeting with Zane, I wanted to scream. He'd promised to keep me in the loop. *On my honor*, he had said.

I covered my face with my hands. Maybe this was just another test. Maybe Zane just wanted to see if Madden would actually try and take Aya to him. I shook my head. I was being naive. He'd threatened Madden's family. More importantly, he'd threatened

Link. He wasn't playing around. I felt angry, disappointed and even a little foolish.

"What does he want with her?" she asked quietly.

"Her destiny is to expose the Revenants. I guess he'll do anything to stop that from happening."

"Maybe," she bit her lip. "Maybe it wouldn't be such a bad idea if they were found. It could solve everything. You know where they are—let's tell the PAE, and Aya doesn't have to get caught up in the middle of it."

"I can't do that. I can't jeopardize Link's life."

"We can have him hide somewhere else," she tried to reason.

"And what about all the other innocent people down there? I can't risk them either."

"And I can't risk something happening to Aya or all the people I love."

"There has to be another way to stop him," I said.

"If you have any ideas, I'm listening."

"I don't know," I said, racking my brain. "What if somehow we set him up? We could make it look like you're following his orders, and then instead you could…" I trailed off. I had no idea what our counter move would be. I shook my head. "Forget it, it's a dumb idea. And it would probably still put Aya in danger."

"No," Madden said, lighting up. "It's brilliant. Aya has major security around her.

Because of my clearance they'll let me alone with her." She paused ever so slightly, probably feeling guilty because she knew it was really my clearance she was talking about. "But they'll still track both of our whereabouts the whole time. She's not allowed to leave Purple without several PAE officers present. If she crosses over, we'll be surrounded in seconds. So if Zane picks a place outside the Purple Zone, we're set. Even if he doesn't, I can still get Aya across the border before the scheduled meet time. I'll tell her I need to make a quick stop. Once I break the border rule, the guards will never let me alone with her again, and Zane can't fault me for not trying."

I nodded. "It's a good plan," I said. "But the Revenants were able to control my tracker. If Zane wanted to, he could just reprogram yours to make it look like you and Aya are still in the Purple ring."

Madden thought about that for a minute, then broke into a smile. "Aya is considered an asset. An extremely important one. The ministry is very careful with her, not only do they hide her destiny and have PAE watching her whereabouts, they gave her an implant in addition to her tracker. That's never done. Zane wouldn't know to look for it. If he tampers with our trackers, then they'll show one location, and Aya's implant will show another. Alerts will go off all over the place."

"It could work," I said, mulling it over. The plan sounded surprisingly simple, but maybe that was the key to it.

"It will," she said. "It has to."

The clock tower bells began to toll in the distance, interrupting our conversation. Class was about to begin.

"Go," she said. "I'll use my injury as an excuse, but you better get there on time."

"Let me know when it's going to happen," I said.

She nodded, and I darted across the lawn toward Spectrum, trailing a mishmash of conflicting emotions. I wanted to be a Revenant, but Link was right. It was time to keep my own council—do what I thought was right. I'd been wrong to trust Zane so easily. It was a lesson I didn't plan to repeat.

FORTY

Madden

Three days after meeting with Dax, I'd been given the coordinates of where to drop Aya. It was in the Purple zone, not far from the Crimson border. The meet was for today. Even though I felt slightly guilty about it, I asked Sol to get involved. I needed a driver who would cross out of Purple with the young girl and not make a big deal about it. Bastin's friend, Brine, had originally been assigned to the job, but I knew he'd never go along with the plan. Instead I had him taken off of my detail, saying I was too uncomfortable working with an ex's confidant. I then recommended Sol for the job. After his "heroic" actions at the UV building, I was able to convince the PAE and my father to give him clearance to be my chauffer. Sol was more than happy to take part; I just hated pulling him into another plan that could land him in trouble. But I needed Zane to think I was escorting Aya to him, then trigger an alarm en route so we'd never show up. Without a cooperative driver the plan failed, and I couldn't afford that. Did I think this would solve the bigger issue, or keep Zane from blackmailing me again? No. But it did what I needed it to do for the time being. It bought me time and kept Aya safe.

The doorbell rang at exactly noon and despite the tension, I found myself nodding in approval. Timeliness was something I always appreciated. I walked down the stairs right as Nora was opening the door. Aya stood there in a violet knee length dress, her dark ringlets framing a huge grin. She was a tiny thing, barely reaching Nora's chest, and brimming with enthusiasm.

"Hi Madden!" she hollered up at me, hopping up and down as she waved.

"Hi Aya," I replied, smiling at her excitement. I held my own dress up as I walked down the stairs.

Nora invited Aya's two escorts in. One followed, the other waited outside our door. I'd gone to great pains to detail how I'd ensure Aya's safety at all times before her team agreed to the outing. I told them it was important for young Purple leaders to stick together, and that after a nice lunch at Perse Manor, I'd take Aya on a private tour of the UV. Once we left my house, we'd be on our own. The guards weren't too pleased with the idea of me being alone with Aya, but my clearance made it hard to refuse. It also helped that her parents were happy for her to get out. Aya's high security made her somewhat of a social pariah among her classmates, so they were pleased to see their daughter get an invitation. I hated that I was going to break the rules and appear untrustworthy, but it couldn't be helped, I reminded myself.

"May I take anything for you, Aya?" Nora asked.

"I'm fine, thank you," Aya chirped back.

"Well in that case, your lunch is all ready. I'll bring it to you both in the sunroom." Nora gave me a quick smile before heading back toward the kitchen, taking the guard with her.

I turned back to Aya. "Welcome to Perse Manor. I'm glad you

could come over. And I can't wait to show you the UV building later."

"Thanks for having me," Aya said. "I was so excited when my parents said it was okay."

"You're welcome," I said. "It's good to shake up your routine, right?" I felt my heart thud. I wondered if her parents would ever let her out again after I took her on an unauthorized trip to Crimson. "So tell me," I continued. "How have you been?"

She gestured to her tracker excitedly. "Good! I have new game I'm playing. I can show you if you want?"

I laughed. "I'd love to see it. How about we have lunch first?"

"Sure," she said, and followed as I led her from the foyer. Our footsteps echoed off of the marble floor as we walked down the hallway to my favorite part of the house, the sunroom. It was a circular room located in the far south quarter. The walls and ceiling were made almost completely out of glass. Center Lake lapped ten feet from the edge of the windows and sunlight streamed through the crystal chandeliers overhead, sending rainbow prisms bouncing over the floors.

"Wow," Aya said. "That's an ultra view."

"Thanks," I said. "I think so too."

Nora brought us sandwiches, and Aya told me about how hard it was to have guards following her all the time. "I can't wait for my Destiny Day. My parents never let me do anything without either one of them there, or my security detail."

Now that I knew Aya's destiny, I wondered how she'd managed to keep it to herself for so long. It must have been hard for someone her age. It was a secret that would have rocked our entire society if it got out. No use dwelling on it now, though. Instead I offered her a bright smile. "Well, parents know best, right?"

She laughed while inside I cringed. After today, my father would be very disappointed in me. I knew better than to bring

Aya outside of Purple, but I had to keep her from getting hurt. She was such a tiny thing. I couldn't let Zane get anywhere close to her, and if that meant looking untrustworthy to my dad and the PAE, then it was worth it.

As Aya and I finished our lunch, I got a ping from Sol.

"Outside now," he wrote.

"Be out soon," I replied.

I looked at Aya, trying to cover my worry with a smile. "Ready for your tour of the UV building?" I asked. I felt my stomach twist. The plan was in place. Nothing would go wrong, I reminded myself.

"Yep!" Aya said. She sprung up from her seat at the table, her dress flouncing around her knees.

"Great," I said, standing to join her. I forced myself to relax. My shoulders were practically bunched up to my ears I was so tense. Everything would be okay. It was just a drive. One that would end with PAE officers swarming our vehicle.

Nora met us at the front door again, fussing over my dress and making sure we'd gotten enough to eat. I think she could tell I was upset about something. She always could.

"We're fine, Nora," I said.

"Alright then," she said easily. "You girls enjoy the rest of your day."

She waved as Aya's security guard followed us out to the waiting black car. He opened the back passenger side door. Aya's other officer was standing by the driver's window, apparently giving Sol the third degree.

"We're fine, I've got it from here," I said to the officers. I tapped my tracker. "You'll know where we are at all times."

Aya hopped into the car.

"Take care of her," the one closest to me said.

"I promise," I said, following her inside.

I couldn't see Sol through the screen separating the passengers and driver, but I knew he would be nodding in agreement. I wished he'd left the divider down, but keeping up appearances in front of Purples—even a young Purple—was important.

I considered telling Aya that we were making a stop in Crimson, but I thought better of it. She knew very well that she wasn't supposed to go there, and if she voiced her concerns, the PAE would come down harder on Sol and me later for breaking the rules. Instead, I had her show me her game to keep her distracted from our route.

She lit up at the chance to show it. After a few touches to her tracker a small 3D city sprang to life. Seven buildings, each at various heights, stood in a perfectly rendered circle. Each one flashed a color of the ring, all in seizure-inducing patterns. "It's called New Ville," she said. "It lets you build a city and then you get to run it. Right now I'm playing Ministry Mode. See, first you have to develop the land. And then you make a settlement, which is really hard. At first I couldn't figure out how to fit the Ash zone in and all of the settlers kept dying. If you don't have all the rings your city fails."

I nodded. "That's a good metaphor. The more the rings can work together, the stronger the city will become," I said, keeping one eye on Aya, the other out the window. We were just about to the border, which meant we were about to cause a huge spectacle with officers speeding to our car.

"Right," she said. "This is the longest I've been able to keep it going. I just got my first Destiny badge today. You have to have…"

I tuned her out as Sol took a sharp right, avoiding Crimson. I leaned forward, rapping on the glass. "You missed the turn," I said, my voice shrill.

I heard a whining sound and then the separator slid down. I didn't know what Sol was playing at. He knew how serious this was. As the panel came to a rest I stiffened, clutching the leather seat under me.

"Yes, ma'am," Zane said from the front seat. His eyes met mine in the rearview mirror, and he touched the brim of his chauffer's hat. "I know a shortcut, don't you worry."

FORTY-ONE

—

Dax

Any minute now, Aya would be safe. I was too wound up thinking about Zane and what was about to happen to stay at home, so I decided to catch the action first hand. I sat in a bench at an air rail stop by the Purple/Crimson border. It was near where Sol and Madden planned to drive by and set off Aya's security alarms. I glanced at my tracker. There was still a little time. Yesterday at school, Sol told me he'd be leaving Madden's place at 1pm.

My tracker buzzed. It was another ping from Theron. He'd written repeatedly to ask how I was doing, but I never responded. Each message felt like a small stab. I knew he was trying to prove he cared, but being around him—even just pinging or holo-talking—was too hard when I knew we couldn't be together. Besides, I wanted to keep him out of my mess of Revenants and fake kidnappings and lies. At least until Madden came clean.

Theron hadn't been the only one trying to get in touch with

me. I had a bunch of pings from Laira. I'd been avoiding her since she went off about destiny breakers and my brother. But I had to give her credit, she was trying. She'd pinged me daily to check in, even going so far as to keep her destiny beliefs out of it. Maybe I'd been too hard on her. It wasn't her fault she believed all the lies the government told her. She tried to be a good friend, and it wasn't like I could push everyone away. I wrote her back and told her we would hang out soon.

Then I checked the time again. Sol should have driven past already. I punched up his location in my tracker to see how far off he was, but it still showed him in the garage. That couldn't be right. He would have left for Madden's estate way before now. He wouldn't risk being late, especially not when it was this important.

Before I even realized it, my feet were moving in Sol's direction. I watched the geolocator, and kept going, following Sol's glowing dot until I was at the government garage.

It was an open-air facility. Sunlight streamed in through the concrete beams around me, casting long shadows. The vehicles here were each locked into individual safety cubes making it impossible to access them unless you had an entry code. I had never seen so many cars all at once. There were about fifty of them lined up, and that was just the first floor. Of course there were officers who drove around in government-issued models, but it was rare to see so many in the open. With the exception of Madden, I didn't know anyone who rode in one. The light rail was the normal mode of transportation, except by the most elite.

"Hello?" I called out. The concrete carried my voice. There was no response. I walked to where the tracker showed Sol should have been. It was an empty parking space, with a storage locker behind.

"Sol?" I called softly. "Are you here?"

Still nothing. I checked my tracker again. I pinged him. "Sol?"

I heard a ding and followed the sound to the next parking space.

"Where are you?" I called louder this time.

That's when I saw him. He was curled on his side behind a parked van, his wrists bound behind his back, a cloth gagging his mouth.

"No," I heard myself say as I ran to his side. "No, no, no, no. This can't be happening."

His body was limp and his hair matted to his head. I touched it and my hand came away smeared with blood. I forced myself to stay calm. He was breathing. That was the important part. Stay calm, I reminded myself. I needed to make sure he was okay and that he wasn't still bleeding. I lifted his head from the floor as gently as possible. I gasped when I saw the lump swelling off the back of his skull. His hair was plastered with blood, but it was starting to dry.

I untied the gag, then the binding around his wrists. My fingers stumbled over the knots. I was beginning to panic when I heard him moan.

"Sol," I said, leaning down over him. "Are you okay?"

"Dax? What are you doing here?" He winced as he tried to move. "Where am I? What happened?"

"You're in the garage," I told him. "Someone attacked you. How do you feel?"

"Awful." He groaned as he pulled himself up to a sitting position. "My head is killing me." He closed his eyes, squinting against the pain.

"Do you remember anything?" I asked him.

"Just getting to the car." His words slurred slightly as he spoke. "I was opening the door and then I don't know what happened," he trailed off, once again opening his eyes to register the empty parking space beside us. "The car's gone."

We just looked at each other. The fear settled over his face—I knew it reflected my own.

"Where's Madden?" he asked.

"I don't know," I said. "She's out of my ping circle. I can't see her location."

Sol's face scrunched up in pain and he held the back of his head. "We have to get you help," I told him.

"No," he said, "It's not me I'm worried about." He squinted down at his tracker, tapping slowly. He looked up, confused. "It says Madden's at the UV."

I shook my head. "If you didn't come for her, she'd be looking for you, not giving Aya a tour."

"Zane," he said. "Somehow he must have found out what we were planning."

"But how could he have known?"

"I don't know," Sol said. "I have to find them. I need my plexi." He looked around him.

My eyes darted around the garage. "Where is it?" I got up, doing a quick inspection. "I don't see anything."

"In my bag." His eyes fogged with pain and he struggled to stay focused. "It's in the car. I put the bag in the trunk."

"Okay," I said. I wasn't sure what to do.

"That's a good thing," he said, his voice getting more animated. "I should be able to track my bag, which means we can find the car." Once again Sol tapped onto his tracker until it projected a map. A stationary purple dot glowed near the Purple running trails.

"That's not too far from here. I know the area," I said. "It's where I met the Revenants last. That must be where he's taking them."

"We need to call the PAE," Sol said. "Get them there before anything happens."

"We can't. If Zane sees the PAE, who knows what he'll do. He'll probably kill everyone—starting with Aya."

"Then what?"

"I don't know. But the PAE isn't the answer. They're the same people who want to kill Link and all the Revenants. They're not exactly the good guys."

"So what are we supposed to do?" Sol asked. "I don't even think I can stand. You can't go after Zane by yourself."

"I'll ping Link. He can meet me there."

"You can't. It will ruin any surprise advantage we still have. They're monitoring everything, Dax. They must be. Otherwise how did they find out our plans?"

"Then I guess that leaves me."

"Dax," he said, trying to get to his feet and failing. "Don't even think about it—it's crazy. You can't stop him on your own."

Maybe he was right, but did I have a choice?

FORTY-TWO

Madden

I wanted to scream, but I couldn't—not in front of Aya. I had to stay calm. I'd been trained to act composed in stressful situations. Despite my façade on the outside, on the inside I was panicked.

How had Zane gotten here? What had happened to Sol? Had Zane killed him?

I couldn't think that way. I tried to ping Sol, my father, Dax, anyone using my tracker, but it wouldn't go through. I looked at the geolocator. It showed we were already at the UV, the opposite of where we were really going. Maybe someone would notice that we never arrived. Even if they didn't, Aya had her chip. It was just a matter of moments until her team noticed it didn't match the tracker coordinates. I had to stay calm until then.

"Aya," I said. "I have some ministry business to finish up before we get to the UV. Do you mind putting up your sound cloud for a moment?"

"Okay," she said.

She tapped her tracker and a ripple of air whooshed around her. The cloud guaranteed that my conversation would remain private. Even so, I spoke in a harsh whisper to Zane.

"Where's Sol?" I asked.

"Where I left him."

"Is he okay?"

"Okay is such a relative word."

I wanted to reach over the seat and throttle him, but I needed to keep my cool. Both for Aya's sake, and so that I wouldn't set Zane off. "Is he alive?"

"I can't give away all of my secrets." He winked at me through the mirror, making my skin prickle. Sol had to be okay. Zane wouldn't be this nonchalant if he murdered him, would he? My head was spinning. I needed to get Aya out of here. Now.

"It's not too late," I said. "Pull over and leave us here. You can get away before the PAE arrives."

"You must still think you're getting saved." He gave a hearty laugh. "Typical Purple mindset, underestimating those born below you. Given your actual standing, you really should reconsider some of those values."

He was wrong, I knew he what he was capable of. He was Blank. But he was forgetting, so was I. "They'll be here."

"Counting on her chip?"

My body tensed up.

"Yeah, I know about that," he said. "Amazing what you can learn when you have access to a minister's accounts. Thanks for that by the way."

I glanced at Aya who was still engrossed in her game. This was all my fault. She had no idea what was going on, no idea of the danger we were in.

"What are you going to do to her?" I asked.

"You're a smart girl, figure it out."

The look on his face told me enough. If I didn't do something soon, Aya and I might not come back from this drive. The car was moving slowly. Zane was probably afraid to get pulled over after what happened at Laira's Destiny Day. I could use that to my advantage. I just had to open the door, grab Aya and jump. Hopefully my body would cushion her fall. I reached for the handle, but the door wouldn't budge.

A flicker of amusement passed over Zane's face. "You really think I wouldn't see that coming?" he asked.

I hated him more by the second. Aya and I were prisoners. A few turns later and we were surrounded by bushes, trees, and dirt. There were no homes or people in sight. We were on the outskirts of Purple, beyond the normal walking trails. I never came this far out. There had never been a reason.

"We're here," he said, turning to look at Aya. "Time to say your goodbyes."

"Wait," I said as he opened his door. "I have a better idea. It can help you, the Revenants *and* keep Aya safe."

"Go on," he said.

"Not here," I said. "We should talk away from her in case she takes down her cloud."

"Don't think I don't know what you're doing. Trying to buy time. But what's a few minutes? I'll admit I'm curious to see what another Blank mind can come up with." He looked at me knowingly. "I'm telling you Madden, when the Purples cast you aside, you'll need an ally. Like is drawn to like."

I'd never work with him. I'd never hurt a child—no matter what it could do for me. I might have been a Blank, but I still knew what was right.

I waved at Aya to get her attention and gestured to let her know I'd be back in a minute. I hoped she'd see the fear in my eyes and somehow understand the need to run. Instead she looked up and nodded happily before going back to her game. I walked out of her view, about twenty feet, with Zane at my side. I looked for a rock or stick or something I could use to fight him, but there was nothing I could reach without him noticing.

"This is far enough," he said. He glanced down at his tracker and opened his screen to a timer. "One minute," he said, tapping in the number. "I do hope you make it interesting." The seconds began to tick down. "Fifty-eight," he prodded. "Fifty-seven."

"You can use me," I spoke as fast as I could, "I'll get bills reformed, I'll make it legal for the Revenants to live wherever they want. Then it won't matter if Aya knows where you are."

"Bills take too long. And they'd never pass. Try again. Forty seconds."

"I'll tell everyone the truth. If my destiny was messed up, maybe other people's were too. They'll want to know. It will cripple the system."

"The Seven will spin it as a fluke," he replied. "There won't be any discord. If there is, the PAE will have the troublemakers removed in minutes." He studied the numbers as they continued to tick down. "Fifteen seconds left. I have to say, this is all a little disappointing. It's like you're not even trying."

The only other thing I could do was beg. "Please," I said, "she's just a little girl. She doesn't want to hurt anyone. What if..." an idea finally hit me, one that could actually save Aya. "What if we let her lead people to one Revenant: Me. I'm already helping you. I'll officially become a Revenant, and Aya can expose me. This can work."

He cocked his head, thinking it over. "Not a bad idea. But exposing one leads to exposing us all."

I started to speak again as the timer hit zero, but Zane shushed me. "You knew the rules. And your time is up." He took out his gun.

FORTY-THREE

—

Dax

A black car was parked near the trail. I snuck toward it, darting from tree to tree, doing my best to stay hidden. I stepped as lightly as I could over the fallen leaves and stones. I grabbed a large rock as I neared, adding it to the collection in my backpack I'd gathered on the way over. As weapons went it wasn't much, but I could improvise if it came down to it. I hoped.

As I approached, I glanced into the car. A little girl sat in the back, huddled over some kind of holograph game. I felt the weight in my chest lighten just a bit. Aya was alive. I crept closer and ducked down near the passenger side to open the door. It was locked. I considered trying to get her attention, but was distracted by voices arguing. I peeked over the car, but I couldn't see anything from where I was. I crept closer, hiding behind a tree stump. The scene playing out in front of me looked grim. Madden was waving her hands in Zane's face, trying to block his path as he headed back in Aya's direction. Her face was twisted into a kind of snarl.

"I'm not going to let you hurt her," I heard her say.

"You're not really in a position to make demands," Zane replied. A gun dangled from his hand.

Don't do anything stupid, Madden, I willed her.

She didn't heed my silent warning. Instead, she lunged at Zane, knocking them both—and his gun—to the ground. Zane might have been thrown off, but as Madden reached for the weapon, he easily beat her to it.

He stood up, brushing the leaves from his pants. "My thanks for that. You know, I had planned to keep you alive for a little while longer. Hoped you'd make yourself useful, but it's probably easier this way."

He aimed his gun at her head, his finger twitching at the trigger. He was going to shoot her. I couldn't wait any longer.

"Stop," I said, revealing myself.

Zane's eyes darted toward me, momentarily taking his eyes off of Madden. His aim didn't waver. "Dax," he said. "Joining our little party?"

"What are you doing?" I asked, feigning shock. "You can't shoot Madden. We need her. For your plan to work, for me to take over as the future minister, we need her alive."

"Dead or alive, it's all the same," he said.

Madden was watching me. The look in her eyes made me think that if I didn't come up with something soon, she'd try to take Zane out again. Only this time she would wind up with a bullet in her head.

"No, it's not," I said moving toward them. "If she's killed before I tell everyone the truth, they'll never believe it. They'll think I murdered her and faked the evidence about our destiny swap. They'd never trust me. Not with her gone."

He turned his gaze to me. "Tell me, are you really concerned about the cause? Or are you just trying to save this Purple?"

I knew what he wanted to hear. "The cause."

"And you had nothing to do with this?" He waved his gun around, toward Madden, toward the car, toward me. "This ridiculous rescue plan?"

"Rescue plan?" I repeated, doing my best to sound confused as I walked closer to them.

He shook his head. "I've been tracking your whereabouts. And I know who you talk to. You've spent quite a bit of time with the Ash. The one I took care of today."

"Sol's dead?" Madden started to stand, but Zane flicked the gun back in her direction.

"Don't worry," he answered. "You'll be joining him soon enough."

The color drained from Madden's face. I wanted to tell her that Sol was okay, but at the moment, the only thing that mattered was keeping her and Aya alive.

I forced myself to meet his eyes and smile. "Zane, think about it. Sol and Madden are the only people who actually know the truth about my status. Or who I can talk to about Link." I gestured to Madden. "But she's too high and mighty to have a normal conversation with, which just leaves Sol. So, yeah, I've spent time with him. It doesn't mean anything."

Zane considered this. "You realize between the two of them, they'd almost ruined everything we've been working toward?"

I pretended to hang on his words. "What do you mean?" I asked.

He glanced down at Madden, his expression darkening. "If they'd had their way, that little girl would have been the death of us all."

I didn't like the way he was looking at Madden. I stalled. "How did you figure out their plan?"

"Once she responded to my first ping, I gained access to her tracker. It was easy enough to put the pieces together from there." He reached out, grabbing Madden's hair to yank her head back. "I would advise considerably more caution in your future, short as it may be."

"Please," I said. "Let her go. *My* future, my destiny depends on it."

"Then she needs to stay out of my way. Aya is going to bring down the Revenants. I need to stop her. One for the many." He waited for me to object. When I didn't, he continued, "You want to save this pretender, fine." He pulled Madden back again. "But you keep her still, while I do what needs to be done. Deal?"

"Deal," I said. I tugged Madden up from the ground and made a show of shoving her arms behind her back.

"No," she screamed as Zane headed to the car.

As soon as his back was to us, I let her go and grabbed a rock the size of my fist from my bag. I slammed it into the back of Zane's head. Probably just like he did to Sol.

"I should have known," he seethed. He had one hand pressed to his head, the other swinging the gun wildly in my direction. "I should have gotten rid of you like I did your brother."

"Link?" Madden said, her voice a whisper.

I recoiled, and Zane just laughed. "The other one. The racer."

"Aldan?" I asked, confused. "His death was an accident. We all saw it."

"You saw what I wanted you to see." He glared at both of us, his hand squeezing the handle of the gun. I'd hurt him with the rock, but it just slowed him down. "He planned to make it a joke. Stop at the top of the track for a little longer than he should, then win the race. Thought it would make a statement."

Zane continued to ramble on, and my chest was suddenly too tight to breath.

"He was always coming down to the underground. He didn't belong. But my sister insisted. Said he could help. Could be the future face of the Revenants. Well, I helped that along. Rigged his board to lock after he was stationary for more than two minutes. When he tried to go down the last drop, he'd be stuck and ultimately lose the race. Missing his destiny by choice. Now *that's* a statement! Had the PAE not caught me and my stolen toys, there would have been an even bigger finale. The whole loop track set to explode. Now that would have been something, though I'd say the ending was still memorable, all things considered."

I tried to say something, but I was at a loss. I opened my mouth, then closed it again, unable to find the words.

When someone finally did speak, it wasn't me. It was Oena, who was crawling out of the tunnels that were just behind Zane. "I don't believe you," she said, disbelief catching at her voice. "Aldan was helping us." Her voice escalated as she stalked toward him. "He was helping the cause. Helping because *you* asked him to!"

Thom, Raze, and finally Link climbed up after her. There was a part of me that was desperately relieved to see them. But that part was muffled by Zane's confession. He was a monster.

Zane turned, his gun aimed toward the new arrivals. He shrugged. "No one is above the cause, sis. Especially not some celebrity Purple."

"I loved him," Oena said, her voice cracking.

"We've all had to make sacrifices. This is war. And right now, our survival is in the hands of an eight-year-old. Since none of you have the guts to do what needs to be done, I'll take care of it myself. You can thank me later." He started to move toward Aya.

"Stop," Oena said, pulling out her own gun to point toward her brother.

He turned back, aiming his gun at her. "I don't want to hurt you, Oena."

"You should have thought of that before you executed the best chance we had for acceptance," she said. "Aldan was going to help us come out. We had plans, Zane. Good ones. That didn't involve killing anyone, let alone innocents."

"Grow up, Oena. This isn't a Purple fairy tale. This is life, and if you want something, you have to take it. It's time for the Revenants to come to power. This girl is a threat. She can expose us. I'm not going to let that happen, not even for you. Now stand down."

"No," she said. Both of Oena's hands were on her gun, trying to keep herself from shaking.

Hesitation flickered over her face. *Shoot him,* I silently screamed.

Zane's gun was still trained on her. "You know I'm a much better shot than you."

"You wouldn't."

He studied her. "I suppose you're right about that. We all have a weakness."

Zane moved quicker than I could have imagined. One minute his gun was trained on Oena, the next he lunged toward Madden, twisting her body in front of his. She struggled against him, but she was pinned too tightly to get away.

"Maybe I can't shoot you, Oena," Zane said, "but I have no problem getting rid of this one." He held the gun to Madden's temple, dragging her backward, toward Aya. "Let me finish this so we can be on our way."

"Zane stop, I'm warning you," she said.

He shook his head. "You won't shoot me either. Besides, you wouldn't risk hitting the Purple. You're good Oena, but you're not that good."

"Luckily I am." It was Thom. He took the gun from Oena and fired.

FORTY-FOUR

Madden

I felt Zane's body jerk away from mine. His hands released their grip on my arms, and I stumbled away from him in terror.

He howled as he dropped to the ground, one hand pressed over the hole blasted through his shoulder. Blood seeped from the wound, dripping from his fingers. It splattered over the fallen leaves. His gun lay beside him.

"Leave it," Thom ordered. He took a step toward Zane.

"Why stop now?" Zane spat at him through clenched teeth. "Complete your destiny. Or get out of my way."

It happened in a flash.

Oena yelled for her brother to stop. Zane lunged toward the gun. Thom bridged the distance between them in three giant steps, kicking Zane square in the face. Bones crunched as his foot made contact. Zane's head snapped back, the momentum knocking him down with a heavy thump.

My whole body heaved as I scrambled further away from the fight. I couldn't rip my eyes from Zane's motionless body. *Was he still alive?* I wondered, and then immediately felt sick. Had the bullet hit two inches to the left earlier, it might have been me lying there.

"Hey," Link said, rushing over. "It's okay, you're okay." He put his arms around me, and I fell into him. He squeezed tighter, and I took in his familiar scent. I just wanted to get lost in it, get lost in him, but I knew I had to pull it together. Aya was still in the car, there was an unconscious, possibly dead man at my feet, and a bunch of Revenants out in the open. Now was not the time to break down.

"I'm fine," I told him. I let myself soak in the warmth of his body for a few more seconds before I pulled away. "Is Zane alive?" Raze was hunched over his body, wrapping a jacket around his shoulder.

Thom shook his head. "Yes," he said, his voice emotionless. "I'm not a killer." He might not have been one, but he certainly looked the part, his expression grim with a gun in each hand. The one he fired and the one Zane discarded. But it didn't matter how he appeared, the reality was, he saved my life.

Everyone went quiet as Oena joined Raze by her brother. She wiped his hair from his forehead before closing her eyes.

"The bleeding's stopped," Raze broke the silence. "He's still out cold and his shoulder's pretty torn up, but he'll survive. Knowing him, he'll probably even brag about it. Just another battle scar."

"Wait," I said, horrified. "You're just going to act like he did nothing wrong? Go back to normal? Like he didn't try to kill me? Kill Aya?"

"What would you have us do?" Raze replied. "Send him back to the holding cells? Your secret would be out the minute Zane came to. Or maybe you'd rather we get it over with and kill him right here?"

I held up my hands as if I could somehow fend off her words. "I didn't say I wanted him dead. But you can't just let him go. What if he comes after Aya again, or—"

Oena cut me off. "Zane will be dealt with." There was a kind of bitter finality to her words "He's going to the crypts."

Raze looked taken aback, but a moment later she nodded her agreement.

"The crypts?" I asked.

"Our prison system. Makes the holding cells look like a Purple dream," Oena said. "Don't worry. None of you will see my brother again."

I wanted to believe her, but I didn't know if I could. Zane was smart. He'd fooled all of us. More times than I could count. "He got out of one secure prison," I told her. "What's to stop him from pulling another escape?"

"Me," she said. "This time, I'll be watching. He won't hurt another soul. I promise you that." She paused to take a deep breath. "And I'm sorry for what happened today, Madden. For all of it." Her expression was guarded, but I recognized the look. I wore my own version when things were falling apart and I needed to appear in control. "You've been a help to us. Zane shouldn't have used you like that."

I felt a sudden wave of sympathy for her. It had to be hard to come to grips with the fact that her brother was responsible for Aldan's death. I tried to remember that as I spoke. "It's not your fault. I'm just glad Thom is a skilled shot."

"I've had a lot of practice," he replied in his stony voice. "I started training at five years old."

I let out a gasp. Five? That was impossible. Only the PAE and authorized officials had access to firearms. A child would never be allowed to use one.

He saw the confusion on my face. "My destiny is to kill," he continued. "No time stamp. No expiration. It's why I defected. The PAE thought I'd make a good weapon. They gave me a gun when most kids were still learning their alphabet. But I never wanted to fight, let alone murder anyone."

My father was in charge of national security. Did he know about this? Was he responsible for putting a gun in a child's hand? I didn't know what to say.

Dax chimed in softly. "Well, what you did today saved lives. Thank you." Her eyes panned over the Revenants and Link. "All of you. I didn't know what to do when I saw Sol..."

I swallowed the lump that was forming in my throat.

Dax looked over at me. "He's fine," she said quickly. "He's alive. I found him in the garage. It's how I knew where you'd be. Zane hit him over the head. He was still groggy when I left him there."

I closed my eyes and breathed in deeply. Sol was okay. I instantly felt lighter. Another question struck me. I looked down at my tracker, realizing it still showed my location at the UV. "How did he find us?" I asked.

"His bag's in the trunk. He used it to track you. On my way here, I pinged Link."

I nodded, piecing it together. We'd been lucky. But we'd made it. "Thank you," I said to Dax. "For everything."

She gave me a smile. A genuine one. "Well, the way you fought for Aya… that was pretty ultra."

Before either of us had a chance to say anything else, Link stepped in. "You two need to get out of here. We don't want anyone to notice you're not where you're supposed to be." He walked toward Zane's still body. "And we should get him underground before he wakes up."

I looked back at the car. "What about Aya?" I asked. "Are we sure she's safe?"

Oena answered. "She should be. If Zane didn't share his plans with us, he wouldn't have shared them with anyone. No one else knows about her destiny." Her eyes narrowed. "Though you should still watch out for her. There are others who are just as good as Zane at finding hidden information."

I nodded, my entire body charged with emotions. Relief that Zane was no longer a threat, but anxious about the future. My life as I knew it was about to end. But that was for another time. Today I'd won. And Aya had too.

We said our goodbyes. Link, Oena, and Raze stayed behind, standing over Zane, probably trying to figure out the best way to move him. Thom took over as my driver. Dax promised to check on Sol before continuing down the running trail. Which just left me.

As I climbed back into the car, Aya looked up, her eyes glazed. She turned off her sound cloud, holding her game up for me to inspect. She had no clue what had gone on.

"I'm back at the beginning," she said, looking at the holograph. "I have to start building New City from scratch again."

"What happened?" I asked.

"I didn't have enough food in the lower rings, so I took some away from the upper rings, but that didn't go over so well. The Purples revolted, and I lost my badges because of it."

"I'm sorry," I said.

"That's okay," she said. "This time I'll make sure the lower rings have enough from the start. It will be better than before. I'll do it right this time."

"Sounds good," I said.

Too bad the game wasn't real life. A do-over sounded like

exactly what New City needed. Like what I needed too. Instead, I was going to be stuck with the rest of the unwanteds in Ash. I needed to come up with a plan. Just like the game, I needed to make New City mine again.

FORTY-FIVE

—

Dax

Nervous energy ran up my spine, and I grabbed Aldan's purple cuff to calm myself down. I had worn it under my gray shirt. Partially for luck, partially to keep my brother with me, and partially to remind myself who I really I was.

I turned to Madden. If she was as anxious as I was it didn't show. "You really think our Destiny Specialist is here?" I asked. I stood on my tiptoes, trying to see beyond the hedges surrounding the property. I could just make out the gabled rooftop of Dr. Og's home.

"Yes," she said. "K.C. Palcove lives with Og. Sol triple checked."

I couldn't believe we were about to confront the woman who altered our whole lives. Especially in the home of the man who created the destiny system. Hopefully this meant the truth would finally come out. It meant a whole new beginning for me. But for Madden… I wondered if she regretted her decision to look into what happened the day we were born.

After we were sure Aya was okay, Madden turned her focus to figuring out why our destinies were swapped. I expected it to be a lost cause, but less than twenty-four hours later she'd tracked the woman at the center of the situation down. Now here we were at the front gate of a minister's mansion.

"You ready?" Madden asked.

I wasn't sure. But I knew I needed answers. I just hoped K.C. Palcove would provide them. I nodded to Madden, and she reached out a violet nail to tap the intercom beside the gate.

I looked around uneasily as we waited. We were in the very center of the Purple zone, and the most exclusive residential neighborhood in the city. It was strangely quiet here. There were no voices, no people. Then again, there was probably less commotion when your nearest neighbor's mansion was a five minute walk away. "I kinda expected guards," I said, careful to keep my voice steady. "Or something."

"He knows we're here," Madden said. She nodded toward the hovercams hidden within the branches nearby. The gate swung open as if to prove the point.

We stood there, waiting, but no instructions came. No voice telling us to come in or go away or anything. We exchanged a long look. Madden wore her usual haughty expression, but I could see the tightness in her face. I guessed she was probably just as freaked out as I was, but then she seemed to make a decision. She strode forward like she owned the place, tossing her hair over her shoulder. I walked beside her, trying to look confident. More like a future Minister. Although it was hard not to gape at my first uninterrupted view of the mansion.

It stood at the end of a long, winding driveway, a lavender, three-story structure with dark purple shutters surrounding the windows on each level. A balcony wrapped around each floor and tens of thousands of purple flowers draped over the sides. A huge expanse of perfectly manicured lawn stretched out around it. I couldn't believe people lived like this. That I would have lived like this, if destiny had gone as it should.

As we got closer to the house I noticed that the flowers weren't as uniform as they'd appeared from the distance. Peeking through the sea of purple were unruly bursts of red and yellow. There were even colors I rarely saw, like orange and pink. Stranger still, the purple flowers had light veins of gray running through their petals. Almost silver in hue. They were two colors that didn't belong together.

When we reached the house, Madden's pace slowed. She fidgeted with the sleeve of her shirt. "Here we go," she said. I wasn't sure if she was trying to convince herself, but whatever she felt, she still sounded exactly like Madden always did—in control.

I tried to mimic her attitude, though inside I was starting to panic.

I walked up the half dozen steps to the porch two at a time, noting the wheelchair lift along the railing. Before we had a chance to ring the bell, a woman, old enough to be my grandmother, opened the door. I recognized her from the picture Madden had shown me earlier that morning. She'd been Dr. Og's personal caretaker for the past few years, though she didn't look like any sort of nurse I'd ever seen. She wore a purple tunic, and a long, white braid hung over her shoulder. Purple flowers had been threaded in and out of the overlapping sections of hair—they were the same ones we'd passed on the walk up. She was a lot older than the photo I'd seen, but she still had the same wide set eyes and square face.

She looked back and forth between us, her expression wary. Most people would have been surprised by an Ash and a Purple standing together, but I could tell she was seeing more than just our colors. "Hello, Madden," she said. She turned to me, tilting her head to one side. "And you must be Dax. It's nice to see you again."

See me again? I sucked in my breath. She knew who I was. What were you supposed to say to the person who took away your standing in the world? "Then you know who I am?" I asked, my words coming out strangled. "And why we're here?"

K.C.'s entire body seemed to wilt a little. She reached one arm out to rest against the doorframe, steadying herself. "I wondered if you would learn what happened, if you'd ever seek me out."

"That's all you have to say?" Madden asked. Gone was the composed mask. I could tell she was fighting not to yell. "All those times I'd see you accompany Dr. Og to the ministry meetings, K.C., you never once thought to tell me the truth?"

"I couldn't. I had to let it unfold naturally," she replied.

My heart was racing and my chest felt too tight, like I had to strain to keep breathing. This woman had actually switched our destinies. "How could you do something like that?" I asked, reeling. "You ruined my life. The lives of my family. Why?"

K.C. struggled to find the right words. "It couldn't be helped. It wasn't my decision." She looked down, her face twisted in misery. "How did you figure it out?"

"You made a mistake," Madden replied. "You left a time stamp for my birth on my mother's file. It led me to Dax. Once we realized there were discrepancies with our destinies, we knew if we wanted answers we had to track down the Specialist who oversaw both of the extractions. Her name was Karina Palcove. Only it looked like she'd disappeared. I couldn't find anything on her. It would have been a dead end, except I recognized the name. Turns out it's the same as the author of a book I've been reading."

Madden reached into her bag and pulled out Laira's destiny book. She flipped to the back, holding the book open to the 'About the Author' page just like she'd done when she'd shown me earlier that day.

"I realized the author looked just like the woman who worked as Og's caretaker," Madden continued. "That is to say, you."

The woman, K.C. Clifton, aka Karina Palcove, took the book from Madden, turning it over in her hands in shock. Her voice was hushed, almost reverent. "I didn't think there were any printed copies left. I can't believe you found this." She stepped back from the door and then looked at us still standing on the porch. "Please," she said, "let's talk about this inside."

Disbelief, shock and anger surged through me. This was it, everything was about to come out in the open. A part of me wanted to scream and shake the woman in front of me, another wanted to fling my arms around her, embrace her for telling the truth. Instead, I kept my cool and walked into the home of Dr. Jebidiah Og. The minister whose position that Madden—scratch that, *I*, Dax Harris—was slated to replace.

FORTY-SIX

Madden

I marched after K.C., my hands clenched into fists at my side. *Keep it together, Madden,* I told myself, breathing in through my nose and out through my mouth. My life was going to be officially destroyed over the next few minutes. But I would still handle it with dignity. I might have a Blank destiny. It didn't mean I had to act like it.

K.C. led us around the large staircase in the front of the house, toward a plush, rich purple-carpeted hallway. The sides of the carpet were trimmed with violet fleur-de-lis. The walls were painted to match. We passed several heavy-looking wooden doors—all closed—until K.C. paused in front of one. She pressed a button and it slid open.

I walked inside to find myself in an old-fashioned library. Hardbound books lined the shelves surrounding the room. An unlit fireplace took up an entire wall and several overstuffed chairs were scattered throughout. A vase of flowers sat on the table between the two sofas in the room's center. The entire room looked like something from a different century.

"Please, have a seat," K.C. said, motioning toward the sofas.

Dax rushed toward the closest one as if she couldn't wait to hear what K.C. would say. Who could blame her? She was about to get the most ultra life there was—mine. I followed more slowly, perching next to her on the edge of the leather cushion. I looked at K.C. as she sunk down across from us. Suddenly all I wanted was to get this over with.

There was no reason to mince words. She obviously knew why we were there. "You switched our destinies."

She nodded. "Yes, I did."

She said it so calmly, like she was talking about giving me the wrong type of tea, not about messing with my whole life. "But why?" I said. "Why would you do something like that?"

She raised her hands in a helpless shrug. "I didn't have a choice," she said.

"Of course you had a choice. There's always a choice," I told her, struggling to remain calm. I waited for her to continue, but she didn't.

Dax spoke instead. "I don't understand," she said. "My brother is a Destiny Specialist. He told me about the process. You wouldn't have been able to switch it without someone knowing."

She paused. "I had help."

"Who would help you with something like this?" I started, and then stopped, groping to find the words. "It could ruin our whole system, cause another Event. No one would risk that."

"Unless there was a reason for it," a deep, creaky voice replied.

I felt my jaw drop open as Dr. Og rolled into the library. He was dressed formally, in a rich, purple suit, his white hair neatly combed to one side. Even in his wheelchair, he maintained a commanding presence. He stopped beside K.C., reaching out to rest his age-spotted hand on top of hers. "I helped Karina cover it up."

"You?" I asked, my voice almost a whisper. "Why?"

"Because I believe in our system, Madden. I was trying to protect it."

I dug my fingers into the sofa cushions. "That doesn't make sense. If you believed, you never would have done something like that."

"Things are not always as they seem," he said.

He nodded at K.C., who took a deep breath before speaking.

"What you need to understand is that I had to do it," she said and paused, looking from me to Dax and back again. "It was my destiny to switch your destinies."

I felt chills go through my body.

"My destiny was one of the first ones ever extracted," she continued. "Og performed it actually. He was just fifteen at the time. A genius even then. He thought it best to keep it a secret, that it could cause trouble for me down the line, so he told everyone my destiny was to be a Specialist. When he told me the truth, I knew there wasn't a choice. I had to do what I was fated for, no matter the consequences."

My body felt heavy. K.C. had acted according to her destiny, and no matter how much I wished I could melt into the sofa, I had to face facts. "So that's it then." I turned to Dax. "You're the future minister. And I'm a Blank."

All I wanted at the moment was to go home, to hide in my bedroom behind a closed door. No witnesses to see the tears that were threatening to fall. I blinked rapidly, clearing my eyes.

Emotions warred in Dax's face as she watched me. This was the biggest moment of her life, but there was sympathy in her expression as well. Her pity made it that much worse, and I turned away.

"Not so fast," Dr. Og wheeled closer. His eyes were bright despite his years, and they bore into mine with a fierce intensity. "There's a reason Blanks have the reputation they do. They're important. You're important."

I looked at him with disbelief. "What are you talking about?"

He reached out and took my hand, pressing it between his own. "You *have* a destiny, Madden. All Blanks do. We just had to hide it—until now."

I heard Dax gasp beside me, and I felt my skin prickle. "What is it?"

The crease in his forehead deepened, and his voice got low. "To take down the destiny system."

About The Authors

Shani Petro is the author of the BEDEVILED series, which includes *Daddy's Little Angel, The Good, the Bad, and the Ugly Dress, Careful What You Wish For,* and *Love Struck.* She also writes for television news programs and several other venues. You can reach her at ShaniPetroff.com or on twitter: @shanipetroff.

Darci Manley works as a creative director, writing and designing for a NYC advertising agency. She is also the author of *A Defender's Tale,* a personalized, interactive adventure tale for the iPad. You can reach her at DarciManley. com or on twitter: @darcimanley.

Petroff and Manley live in New York City. They were destined to write a book series together.

Acknowledgments

ASH is much stronger because of the friends and family members who supported us along the way. Many, many thanks—your feedback and encouragement means a lot. You are, in a word, AMAZING!

Jason Pinter, thanks for believing in this project and for being all-around fantastic. ASH wouldn't be what it is without you and your team. Craig Cohen, thank you for your guidance and expertise in helping us navigate the publishing process. Jen Malone, your feedback was invaluable. This book would have ended in a very different way without your suggestions. And a shout out to Sammy Yuen for designing such a striking cover.

To Micol Ostow and the Mediabistro gang, some might say walking into that classroom was destiny—and the foundation for a very important new currency.

To our coworkers at Fox 5 News and thelab NYC, we heart you. This kind of project gobbles up a lot of time, and you helped us manage the juggling act.

Even more hearts go out to our friends. Both of us have been serious hermits and we've missed some important stuff—birthdays, anniversaries, nights out, girl gabbing marathons and more. But part of what makes you incredible is that you are all still right there, waiting for us on the other end.

A special thank you to Millie Sensat for thinking through flowers and typography, Ted Schantz for the photo shoot, Shana Grossman-Heller for her photo expertise, and Anna Schumacher for helping us sum it all up. Additional thanks to Nina Dinoff, Charla Myers, and Justin Hahn for being early readers and champions.

Lauren Scobell, you are an amazing cheerleader. Thank you for reading and rereading, talking through every last detail with us, and for being our go to on all things swoonworthy.

David Hohusen you are better than ultra. We don't know where we'd be without you. You are the master of tricky plot points and helping us get our thoughts in order. And Darci thinks you are some kind of dreamy husband, best friend, and confidante. Every single thing in her world is just a little better for sharing it with you.

To the rest of Darci's family, thank you. To Joy Manley, who taught Darci to love books and words and writing in general, and to Norm Manley, who taught her to laugh at the oddest of moments, and is still her favorite storyteller. To Katie Manley, for being a best friend along the way and a critical reader in the final hour. And to Darci's grandparents, Ed and Nancy Stewart, who always take the time to cheer her on. You are all so important and wonderful and supportive. She's lucky to call you all family… and share your kindle plan.

And to Shani's family—all the cousins, aunts, uncles, and Christina Park, who Shani sometimes forgets isn't actually her sister—thank you for always being there. To Marilyn, Jordan and Andrea Petroff, your love and unwavering support is tireless. She is lucky to have you. To her grandparents and Robert Petroff, who taught her to love books and follow her dreams, while you are no longer here in body, your memories live on. And to Liam and Alice Petroff, who already have Aunt Shani wrapped around their little fingers, she can't wait to see the wonderful things destiny has in store for you. You all mean the world to her.

Coming Soon

The "Destined" series will continue

ULTRAVIOLET